Patti Hill finds the most amazing 1
San Clemente Bait Shop and Telephony is no exception. In this
Magical Realism story, a ringing telephone is no ordinary
occurrence, and if you dare to answer, there's no telling where
the call will take you. An excellent story told by an excellent
storyteller.

~ Sharon K. Souza, author of *The Color of Sorrow Isn't Blue*

In the midst of an imaginative, mysterious telephony, Patti
creates rich and complex characters who draw us in and invite
us to find a deeper courage—the courage to hope and to
change.

~Sharon Hinck, award-winning author

Patti Hill is a master at writing the deeply flawed, vulnerable,
and shockingly real characters that work their way into the
heart of the reader. Jenna Archer of *The San Clemente Bait Shop
and Telephony* is no exception. Hers is a story of loss, rejection,
dysfunction, and ultimately hope in the midst of so much muck
and mire of life. Walking around in Jenna's flip-flops wasn't
always comfortable, but it did change me in no small way. And,
for that, I am once again grateful to have read Patti Hill's work.

~Susie Finkbeiner, *A Cup of Dust*

Patti Hill knows everyday magic can transform ordinary lives: a
kind word, a window open to the sea breeze, the ring of a
telephone. *The San Clemente Bait Shop and Telephony* is that rare
novel with the power to pick you up by the ordinary and
transport you to the magical where you will wish to reside long
after you turn the last page. You'll cheer for Jenna, and for Patti
Hill.

~Bonnie Grove, *Talking to the Dead*

THE SAN CLEMENTE
BAIT SHOP
&
TELEPHONY

Enjoy!

Patti Hill

ALSO BY PATTI HILL

The Garden Gates Series

Like a Watered Garden
Always Green
In Every Flower

Stand-alone Novels

The Queen of Sleepy Eye
Seeing Things
Goodness & Mercy

THE SAN CLEMENTE BAIT SHOP
& TELEPHONY A NOVEL

PATTI HILL

GARDEN WALL PRESS
COLORADO

THE SAN CLEMENTE BAIT SHOP & TELEPHONY

Copyright © 2016 by Patti Hill.
All Rights Reserved.

ISBN 978-0-692-65923-6

Cover photographs by Claudya Plebani
Cover design by Tania Settje of www.CatchingKeepsakes.com.

Visit Patti Hill's website at www.pattihillauthor.com
www.Facebook.com/PattiHillAuthor

TO MY READERS...
you're the best!

The feelings that hurt most, the emotions that sting most, are those that are absurd - The longing for impossible things, precisely because they are impossible; nostalgia for what never was; the desire for what could have been; regret over not being someone else; dissatisfaction with the world's existence. All these half-tones of the soul's consciousness create in us a painful landscape, an eternal sunset of what we are.

~ Fernando Pessoa

1

I'm no Cinderella.

Enchanted pumpkins and singing mice have nothing to do with my story. The regulars who came to the telephony to chat with people from their pasts—some I suspected to be quite dead—simply provided a rhythm to my day, but nothing much changed.

I woke each morning to the nagging whine of Brian's alarm clock, an uncomfortable reminder that my life had forever changed and would forever be the same, magic or no.

Think about it, real people don't actually live in enchanted woods, where the only jobs are evil step-mother and handsome prince. In the real world of bills-must-be-paid, I managed my family's bait shop and telephony (read that: telephone museum) across the street from the San Clemente pier. My own encounters with magic were purely secondhand in the beginning.

The first tick of the clock found me refreshing the newsstand with current editions. Next door at Canatello's Ristorante delivery trucks dropped off produce and wine. At 5:20 a.m., Eric dollied frozen bait through the door and begged a cup of espresso for the drive back to the harbor. If he arrived fresh-shaven and lingered, glancing toward the back of the bait shop to my bedroom, he stayed longer and the shop opened late, a simple hiccup of time easily recovered.

Tick!

On those mornings of disappointing delight, the fishermen huddled on the sidewalk past our usual opening time. They bypassed the espresso—too fussy—for drip coffee, which was strong and burned by the time I unlocked the door. If customers must be faced early in the morning, fishermen were the easiest to please. As a group they defined their suffering more sparingly than others.

Herb, a Vietnam vet with a salt-and-pepper braid, bee-lined to the counter. "Hey there, Jenna, you got any of that sludge you call coffee?" Like I said, easy.

We generated absolutely nothing toward the bottom line from the adjoining telephony—a creation of my father's. Regulars visited the telephony daily. First came Ginny, a woman with tangerine spikes of hair and an electric alertness, just before nine to wait by Model 302, the first Western Electric telephone to include the ringer and network circuitry in the same desktop unit. Ginny's appearance cued me to chill the soft-serve mix to be ready for the beach crowd.

Tick!

In the beginning, the bait shop had been larger. Instead of old telephones, the connecting space housed the Pierside Rental Shop. Every kid coming from the Inland Empire needed a surf rider to experience a better-than-average day at San Clemente beach. And we'd actually made money renting the things to the little boogers.

But Dad had needed a place—and a reason—for all the telephones he'd collected in the years since Brian's disappearance. The doorway between the two storefronts had been narrowed to increase wall space for day-at-the-beach essentials on the bait shop side and countless telephones on the telephony side, which made keeping an eye on the regulars difficult, not because I didn't trust Ginny. She could take as many telephones home as she could carry in her knitting bag and I wouldn't care, but she would never do such a thing.

The truth? I liked to watch and listen.

While she waited for the 302 to ring, she knitted caps for orphans somewhere in Central America, a place where people wore snake boots to walk through the forest. Costa Rica? It might have been Nicaragua. Anyway, I couldn't actually hear the telephone ring for Ginny, but I could hear her talking, although not her words. Her voice fluttered like a bird caught in a trap.

Most days I delivered a cup of tea to Ginny, my way of snooping without being obvious. I usually found her leaning over the small desk, perched on the chair with butt-biting springs and her knitting discarded in a heap. She acknowledged the tea with a pat on my hand but kept talking.

"I hear you, Frank. You don't have to yell … No one's listening. I can tell when Debbie gets on the extension … It's been so long. I can't bear not knowing another minute. When will you forgive me?"

If the 302 didn't ring for Ginny by nine-fifteen, her knitting needles clicked a distress signal, much more discomforting than her pleadings with Frank. And so, I delivered an extra-large cup of tea with cream and sugar, the Valium of the British and cap knitters everywhere.

At the end of her time in the telephony, around ten-fifteen, she insisted on paying for the tea she didn't order. I refused her money, but each Christmas she knitted me something—at least a dozen caps over the years, plus a family of mice and some socks meant to look like watermelons, which I wore to bed all year long.

Soon after Ginny slipped out, Mr. Foster shuffled in, leaning hard on his walker. He arrived at ten-thirty.

To my knowledge, the Kellogg ashtray telephone had only rung three or four times for Mr. Foster. There was no need to serve him tea to hear what he said. He yelled loud enough to drown out the sinners in Dante's third ring of hell.

"You have got to believe me! I've never lied to you. And I won't start now!"

When my stomach gurgled around noon, I knew Tim

would soon arrive.

Tick!

He was a buttoned-up accountant with round blue-gray eyes and a face that was boyish but serious. He moved like an athlete, although I doubted he stood a full inch taller than me, and no one had ever accused me of being tall.

More than once I'd thought of reaching out and undoing the top button of his shirt. He looked positively choked, especially in the heat of summer. Unreasonably pleasant and earnest, Tim probably recited the Boy Scout pledge in the mirror before leaving for work.

Tim brought two containers of leftovers to heat in the microwave each visit—one for him and one for me. He liked to experiment after watching cooking shows. Mostly, his experiments resulted in restaurant-quality food. His culinary skills made him my favorite.

The Snoopy telephone rang for him during his lunch hour, Monday through Friday, again without my hearing. He talked to his younger sister Amy. Brian had been gone for seventeen years, but the way Tim talked to Amy made me miss my brother all the more, even though Brian had never shown me much concern. Memories are odd that way.

I displayed the Snoopy telephone on a nightstand in the front window. Tim never flinched at the attention he drew from passersby, although some considered a grown man talking on a Snoopy telephone hilarious enough to point and laugh. I didn't move the telephone, which I probably should have, but the placement of Snoopy kept Tim in my line of sight and only ten feet from the cash register. I heard every word from his end.

"You shouldn't worry about them," he said. "Guys can be cruel. They say stupid stuff they don't mean, not just to you, to everyone. You're beautiful ... Brothers know these things. I have a reputation to uphold ... I would hide you in the attic if you were that ugly."

On his way out of the telephony at twelve forty-five, Tim collected the washed containers from the previous day and thanked me for letting him come. In the typical gloom of June, when fog clung to the coast and customers were sparse, he sometimes broke off his conversation with Amy early. He leaned against the counter to ask about my day or to tell me about his most recent orienteering event. He recounted every obstacle in painstaking detail—the views he enjoyed at the pinnacle of an ascent and the advantage some opponents gained by not following the rules in spirit, whatever that meant. When the day came for Tim to finally win, I hoped he won big.

More than once I'd been tempted to ask if he had a younger brother, one as good at the stove but more dangerous, less predictable, taller. I didn't have the heart.

In between customers, I spent the afternoon doing the perfunctory jobs around the shop and telephony, which included restocking merchandise and placing orders, plus ridding the glass cases of fingerprints and the telephony of dust. And paying bills when I had the money.

At three p.m., Dad arrived breathless from dashing to the store from his workshop, where he refinished and repaired telephones to sell on eBay and at telephone-lover conventions. Sad but true, he wasn't the only telephone-crazed person on the planet.

Tick!

He knew not to be late. While he played barista and clawed through the freezer to find squid or mackerel for a fisherman, I ran errands for myself and Mom. I raced to be back before my last regular of the day arrived. She liked to slip in as the Metrolink passengers selected snacks for the 5:02 inland, the busiest time of our day.

I'd not managed to learn the woman's name, but she sat in front of the Whitman & Couch fiddleback, an odd telephone choice for a woman in her twenties. She spoke too softly for a word to be heard. And I rarely saw her leave. She dissolved into the ebb of the late-day crowd.

I didn't mind that the telephones in the telephony didn't ring for me. Dad had warned me about involving myself with those on the other end of the line. Such carelessness, he assured me, only led to heartache. I'd heard for myself the frustration of the people on this end of the line and decided not to get involved.

I locked the door at five-thirty and headed upstairs to eat dinner with my parents. Thirty-four, single, and sleeping in the backroom of a bait shop. If my very own fairy godmother showed up, she would cinch closed her bag of magic dust and fly off to find a more hopeful recipient of her goodwill.

Tick. Tock.

2

I found the boxes of hair dye under the passenger seat. They'd been in my car for at least two weeks.

Clairol had yet again discontinued Mom's hair color. Why the company felt compelled to take a perfectly good hair color and toss the formula to the wind, I would never know. I'd traipsed to every drugstore in south Orange County. I'd even slipped a clerk a five at a store in San Juan Capistrano to search her storeroom for returns.

No such luck.

Now I stood outside the apartment, constructing lies and excuses for being late to color Mom's hair. For good reasons Mom held little faith in my chemistry skills. I'd convinced her to mix colors before with disappointing results. I stuffed the boxes inside my purse and opened the door.

She stood studying the view, a tiny paintbrush poised in her hand before an easel. The breeze rattled the vertical blinds and lifted her bangs. I expelled a long-held breath. She squinted down on the vista, painting the landscape on the inside lid of a cigar box. Her scrutiny reassured me, ever so slightly, that the play of light and shadow, line and form still roused her to life. This was the mother I remembered from childhood and into my teens.

Mom dabbed at the clouds in her painting and stepped back, tilting her head. "Finished?"

I stepped behind her. The scene was familiar, the one scene my mother painted, the San Clemente pier. Only the participants changed. In this painting a group of surfers huddled to pass a joint, a mother pushed a double stroller—she should not have been wearing a bikini—and an old man bent over to offer his attentive Yorkie a treat. He should have been wearing a belt.

I looked out the window to see the echo of her painting. She'd caught the blushing gold of the fading day and the long arm of the pier reaching toward the horizon. "Your best ever. The sky is perfect. I'll take the box down to the shop when it dries. This one will sell within the week."

She ran a hand through her short hair. "My hair feels like straw. You promised me a haircut ages ago."

I pulled the first lie from my hat. "I like your hair a little longer. It's cute."

"Brian won't recognize me. And my color. Jenna, let's cover this gray before dinner. I would hate for him to come home and see me like this."

Rather than allowing her desperation to gutter me, I studied the shimmer of light off the water, selecting my next combination of lies carefully. "I need to do an inventory in the shop and make a run to Walmart. We're getting low on sunscreen and diapers. And I'm thinking about picking up a case of baby formula. A frantic mother came in last week. We're missing a market there."

Mom narrowed her gaze. "Since when are you in a sweat to shop Walmart?"

Dig deeper. "I think you should consider letting your hair go gray. We could get some gel, spike it. Nothing could be easier." I lowered my voice. "And don't forget the chemicals in the dye. No one knows how they pollute our bodies over the long term."

Mom's eyes welled with tears. "You know how important this is to me."

I knew too well how irrationally non-negotiable she'd become about keeping herself and the apartment as Brian had last seen both. Keeping the aging appliances running, the hinges from rusting off the cupboards, and the carpet from becoming a tripping hazard fell to me.

Rather than scream over the hair dye, I introduced unvisited logic. "Brian will be different too. He's older. He's probably thinning on top and has grown a beard to compensate. Knowing Brian, and you know this to be true, he's shaved his head to spit in the eye of balding." Never in the seventeen years Brian had been gone had anyone in my family suggested he could be anything but exploring the world, certainly not that he could be anything but alive and well. Not to Mom. Not out loud. "I'm betting he has a potbelly, like Dad."

She slumped into her recliner and worried the exposed piping like a rosary. "Everything has to be the same."

No problem there. Nothing had changed. True, the furniture had frayed and sagged with age, but the push-button telephone still hung on the kitchen wall; and the family photographs scattered about the apartment all predated the year Brian had disappeared.

I certainly wasn't the same. I was young enough but no longer fresh. If Mom looked closely, she would see gray hair at my temples. I wouldn't color my hair for Brian or anyone else. The clerk at the drugstore had leaned in close to suggest an eye cream, but I'd opted for bug-eyed sunglasses.

I draped my arm around Mom's shoulders. She was all rafters and beams under my touch. "They've discontinued your color."

Mom stifled a sob.

I continued quickly, hoping to staunch a full-blown cry fest. "I bought two boxes, one shade a little darker and another bottle a shade lighter. The mixture should be perfect, really. The clerk helped me." I omitted that the clerk looked twelve and dyed pink streaks through her hair.

Mom ran to her bedroom and sprawled across the bed. I

followed, knowing I'd emptied my pockets of logic and lies, and all the stale platitudes I'd whispered into her ear over the years. I certainly didn't believe them, and I feared she no longer believed them either.

I crawled onto the bed and rested my hand on her heaving back. I squelched the urge to mouth her muffled words. I lay there, instead, as helpful as a mustard plaster.

Mom's bedside clock clicked with each passing minute. Outside, the Metrolink crossing clanged, and the train's horn bellowed. Her breathing slowed. "I can still smell his milk breath, feel his puffs of breath on my face. The heat of him against my chest. He packed a fire even as a baby. I remember everything about Brian."

"I know."

"Brian," she whispered, and her tears redoubled.

A bar of sunlight rose toward the ceiling. The front door opened. Dad said Mom's name—no need to shout in a one-bedroom apartment. I answered, "We're in here."

"I'll be back late. Thought you should know." The door clicked shut.

"Are you hungry, Mom?" I said to distract her from Dad's sidestepping of her pain.

But if she'd heard him—how could she not?—she didn't react. She rolled onto her back. "I woke up every morning to find Brian sleeping on your father's chest. He adored him."

"Brian was special," I said, remembering a much different brother than she described. I would now hear how he'd never cried or whined or thrown temper tantrums. In her mind, Brian was sunshine to my dark side of the moon. He shone like a fresh summer day. I was the storm arriving like clockwork over the prairie with billowing clouds and strikes of lightning.

"Do you think the dollar store might have my color?" she said, her voice clogged with phlegm.

"Been there. Actually, I've been looking for weeks,

everywhere. We either try combining the two colors I found, or you'll need to go see Suzanne."

Mom blanched. "You know what that woman does to me."

I'd just committed emotional terrorism on my very own mother. There wasn't a boundary Suzanne wouldn't climb over, cut through, or plow down.

"As long as the clerk helped you," Mom said, reaching for a Kleenex to blow her nose.

The clerk had told me which aisle to search. "Of course she did."

"Well then, I have no choice but to trust you."

I wasn't a praying woman, but I did wish for a happy collision of *Coastal Sand* and *Sunflower* as I mixed and shook the applicator bottle. When we finished, Mom stood in front of the mirror, freshly coifed and hair-sprayed. She arrived at the dinner table wearing mascara and lip gloss. She looked better than I'd seen her in over a year. Mom went to bed early that night. As far as I knew, Dad never came home.

I worked at making cover-ups from faded San Clemente T-shirts and flounces of old curtains at the dining table. Selling the cover-ups gave me some pocket money. Women will buy anything to cover-up cellulite. When Jimmy Fallon finished his monologue, I headed for the bait shop and bed.

Yet another wondrous night in paradise.

3

Playing hairdresser to Mom revived dreams of stuffing my rubble into a Trader Joe's bag and driving as far as my pitiful 1990 Daewoo Le Mans would take me. Hesperia? Barstow? Probably Tustin. Not far enough.

Besides, who would buy Mom her paints, fill her cupboards with groceries, and hunt every store in south Orange County for a discontinued hair dye? And who would work for practically nothing to keep a failing business afloat?

Dad?

Not likely. Even less likely now that he was the one packing his suitcases and piling his miscellany into beer boxes.

I sat on the edge of his chair and watched as he selected books from the shelf. By habit I sat out of striking distance and poised myself to flee, keeping one eye on the veins in his temples. I hadn't been this wary since high school but neither had I been this angry. I worked to keep my tone inquisitive rather than accusatory. But I was feeling reckless.

"You're leaving her? Now? How will she...do anything?"

Dad threw a few books in a box and turned toward the dresser that served as a TV stand in the living room. He lifted a handful of black socks and dropped them into his suitcase. "How long has it been, sixteen—?"

"Seventeen," I corrected.

"What?" he asked, surprised, stopping to look at me, frowning as he counted back the years.

"Seventeen years, Dad. Brian has been gone for seventeen very long years—a lifetime, half of mine."

Dad glanced toward the bedroom. "Your mother hasn't

adapted well."

A slap would have hurt less. This proved Dad hadn't a clue about what his leaving meant to us. He might not have been the most pleasant person to have around, but he was a person who knew how to dispense drugs and be somewhat present. My hurt morphed back to anger. "How, exactly, do you adapt to your son disappearing?"

"We do what we have to do," he said, matching my anger with condescension.

Geesh, he was bumptious (new word: self-assertive or proud to an irritating degree).

He drew in a breath. I prepared for an outburst of indignation and a generous spray of spittle. Instead, he released a slow, even breath. "Listen, Jenna, we both know your brother was a lost cause by the time he left. We gave finding him our best shot, but he's out there—and you know this is true—he's out there, somewhere, having a heck of a good time, leaving us to handle your mother like a basket of eggs. Well, I'm done."

I did not know anything about Brian. In fact, I'd spent most nights between wakefulness and sleep, picturing Brian in every possible situation, most of them horrific—a prison in Turkey, a diamond mine in Angola, forced to fight in the Congo.

"Brian will be found when Brian is found," Dad said, putting a period on the conversation.

Not so fast. "Who's looking? Are you?"

Dad opened the second drawer to retrieve plaid boxers. "Brian has moved on. We need to move on too. If he saw us holed up like this, he'd have a good, hard laugh on us. There's no denying what's true."

"Can you wait until Mom calms down to talk about this?"

Dad gestured toward the closed bedroom door and dropped his arm. With a crooked grin, he said, "She's gleeful over the extra closet space. She now has plenty of room for everything she buys on QVC. See, everyone's happy." Dad lifted a stack of undershirts from the bottom drawer. He zipped his suitcase closed and opened his wallet to fish out a business card. "You can reach me here, at the home number. And I'll come by to relieve you in the afternoon, as usual."

The business card belonged to a Realtor, a blonde, cute in a Botoxed sort of way. Sally McCallister. For all of my life, Dad had referred to Realtors as glad-handers and bottom-feeders, swimming down there with lawyers. And now he was living with one.

He hefted the suitcase to the floor. I looked around the apartment, all but the bedroom and bathroom visible from where we stood. Nothing of my father remained, not his crossword puzzle books, not his collection of antique telephone catalogs, not even the rug Mom kept in front of his chair.

"Sally's a real nice gal, likes to travel and go out to dinner," he said.

My heart thumped. He was really leaving. I spoke through clenched teeth. "You're abandoning Mom!" And me, Dad. You're abandoning me.

"Jenna, your mom and I haven't had a real marriage in a long time. You're old enough to understand."

I cast caution to the seagulls and pulled Dad onto the balcony. The sliding glass door closed with a thud. Below us, beachgoers walked languidly. He needed to understand certain things too. "I'm leaving. I've been accepted in Rochester—"

"New York? That Rochester? Or Minnesota? It's cold in Minnesota."

"New York, Dad. I've been accepted into their sonographers program. I've waited—"

"And how will you pay for this?"

Leave it to Dad to deflect the real issue. I pivoted away, stopped and turned back. He could fear my spittle for a change.

"I plan on doing what I always do, work my butt off."

I repelled from his touch.

"You should go," he said. "We can hire someone to work the shop. Selling beach garb isn't exactly rocket science."

"And Mom?"

"She'll be fine."

There had been a time when I'd believed this too. Mom needed to get out of the apartment, and the motivation would magically appear with us refusing to meet her every whim, calling her bluff, letting her get a little hungry. I didn't believe in magic anymore, not that kind. Mom had changed. She'd slipped into a darkening place. She gave the same excuses for not leaving the apartment, but her eyes no longer reflected light. What had started as a vigil had become a prison. The world, even the world of sand and surf across the street, a paradise to most, threatened her.

"I don't think so, Dad. She's changed."

He shrugged. "We can't help someone who won't help themselves."

"But we could try being decent. You know, sticking by her in her time of need?"

He pushed past me and re-entered the apartment. He spoke over his shoulder as he stacked boxes. "Do whatever you want."

"That's not an option, thanks to you. You're leaving me here to rot."

Dad's voice turned velvety. "Only if rotting is what works for you."

Where did that come from? I studied the Realtor's card. A woman in a navy blazer smiled back with teeth the size of movie screens. I held the card in front of his face. "That sounds like something Sally here might have heard at a real estate agent's convention."

He stepped toward me and I backed into his chair. But Dad

wasn't angry. He looked like he'd dropped his ice cream on a hot sidewalk.

"You're not being fair."

"Just following your lead, Dad. Does Mom know about Sally?" How could she not?

He balanced a stack of boxes on one arm and opened the door. At sixty-three, I still marveled at his strength. "I'll see you at three."

He turned to quickstep down the stairs to the sidewalk and his waiting car. If he drove away from me now, I would be stuck with the telephony forever, which would keep me living with Mom. I swallowed hard and followed. I stepped between him and the car door.

"This is ridiculous," he said and dropped the boxes to the street.

A pair of surfers stood at the counter in the bait shop, shifting from one foot to the other. They could wait for their board wax.

I turned back to Dad who stared at the horizon, a convenient delaying tactic for all of us who lived on the coast. I put my hand on his arm. He startled, but he looked at me. "Dad, there are other things we need to talk about. Profits are close to nil. We should move the telephony to make room for something that makes money."

"I'm not comfortable moving the telephony. Who knows what might happen?"

"What could happen? You move the telephones from one place to another, and the retail space starts bringing in income."

"And our regulars?"

Dad knew the regulars were my pets, the rhythm of my day. My whole world. I would miss them. On the other hand, I didn't see the telephony making them happy. "We might be doing them a huge favor. You could sell the telephones on eBay and take Sally someplace nice."

Dad shot me a warning glance. "I need time to think." This was Dad-speak for: the telephony will stay put.

I gambled on upping the stakes. "Maybe Mom could move in with you and Sally."

"End of conversation. I'll see you at three." He threw the boxes into the back seat and zoomed up the hill and disappeared around a cliff of apartments. Something in me snapped and slackened.

I FOUND MOM LAYING her clothes out on the bed by color and type of animal print with a heap of newer things on the floor. She gestured to the pile dismissively. "Brian's never seen me in those. Take them to Goodwill on your next trip."

What did people say at the end of a marriage? "I'm sorry, Mom."

She stopped, frowned. "Sorry?"

"Dad leaving." Me staying.

"For heaven's sake, he was never here. And look at the closet space. There are things in this closet I'd forgotten about, but Brian will remember." She pulled out a periwinkle golf shirt. "I wore this to his fifteenth birthday party. I'm finding treasure, Jenna."

My knees softened. Mom hadn't demonstrated this kind of exuberance since before Brian hit puberty. How could I have missed her ambivalence over Dad? Maybe I hadn't. Maybe I'd ignored her detachment, or was I too busy trying to keep her keel in the water? Whatever my culpability, the changes in her felt like a millstone.

"We're down to me and you," I said. "Maybe you could try going out, not far. A trip to the post office would be nice. We'll be back in ten minutes."

The color slid from Mom's face. "And if Brian comes home?"

"We'll leave a note. And we won't lock the door."

She dropped the golf shirt to the floor. Her hands fluttered over her heart. "He'll think we've forgotten him."

Forgotten him? Forgotten I was parked in the brush behind the high school, losing my virginity, when I should have been riding the bus home with my younger brother? Forgotten that we hadn't seen Brian since? That I had to learn to fall asleep without the sound of his breathing in the room, or that my heart had been stuck in neutral for seventeen years, where I feared it was forever lodged, that his absence served as the great black hole that pulled every particle of joy from my life? Forgetting Brian wasn't possible, not for a minute.

I pulled her into my arms. "I'll find him, Mom. I will find Brian, and I'll bring him back to you."

4

I traced the muscles of Eric's back, naming each one as I ran my finger over his smooth skin—"Trapezius, deltoid, latissimus dorsi." And back up to his neck. Under the trapezius, the levator scapulae, supraspinatus, infraspinatus—

"I need to get back," he said, shifting.

"In a minute. I'm almost done." I kissed the tattoo of a Chinese character on his shoulder. I felt his pulling away through my lips. "Teres minor, teres major, and rhomboideus major." I poked him under his eighth rib, making him arch his back. "Go on, get outta here."

Eric climbed over me and out of bed like a wildebeest with a lioness on his tail. For that and about a million other reasons, I didn't like him very much. Plainly, he didn't like me very much either. "I thought you were done with the muscles and bones stuff," he said.

"You mean anatomy?" I'd spent two years with textbooks and coloring books of the human body to learn every muscle, bone, and nerve, all in preparation for going to Rochester. A head start couldn't hurt.

Eric's question forced me to face the dismal truth of my non-future. What did I need anatomy for? With Dad over-and-out and Mom growing more dependent by the day, I wasn't going anywhere. Not to Rochester. Not even to Saddleback Junior College. Making espresso, restocking, overseeing the regulars at the telephony. This was my star-studded destiny.

My stomach churned.

"Whatever you call it," he said. "You aren't going anywhere, right?"

I dug under the covers for my clothes. "No, I'm not going anywhere."

"Good," he said, stepping into his boots. "I would miss…this."

I froze. He would miss *this*. Not me. Not playing name-that-muscle. Not the scent of my skin. He would miss *this*. I vowed, yet again, to tell him our hooking up no longer satisfied. And then he leveled lagoon-green eyes at me.

"See you next week," I said.

The bell above the door jingled. Only then did I rise. I twisted my hair into a coil and clipped the knot into place. Like the Sirens, the fish that swam between the pilings had tempted the fishermen beyond patience. Herb had probably tried the door and thought, *what the heck?* I saw no problem with Herb and the guys filling their own insulated mugs. Why should they wait while I contemplated my dismal prospects?

I tied my bikini top at my neck, slipped one of the cover-ups over my head, and pulled on a hoodie. Such was fashion in pier-side bait shops. As soon as I rang the fishermen up and collected payment, I turned the open sign over and locked the door.

I waited for a break in the traffic along Avenida Victoria and ducked under the railroad crossing gate. I walked past the pier entrance toward the beach to run toward the water's reach. I plopped in the sand, stared into the fog, and clawed down to the wet sand and squeezed a handful into a walnut-sized ball.

Surfers studied the swells for a wave worth riding. The fishermen nattered over bait and catches. The train blew its horn and sped through the crossing. I turned away from the pier to pop the ball of sand into my mouth.

And chewed.

Slowly.

A shivering crackle throbbed through my jaw, down my neck to my clavicle, telegraphing the message: All is well. All is well. All is well.

I rubbed the sand against the roof of my mouth until the metallic taste of blood seeped through the grit. I lay back in the sand. A wave reached my feet. The cold sent a shudder through my body. I softened my muscles and waited for the next touch of water and foam, to lay there until the water covered me, past the first chill until no divide of degrees separated my body from the water, to be lifted by the surge and plummeted into the deep, swirling darkness.

I sat up, brushed sand from my legs and cover-up. The swirling darkness would not claim me that day. There was no one to make lattés or iced mochas with crème. Mom would forget her midday Xanax, and who would adjust the prices on the sardines and squid?

I walked back to the bait shop, where I made my bed and checked my teeth for grains of sand before reopening the shop.

MOM HAD ALREADY SETTLED in front of the TV for *Ellen* when I came up from the bait shop. She didn't need anything, not with Bradley Cooper making an appearance on the show. I took the stairs two at a time to Larice's apartment. Sitting at her bistro table was the closest I got to a vacation. She slid the rent check across the glass-topped table.

"That's not why I'm here," I said.

"I have the money now. Better it's in your hands than mine."

I pictured Taylor, her daughter, doing homework where I sat, and Larice twirling spaghetti around her fork. A jar of Prego went a long way on her salary. In Mom's apartment, we used TV trays, and the vertical blinds remained closed to keep the glare off the television, unless Mom chose to paint or ride her stationary bike. Then, and only then, the ocean like a great mirror held to the sky filled our view as far as we could see.

Larice's and Mom's apartments stacked like tiers on a

wedding cake, sharing a floor plan but not the same centuries. Larice inhabited the twenty-first century with ease. She wasn't interested in maintaining a museum of 1994. She'd kept a few *tchatchkes* from her grandmother's estate, like a selection of crystal bells that she complained about dusting. But she managed to limit the requisite beach-themed paraphernalia to a pillow with a graphic of a scallop shell, which I'd never seen on a San Clemente beach, and a nautilus, also a no-show, mounted like a sculpture. All very classy and simple. No dolphins. No seahorses. And hallelujah, not one sea gull in sight. Such nasty, opportunistic creatures had no place in decor. I'd never understood Mom's fascination with the birds.

Larice not only lived above me, she rose above me in all things. She switched from scrubs the moment she walked through the door, changing into clothes I once considered suitable for the prom, but she claimed made her feel put together—gossamer blouses and lacy sundresses. I still wore my bathing suit top as a bra. Her nails were perfect, and she'd mastered cat-eye makeup. She was California blonde perfection. Straight nose, azure eyes—with the help of tinted contacts—and the softest dimple of a cleft in her chin. If I didn't love her, I would have hated her.

Sometimes I did.

"So how are things at the nunnery," I said, hoping to commiserate over our common weakness.

Larice poured cream into her coffee and stirred. The result was a cup of dirty-looking hot milk. I sipped from the to-go cup I'd brought with me. I'm such a coffee snob.

"You're making fun," she said.

"And Taylor is going along with your plan?" Did teen girls know virgins lived past eighteen?

"Taylor is a lot smarter than the both of us. She has plans for her future, and she doesn't mean to lose out because she can't keep her pants zipped," she said and sucked her lips into a hyphen.

When would I learn to keep my mouth shut? The afternoons I visited Larice, when the sun punched through the glass to intensify even the shyest colors—this was my sheltered place, where my past and present didn't thumb their noses at me. And I'd angered her. Instead of antagonizing her, she deserved a pat on the back for her efforts.

"You picked yourself up pretty well," I said.

"Nice of you to say so. I'm living over my best friend and her parents, paying rent far below market, and I've had more loser guys in my life than I can count. Married and divorced twice, and I'm really, really tired."

"Taylor is wonderful. You can take credit for her."

"She's one resilient kid, all right, in spite of me. But I'm trying harder to be what she needs. A good example, for one. No men for me until she graduates. That's what the nunnery, as you call it, is all about. I want her to see me standing on my own, so she'll know she can do the same."

Larice wasn't exactly standing on her own. She'd been right about the rent. The apartment was worth four times what I collected, and her parents often brought groceries, along with bags from trendy shops loaded with clothes for her and Taylor. Living in paradise is for the rich, the doggedly determined, and the subsidized.

Still, Larice was as grown up as anyone I knew from my high school days. She'd trained for a good-enough paying job as a dental hygienist, lived in her own apartment, and, most importantly, she parented her daughter from the heart, even when she totally screwed up. And boy, she had really screwed up.

Larice tilted her head and lifted a brow. "Maybe you should join us."

"Where? Abstinence? Taylor doesn't graduate until June." That was a year from now. "There's nothing wrong with sex. I like sex. You like sex, don't you?"

She fingered the fringe of the placemat. "What's Eric's last name?"

I didn't know, didn't want to know. "Smith."

"Has he ever taken you out?"

No.

"Have you met his parents, a sister, a friend?"

No, no, and no.

"You deserve better, Jenna."

Time to change the subject. "My parents are divorcing."

"Since when? They've been married forever."

"Dad moved out."

The skin between her brows puckered a question. "I saw him in the bait shop yesterday. He smiled and waved."

"He's keeping good, so far, on his promise to relieve me for a couple hours each day, mostly to appease his conscience, I'm sure. He's living with his girlfriend."

"And you've changed the subject."

Having a teenager had made Larice a gifted interrogator. "No, really, that's what I came up to tell you. Mom and Dad are divorcing, and school is no longer an option."

Larice leaned forward and took my hand in hers. "There has to be a way."

My eyes burned with tears. "Nope. There's no way I can leave Mom."

"There are people who can help. I'll ask around."

I'd already checked. We owned too much property, according to the county welfare folks, even though our income qualified us for assistance. The cash flow for extras, like help for Mom, didn't exist. All those smiling angels in the telephone book ads charged plenty for their heavenly care. This would be simpler if I felt qualified to actually help Mom. I'd read every psych book in the library, but we still lived under a veil of delusion.

If I cataloged all of my reasons for kissing school goodbye, Larice would read between the lines and insist on moving. A new tenant would boost our ledgers, no doubt about that. But as my only friend, I needed her close, especially since I would be working at the bait shop until I mummified.

I wiped my eyes and pushed my chair back. "I better get back. The rush is coming."

"Eric is your business. I'm sorry, Jenna. Stay a little longer. I have more coffee. Taylor will be home from soccer practice soon." Larice turned her pleading eyes on me. "I love having you, a real adult—not a child who is more adult than me—to talk to. Can you?"

Only a friend would pretend to need me. And I loved her for that, even though I wouldn't drink her coffee on a dare. "You're being hard on yourself."

"Remember when we were kids? We never questioned whether we deserved happiness or not. I want to be the person I thought I was back then. We belonged to the service club and volunteered at the hospital." She held my gaze as she sipped her coffee.

Maybe Larice had been sucking on the nitrous oxide meant for her patients. We weren't angels, not ever. But I wasn't about to sully her memories. Friends allowed friends their distorted recollections.

"You visited Mrs. Frye every Saturday," I said. "And ate her stale cookies in her oven-like apartment."

"You helped the kindergarten teacher with Abbie. No one could calm that girl down from her tantrums. We all held our breaths, but you got on the floor with her and talked to her about your cat. You didn't have a cat, but somehow you figured out Abbie would do anything to hear cat stories. What became of her?" Larice shivered at her question.

I filled my mouth with the last of the coffee and swallowed hard. "We were pretty naïve back then."

She set her cup down. Her eyes brightened the way they did when she talked about a new guy in her life. I was right, the nunnery stuff couldn't last. "You aren't going to believe this," she said. "I've started praying. Surprising, huh?"

"To God?"

"I think so. At least, that's my intention." She led me to the entry closet. "Look at this."

She'd nearly emptied the closet, quite a feat since she hadn't started with much closet space. A cushion filled the closet floor. "I sit in here. That's about the only thing I remember from youth group, to go into a closet to pray."

I would have picked a fatter cushion, that was for sure. And I would not have considered praying, no matter how desperate I got. "Why?"

"Taylor. You wouldn't believe what she's up against. It's nothing like our days in high school, and that was pretty bad. It can't hurt to ask for divine protection. And there are people who come into the dental office. If my hands aren't in their mouths, they're spilling their guts. Some of what they say is terrible stuff. Yesterday, a lady whose teeth I've been cleaning for years told me her son called from college, said he didn't think he wanted to live anymore. I had no answers for her. So I told God everything she'd told me and asked him to save the day."

It was the all-knowing and all-seeing part of God I remembered, which went a long way to explain why I felt awkward even looking into Larice's closet. "Shouldn't he already know about the lady's son?" Did she pray for me? For Brian?

She lifted her head, a mix of surprise and disappointment flashed in her eyes. "I guess so."

Sometimes I hated myself.

I WOKE MOM AFTER the news to tell her to go to bed. As I

helped her out of the recliner, she said, "I can't seem to stay awake."

"You didn't miss much." She didn't need to hear about an Amber Alert in Texas or bone loss due to vitamin D deficiency. Who did? I only knew because I'd been sewing at the table and heard every life-crushing detail. Creating something to the sound of TV made me feel superior, like the thing hadn't managed to rob my soul.

Once I heard snoring from Mom's bedroom, I turned off the TV. I'd done some experimenting with the tulle I'd found on sale at Walmart. I didn't see a long future for me and the netty stuff. It groused in my fingers, tugging and pulling when I tried to pin it to the flouncy hem. Enough of that. I left the apartment for the bait shop. Inside my bedroom, I dug in my closet to find the scrapbook of clippings I'd compiled about Brian. Maybe I'd missed something. Maybe there was a clue in the pages as to where to find him.

The scrapbook contained pictures and articles from the *Orange County Register* and our local paper, the *San Clemente Times,* plus some coverage I'd printed from the internet when I'd googled Brian's name. I seldom read the internet stuff. People had posted pictures from their time in the hills hunting for Brian. They leaned together to smile for the camera, which creeped me out. Each and every writer had a theory about his disappearance. I shared the collection with no one.

At first, the news stories about Brian, especially locally, rallied residents to help with the search. And people had come out, donned orange vests, brought their dogs, and poked through the chaparral with walking sticks, probably more to roust rattlesnakes than with any real expectations of finding a kid over six feet tall.

I turned the page to find pictures of Dad accepting checks for a finder's reward, others of people searching the arroyos and hills for any sign of Brian. Eventually, the stories included pictures of Brian's be-studded and leathered friends, talking about how much they missed their friend. I stopped numbering the pages after fifty.

On the first anniversary of his disappearance, a reporter from the *Times* showed up to interview all of us. Mom refused, of course. Dad and I gave circumspect answers about Brian's brush with rebellion, trying to emphasize his youth and inexperience, which at fifteen was true enough.

The story included his freshman picture—with a smile bordering on a sneer—and a family shot from a trip to the San Diego Zoo taken the summer before his disappearance, a rare excursion for a family that ran a retail shop opened seven days a week, 363 days a year. In the picture, Brian looked like he'd eaten bad fish. The rest of us didn't look much better. We stood in front of the penguins, making scant effort to feign happiness for the camera.

The following scrap pages would have been blank had I not pilfered photographs from the shoeboxes under my parents' bed. The world had too quickly forgotten I'd lost my brother, so I'd filled the remaining pages with the two of us hamming for Dad's camera on Christmases and Halloweens and birthdays.

I lingered over the shots I'd taken of him for my photography class, all very moody and grainy black and whites. He had loved those pictures, too, especially the one where I'd found a cigarette, nearly whole, for him to dangle from the corner of his mouth. He'd taken off his shirt to stuff in his back pocket. He wanted to look like a renegade in the worst way. A forehead dotted with angry pimples ruined his efforts. The disparity between what he'd wanted to convey and what the pictures revealed would have been comical, if these hadn't been among my last memories of him.

I closed the book but didn't return it back to its hiding place. Instead, I held it like a shield to my chest as I slipped under the covers and turned off the lights. I remembered everything about the day Brian had gone missing.

I'd talked Ryan Knight, the president of the school's senate, into taking me up into the hills after school. Emboldened by even that minor accomplishment, I crawled onto his lap and guided his hand under my T-shirt and kissed him full on the lips, the lip-chewing kind of kiss I'd seen in the movies. He hesitated. He actually hesitated, which embarrassed me. I wasn't good enough? What was I thinking? This guy could have any girl he wanted. Finally, his face contorted with longing and pain.

"Are you all right?"

"Should we be doing this?" he asked, gasping for air.

According to Larice, everyone but she and I were doing this. I added Ryan to the list. For both of our sakes, I pulled off my T-shirt. Larice would not win this race. "Absolutely, Ryan, we definitely should be doing this."

When he lay heaving and sweating against me in the back seat, he was grinning, and I was no longer a virgin. He would have pledged his eternal love had I asked him to. But I wasn't sure I wanted to see Ryan at school the next day. Sex had proved to be mechanical and awkward but also less gross than I feared. There was no sense getting all moonstruck.

Still, after Ryan dropped me off, I ran up the stairs to the apartment embossed with a strange sensation of connectedness. I hovered in a different dimension, or so I believed until I heard Mom's keening through the door. I entered the clabbered air of the apartment to face her.

"Your brother hasn't come home," my mother said, blotch-faced and wide-eyed. "Where have you been? Where's Brian? What have you done with him?"

Dad raised his head. "The police won't do anything for twenty-four hours. Who are his friends? We need to make some calls, see if we can find him. The police are idiots."

My heart thudded. "Wait. Slow down. Brian didn't come home?"

"And where have you been? Your number one job is Brian," Mom had snapped. "He could be anywhere."

From out of my memories Mom's despairing eyes accused me. I slapped the scrapbook closed. There would be no sleep for me. Such was the danger of the scrapbook. I returned to Mom's apartment, turned on the kettle, and sat down at the sewing machine. By the time the fishermen came, I'd tamed the tulle to peek under the flounces of three cover-ups and a skirt.

That was enough regret for one day.

5

I swooned over each bite of Tim's creamy pesto lasagna.

The fog shrouded the pier from view, a typical day in paradise for June. Only Tim and I occupied the space, me in the bait shop and Tim talking to Amy on the Snoopy telephone in the telephony. From where I stood behind the counter, I heard every word he said.

Truth was I could mouth most of his words.

"I'm glad you called ... Nothing much, studying for a statistics class. And you? ... The secret to biology is reading the book and memorizing a few terms. Nothing to it. You'll actually use that stuff, eventually ... Yeah, well, I am an old man. How are Mom and Dad? ... You're hard on them ... Sure, they worry. It's their job to worry.

"I *am* on your side. But I think they're right about the quarry. You're too young ... I do, don't I? ... Okay, okay, I promise.

"Hey, before you go, I hear the bowling alley closed ... Try something else."

I heard a rustling of papers. At this point in the conversation, Tim suggested an activity for Amy to try, something to keep her from going to the quarry. "Ask Mom and Dad for karate lessons."

Karate lessons?

"Knowing some self-defense is a good idea ... They're not pajamas. Karate is a sport of self-discipline and inner strength ... You're laughing now, but you'll thank me someday ... You're right, but don't forget your promise ... I mean it, Amy. You don't know what you're up against."

The bell over the door jingled. A pair of teen girls strolled in, scanning the merchandise, wrinkling their noses at the bait freezer and disappearing into the back of the store. The June gloom had robbed the girls of the chance to deepen their tans, and they now trolled for something to do until the train came. They might even be willing to shoplift. I should have followed them, but I wanted to hear the end of Tim's conversation.

Maybe this time.

"I have to go. Say hi to the folks." And here he paused, as usual. "Amy, you're very special. Don't forget ... Yeah, well, it's the truth." He lowered his voice. "Think about the karate classes and take care of yourself." He placed the receiver back in Snoopy's hand.

The girls walked out, hands deep in their pockets. At worse, they'd pocketed stale Cheese Puffers from last year. I let them go.

Tim looked up, shoulders sagging. "How was the lasagna?"

"Dreamy, as usual. How's your sister?"

"Vague. Determined. Distant."

I came around the counter to collect his dishes. Our unspoken agreement meant he cooked and I washed the containers.

He touched my arm. "Do you have a minute?"

I looked out the telephony's window. Only surfers ensconced in wet suits dared the water, and the fishermen had come and gone long ago. "I have nothing but time."

Tim rose to grab a chair and held it until I sat. "My sister is a couple years younger," he said. "Her fortieth birthday is next month." He receded behind closed eyes for a moment. "If she's still alive, that is. She got caught up with the wrong crowd when I went away to college—drugs and all the stuff that goes with drugs." He looked out the window for a long moment before turning back to me. When he did, his eyes had changed from blue-gray to flint.

"She called me at school all the time, tried to keep the connection between us, but I put her off. I blamed my abruptness on projects, weekend trips, a test, a party. I once told her I had to change my sheets. I never changed my sheets, not in four years. She probably thought I was gay."

And you're not?

"You know, I was putting her off. She was my pesky little sister, a true brat of colossal proportions."

Tim looked down at his opened hands. They looked soft. His fingers were long, no calluses but some impressive scars marked his fingers. When he didn't look up, I had to wonder what he saw in his hands—opportunities lost, chains around his wrists, blood like Macbeth?

He shook his head tightly. "She wasn't all that bad, not really, only when my friends were around. My parents didn't have a clue what she was doing. I should have said something. Talk about myopic. I didn't care enough to bother.

"I haven't seen her in twenty-three years. We last heard she was in a halfway house in Seattle. She'd just gotten out of jail for prostitution—my *baby* sister. She said she was ready to come home, but when my folks got there, she'd disappeared. Back to her pimp. Back to heroin. God, how could I have been so stupid?"

Seeing Tim in agony brought on a sudden impulse to clean the espresso machine, wipe out the bottom of the bait chest, and scrub the urinal. "You're too hard on yourself. You were a kid. All kids go wacko when they're let out of the nest."

"You listen when I talk to her. You hear I'm trying to be the brother she needed."

He sounded more like an anxious father. "You're doing a great job. I would have been a much better person with you as my brother."

"But nothing has changed."

"Tim, what do you want to happen?"

"Could you help me? If I say the right thing, maybe she won't settle for the party life or get mixed up with those kids."

I knew my limitations. I could make him a killer serving of nachos, but saving a sister from a life she'd chosen twenty-three years ago? "Let me give this some thought. I'm not exactly overqualified for what you're asking."

"You're a woman."

I was that. "I have to ask you this again: what do you want to happen?"

"I want Amy back in our lives, healthy and whole."

Oh boy.

THE SUN FINALLY DISSIPATED the fog about two-thirty, too late to have a good sales day with beachgoers but in time to keep me from going nutty with boredom. I handed a latté to a woman dressed to avoid exposure to the sun—a broad-brimmed hat, long sleeves with slacks, and gloves. She slipped on sunglasses as she stepped out the door. I released a shot of steam to clean the wand on the espresso machine.

The bell sounded above the door and in rushed a tall man dressed in Tommy Bahama from his cap to his boat shoes. Boat shoes? Really? So inlander. I looked down at my hoodie, the one that smelled of sour milk and glistened with rivulets of flavored syrup.

The man searched the shelves hurriedly.

I slipped off the hoodie and dropped the nasty thing behind the counter. "Can I help you find something?"

"You don't carry diapers, do you? And I need some sunscreen." He read from a piece of paper he'd pulled from his pocket, "Without retinyl palmitate or oxybenzone, and it can't have a SPF over fifty, and must protect against both UVA and UVB sunlight." He eyed me with the panic reserved for a severed limb. "Got anything like that?" Outside, a woman with a stroller the size of a barge tried to soothe her baby without unlashing the protective harness.

"I have diapers in the back, on the right." He left the counter, scanning the shelves. "I keep the Beach Baby lotion under the counter," I called back to him. "It's exactly what you want but kind of pricey."

The dad stood before me, diapers held to his chest like a prize. "How pricey is pricey?"

"Twenty-one dollars for six ounces."

His eyebrows rose.

Selling him the sunscreen could make opening that day worth the trouble. "Beach Baby is gluten-free and dairy-free. If you get hungry, squeeze a little on a cracker, which I also carry. Delicious."

The woman with the stroller yelled in the door, "Connor, what's taking so long?"

"I'll take it," he said, slapping down a golden charge card.

With the diapers and sunscreen bagged, he returned the signed credit card receipt and lifted his chin toward the telephony. "Aren't you going to get that?"

"Sorry?"

"The telephone, and it's an old one by the sound of the ringer. Brings backs memories." He shuddered.

"I don't hear anything. The telephone must be for you." I gestured toward the telephony. "We have all kinds of telephones in there. They only ring for certain people."

"You're pulling my leg," he said, but he stepped toward the door between the bait shop and the telephony.

"Go on in. There's no admission."

He returned to the counter to leave his purchases with me, looked out the window to the woman and baby. The woman had settled onto the bench outside the door, gently rolling the stroller forward and back.

He stopped at the threshold of the telephony. "The ringing sounds like my granddad's telephone, the one he kept on his desk."

"A black thing with clear buttons along the bottom?"

He looked over his shoulder at me and smiled. "Yeah."

"Right around the corner to the left."

The man disappeared into the telephony, and a good while passed before he spoke. "Hello? ... Who is this? ... What kind of cruel joke is this? ... I remember all that differently ... You'll burn in hell before I forgive you."

I had only a moment to open a magazine and fake interest before the man returned to the bait shop. "I'm outta here!"

The woman opened her hands as if to ask if he'd gotten the diapers and sunscreen.

"We're going home. It's late. They only carry junk in there." He swung the stroller around and headed toward the parking lot. I left the counter to check the Western Electric the man had answered. The receiver hung by its coiled cord off the table's edge. I put it to my ear.

"Hello?"

Silence.

"Hello?"

I hung up the receiver and straightened the telephone on the table.

I really hated when that happened.

THE DAY HAD BEEN less than stellar sales wise, but a minor rush preceding the 5:02 helped. I waited for the last customer to leave before asking Dad about what had happened with the Tommy Bahama-clad young man and the Western Electric.

"Did you talk to anyone?" Dad asked, his forehead corrugated with worry.

"No, I talked into the receiver, but the thing was dead silent."

Dad exhaled. "That's good. Don't forget what I told you."

He looked great, relaxed but interested, alive. Was this new?

Was this Sally, or was this what getting away from Mom and me looked like? Knowing the answers to those questions would yield me exactly nothing, so I used the rare moment of being alone with Dad to ask other questions to help our regulars.

"Dad, a man has been coming in regularly. The Snoopy telephone rings for him every time. That's pretty unusual, right? But with Tim—"

Dad stopped wiping the counter. "I wouldn't get involved with these people, Jenna. I'm not sure how things work all the time. I would hate for you to get dragged into something."

Where did he think I'd been for the last seventeen years? "I'm in, Dad. Every day I'm in this place with the people who answer the ringing telephones. If you think the telephony is dangerous…"

"It's not dangerous, not how you're thinking, exactly. I wouldn't leave you here alone. I'm saying to be careful." He scrubbed hard at the counter.

I could be careful. I had been careful. And now I cared more than I wanted to about what happened to the people who wandered into the telephony. "A man asked me to help with his sister."

Dad straightened. "He doesn't want you to talk to her, does he?"

"I wouldn't."

"Good."

I expected Dad to dart off to Sally, so I started dismantling the espresso machine. Doing the messy job was my gift to Dad. Later, I would sew a couple skirts from my stash of curtains.

Dad said, "Are you and your mother doing all right?"

"Not much has changed."

"Well, I should be going then."

"Dad," I blurted to his back. "Have you ever talked to anyone? Has a telephone ever rung for you?" He'd always insisted that he hadn't spoken on the telephones, but I was older. He'd asked if I was all right. I felt perfectly justified pressing the point.

He shook his head slowly, looking to the ceiling for his answer. "No, never, and if a telephone did ring, I wouldn't answer it."

I didn't believe him, and I couldn't see the harm in talking to someone on the telephone. I walked into the telephony and waited.

Ring. Ring now.

6

There's nothing quite as irritating as perfect strangers enjoying a boisterous good time. My only plan—by contrast—included seven, maybe six-and-a-half, hours of sleep.

The partiers in the vacation condo above Canatello's—best tiramisu in town—had opened every window and door. The bass line of their music dragged the Mariana Trench. They also considered each other's stories uproariously funny. No one was that hilarious.

I slept fine through train horns blaring only yards away and the warning clang at the crossing, but other people having fun alerted me like a double espresso. I finally turned on the light, considered sewing but grabbed a novel from the stack on the nightstand instead. I settled into the story after turning back a few pages to remember why the detective was spewing broken glass and blood. Egad, another fight with an obscenely muscled enforcer over a misunderstood hooker. Could we have an original story line, please? The bland story angered me. I closed the book to play connect-the-dots with the spit wads on the ceiling, a leftover from Brian.

Still, sleep would not come.

Anyone who believed in the restorative power of beach living had not lived within shouting distance of War of the Bands. And yet, people happily took out ridiculous mortgages for the chance to listen to squawking sea gulls and to tame—couldn't be done—fog-frizzed hair.

I drove my thoughts somewhere else.

I didn't have a clue about how to fulfill my promise to Mom to find Brian, so I pictured walking him into the apartment to a waiting Mom. Their reunion is all hugs and tears and trembling smiles. They sip iced tea while Brian explains that he was held by pirates all these years. I'm bruised from fighting my way into their lair to rescue him but happy. Very, very happy. And there's a suitcase packed at my feet.

The vision did not make me drowsy.

Maybe a walk on the beach would settle me, but the clock read 1:32. The beach had closed at midnight, a rule I'd broken plenty of times, but I'd always been with someone. I reached for the novel again.

A ring sounded from the telephony.

I sat up. The book slid from my lap to the floor.

The telephone rang again, a ring I didn't know. The Piano telephone? The Princess?

Dad's warnings echoed through my thoughts. I fell back on the pillow and covered my head with the blankets.

The telephone rang. Again. And again.

I threw back the covers with the intent of discovering which telephone rang for me. By the time I reached the telephony, the ringing had stopped. Even with the party raging on, the silence pressed. I turned, daring the telephone to ring again. Only compliance from the telephone would solve the mystery. But not one of the telephones raised its voice to say, It's me! I rang!

Part of me felt like I'd dodged a bullet; the other part still felt excluded from the party. Perfectly wonderful people received calls in the telephony every day. Shouldn't I? Dad exaggerated like the fishermen.

But who could have called?

I'd been watching and listening to the telephony regulars long enough to know they all dealt with unresolved business with those who called. They left the telephony more unsettled than when they'd arrived. I heard pleadings and disbelief and anger from this end. Perhaps I'd dodged something more like a cannonball.

But who?

Andy from high school? He'd left for college a semester early. I pretty much killed his chances of being a pastor by showing up in his dorm room. I never heard from him again. He probably hated me.

In my less than generous moments, I pictured him working in a convenience store and drinking Mountain Dew nonstop to stay awake, a holdover from his days as a meth addict. His teeth had rotted out while waiting for Medi-Cal to pick up the expense of dentures.

I did not want to talk to Andy, even if the opposite were true, that he'd managed to find a seminary to take him, and he now pastored one of those supermarket-sized churches in the south. Surely, he would feel obligated to save me. Was that even possible?

I dated a guy seriously after high school. We'd—okay, *he'd*—talked of marriage. What was his name? We didn't separate on the best of terms. He got squeamish when I used his toothbrush. I didn't want to talk to him either.

Grandma? She believed the sun revolved around me. I could do no wrong. She made the best molasses cookies, and the simplest chore turned magical. The giant bubbles. The Little Mermaid costumes, for land and sea. My very own room, and it did not smell like mackerel. But Grandma died months before my brother—

My brother? And I'd pulled my covers over my head? How many times could one woman let her brother down in a lifetime?

Evidently, I was poised to find out.

7

Mom traveled the world on her stationary bicycle.

I checked out travel DVDs from the library—Rick Steves' were her favorite—and she pumped like a mad woman during the entire program. Every Monday, Wednesday, and Friday she opened the sliding glass door for the breeze to lift her bangs as she pedaled and experienced the world vicariously.

Mom pedaled hard with a sense of purpose. She dared not weigh one ounce more than when Brian last saw her. Never mind she needed a diaper pin to cinch her jogging pants in place. How the brain clowns with our thoughts when we surrender to the unreasonable.

"I'll need more DVDs, and I have a bunch of books on hold at the library," she said. "You better pick them up today. You were late last time, and they sent the books back to the Costa Mesa branch."

I didn't look up from a three-year-old issue of *People* magazine. "Please?"

"Please? Oh, yes, of course. I thought I'd said so."

Mom didn't dabble in such pleasantries, ever. Not with me. I suspected she knew my true role in Brian's disappearance, and all of her neediness served as torturous revenge. Discovering whether or not my skepticism was warranted required too many ugly questions and the subsequent unraveling of Mom's relative calm.

A telephone had rung for me. That created more important questions to be answered. I tossed the magazine back into the heaped basket. "So, Mom, have you ever talked to anyone on the telephones?"

"*The* telephones?" She stopped pedaling. "You mean in the telephony?"

"Just curious." I tried to sound nonchalant. "Have you ever heard one ring?"

She resumed pedaling, faster. "Ask your father."

"I already did."

"There. Problem solved."

"The problem is not solved." I smiled to take the sting from my words. "He stonewalled me much like you're doing."

Mom coasted and the wheel spun without sound. "You have such a vivid imagination. You always have. Each of your dolls spoke with a different voice. One merely squeaked; another sounded British. Since you gave the redheaded doll your own voice, I figured she was your favorite, and why not? You looked so much alike. The things you made those dolls say, outrageous things about unicorns and talking bunnies."

I almost asked where those dolls ended up. That would have started a conversational goose chase, one that I'm sure she would have preferred. Since she didn't deny talking on the telephones, I took her sidestepping as an admission. "When was your last call?"

She dropped her arms to her side. "You're putting words in my mouth."

"You didn't answer my question."

"I don't have time for this." She pedaled on, ignoring the images of Stonehenge on the TV to face the smothering gray outside.

"Going somewhere?" I said, not trying to hide the irony in my voice.

Her head snapped toward me. "This conversation is over." She climbed off the bike, stomped the five steps to her bedroom and slammed the door. Her jagged cries bled through the door.

After I paced and fumed, felt alternately guilty and furious,

I knocked softly. "Mom?"

She blew her nose. "I've never—cross my heart and hope to die—been involved with the telephony. I wouldn't." She opened the door a smidge. "The telephony is your father's number one love. He has his blonde bimbo, but she'll learn soon enough your father's heart belongs to the telephones. He's incapable of loving in the truest sense. I learned this the hard way and so will she."

"I'm sorry." I looked at her more closely, saw the bend of her shoulders, the sadness held in the creases of her face. She made one horrible decision to marry Dad, and this was where she ended up, so very far from the mom I remembered from my days with the dolls.

"I know you're sorry, Jenna. We don't need to speak of the telephony again. *The Young and the Restless* starts soon. I do believe Victor is somehow responsible for Summer's visit to the hospital. She nearly died. Money and power, that's all Victor really cares about."

The bait shop's bell jingled below, meaning the rush had started. I turned to leave.

"Don't forget about the library," she said.

She'd dashed any prospect of preparing for the next time a telephone rang, mostly because I feared her plunge into the irrational if I pushed too hard. True, I'd frittered my life placating her, but I was good at what I did. Why stop now?

Later, at the library, I fought the urge to check out Daniel Defoe's *The Journal of the Plague Year*, a dreary and redundant account of the Black Death in England. Mom's tastes ranged from Victorian romances to Danielle Steele. Realism didn't suit her. And passive-aggressive behavior was too cowardly, even for me. I took the high road and gathered a pile of Victoria Holt along with a variety of novels with covers boasting ab-pumped heroes who couldn't keep their shirts buttoned. I also found a Rick Steves DVD about Christmas destinations in

Europe.

I doubted my future included a walk through the undulating hills of Ireland or an afternoon at the Louvre at Christmas. I hadn't been away from Orange County in ages. As isolated as I felt, I also sensed the rumblings of a coming adventure. I would hear a telephone ring and join the ranks of Ginny, Tim, Mr. Foster, and the girl with slick hair.

But who would say hello on the other end of the line?

8

No one is perfect.

I'd long ago released Mom from any goddess-like expectations, as every child does. She was frail, so I didn't expect much, but I also didn't expect her to brush away her footprints when following her lead would have helped me, her daughter, navigate strange territory. In other words, Mom lied when she said she'd never spoken to anyone in the telephony.

I wasn't surprised. Hardly disappointed. Saddened, really.

The sound of Mom's voice woke me. By Brian's alarm clock, it was nearly two. At first I figured Dad had come by on one of his hunches a fire or a tsunami threatened his beloved telephones. He usually woke me, not Mom, and we nosed around the telephony for hot wires and leaky pipes. His clairvoyance had never harkened reality.

To protect Dad from Mom's indifference and to shelter Mom from Dad's obsession, I threw back the covers to join them in the telephony.

Oddly, I only heard Mom. She did not speak with her usual schlepping-through-mud voice caused by Xanax. She spoke with a sweetness and determination that flushed out a caravan of unexpected memories—of organizing surprise parties for Brian's birthdays, of co-conspiring escapes into normalcy, which meant a stop at the ice cream parlor, of Mom convincing Dad, finally, I needed a bra.

I slid down the wall in the bait shop to listen, pulling my hoodie over my legs. I imagined Mom on the Princess telephone, like the one she still kept on her nightstand upstairs.

She said, "I can't get away. Jenna is sick … I know, I want

to see you too … It's only been a week, but it seems like a year … She has a cold, nothing really. I could send her back to school after lunch and bring Brian. He naps like a champ every afternoon.

"Kevin, darling, we need to be very sure about what we're doing. Where are we headed? … You seem so unhappy with Denise. She's all you ever talk about … Have you asked? You don't need her permission.

"Of course, she gets upset. She's manipulating you. As long as you appease her, nothing will happen, which leaves me in a terrible situation. Ron grows more volatile by the day.

"Won't you talk to a lawyer? I'm serious about this, Kevin. I'm only truly myself when I'm with you. Continuing to live a lie is killing me … This has nothing to do with being brave. We deserve to be happy. Don't you see that? Life is too short. Seeing my mother die, well, waiting doesn't make sense … I agree, we made horrible choices the first time around, but nothing forces us to remain stuck. This isn't the eighteenth century, for heaven's sake."

Mom went quiet for a long time.

"Of course, I need to see you too … Yes, then, this afternoon, no matter what. I'm not giving up on being happy. I won't, not ever … Leave the door ajar, my love." The handset clicked into place.

I jumped behind the counter before Mom walked through the bait shop to the front door. She slid through the opened door with practiced ease to avoid ringing the bell.

Back in bed, I lay straight as a sentry with my eyes open. My mother had been—was she still?—in love with a man named Kevin, and she'd planned a rendezvous with him in spite of me, a much younger and vulnerable me, being sick. And she had walked down the stairs to the telephony to talk to him without any hesitancy or drama. I didn't know which of these truths to resent more.

The past and the present melded oddly for a moment. I forced myself to remember Mom hadn't spoken to a present-day Kevin. She'd talked to the Kevin of her past. And she held no regrets about slipping away with him and would happily do so again. That stung.

My mother—the one who had taken us for walks on the beach when winter storms blew ashore, who baked cake with Coke, and loved Miracle Whip sandwiches on white bread. She taught me how to use tampons. She sewed matching outfits for the family every holiday. You couldn't get much more maternal than that. I cringed with the truth and contradiction of who she really was.

Despite all her blasé domesticity, she'd had an affair. With a married man. An unhappily married man. And the secret love they shared had made her no happier. That Mom and Dad hadn't divorced earlier had always been a puzzle, even without knowledge of her relationship with Kevin or Mom's long, cool slip into craziness.

The worst—if there could be a worst part to this revelation—was that I did remember Mom sending me back to school with a fever, saying I wasn't sick enough to stay home. Rather than drive me to school herself, she'd called a taxi. She paid the driver in ones she'd retrieved from the sugar tin. I was young, probably five, a kindergartener. This predated any recollections of Dad's infidelities.

Why hadn't I seen their duplicity sooner?

The answer was simple: they were my parents. Parents behaved like parents, not characters in a movie. Certainly not badly. This was how things were done. Sending a sick child back to school? This passed for normal in the Archer household.

Perhaps Mom and Dad had an understanding, a pact, *a vivre et laisser vivre* approach to the marriage contract. My father, who didn't exactly fit any categories of suave or debonair, was a tomcat in his own right. Discovering Mom's tryst complicated my loyalties. Considering my mother complicit and participatory shifted my world off its axis. I reached out for something solid. I grabbed at a fistful of bedding. I deeply regretted listening in on Mom's telephony conversation but knew, given the chance, I would listen again, even though doing so had forever shifted my sense of time and reality.

This must have been the danger Dad had warned me about.

9

Larice's coffee-making skills should have disqualified her as my confessor of choice. The afternoon light shone through the reddish-gold stream filling my cup. Hardly worth drinking.

Coffee, good or bad, wasn't the point that day. That I'd left the bait shop too fast to grab an espresso was my fault. I'd come to talk to Larice about Mom's conversation with Kevin. Old news had become new. I'd replayed my childhood, bouncing between a little girl's lost dreams and the clues of Mom's philandering all through the comings and goings of my regulars.

I needed to vent.

Larice asked me to repeat the story. I'd never told her how the telephony actually worked, family secrets and all that. Besides, asking my best friend to believe telephones only rang for certain people had seemed risky. What was my best-friend quota? I didn't expect anyone like Larice to happen along again. It had seemed wiser to let her believe the telephones simply represented Dad's need to stuff something into his shallow life. I told her everything, not holding back one detail about the telephony.

As much as I hated overwhelming her, I needed to tell someone, and that someone's top job required secrecy. Larice had more than proven her loyalty. After all, I'd never been arrested. How did she respond to the big reveal of my family's close encounters of the bizarre kind? She yawned until a tear seeped out and slid down her cheek.

She spoke through her hand. "Sorry. Late night with the bills. I can't believe you haven't told me this before. You've been entrusted with something wondrous, strange, and a little spooky."

"You don't think I'm crazy?"

"Never. But have you looked through your mom's address book to see if a Kevin is in there?"

I didn't care about discovering Kevin's identity. I wanted to find some solid ground to stand on and to reconcile what remained true in my life and what might prove false. Mom should have been my first stop on that discovery trail, but I'd only slipped in and out of the apartment to make sure she was properly medicated. After all, my mother had lied to me in a big way, and by doing so had refused to help me. She alone could coach me through what talking on the telephones meant. And she chose not to.

Larice tapped my arm with light fingers. "Jenna?"

I startled. "Sorry."

"So, have you checked her address book?"

"What's the point? I would know Kevin's last name and where he lived, but what does that tell me about my parents? Who are they?"

"I can remember thinking the same thing when I was eighteen. One day, my parents walked godlike, could do no wrong. The next day, I lay in bed for hours wondering if I could ever like them again. They'd turned into freaks."

That had been sixteen years ago. "So I'm developmentally delayed, is that what you're telling me?"

"You're in the middle of something totally weird. You have no reference points. And I have no idea what to do with people who talk on the telephone with old lovers who aren't really there or aren't there when they should be." She laid her head back on the sofa and draped her arm over her forehead to stare at the ceiling. I followed her gaze to the yellowing popcorn ceiling. She straightened, looked me in the eye. "I wish I could do more, give you the answers you're looking for, tell you everything is going to be okay. All I'm really good for is listening and reassuring you of your sanity. And I can pray."

My eyes filled with grateful tears. I didn't deserve her loyalty, but I wasn't going to refuse her kindness. "Kevin could be dead."

Larice gave me that I'm-glad-you-realize-that look.

"Or not. Kevin could be living down the street or in Timbuktu, a missionary doctor treating malaria and whatever else plagues the fine residents of Timbuktu. The point is this: Mom is talking to a younger Kevin with no knowledge of his future self. Younger Kevin doesn't know where he is now—*our* now—especially not if he's alive or dead." I covered my face in my hands, just as flummoxed as Larice over the logistics of talking to someone stuck in the past. "I haven't scared you, have I?"

"Crazier things have happened. I thought stuff outside explanation was the result of someone's overworked imagination. This is different."

What had seemed normal only hours earlier, when I sat with Tim to talk about his sister, now seemed too close and personal. And yes, crazy.

Larice lowered her voice. "Don't talk about this stuff around Taylor, okay?"

"I shouldn't have said anything. My job is to contain the family weirdness. I don't suppose you can forget about the telephony?"

Larice glanced toward the entry-closet-turned-prayer-closet and back to me. "I don't have any answers for you. Maybe you should pray, light a candle."

"Is that safe?" Dad would evict Larice in a minute if he knew she burned candles in the closet.

She squinted down on an idea. "Praying? Definitely not safe, especially if you don't like change. Anything might happen. You'll be fine, though. You're used to stuff happening."

I excused myself and left without crawling into Larice's prayer closet. What could I possibly say to God? I was no saint. I'd fudged the taxes more than once and fornicated my way through my twenties and into my thirties. A polite distance between me and God seemed prudent. Besides, it would take a lot more than a candle and a quick prayer to fix my life. Larice was right that I'd gotten used to stuff happening, but change via God sounded even more dangerous.

As I pushed through the bait shop door to help Dad close up for the day, I winced at the thought of God noticing me at all. I paused, looked toward the waves north of the pier. Could the waves cease? Would the moon turn to dust and powder the earth? Could the earth's rotation reverse? Absolutely not. And Jenna Archer could not, would not, change.

End of story.

10

A mother with an air of mystique is a creepy thing.

For good or bad, mothers are constant, right? Once I knew my mother slunk into the telephony to talk to Kevin, I kept one eye on her whenever I came to the apartment. Who knew what she was capable of? I thought I understood her innumerable limitations and fears and disappointments. Evidently, I understood less than I thought. That made me wary.

There were logistical questions. How had Mom heard the telephone ring from the upstairs apartment, and why hadn't I heard her talking?

I started noticing things.

Mom always left her bedroom window open. Since I now expected to hear her at two a.m., her footsteps woke me as she moved from the bedroom to the front door.

Her late nights explained her daily naps. I'd always considered them a coping mechanism, a way to blunt reality for an hour each day, and I'd envied her ability to do so. In truth, she was simply tired.

Although she came to the telephony most nights, Kevin didn't always call. On one of those nights, when the fog dampened the constant throbbing of the surf, she left the telephony after only a few minutes. I turned toward the wall and waited for sleep. Instead, I heard a ringing from the telephony. This time I didn't bury my head in blankets. I ran to the telephony in my T-shirt and panties.

I picked up the Princess handset, sucked in a breath. "Hello?"

No reply or dial tone, nothing. A telephone continued to

ring, stifled but near. I tried answering a novelty phone that looked like a piano.

Silence.

A metal desk nearly the size of my Daewoo sat in the middle of the telephony. Every kind of desktop telephone ever made covered the glassed surface. Not one of them rang, but the sound of the ringing phone was close.

The ringing grew louder when I opened the bottom right drawer. Inside, telephones lay in a jumbled mess, awaiting Dad's skilled hands. I pulled out telephone after telephone, uncoiling cords, and putting the handsets to my ear.

"Hello?"

"Hello?"

"Hello?"

The telephone rang on. The last, a Western Electric model 354 with a cracked case and exposed wires, vibrated in my hand. If I remembered correctly, Western Electric had made this telephone in the early 1950s, about the time my grandparents were dating.

"Hello?" I said, my heart pounding.

"Are you the girl with the missing brother?"

A man's voice, older but not elderly and certainly not anyone I recognized, spoke. "Who is this?"

"Doesn't matter. I read the story in the paper. Got your telephone number from the operator."

We'd had plenty of calls from strangers once news about Brian hit the media. My dad, from chivalry I supposed, insisted on answering all telephone calls. He stood by the avocado-green wall phone for days. From listening to his responses, I learned people with do-gooder sensibilities said incredibly stupid stuff. This guy reminded me of all that. "You've got to be kidding me," I said.

"I'll hang up, if that's what you want."

I don't know if it was the intrigue of a call coming to me or that the man might know something about Brian, I couldn't hang up. "Wait!"

"There's no need to shout, girlie. I can hear just fine."

Girlie? He heard my younger self, like Amy heard college-aged Tim. "What do you know about my brother?"

"Cool your jets, girlie. I got my own questions."

"Where's Brian? Is he all right?"

"You're not listening."

I thought of Ginny's patience with her Frank and Tim's pleas with his sister. Maybe this man did know something and getting results required finesse. After all, I couldn't call him back. Not one of the regulars had ever telephoned anyone. They only waited. The man on the other end of the line controlled everything. "I'm sorry. Of course, your call is greatly appreciated."

"Your brother don't have much to say about your dad."

"You have questions about Dad?"

"There's a reason your brother is gone."

If he wanted to know about Dad, Mom, or me, I was prepared to talk. I would tell him all about my family. Well, some things. Not everything. "Brian and Dad fought a lot. Brian pushed and Dad pushed back. He was pretty hard on Brian. Dad wanted him to go to college, to be successful."

"And Brian didn't care about none of that, did he?"

I fought to hide my contempt, to stay optimistic and polite. "Did you talk to him, sir?"

"I talked to him, all right."

I reached for the chair Ginny used and sat down slowly. "When?"

"You planning on being a cop when you grow up, girlie?"

Mentioning a cop flashed memories of blue-uniformed men with squeaky leather holsters and padded chests asking pointed questions. Perhaps this man spoke cryptically to protect himself. Stay calm. Be honest. Do not think of cops or why people need them. "I miss my brother."

"He ain't missing you."

"But we were close. We shared everything." We were close enough. We'd shared a bedroom and whispered things we didn't want our parents to know. Mostly, we covered for one another, even though I resented more than appreciated Brian. He was younger, yes, but Mom and Dad treated him differently. Mom doted on him, and she pushed me into the role of second mother. He was never to be alone, never to be hungry, never to be with anyone of questionable character, which turned out to be a long list of freshmen. She forbade skateboarding with his friends or swimming in the ocean. We lived across the street from the Pacific Ocean, the largest ocean in the world, and Mom didn't want him to get wet? You can't get much crazier than that. So I taught him how to body surf when he turned seven. The kid was a fish.

Dad's feelings toward Brian confounded me. He took him to Angels games and anything to do with fast cars. He even bought Brian a skateboard and drove him to remote places for him to hurl down steep streets.

But the taller Brian got the more distant and brooding Dad became. I chalked his contrariness up to two guys in a shoving match, father and son vying for supremacy, only Brian didn't play the game. Anyone would describe Brian as mellow until Dad started goading him. The man on the telephone didn't need to know that. He didn't seem to have the patience for family saga stories, so I said, "I can keep a secret."

"I don't know."

"I'm good at secrets. There's lots of stuff I've never told my parents."

"You're one of them kind of girls, are you?"

I was. "Yes. I got—*get*—in trouble a lot."

"I made a promise." Finality weighted his words.

"Please, don't hang up."

"I gotta think on this."

"And then you'll call back, promise?"

"No promises."

And the telephone went dead.

I lay in bed—not sleeping, definitely not sleeping—with the telephone on my chest and every light in the bait shop and telephony blazing. Before lying down, I'd checked and double-checked the front door. I replayed every word of my conversation with the man who had spoken to Brian. About the family. About how hard things had been. This man had spoken to my brother.

I would outwit the man, discover what I needed to find Brian. I wasn't the seventeen-year-old he believed me to be. I'd had lots of practice being calculating, secretive, stubborn. The man on the telephone had no chance of protecting what he knew of Brian.

I shook my head. Who was I kidding? I was no mastermind.

Delusions ran in the family.

11

I carried the cracked Western Electric 354 everywhere in case the man called again. I left the telephone on the bathroom floor as I showered, I stowed it under the counter as I waited on customers, and, very weird, I slept with the thing on my chest.

But the 354 did not ring.

To avoid explaining why I carried around a telephone, I ate dinner in my bedroom every night and made up vague excuses for Mom. She couldn't know I had a caller with information about Brian. I'd seen her plummet into despair too many times when a lead didn't pan out. Dad couldn't know either. I didn't want a lecture from him on the dangers of talking on the telephones. I feared I would snipe back with admissions of hearing Mom in the telephony, which would only deepen the mess I trudged through.

On the first night of subterfuge, I said to Mom, "A customer is coming by to look at one of your boxes." She nearly exploded with excitement. I vowed never to use her art as an excuse again.

"I'm reading a great book," I told her the next night. She almost didn't buy that excuse, but I was reading a fabulous story about a daughter who lifted a car off her injured father in *Reader's Digest*, so I didn't lie, not exactly.

By the third night, I was desperate for a reason to miss dinner with Mom. "I need to update the software on the POS system." I experienced some pride by coming up with an absolutely true reason to be in the bait shop. Mom had no way of knowing I usually waited until the very last moment to update anything. Software companies are extortionists.

During the day, I took the telephone on errands around town. The 354 sat like a goldfish bowl on the Daewoo's seat. When I went to the thrift store to hunt down vintage linens for the cover-ups, a volunteer charged me five dollars for the 354, thinking I'd plucked the telephone from the broken electronics bin. I could not convince her otherwise. A man at the pharmacy quipped that a cell phone would be less cumbersome. I wanted to kick him in the shins.

And I slept with the telephone on my chest like a paperweight.

It did not ring.

GINNY LEANED OVER THE counter of the bait shop to whisper, "It's never been this long between Frank's calls. Is something broken?" Her eyes glistened and her spikes lay flat against her scalp.

Ginny and I weren't the only ones disappointed by the hollow silence. Tim hadn't had a call from Amy all week, nor Mr. Foster or the girl who came late in the day.

"Not that I know of," I whispered back weakly. No one wanted the telephones to ring more than me.

"I knew this could happen." She stepped aside to let a young mother order two hot chocolates. When the door closed behind the mother and her child, Ginny spoke up. "There are still things I need to say to Frank. And more importantly, there are things he needs to say to me. Never was a more stubborn man born on the face of this earth."

"Care for some tea?" I said, hoping to distract her.

"I care to hear his voice again. Just one more time. That's all. Then I can be content. I won't be so grumpy the next time he calls, I can promise you that." Her eyes widened in panic. "If there is a next time."

"I'll see what I can do," I said, but I hadn't a clue where to start. The telephones rang; the recipients heard the rings and answered. Some telephone calls made the recipients happy, others not so much. I did absolutely nothing to make any of that happen. That meant, as far as I was concerned, fixing the system fell to Dad.

Asking Dad for help would require admitting I'd taken a call, which meant telling him about the call from the cranky old man about Brian. I didn't worry about Dad's mental stability the same way I fretted about Mom's, but I didn't relish being a co-conspirator. I would work this out on my own.

"Have a seat, Ginny. I'll bring you some of that pomegranate tea you like. Frank may call yet. You can stay all day, if you want."

"You're so very kind. Yes, the tea would be lovely." She crossed her fingers. "All we need is a little luck."

TIM WALKED IN AT his usual time with a grocery bag of goodies for our lunch. His smile was obligatory at best. Inclement disappointment hung over his head like a cloud. "Are the telephones ringing today?" he asked, like the fishermen will ask what kind of fish are biting.

I hated seeing him like this. "Not yet, but things change." Even with my forced confidence, Tim's boyish earnestness sloughed from his face.

"Perhaps a solar flare or a disturbance in the force has stalled the telephones."

"Those are the best theories so far."

He smiled genuinely. "Care to join me for lunch?"

I looked out to the sidewalk and the entrance to the pier across the street. The sidewalks remained empty, thanks to the persistent gray. Only the stouthearted came to the beach if the sun didn't shine.

He handed over the bag. "Let me heat these up," I said. "I'll meet you by Snoopy."

He'd made poblano and spinach enchiladas and a Mexican

rice dish. He was quite proud of himself for making the enchilada sauce from scratch and told me about doing so in stunning detail. The chilies ignited my tongue. I filled our water glasses three times.

The silence of the telephony pressed like a grindstone. The more I tried to cover the silence with conversation, the more we talked about the food. "And the beans? Homemade?"

"From a can, I'm afraid."

"But you've added something."

"Green chilies and some adobo seasoning."

Tim finished his lunch and leaned back in the chair, glancing at Snoopy as we talked.

"Do you have an orienteering event this weekend?"

"Yes, in San Diego, and I have a better than even chance of winning. Old Bullard has sprained his ankle. I shouldn't be happy, but he's insufferable, and I suspect he cheats, although doing so is nearly impossible. Still…"

I spoke around a bite of enchilada in my cheek. "If you win, I'll buy you a drink. We'll toast Old Bullard to appease your conscience."

He leaned forward and smiled, warmly. He looked like the shy boy who had just gotten a yes for the prom from the cute girl in American History. I wanted to touch the patch of silvery hair above his forehead. I'd wondered for a long time if the hair was as silky as it looked. I raised my hand, but the bell on the door rang.

A customer called out. "Excuse me! Could I get a couple of lattés?"

I met Tim's gaze. His eyes mirrored the mood of the sea. Today, a deep gray, colorless but bright.

"When's summer going to get here?" the customer said, spotting me in the telephony.

Tim rose. "I need to get back to work. Amy won't call today."

As he pushed open the door, I called after him, "Lunch on me tomorrow."

His eyes widened. He seemed pleased and worried by my invitation.

And he had every right to be worried. I excelled in reheating hermetically-sealed burritos, not deepening the flavor of anything.

THE FOG GREW BRIGHTER and finally lifted around two. And then the crowds pressed. Dad arrived at his usual time, but I didn't dare leave him to run errands. A busload of tourists from Laguna Woods had traveled from their ensconced lives to walk the length of the pier, some with the aid of canes and walkers, others with helpers to push wheelchairs. They all found the telephony a refuge from the wind.

We brought kitchen chairs down from the apartment for those who needed to rest. Dad disappeared into the telephony to deliver a rooibos tea. He answered questions and listened to the stories of the older folks, who found the telephones a reminder of simpler times.

This was what Dad had always intended the telephony to be, a lively place for appreciating craftsmanship and remembering a rose-colored past. As the ambassador of telephones, he made sure each guest returned safely to their seats on the bus. I'd never seen him happier.

Because of his good mood and his eagerness to be on his way to Sally, I chanced to ask him about why the telephones might not be ringing.

"You're asking me? Enjoy the quiet," he said, waving over his shoulder as he left.

I found a folded piece of paper behind the counter. A note read, "Please, please, please fix the telephones." There was no name at the bottom. The young girl who came to sit in front of the fiddleback came to mind.

MOM STARED INTO THE freezer. Boxes of frozen entrees filled the compartment like the hold of a cargo ship. "Does any of this look good to you?"

I stepped beside her to read the sides of the boxes. "You like the sweet and sour."

"Didn't I have that last night?" She pulled out a box of the sweet and sour and ripped open the tab. She stabbed at the plastic covering over the frosty noodles, vegetables, and anemic pork with a sharpness that concerned me. Mom didn't grouse about the small things unless something overwhelming loomed. This raised the possibility of a suffocating depression that would keep her bed-bound for weeks. Did I do something? Not do something?

"I'm sorry I didn't get to the library for you today," I said, fishing for a clue.

"Is today Wednesday? Are the books due? I haven't read the new Picoult yet."

"Only the DVDs are due, and I can take them tonight."

"Whatever works."

Mom's devotion to due dates orbited close to religious zeal, especially since I was the one who returned all her library materials. "Is everything okay?"

"I'm fine," she said with the sort of blasé indifference you would expect from a wallflower at her last high school dance.

Maybe she needed to lower the dosage of her anxiety meds. "It's been a while since you've seen the doctor."

"The doctor? That old boob? He'll only prescribe more pills. He's an idiot."

Her calm perplexed me more than her anxiety. I wrapped the noodles from my teriyaki beef entrée around the fork and paused. Other things pressed. I'd promised lunch for Tim the next day. "Mom, do we have a cookbook?"

"Never needed one." She tapped her temple. "Here's my recipe box."

Tapping my temple would only raise dust and disturb cobwebs. "I'll go to the grocery store after the library. I need to cook tonight. I have a friend coming for lunch tomorrow." I winced, hoping she wouldn't ask who. I should be long past explaining who I entertained at lunch, but if she asked, I would answer. And then I would have to explain how Tim and I were just friends, which we were, but her eyebrows would dance, and she'd ask for more details about my so-called friend. I desperately needed my own life.

"You haven't invited that bait fellow, have you?" she asked, not looking at me, which made the words more menacing than wiggly eyebrows.

How would she have known about Eric? She slept way past the time of his visits. I played dumb. "What bait guy?"

"Jenna, honey, the walls are very thin. Do I need to say more?"

She did not. "I haven't invited the bait guy."

Her eyebrows rose anyway.

I buckled and told her about Tim. Not about the patch of silver in his hair or how he brought lunch every weekday. "He's one of the regulars who come to the telephony."

"So he's upset about the telephones not ringing? I'm happy to see you doing something for him. How about the others?"

Of course she knew the telephones hadn't been ringing. She hadn't talked to Kevin for over a week, at least. This had to explain her melancholy. Her loss of contact with time. Her loss of taste.

She laid her fork down and gazed past my shoulder to the horizon. And then her eyes settled on me, studying me, looking for something below the surface, which made me squirm. "Tell me about the man who comes to see you in the morning."

"Eric? There isn't much to tell. He's tall, very good looking in a scruffy sort of way you wouldn't like, and he's nicely muscled. Also, he's punctual with the bait delivery."

"There has to be more, Jenna. Do you see him away from the bait shop?"

"We're both a little busy for a relationship."

"You don't have a relationship? What do you have?"

We had convenience, a distraction from the crushing loneliness, and an admission that the real thing most probably wouldn't be coming along anytime soon, if ever. "We're trying to figure that out."

She reached across the table to touch my hand. "You have no reason to believe I'm made of flesh and blood, or that I still want to be a good mother, but I am and I do. You should get out more, Jenna. There are nice guys out there looking for a girl like you."

"Maybe ten years ago."

Mom pressed back into her chair. "You haven't given up, have you? You can't. Love will come. Young people are getting married later, certainly not as young as when I married your father, which is a good thing, I think. They're waiting for the right person to come along, not the most eligible or best looking, but the one who is kind. All these people must be meeting each other somewhere. They talk about using computers."

"Online dating? Mom..."

"They have computers at the library, don't they?"

"The library isn't the place." I almost asked her where she'd met Kevin, but a snide question like that would not help me become a gourmet cook in an hour or two. That conversation required time for histrionics for Mom and quick backpedaling on my part. "I'd better get going." I turned toward the door, stopped. Mom needed a dose of reality. "I work seven days a week. When would I actually meet a man on the internet or anyplace else?"

The furrows between Mom's eyebrows deepened.

"I'll be home in an hour, probably less"

I FOUND THE COOKBOOK section at the library. The titles either struck me as irreparably optimistic or intentionally intimidating, all of them too self-important for my taste. Besides, most of the ingredients sounded too exotic for our Ralph's Market. I left with a stack of DVDs and a Picoult novel I wasn't sure Mom had read, but without a cookbook. I headed for the grocery store with nothing to go on.

Ralph's should have been like coming home. This was the go-to store for people who lived in south San Clemente. I usually ran into at least three people I knew and played slalom with my cart around locals who stood in the aisles chatting. That night, I stood in a stupor in the middle of the produce section, hugging a bowling bag with the model 354 to my chest.

"Jenna? You look like you've landed in Oz, my dear."

My knees warmed at the sight of Ginny. If only I had landed in Oz. The Wicked Witch of the West would be less menacing than cooking. Even I could throw a bucket of water to melt a witch.

Ginny watched me expectantly. My words came out fast and desperate. "I agreed to make lunch for a friend who watches cooking shows and cooks like a chef. On the other hand, I rip open boxes and add water, sometimes margarine and whatever they put in an envelope. I'm way over my head."

"Lucky for you, I'm a master at deceptive cookery. I've been pretending to be a good cook for decades." She lowered her voice and leaned in. "I would rather knit than just about anything, including cook."

She took me by the arm and we strolled into the bowels of the beast. "It's easier than ever to pull off this ruse. And here's the secret: let the nice people in the grocery store kitchens cook the dishes that can go wrong, and you tackle the no-fail stuff. You get to create the fresh-out-of-the-garden goodness that will impress your guest. Remember too, we eat with our eyes, so we'll want to put a lot of color on the plate."

I remembered an unfortunate visit to the ER. "Will there be lots of chopping involved? I'm not good with knives."

"Only a minimum. Remember, we're only pretending to be good cooks." She squeezed my arm, and we commandeered an abandoned cart. She explained how to cut up a roasted chicken, the kind they keep under heat lamps. When I frowned, she asked, "You do have poultry shears, don't you?"

"I have wire cutters."

"Use a knife, then." She fished a tablet from her purse and drew a diagram of a chicken with little hash marks across the places to cut. "Let's move on to the potatoes." She stopped in front of the ready-to-serve case. "I'm assuming this friend of yours is a man."

I nodded, reluctantly. I didn't want Ginny to think I was preparing a romantic lunch. In fact, what kind of lunch had I invited Tim to eat? Why had I done this to myself? I remembered a sense of appreciation for all the lunches he'd prepared and a sense of responsibility for the broken telephones. There were worse reasons for cooking, I supposed, but they'd never actually thrust me into the deep end of incompetence before.

Ginny wound through the shoppers, talking over her shoulder. "You can't go wrong with mashed potatoes. There isn't a man alive who wouldn't cross a lake of lava for a heaping portion of mashed potatoes." She lifted a tub from the case. "And lucky for you, here they are." She scribbled notes on her pad. "Right before you serve the potatoes, add a little hot milk and butter. It's impossible to put too much butter in mashed potatoes, so don't be shy. That's God's honest truth."

I could steam the milk with the espresso machine. Confidence swelled where a niggling panic had parked in my chest for most of the day.

"Now for the panache. Let's head back to produce. That's

where we get the color and freshness." She eventually noticed I wasn't following her. "Are you a woman or a mouse?"

"In the kitchen?"

"Those days are behind you. Charge!"

Ginny's enthusiasm proved impossible to resist. She walked me through how to roast asparagus with garlic and olive oil. No chopping, only snapping was involved. I could snap with the best of them. Whatever she saw in my face told her I had the confidence to attempt a tomato relish.

"You can make the relish tonight," she said, like making something by the dark of night made anything possible. "Clandestine cookery calls for stealth. I do my best work with no pressure and no prying eyes." She turned sharply to face me. A look of expectancy brightened her face. "What's for dessert?"

Tim never brought dessert. "I wasn't planning on anything."

"That's just wrong. You are trying to impress this young man, right?"

"No," I said too strongly. I tempered my words. "No, he's been going through a rough patch, some disappointment over a relationship. He's a friend. He's quite a bit older. He has some gray hair."

"Impressing is easy, but lifting up a friend, that takes something extra."

"I *am* making a tomato relish."

"The relish is for distraction. The dessert is for compassion and love."

Ginny's hopes were unrealistic. Maybe a peanut butter and banana sandwich would suffice. I would eat one every day, if I could. "I don't bake, Ginny."

"Thank the Lord that Sara Lee does. The pound cake is your best-kept secret. Why, you can make trifle and shortcake and—"

"Remember my limited knife skills."

"I won't steer you wrong." She explained how to cut the pound cake into cubes and top them with sliced strawberries. "They're heavenly right now. Add a thin drizzle of chocolate sauce, found right at the end of the ice cream cases. You can do all your knife work tonight."

My confidence trembled under the weight of so much cubing and slicing. "I like Pecan Sandies, the kind the Keebler elves make, also friends of the inept."

Ginny looked at me over her glasses. "You can do this."

Tim had a trained palette. Ordering a pizza from Canaletto's tempted me, but doing so seemed ungrateful and a bit like shortchanging a man who had cooked for me for nearly two years.

"Where do we find this Sara Lee person?" I asked, surrendering yet again to Ginny's conviction that I was capable of tricking Tim with an almost homemade meal. What unnerved me was how easily Ginny had swayed me into this counterfeit confidence. How did that happen? True, Tim's generous offerings had filled me with gratitude, but I usually found more motivation in guilt. Or did I believe I could actually help someone who seemed so very capable? That seemed a bit ridiculous.

"On second thought, raspberries instead of strawberries might ease your worry lines, giving you one less slicing project," Ginny said. "Simply rinse the raspberries off and set them to dry on paper towels before putting them in the fridge. But if you do raspberries, you have to add a splash of Chambord, a raspberry-flavored liqueur. Oh my, we're on a roll now."

I'd succumbed completely to Ginny's optimism. "Lead the way."

We exchanged telephone numbers in the checkout line. "How late do you stay up?" I asked.

"You call any time of the day or night." As we prepared to

go our separate ways, she stopped me. Her face slackened. "Did the telephones ring today?"

"Sorry, no. Do you want me to call when they do?"

"No, I'll be in tomorrow. I would hate for Frank to miss me."

I left the store with food that actually smelled like food. Maybe cooking wasn't as hard as people made it look. Driving through the winding streets toward the pier and home, I couldn't shake the last look on Ginny's face. She looked like she was about to be sick, but a sparkle flashed from her eye. Such contradiction wrung my trapezius muscles.

The telephones had to ring, and they had to ring soon.

12

Tim leaned back in his chair. He blotted his mouth with a napkin and tucked it under the edge of the plate. He wore a gray striped shirt with his tie loosened and cuffs rolled up. His eyes shone blue.

"Amazing." He scraped at the chocolate in the bottom of the bowl.

"You seem surprised," I said with mock indignation. He'd commented several times on the tomato relish and asked for more mashed potatoes, the very things meant to tease him into believing cooking came naturally to me. I owed Ginny something much more wonderful than a cup of Earl Grey for pulling off such a gargantuan ruse.

"I didn't mean—" he started, his smile gone, the earnest Tim returned.

I reached for his dessert dish. "You should be surprised. *I'm* surprised. I'm the queen of the microwave." A cautious smile returned to his face. He'd smiled more today than any other time he'd come to the telephony. "You're in a better mood than yesterday."

He shrugged, opened his hands. "The meal. The conversation. Thank you."

I looked away from his gaze—where else?—to the horizon. A faint outline of Catalina Island rose from the startlingly blue ocean. "And the sun is shining. That's something for June."

The bell over the door rang. A customer. I stood, dessert dishes in hand. "This will be the day," I said. "Amy will call."

He rose. "You have to get back to it, I suppose?"

The door of the cold display case slammed closed. I hated

the bait shop more than ever. "Duty calls," I said, cautious but not too disappointed about the interruption, or so I wanted him to believe. He was older, more of an adult, really. Stable and intelligent. Nice. Too nice. "I'll be back if I can, but you'll probably be on the telephone."

After I'd waited on a few customers, Tim stood before me. "Is there something I can do while I'm waiting? Do you need help?"

I'd been meaning to replenish the lip balm display for days. I handed him the box from under the counter. "Would you mind?"

"This is perfect. Thanks."

In between customers, we talked. Mostly, I answered questions. "You do take days off, don't you?" he asked.

"Only if I'm near death, and then my father pouts and stomps about until I drag myself out of bed. He hates being away from his workshop. And now there's Sally. He would prefer snipping off his pinkies than stay here one minute longer."

"So these are his telephones. I'd been wondering. You don't seem the type to collect antiques."

I stood before him dressed in a faded San Clemente T-shirt with an attached skirt that used to hang in someone's kitchen window. What kind of person was I?

"Had you ever thought of charging people to use the telephones?"

"We tried, but people aren't interested in museums at the beach, much less in paying to see what's inside. Besides, not everyone gets a call. To most people the telephony is a bunch of old telephones so far removed from what they know of phones today."

He ran his hands through his hair, leaving the gray patch deliciously disheveled. "You will tell me, won't you, if I cross the line with my questions?"

What's this?

"This space needs to work for you. I'm a numbers guy. I can't help thinking of this stuff, even when I'm begging Amy to take the high road. I look around the telephony, imagining a tenant paying rent and a percentage to you each month. You could take days off, enjoy life."

He hadn't thought this through. "You would miss your talks with Amy."

"Sell me the Snoopy telephone. I'll talk to her at home."

I hated that idea. No more scrumptious leftovers, for one. And how would I know the time? "I'm not sure the telephony works that way."

"Your father must know how the place works."

"He doesn't say much."

Tim looked at his watch. With his head down the silver patch was so close. "I better get a move on." He leaned in a little. "There's an orienteering event in Temecula this weekend. The change of scenery would be a nice break for you. And I would enjoy your company."

He said all this lightly with no hint of expectation, but I'd just pretended to cook him a gourmet lunch. The experience had tilted my reality. Who was this guy? We were acquaintances bordering on friends. We'd seen each other for forty minutes Mondays through Fridays. He wanted a whole day together, in a car, and eventually watching old guys sweat as they ran through snake-infested chaparral. That added up to more than dicing tomatoes and a splash of hot milk.

"Weekends are our busiest days," I said. My voice unwittingly revealed my disappointment.

"Do you have anyone to spell you besides your father? Everyone needs a break." His eyebrows rose. If he'd been begging on a street corner, I would have emptied my wallet. The man had my number. He made me feel vulnerable. I didn't like feeling vulnerable. I'd spent all of my twenties becoming impervious. I set my resolve, even though I stammered through my answer, a lie meant to show I was a thoughtful businesswoman who couldn't be replaced. "Yes. Sure. She requires a six-week notice. Dad hired her. She works cheap. A real charmer. Sales usually dip."

"Six weeks? There's an event at Mt. Laguna in San Diego County about then. Book her."

Book her? Had the trifle meant more than I'd intended? I squirmed. "I don't know, Tim. I'm sort of seeing someone."

His face fell.

Before I could stop myself, I said, "If you win tomorrow, I'll buy you that drink I promised, after work, on Monday." I banked on Tim's chances at winning being slim. I trusted Old Bullard had regained his championship form.

Tim brightened more than I'd expected. "A drink is incentive enough. I'll see you Monday."

After he left, I barely noticed the customers. Yes, I waited on them, sold them fat-laden snacks and concocted iced coffees at breakneck speed, but I dedicated my limited brain mass to estimating Tim's age. I remembered him saying that Amy would soon turn forty and he was a couple years older. Gads.

But really, what did his age matter? He wasn't my type. Nothing to consider there. He was short. He needed a fashion overhaul, and by that I meant he looked too together. And old acne scars pitted his cheeks, hardly noticeable, especially if you weren't looking for them. Yes, he was smart, a great cook, and assured of himself in a quiet way that completely rattled me. I liked my men tall, dumb, and insecure.

Truthfully, and even I could be honest when it came to matters of the heart, a nice guy who called his sister five days a week on a Snoopy telephone deserved better than me, no matter what his age.

LARICE LOOKED ME UP and down and determined I needed exercise when I really wanted sympathy.

I hunted through my car for twenty minutes before I found my running shoes and sports bra. We eventually jogged across the street and veered left to the walking trail. Let it be known that I hate running. I'm strong from hefting cartons of merchandise, and I can swim all the way around the pier. But running? By the time we reached the first lifeguard stand, I bent over to gasp for air.

"Age is only a number," Larice said, not winded at all. "Guys of any age can be a dream come true or your worst nightmare."

She wasn't helping. I re-tied my shoe to buy more recovery time.

Larice jogged in place over me. Her endurance was irritating. "So how old do you think he is?"

"He has a solid gray patch right here."

"A gray patch? Really? That's so sexy. You're lucky I'm not interested."

She wouldn't be, would she? "A gray patch could be a warning sign: I am marked by—"

"The devil? Since when have you been superstitious?"

I sidestepped a dachshund pulling a woman. The soft hour before sunset brought the good residents of San Clemente out to the walking trails with their pets. The pets had been fenced in all day, but the pet owners hadn't fared much better. They'd fought their way to and from work on the 5. Both seemed relieved.

I still troubled over Larice's question. Was I superstitious? Did overseeing telephones with callers from the past classify me as superstitious? Would I soon be filling my pockets with rabbits' feet and four-leaf clover key chains? Never! "I am not superstitious. It's just that—"

"It's just that you don't know what to do with a nice guy.

He is nice, right?"

"A little too nice. He's probably gay."

Larice looked at me askance. She wouldn't chase that rabbit. "I once dated a guy twelve years older than me. He had nothing to prove. Life had tested him, and he'd met the challenge. In short, he was a man."

I slowed a skosh, hoping Larice would match my pace for a change. "Which one is this?"

An annoyed Larice only kicked harder. "You didn't know him."

"What happened?"

"I probably shouldn't tell you."

"Was he married?"

"No."

"You're sure?"

"Taylor and I lived with him for a while. She was three or four. Four. Definitely four."

Where had I been? "My happiness is in your hands." I gasped for air. "You can't leave me hanging."

"I didn't think my parents would approve."

I put out my arm to stop Larice. "We run...or...we talk. I can't do both."

We stopped. I bent over, trying to keep dinner down.

"You're running with me every night," Larice said. "No more bingeing on syrupy-sweet TV shows with your mother."

The thought of wheezing for every breath night after night appealed about as much as an appendicitis attack, followed by septic shock. But if I wanted to hear the finale of Larice's story, this was no time to get in a spitting match with her. I brought the conversation back to her old guy. "Your parents didn't approve, so you moved out, right?"

Larice walked in a small circle, hands on hips, head down. "He died. A heart attack. I found him in the shower."

I put my hand to my chest, where my heart beat like a war

drum. I did the arithmetic. "Are you kidding me? He was our age."

"He had a heart defect. No one knew."

I leaned on my knees. The guy had died. A perfect guy had gotten in the shower and died. Old guys came with a limited warranty. I didn't need that kind of trouble.

She put her hand on my back. "How much time do any of us have?"

Larice wouldn't expect me to know the answer, which was good.

"He asked me to marry him, and I planned on saying yes, but I hadn't yet. I'm so sorry I didn't." She wiped away tears. "The good ones don't come to us packaged quite like we'd dreamed when we were in high school, but those are the keepers, Jenna." She pulled my arm as she broke into a run. "Race you to the lifeguard tower."

I stood there, holding the burning place in my side as Larice ran like a puma. I thought of finding Tim dead in the shower, and my heart thumped against my ribs, a warning beat. I wasn't built to survive a shock like that. I would be polite to Tim, give him a place to talk to his sister—if and when the telephones started ringing again—and eat the lunches he brought. I would do my job. Period.

Then I remembered the chipped 354 telephone I'd left on the bed. I ran past Larice north of T-Street. Back in my room, I held the telephone in my lap and leaned against the wall. I bowed my head to touch the cool plastic. "Did you ring? I'm home. Try again. Please, please, please ring."

THE MODEL 354 DID not ring, not when I removed the casing and smothered the innards with WD40, not when I lit a hundred candles in my room, and certainly not when I'd doused the thing with tears.

I'd done what no one else had managed. I'd broken the

magic. The spell? The voodoo? I still carried the model 354 everywhere I went, but waiting for the thing to connect me with the old man, and, hopefully, my brother had been a bust. I'd mostly ignored my mother during the week I waited, so I carried the telephone up the stairs and set it outside Mom's door, where I could hear the stupid thing ring, if it did.

I wasn't prepared for what I found inside the apartment. Coffee stained the front of Mom's robe, and tufts of hair rose like feathers from the crown of her head, the worst case of bed head I'd seen outside a nursing home. And she smelled sour under a veil of Tabu perfume. Always thin, her cheekbones now rose precipitously over the valleys of her cheeks.

To find my brother and to release my mother from her prison of uncertainty, I would carry the 354 with me until I drew my last breath. Was this what believers called faith, being completely disappointed by a telephone and still certain salvation lay within its ring? To step away from the telephones meant disaster. No other portal to my brother existed. Maybe Larice had been right. My faith masqueraded as distress redoubled by superstition. I had nothing to go on but the old man's telephone calls. How long could we both wait? Could Mom regain the lost ground?

"Have you eaten?" I asked Mom, but I already knew the answer.

"What?" she said, dazed by the question.

"It's nearly seven. Dinner, Mom, have you eaten dinner?"

An empty bowl sat in the sink encrusted with cereal residue. I showed her the bowl. "Have you eaten since breakfast?"

She lowered her head, drew a deep breath that she expelled sharply. "I don't remember."

I dropped the bowl in the sink and rushed to her, sitting on the floor at her feet and laying my head in her lap. "Mom, what's going on?"

She laid her hand on my head. "The apartment is so quiet."

I deserved any scolding she dished out. And yet, I reverted to old habits. I redirected. "You complain about the trains constantly."

"Not that sort of quiet."

I could be repentant. "I've been downstairs too much. I'm so sorry."

"Jenna, I fully expect you to live your life." She didn't, really. How could she stay in this apartment, refusing help from anyone but me, and say she expected me to live any kind of life but a very tightly-knitted one? She whispered as she stroked my hair. "I have a confession to make."

I waited. When she didn't speak, I raised my head. She chewed her bottom lip.

"You don't owe me any explanations." I said this, but I very much wanted to hear who or what she blamed for the quieting of her days. I suspected my father's infidelity had finally sunk in.

"I lied to you about the telephones. I do get calls, or I did get calls, all the time."

"I'm sorry you felt like you had to lie. I'll believe anything you tell me. I'm in no position to judge."

She folded into herself to consider my words. She must have thought me trustworthy, because she blinked a few times and spoke with clarity. "The telephone calls came from a man, a man I once loved and probably still do. I suppose that seems odd to you. Look at me, I'm no ingénue. It's all pretty silly. But what I feel or don't feel doesn't much matter anymore. He hasn't called in over a week." Her voice grew tinny with panic, and her hand covered her heart. "Oh my, what am I to do? Something is very wrong, and I don't know how to fix it. I'm so sorry, Jenna."

"For what?"

"I've been unfaithful to your father."

I rubbed her leg. "Mom, Dad's living with another woman. Besides, we both know this isn't his first affair. Am I right?"

"Yes," she breathed. "We all hope our children will hold us in high regard."

The temptation to go snarky nearly toppled me. I could have capsized Mom's mental health boat in five words: You should have tried harder. Maybe exhaustion had softened me. "You, on the other hand, are talking to a man on the telephone. There's a whole world of difference between moving in with little Miss Sally and talking on the telephone."

"Your father is only looking after his happiness."

"No kidding!"

"Sarcasm is beneath you, Jenna."

Did she know me at all?

"Your father has endured a lot. He deserves the comfort of a companion as much as anyone else."

"Like us?"

"We do all right."

Mom and I traveled far outside the solar system of all right. All right would be a mother who saw the sun rise over the water and made plans for lunch with friends, or to play a round of golf, or hike along the Forster Ranch trail. All right would be a married daughter bringing grandchildren to the beach for a day of sand castles and catching buckets of sand crabs. Dad would be all right if he felt loved and respected within the four walls of this apartment, and all right meant old telephones did not ring in the middle of the night. And all of us would be all right if Brian had never left us, even if that meant visiting him at the cemetery. The not knowing filleted muscle from bone.

"I'm going to run a bath, and while you're bathing, I will create for you a culinary treat beyond your wildest expectations." Thank God for leftovers from lunch. "And then we'll watch *That Girl*, the whole last season if you want."

"I don't know."

I moved toward the bathroom. "I'm adding lavender crystals. No arguments. I'll be right back."

If I started with the ordinary things—a bath, fresh clothes, and a meal almost prepared from scratch, perhaps she would rally. If not, I had no idea how to help her anymore.

But maybe Dad did.

SALLY PROVED EVEN NICER in person than on her business card, and not at all realtorlike. She wore tight, faded jeans and a Charger's jersey. Her hair had deepened in color since the headshot for her business card—more honey than glitter. She welcomed me at the front door like a long-lost, rich relative, even though the clock ticked perilously close to eleven at night. I carried the model 354 in the bowling bag.

She offered a drink I didn't refuse. Sedation could only help. My father's paramour, after all, had greeted me at the door. I waited in the living room while she went to the kitchen. The room felt like a furniture showroom. Conversational groupings of couches and overstuffed chairs filled the room, not one La-Z-Boy in sight. She'd decorated to entertain or to duplicate her favorite hotel lobby. Dad hated entertaining and travel.

Where was Dad? Probably snoring in a bed with a comforter a mile thick. I should have come in the morning, but then, who would watch the store while I visited him?

I leaned back into the embracing chair. The view of the courtyard patio filled a wall of windows, a space larger than Mom's apartment. A forest of potted plants lined the courtyard wall and a lighted fountain splashed happily.

On the ocean side of the house, another wall of windows offered a competing view. Lights mounted on the roof illuminated the waves as foamy fingers reached for the high tide line. A fire blazed in the fireplace. Perhaps Sally had a spare room.

Sally returned to the living room carrying a tray with three glasses and a bottle of wine. "Your father will be home from the workshop in a minute or two. He better not drive too fast. I've longed for a chance to get acquainted with you."

She handed me a glass of red wine that caught the reflection of flames from the fireplace. She returned to the kitchen for a platter of cheeses, crackers, and fruit. Had I fallen down a rabbit hole?

A clock chimed eleven hours. "I'm sorry for my lateness."

Sally settled into a chair across from me. "You're always welcome, Jenna. Your father and I are both night owls. We get our best work done when the rest of the world settles in for the night."

Dad had always risen with the sun and sped off to work without breakfast. He snored through the early news. I wondered if I'd come to the correct address. "Ron Archer? *The* Ron Archer?"

She laughed. "One and the same." Her expression shifted from Martha Stewart to Mother Theresa. "I hope nothing's wrong at home."

"Mom and I are doing great. Never better. There's absolutely nothing to concern yourself about. I only have a question about the telephony for Dad. Our regulars would appreciate an answer as soon as possible."

Sally brightened. "My first husband had a passion for trains, the play kind that run on tiny tracks. He filled the basement with miniature towns and rolling hillsides. The constant tooting of horns, not to mention the dinging of the railroad crossings, nearly drove me mad. If he didn't have money in his pocket to spend at the hobby store, he puttered in the basement, always planning ways to expand his empire."

I swallowed hard on a mouthful of creamy brie and sesame seed cracker. "I can see how such preoccupations could affect a marriage."

Sally lowered her wine glass. "I never saw Tristan's trains as a problem. A man with passion understands a woman with passion. And he understood me. No, our differences turned out to be more complicated than toy trains, but isn't that always the case?"

I feared answering her question might bring us to Mom and Dad's marriage. I wasn't ready to go there. In fact, I felt downright treasonous, sipping what I'd identified as a velvety pinot noir and sampling a variety of cheeses and gourmet crackers. I decided to move the conversation out into the safety zone of brick and mortar. "Your home is lovely. And what a great location. I'm sure your view is amazing during the day."

"And at night we have the constant song of the waves. Still, the house needs lots of work. The kitchen is beyond dated. But I couldn't pass up the opportunity to live with this view." She turned toward the ocean side of the house. We watched a set of waves encroach the beach before she turned back to me. "I have a contractor coming next week. He's worked with me on lots of houses. I trust him implicitly."

I'd lived most of my life in the apartment above the bait shop. "Do you move a lot?"

"No, not really. But I've done some investing. Charlie, the contractor, knows what my clients like. He's very fussy, even fussier than me, if that's possible."

I thought of Dad leaving his socks and underwear in the bathroom, and made a conversational jump into the volcano. "How did you meet Dad?"

"I've known Ron for years. We often rubbed elbows at Rotary events. He asked for my card when he discovered Roger and I had divorced. I thought he wanted to buy real estate. Instead, we went to dinner." She smiled conspiratorially. "Your father isn't the most handsome man I've had in my life, but he is the kindest."

So kind that he went out on dates while his wife sat at

home?

Sally swirled her wine. "Are you involved with someone?"

Getting acquainted meant talking about school and jobs. Romantic involvement questions felt like something else, something intimate. I now regretted opening that door. I flipped my switch to vagueness, my default setting. "Yes and no. I'm taking stock. Considering my options." I looked out to the courtyard, hoping to see Dad walking toward the front door. Like me, he avoided any talk of romance. Landscape lighting filled the courtyard with elongated shadows of birds of paradise and palms but no Dad.

"You're too young to be sure. You're being thoughtful, purposeful. I like seeing young women taking their futures seriously." She lowered a knowing look at me. "My own daughter isn't so circumspect."

I scooted to the edge of the chair and gathered the handles of the bowling bag. "When do you expect Dad?"

"Always longer than he says, but he seemed intrigued that you had stopped by."

I stood. "If I'm keeping you from anything, I can wait in my car."

Keys worked the lock. Sally stood and went to Dad. "Speak of the devil."

I looked away as Sally stepped into his embrace. I could not tell you the last time I'd seen Mom and Dad stand close, never mind embracing. Sally poured Dad a glass of wine and excused herself. He settled into a chair. He looked comfortable, settled, content.

For a minute I'd liked Sally, which made me hate myself. Parents, in their quests for happiness, dragged their children into conundrums of loyalty. That made me angry. I was thirty-four, not a child. I should have been beyond being polite to people who had upended my life.

I itched to leave.

But while I wanted to scold Dad for his cock-in-the-henhouse ways, Mom hadn't seen his relationship with Sally in those terms. She'd become the realist. In fact, she seemed more comfortable with him gone. I could learn something from her. I reminded myself why I'd come.

"Dad, the telephones aren't ringing, and I need to know why. Is there something we can do to fix them? Has this happened before? What did you do?"

Dad's palms went up. "Wait a minute. Aren't you going to say hello? What do you think of Sally?"

I heaved a sigh like a teenager. "Our regulars aren't getting their telephone calls. They're crazy upset. I would like to help them. Wouldn't you?"

"I can't help you, Jenna. I want to, honest, but the telephones have always rung. Something must have disturbed the balance or something."

"Perhaps when you moved out?"

Dad tapped his chin. "But the telephones kept ringing after I left. I saw the young girl come several times. When did they stop?"

I counted back on my fingers. "Nine, maybe ten days."

Dad scooted forward in his chair. "Think back. What happened?"

Only the usual—Eric—occasionally, Ginny, Cranky-Man Foster, Tim, the young girl. Me. "I got a telephone call, Dad."

"In the telephony? Jenna, I told you—"

"So I'm the one who unbalanced...whatever? How convenient. You leave and I'm the one who tips the scales." I stood, hefted the bowling bag. "I don't know what I expected from you." I scanned the room, taking in the showboat elegance of the furnishings. "You've got a pretty good life here, Dad. You better appreciate Sally."

I wanted to tell him not to bother coming to the bait shop in the afternoons. In fact, I wanted to tell him to have fun looking after his own happiness, but I needed him. Hiring someone to take his place would drain the bank quickly, and I wasn't ready to give up two hours of freedom during the daylight hours. Was this how Mom had felt all these years since Brian disappeared, needing but not wanting Dad?

How had we all landed here?

13

Tim opened the door to the Fisherman's Restaurant, guiding me along with his hand to the small of my back. Men still did that? Never before for me. Winning an orienteering event had certainly changed him

Or was this the man Tim had always been?

I unzipped my hoody, and he offered to take it, but I rethought unveiling the wrap-around dress I'd stitched from thrift store curtains. I'd spent most of my life in a bikini, and now I felt self-conscious about exposing my shoulders. I had no idea where that measure of modesty came from. "No thanks," I said, looking for a place to park the bowling ball bag with the 354. "I'm comfortable." The bag plunked against the floor when I misjudged the distance.

Tim looked surprised. "You're not carrying a gun, are you?"

Living as I did with my mother above me and sleeping in a back room of a bait shop had left little room for mystery. I grabbed my chance. "One never knows."

My cryptic words earned a nervous smile. Larice had warned that my sense of humor could be off-putting, so I leaned my chin on my palms and batted my eyelashes. "You may think this is natural beauty, but I use an arsenal of makeup to look this genuine." I nodded toward the bowling bag. "I carry thirty pounds of cosmetics in that bag."

He laughed, and I realized I hadn't seen him smile since we'd had lunch. He looked good, a little sunburned from running around in the hills, but he'd abandoned his accountant attire to dress like a local in baggy shorts, a Hawaiian shirt, and sandals. He'd buttoned the top button of his shirt, though. I got all choky looking at him. I sneaked a look at his toes. They were plump, not skeletal like so many guys. Very nice. His first-place medal lay on the bar between us.

He picked up the medal. "I earned it fair and square." He turned the medallion over to reveal the engraving. "Check it out: I ran the course in record time."

The bartender laid coasters in front of us. "Whaddya have?"

Tim ordered a beer as dark as coffee. I'd not pegged him for a sweet-and-strong beer kind of guy. They wore kilts and braided their hair for battle. For two years I'd shared lunch with Tim from a distance. I thought I knew him. Then he touched my back and ordered a most unlikely beer.

My pits got sticky and my palms turned damp. I sloughed off my hoody. I needed air. Benign, blah, and buttoned-up Tim had ruffled me. Men did not ruffle me. Unnerving was my specialty. I ordered a strawberry daiquiri, something I could drink fast to fulfill my promise and leave quickly.

As we waited for our drinks, I played with the hem of my dress. Tim raised his voice over the crowd and the televisions. "I see you five days a week, but I know very little about you. Tell me something, anything."

He certainly left a lot of rope for a girl to hang herself. Didn't people practice safe conversation anymore? "Wait a minute. I'm paying, so I get to ask the questions. What got you started with orienteering?"

"I thought you'd want to know if I'd been married."

Past relationships and marriages provided screening questions. This wasn't the bait shop or the telephony, not tonight. His question, even more than the hand to the back, told me Tim thought of our casual drink as a date. If he'd been a true local, he would have known drinks on the pier didn't qualify as a date. "I thought you were gay."

He ran a hand through his hair, laughed knowingly. "You're

not the first. Even my mother says I'm too nice. But I was married, once, to my college sweetheart. She left me for her orthodontist, to whom I paid a pirate's ransom to straighten her teeth. He'd been in practice long enough to have a very sweet lifestyle—the Porsche and the house on the beach, trips to exotic places. My accounting firm had barely gotten on its feet. I worked long hours to keep the lights on. That's gone too. After dividing the practice in half, there wasn't much left."

"I'm sorry." And I was. Betrayal and loss of any kind stung.

"Don't be too sorry. Her front teeth have a gap as wide as the Suez Canal. And I'm here with you."

I squirmed on my stool.

He touched my hand lightly. "Can I give the maitre d' our names? On me?"

When I hesitated, he said, "So you think I'm too nice?"

He was nicer than any man I'd ever known, and I'd accumulated quite a roster of known men. Truth be told, Tim out-niced my dad by a long shot. I wanted to believe Tim was what we were all supposed to be. "Actually, no. You're refreshing, and not a bit too nice. I'm sure there's darkness crouching in your heart somewhere." Who was I kidding?

"My mother would love to hear you say so. Do you have proof?"

"None I'm willing to divulge at the moment." I had nothing on Tim. His kindness was as rare as a blue-footed booby and just as authentic. I reached out and unbuttoned his top button. "Better?"

"The girls in the office insist buttoned up is cool."

"Only if you're Forest Gump or a hipster."

"And dinner?"

I'd washed my hair, shaved my legs, and put on a new dress. Any reasonable observer would surmise I'd expected a date. I'd only meant this to be a friend helping a friend celebrate an overdue victory, plus an apology for having cut the connection he'd made with his sister. Eating dinner, not sharing the tab, that was a date, right?

"I have plans." And I did have plans. A bag of overdue library books filled the passenger seat of my car. And Mom wanted to watch *You've Got Mail* for the gazillionth time. Those were rock-solid plans for a Monday night. I finished my drink and slid off the stool. "I'm sorry. Maybe another time."

From the look on Tim's face, he figured there wouldn't be a next time. Of course, I second-guessed myself immediately. But, honestly, getting involved with someone seemed pointless, not now, not even with someone like Tim. I had Brian to find, my mother to appease, and don't forget enigmatic Eric. I'd cataloged my shortcomings plenty. Being a two-timer wasn't one of them.

The bartender picked up my glass and offered another. I ordered a chardonnay and climbed back on the stool, because I'd memorized all the dialogue in *You've Got Mail,* and I had one more day of grace on my library books. Knowing the system worked for me. Eric was Eric.

"Maybe you're hungrier than you thought?" Tim said.

Ravenous. We sat on the edge of the pier next to the glass, where the floor swayed from buffeting waves. We didn't talk about telephones or missing brothers and sisters. We talked about orienteering, which sounded like way too much work for a good time. But Tim made playing with a compass sound like an acceptable sport to observe. He also insisted he'd never come across a rattler. Surely he hadn't looked for snakes. They were out there, waiting for me.

Our waitress walked our orders toward the kitchen. A couple dressed in California chic, the woman in a silk sheath of palm fronds and the man in a shirt that filled and fluttered in the breeze, stopped at our table. They knew my name, smiled knowingly at Tim, and shuffled off quickly.

From the way they scampered off, Tim had talked to

people, specifically a woman, about his plans with me. "Who is she?"

"Linda? She works in HR," he said, twisting his beer in a puddle of condensation.

He asked what kept me at the bait shop. Explaining Mom's aversion to change and leaving the apartment led to the story of Brian's disappearance. I teared up telling him about Dad leaving, which surprised me because I believed I'd accepted his absence. Tim dug out his hanky. He moved to blot my tears but thought better of the move—had I backed away?—and handed the hanky over.

While I considered the appropriateness of blowing my nose on someone else's hanky, Tim greeted a trio of people, all sinewy and tan, that he knew through orienteering. Tim made arrangements to caravan to the next event with them before they left.

He turned to me and asked, "What would you be doing, if you were free of the bait shop and the telephones?"

"I was accepted into a sonographer's program this fall in New York. I like to help people when there isn't blood or bodily fluids involved. Dad leaving scuttled that plan."

"Do you have a plan B? You could go to school in Orange County."

"No plan B. Anywhere in Orange County is too close to home. Besides, I'd gotten a scholarship to Rochester." He waited, probably hoping I'd given more thought to my future. "I'm going to find my brother. I don't see my mother getting well without definitive news about him, good or bad. Without Brian there are no plans."

Because Tim didn't laugh or try to console me about my grim future, I let him pay for my mahi mahi dinner and walk me back to the bait shop, where he dared not play the entitlement card, not even for a kiss. I needed his friendship more than another entanglement, although I had no idea how

friendship with men worked. I would probably need to learn
how to spit.

14

Never big on afterglow, Eric patted my shoulder and threw the sheets back.

Hefting crates of bait had swollen his biceps, forged broad shoulders, and built pectoralis major and minor that made me swoon. In general, everything from his sea-glass green eyes to his belly button and beyond screamed perfection.

I pulled the sheet up to my neck. Eric deserved a chance to prove he owned a heart to match his brawn. "Do you have to go?"

"I have five more deliveries before lunch."

That made five deliveries in six hours. We had time to talk, but no one unveiled their heart to a shrew. I used my come-hither voice. "We don't get to talk very often." I patted the bed, but he reached for his jeans.

"About what?"

"Normal stuff, like the weather or our dreams. You know, conversation?"

He laughed tightly and grabbed for his shirt. "What do you want to know?"

I should have thought this through. "Let's start at the beginning. Where were you born?"

"I'm sorry, Jenna. I don't have time for a full-blown history lesson." He sat on the bed to put on his socks and boots.

I sat up, made sure my hair fell over my shoulders. "Do you like your job?"

He looked relieved. "Fishing? Yeah, fishing pays the bills."

I remembered Larice's questions about Eric. Asking to meet his parents seemed too ambitious. Instead, I asked,

"What's your favorite food?"

He paused tying his boot. "I never thought about it. In-N-Out, I guess." He tucked in his shirt and threaded his belt through the loops of his jeans.

I fired questions at him. Eric spouted answers like a winning slot machine. I should have compiled a list. "What's your greatest fear?"

He fastened his belt. "I don't know. See ya Friday?"

I grabbed my robe and followed him from the bedroom. "What do you avoid? I hate snakes, so I don't go hiking in the hills."

"I saw a rattler on the walking trail."

Where Larice and I had just jogged? "You did not!"

"You betcha." He stopped and turned back to me. "What's this about, Jenna? I thought we had an arrangement." He threw up his hands and turned for the front door.

I thought of plenty of questions as Eric revved the delivery truck motor and pulled away from the curb. Do you like me? Do you think about me when we're not together? Do you see me in your future? And the question I dreaded the most: are you married? His answer held the power to turn me into the very thing I loathed, the other woman.

I threw on some sweats and a hoody to meet the fishermen at the door. Thankfully, they took one look at me and knew I was in no mood to banter about which fish were biting. Once they left, I turned the sign over to the closed side. I didn't bother locking the door. A thousand thieves could walk in and take everything. I did return for the bowling bag and the model 354 before running across the street, over the tracks, and to the waterline.

The grit of sand against my teeth and the saltiness of the water slowed my heart rate, but the stew landed hard on my stomach. Still, I formed another ball of wet sand, scanned the beach for onlookers, and popped the clod into my mouth. This time I held the granules in my mouth, playing with the cutting edges against the roof of my mouth and inside my cheeks, letting the sand swim with saliva under my tongue.

I caught the motion of a fisherman dropping his line into the water. Thinking of fish in the water reminded me that fish pooped. I unzipped the bowling bag to find the water bottle stowed there. I swished and spat the noxious brew of sand and who-knew-what from my mouth.

The waves expelled their foamy breath at my feet, and the water inched closer through the 6:09 and the 6:57 Metrolinks. The clanking, bellowing, and clattering of the trains accompanied the chaos of my thoughts. In the end, one idea crystallized: I knew as much about Eric as I would ever know.

I turned toward the crossing in time to see the tail of the Metrolink train slink northward. Watching the train recede, I made a promise to want more and expect more. There weren't enough beaches or sand in the world to make me feel better about who I'd become.

15

I watched back-to-back episodes of *The Twilight Zone* until Mom's sobs transitioned into airy gasps and, finally, to snores. I clicked off the TV and left the apartment, careful to close the door without making a sound.

Back in the bait shop, I felt strangely light. I'd left the bowling bag with the model 354 in Mom's apartment. I climbed back up the stairs. There was no point following through with my plan to exorcize the quiet from the telephony without carting my own demon along, for I considered the 354 no less than a tormentor. At first, the telephone had created a flicker of hope. And then, when the thing clammed up, nothing but angst.

Inside the telephony, I watched the occasional knot of walkers stroll by the large windows, some leaning on their friends for support after a night of gorging lasagna and drinking glass after glass of wine.

I pressed my face to the window of the telephony to look toward the restaurant. The sidewalk had emptied of foot traffic. I'd turned the lights off hours earlier, but streetlights flooded the interior of the telephony, stretching shadows across the floor. There were the fiddleback and the ashtray, the desktop of monotonous office telephones, the switchboard veiled in shadow, and, having turned full circle, the Snoopy telephone grinning sinisterly at this hour. My only strategy to restart the ringing was to convince whatever powers controlled the connections between yesterday and today to see things my way.

Talking in the room seemed sacrilege. Don't ask me why.

Interrupting silence, whether the library's or a telephony's, affected me the same way, so I whispered. "Something has happened to quiet you. But any missteps shouldn't be taken personally. We're dopes when it comes to how things work. Dad hasn't a clue. Mom is heartbroken. Please, for the wonderful people who come here, could you please let the telephones ring again?"

The condensers on the refrigerated cases clicked off and hummed back to life in turns. No telephones rang.

I finally dumped the model 354 from the bowling bag and pushed the display of telephones from the desk to the floor. I set the 354 smack dab in the middle of the emptied space.

"I'll know my pleadings have changed your mind when the 354 rings. I don't hear the others, so if the 354 could jingle to let me know my words have caused a change of heart, I would greatly appreciate that kindness."

The telephony was never truly silent, not with the relentless pounding of the surf and the mandolin music piped onto Canaletto's patio. But that night the silence of the room sat on me like a wet coat. I slumped to my knees.

I'd spent enough time in youth group to know praying to inanimate objects ticked God off. And making God mad certainly wouldn't help my cause. Fairness required he should be allowed a chance to pull off a miracle too. I put my face to the floor and pulled myself into a ball. Perhaps God wouldn't recognize me all wadded up.

"Hey there, God. I'm probably the last person you expected to hear from tonight. You should know, before we continue, that I'm breaking up with Eric. I do realize beseeching the telephones to ring was probably inappropriate. I apologize, sincerely. Awakening a silent telephony doesn't seem like your area, but if you're feeling magnanimous, thanks for considering it. I'm sorry for not asking you first. So, could we come to some kind of understanding here?

"I have a mother who's on the verge of..." Tears streamed my cheeks, and I no longer whispered. "I should have come straight home that day. If I'd been on the bus with Brian, none of this would've happened. But I took a stupid bet, and my mother is trapped in her apartment. She's changing. I'm sure you can see she's getting much, much worse. I don't know what to do, except to find Brian.

"Could you, *would* you, reconnect me with the old man, the one who saw Brian that last day? And reconnect Amy with Tim, too. I might have a plan you would like, but he needs to hear from Amy one more time. Just once. I'm not asking for myself, except that bit about Brian.

"I don't have anything else. I know I'm a pig and don't deserve any favors from you. But I have absolutely no idea what to do. I hate this feeling, so I'm begging for your help."

I waited and the silence mocked me. I squeezed into a tighter ball and sobbed until my throat burned. Blubbering didn't help anything, but I couldn't stop. I must have fallen asleep. I woke with a start when a group from the restaurant staggered by, laughing and yelling under the influence of the drink du jour.

Once they passed I stood at the window. The mandolin music at Canaletto's stopped abruptly. I put my hand to the cool glass to feel the reverberation of the waves. Only the Pacific Ocean and I remained.

I've only been caught in a riptide once. I knew to look for the churning of sand under the water as a warning. I was fourteen. Preoccupied. And a little stupid. Definitely immortal. The sucking tide pulled me farther and farther out. I swam parallel to the shore as Dad had drummed into Brian and me. Fear hadn't even quickened my heartbeat. And then something rough brushed against my leg. I imagined Great Whites circling. But the rogue tide still held me. My heart raced. And then I got angry. I plowed through the water, kicking with all my might to escape the current.

That was exactly how I felt in the telephony, facing the unblinking telephones—pulled by an unseen, relentless power toward an expanse of colossal threat. Kicking had worked for me before. I swung back and landed a solid kick at the desk. The crammed drawers dulled the drumming. I leaned on the desktop and kicked and kicked and kicked at the drawers. I only stopped when a drawer handle flew off.

"You stupid, stupid telephones!"

I plucked the 354 off the desktop, opened the bottom drawer, dropped the telephone inside, and slammed the drawer closed. I kicked the drawer once more for good measure. "Take that!"

And then I crumbled to the floor and spread out on my back. The ceiling fans twirled in lazy circles, and for some unfathomable reason, that spurred more tears. "What's wrong with me?"

A telephone rang. Subdued, yet insistent.

I opened the bottom drawer. The ring pulsed louder. I pulled the telephone out and leaned against the desk. With my hand on the receiver, I whispered, "Thank you." I couldn't tell you who I thanked, but as soon as the words escaped my mouth, I worried I would mess up with the cranky coot again.

"Help me." Those words, I knew, were a prayer.

The telephone rang in my hands. I lifted the handset to my ear. "Hello?"

"You're a hard one to get a hold of," the old man said.

"I've been helping my parents look for Brian," I said, reminding myself to be seventeen-year-old me.

"I seen you on TV. You ain't going to find him, not where you're looking."

"Where should we look? Is he close by?"

"I'm not finished asking questions. You got a problem with that?"

Yes. "No sir, I'm ready. Ask away."

"There's no sense calling me sir, girlie. I ain't never been a sir."

"I figured you for a Marine. You talk like one."

"I wouldn't go speculating unless you're tired of talking to me."

I sat on the floor and leaned against the desk. A drawer handle poked me in the latissimus dorsi. "I'm sorry. Ask me anything."

"Tell me about your family, and don't leave anything out."

I couldn't make my family look like the Von Trapps, so I pressed on with the truth. "We price merchandise in the bait shop for the tourists. We expect them to be desperate and for their kids to exploit their weakness. I suppose that's extortion."

"You would be stupid not to charge them suckers through the nose. I hate tourists. They're everywhere and the traffic...don't get me started."

The old crank's near miss at commiseration opened a floodgate of muddy water about my family. "Mom and Dad make us sleep in a tiny room at the back of the bait shop. We haven't eaten dinner together in years. Instead, Dad watches the news. Brian is failing most of his classes, even though he's tons smarter than me. I once saw my dad kissing a lady on El Camino Real. And she wasn't my mom."

When I took a breath, he said, "Your dad's a real prince. Does he wallop Brian?"

I marched on, knowing I wouldn't tell the whole truth. "Brian can get mouthy. Dad slapped him a couple times. He left red marks on his face, so Brian missed a couple days of school."

"You're hedging, young lady. Protecting your dad ain't going to get you what you want."

Withholding information about Brian wasn't right either. But he made a point. Dad's anger pummeled Brian, literally.

He'd outweighed Brian by a hundred pounds. And his voice
boomed like a canon. There was nothing fair about the fights
between Dad and Brian. Brian had the quick-draw mouth, but
Dad owned every advantage physically.

Family loyalty is a funny thing. Not always deserved, but we
only get one family. Does sharing DNA buy us a rooting
section? At the moment, cheering Dad struck me as pathetic.
Besides, the crank saw right through me. Appeasing him
required steering clear of Dad. "My mother treats Brian like a
king."

"You don't like that much, do you?"

I held out the receiver. Either Brian had told the old man
everything that happened in our apartment, or the telephony
held powers I didn't know about. In any case, he knew too
much.

No, I didn't like Mom's preference for Brian then, and her
mooning now was a thousand paper cuts to my heart. If I heard
about his milky breath one more time...what? What would I
do? Would I leave my mother to fend for herself? Not likely. I
forced myself to focus on the old man. Perhaps he'd sired his
own family of disappointments and sheltering the truth about
Brian brought him a kind of absolution.

"Mom's adoration of Brian did hurt," I said. "I never
figured out what made me the lesser."

"So you've become the lesser, haven't you?"

I came perilously close to hanging up on him. He couldn't
have known this from Brian. I hid my worst rebellion from my
impressionable brother. Whenever he needed me, I ran to him.
All except that one day. "Who are you?"

"I'm the one asking the questions."

"And I'm answering. Now tell me who you are."

The line went silent. "Hello?"

"I'm here, girlie."

Another long pause.

I waited. A lone man teetered past the telephony's window. I recognized him as Canaletto's cook, the son-in-law of the owner. His chef's coat flapped in the breeze to reveal a tomato splatter T-shirt.

"My name's Jerry."

I found a pen in the desk drawer and scribbled his name on my hand. "Did Brian know you?"

"No more questions."

My voice squeaked. "You have to tell me something about Brian, please."

"Be sure you want to know the answer."

"Hello?" I said over and over, but Jerry had hung up.

I LAY ON THE BED staring at a quiver of light dancing on the ceiling, a happenstance of light and water thanks to the fountain next door. My conversation with Jerry buzzed in my head. I'd told him plenty, practically laying out the history of my family and divulging feelings I'd nurtured for years without naming. All I knew about him was his name.

Jerry.

For two weeks I'd been sleeping with a telephone, and all I got from him was a name, his very useless first name. I didn't remember any Jerrys, except for my favorite teacher, Gerry Wigent. She'd made fifth grade worth attending. She taught us how to draw from the right sides of our brains and how algebra worked, and she read to us every day after lunch—magical books that made me fall in love with reading.

Jerry was no Mrs. Wigent. He was vituperative (new word: bitter and abusive). He sounded like a psycho, which scared me very much for Brian. I shook away a vision of Brian deflating into the damp earth of an arroyo somewhere in southern California, his eyes white as cotton balls.

If not a psycho, Jerry bordered on control freak. At this rate, I would be seventy by the time I learned where Brian had gone, and Mom would be dead. I couldn't let that happen. I needed to be smarter, sneakier. I needed to find Jerry's weak spot.

My weak spot, of course, was obvious, but I planned on settling the Eric problem at his next delivery.

16

Sad but true, self-loathing does not change behavior.

Otherwise, I would have been Mother Teresa, or at least Mrs. George H. W. Bush, the patron saint of first ladies. There had to be another way. I'd tried everything, including prayer, for heaven's sake—and my sake too, I guess. All of this because I could not say no to Eric. I needed Larice.

I heard her sensible dental hygienist shoes clomping up the stairs. Perfect timing. I gave her five minutes to change her clothes before I double-stepped up the stairs to ring the doorbell. She took another five minutes to answer.

Sweat pasted her bangs to her forehead. She wore a silk robe over her SpongeBob scrub pants. She also wore the don't-ask-one-more-thing-of-me look. A better friend would have let her take a shower and drink the tea that relaxed her in the afternoon.

"What's wrong?" she asked.

I pushed past her and headed for the kitchen and the refrigerator. Larice's mom kept it stocked with the healthy drinks Taylor craved. I grabbed a Vitamin Water. "I'm ready to join the nunnery. Tell me what to do."

"Could this have waited until I went to the bathroom?"

"Go," I said and shooed her toward the bathroom. "But come right back."

Larice looked me up and down. "You look awful."

I'd gotten less than an hour's sleep before Eric arrived with his delivery and enough passion to unseat my resolve lickety-split. Not long after, the fishermen pounded on the door, so I hadn't changed my clothes from the day before. I hadn't brushed my teeth either. About two, I finally ran a brush through my hair when I'd caught my reflection in the espresso machine.

"I had a rough night."

"Eric?"

I took a long swig of Vitamin Water. "He's out, totally gone from my life. No more Eric. He's g-o-n-e, gone."

"You haven't told him yet, have you?"

The teapot whistled. "I thought you had something to do, Larice." Her know-it-all side always seemed to make an appearance when my tail feathers mopped the floor.

"I can be there when you talk to him."

I set her teacup on the counter with a clatter. "You have no faith in me."

"I've been right where you are. Breaking ties is hard, especially muscular ones. Backup can only help, sweetie."

"What ties? I can't get the guy to talk to me for five minutes." I'd promised myself I would not cry, but here came the tears. Larice pulled me into her arms. Once the tears started, there was no stopping the flood of snot. I wriggled from her embrace to grab a Kleenex. Larice watched me blow my nose with her arms hanging to her side. I'd completely deflated her.

"You don't want a bladder infection." I shooed her toward the bathroom again. She didn't move until I assured her I would be all right.

Would I?

I was blubbering over a man who couldn't be bothered with simple conversation. The tears were fueled by anger, right? Eric treated me like a—oh boy, I sure didn't want to go there. But who had made his evasiveness okay in the first place? No one but me. I cried harder. I could be so stupid.

Larice carried our drinks to the balcony. "We need to dry you out before we can talk. I'll be right back."

The day had dawned bright and clear. Everyone who'd come into the bait shop declared June gloom dead and gone. And now the day waned. The water shifted from Coke bottle green to a sensible blue-black, startled only by the whiteness of foam. If there had been an on-and-off switch to a day like this, no one would ever turn it off. Not too hot. Not to cold. This was Goldilock's day at the beach, the day we all remembered and used to measure the goodness of every other day.

I settled into a deck chair. Below me, Crayola-colored umbrellas sprouted from the beach, where mothers gathered their children for sand-encrusted afternoon treats. A few hardy surfers rode the undulating swells, waiting for a wave with enough *umph* to curl and break. Some gave up and paddled in. Only a lone kayaker seemed content with the lethargic action— or inaction—of the waves, none of them regretting their day of sun and sand and sky and sea.

I felt horrible.

Larice sat beside me, now wearing a pair of shorts and a T-shirt from a family reunion in Lake Okoboji. "Is there someone else?"

I thought about my dinner with Tim, how he'd been pleased to be with me and to show me off to his friends. But if he knew the real me, the disappointing me, there would be no dinners on the pier or invitations to orienteering matches. I would have sworn such losses meant nothing to me, but they did. I shook my head, more to clear my mind of Tim than to answer Larice's question.

"Really? No one? I don't believe you. He better not be another hottie because I'm telling you, Jenna, those guys are nothing but trouble. No one shreds a woman's heart more than a guy who's hot and knows it."

"My problem isn't hotties. I'm a mess. I screw up constantly. I'm prepared to be single for..."

Larice reached over to rub my arm. "You need to prepare

for a relationship that matters. It's going to take some time to be ready. I can't lie to you. It's hard. At least, that's what I hear. There are days when I say to myself, Girl, you're good to go. And other days when I should crawl under a rock and stay there."

Larice under a rock? I belonged under Mt. McKinley.

She waited for me to return her gaze. "You're not a mess, just beat up."

That was generous. "I've never brought a guy home to meet my parents, ever. I couldn't face their expectations. Mom would want to shop for wedding dresses, through QVC, of course. Dad would ask to see the guy's bank statement. I'm better off alone. Forever."

Larice flipped a dismissive hand. "You're not in a place to make that kind of decision. You deserve a good guy. You're the one who has to believe that before any guy will. And then the good ones will come around."

"And they're coming around you?"

"A couple have. I told them to look me up next summer."

"And they agreed?"

"One has. I'll be disappointed if he doesn't call after Taylor graduates. I got his address, so I can send him a graduation announcement. I'm not too proud to remind a guy I'm alive and well. He's a patient at the office. And so cute. A little younger than me but nothing indictable. He's a radiologist at the oncology pavilion. He genuinely cares about people."

"And the other?"

"When I told him why I was waiting, I learned some new swear words. He turned out to be a jerk."

That sounded like a fifty-percent success rate to me. "So how do I enroll in the nunnery?"

"You won't be a nun. Real nuns marry Jesus. I'm sure doing so is nice for them, but I want a man with flesh on. Some days are hard. Again, I won't lie to you. We don't live in utopia.

I have patients—some guys too old even for me—who come on to me while their wives are sitting in the waiting room. I can't believe their gall. They tell me how pretty and fit I am, and then they ask me out to lunch or for a drink. I get lonely. I'm not made of stone. Their company is tempting, real tempting. So far I haven't taken them up on their offers, but I have hosed a few with my water syringe."

I had no idea.

"You need to know, honey, that I have failed. Some guys know how to get what they want, and I'm weak enough to fall for their moves. I hate myself afterward."

"And Taylor knows this?"

"No. I thought about telling her, but the receptionist—we have lunch once a week—"

"You never told me."

"Jayne's been through a lot with her daughter. It turns out I'm not that original with being a mess-up. I really appreciate her honesty. Jayne knows a different God than the one we learned about. He's a father."

I stood up. "This is getting weird."

She tugged on my skirt. "Sit down. I'm done, but I wanted you to know. I'm as human as you are."

I sat back down and studied Larice's profile. Now that she'd changed her clothes and washed her face, she wore the day like a champ. She wasn't really a mess or beaten up. Even at this hour of the day, when the breeze held its breath and the temperature peaked in the apartment, she seemed certain, honest. For that kind of resilience, she had to sleep like a baby.

"So what's your plan?"

"After much trial and error, and with some help from good people, I've come to a conclusion: I can be a good example for Taylor without being perfect or having a perfect past. The important thing is to brush myself off and keep trying. I also spend extra time in the prayer closet. Sometimes a girl needs help forgiving herself and moving on."

I knew all about being stuck. "And sitting in a closet helps?"

She rolled her eyes. "Eventually."

Stepping into a closet, sitting on a cushion, and sliding the door closed made no sense to me whatsoever. What good, anyway, was a God who lived in a closet? I stood up again. "I really do have to go. We're out of milk, and I have to stop by the clerk and recorder's office."

"What in the world for?"

"Stuff for Dad. Property stuff. Nothing important." To find Tim, actually. I had no idea where he lived. He needed to know the telephones were ringing again.

17

Tim lived in a home worthy of the most uptight, persnickety retiree known to man.

Not one dandelion marred the rigid plane of his lawn. Beyond stood a beige shoebox of a house with a red door—the one and only bolt of color—and a one-car garage painted a shrill white. Two palm trees, the ubiquitous plant of our tender climate, cast reaching shadows on the lawn.

I wasn't there to give Tim landscaping advice. I was there to reconnect him with his sister. I walked along the street to the driveway, so I wouldn't leave footprints in his grass.

A woman answered the door, holding a glass of red wine in a fish-bowl sized glass. I checked the house numbers against what I'd written on a piece of paper.

"Can I help you?" she said.

I took the woman to be older than me and certainly tidier, dressed for work but not rigidly so. She wore linen slacks and a crisp chartreuse blouse. She also wore ridiculously high heels. I wished I'd slipped into my Rainbow sandals—my dress-up flip-flops rather than the faded pair I wore—before leaving the bait shop.

And she was pretty in a favorite book sort of way, even though her features gathered unimaginatively on her face. She could have modeled for a Republican fundraising brochure. Very Nordic. An aging high school cheerleader. Perfect for Tim. Why did that matter?

"Tim doesn't live here, does he?" I said.

She turned into the house. "Tim, you have company."

The woman looked me up and down. What did she see? A

girl who had never stepped into linen slacks or styled her hair, who wore a dress made from three post-war era fabrics. My beauty routine included running a brush through my hair and applying lemonade-flavored lip balm. I flipped a length of hair over my shoulder because I could. Lady Green-Shirt frowned.

The door opened wider. Tim stood there, open-faced, smiling like a goof. "Jenna! Come in."

I looked to Lady Green-Shirt. Her expression idled in neutral. "You have a guest," I reminded him. A wife? A girlfriend?

"You must join us," she said, with zero enthusiasm.

I smiled reluctantly. "Thank you." I stepped over the threshold into an alternative universe with wide-planked, distressed floors, an open-beamed ceiling, and a kitchen suitable for Giada de Laurentiis. A sectional faced a limestone fireplace, comfortable and perfectly proportioned. Not boring. Not persnickety.

"Nice place," I said.

"It's not exactly what I had in mind. I bought the house from my parents after they'd done all the renovation," Tim said, shoving his hands into his pockets. "They meant to retire here. When the time came, Mom wouldn't move. She wanted Amy to be able to find her way home. My only complaint about the place is not having a spot for my coconut gorilla collection."

Had I figured Tim wrong? I couldn't read his face. Perhaps he played poker. I lost my chance to call his bluff. The woman extended her hand. "I'm Connie. I work with Tim. We have a big meeting tomorrow."

I stepped back. "Then I shouldn't intrude. I dropped by with news of the telephony."

Tim went alert. "You're getting calls?"

I glanced at Connie. She didn't seem the sort to dabble in the whimsical. "Yes."

"Did *you* get a call?"

I hadn't told him about Jerry. "I don't know what you mean."

Tim took my elbow and pulled me outside, closing the door with Connie inside. He escorted me across the lawn toward my Daewoo. I stopped short of the car/closet/purse/trashcan. The lawn felt like a sponge under my feet. "How did you know?"

Connie waved at us from the front window. He followed my gaze back to the house. "Never mind her. We have time." He pulled me to the street side of the Daewoo. "Are you all right? Who called?"

I wanted to cry on his shoulder. Instead, I told him about Jerry, how cantankerous he'd been and secretive, how he hated answering my questions. And that he had been the last one to see my brother. "He scares the poop out of me. His voice—"

"Can he help you find Brian?"

"Only if I get much smarter before he calls again. He knows things about Brian he isn't sharing. That's the scary part, the really scary part. What does the man know?" I flinched at the question. "To find out, I'll have to trick him into saying something, anything."

"I could be there when he calls." He stepped closer. "Clearly, he scares you."

"He calls in the middle of the night." I pictured dropping the 354 into the drawer and the ring that followed. A wave of guilt washed over me. I confessed I'd caused the silencing of the telephones by carrying the 354 with me everywhere.

Tim scratched his chin. "So everything has to be in its place, or in the telephony, for the thing to work."

I nodded as if I'd already discovered the secret to restarting the telephony. What he said, though, made sense. Order ruled the telephony. Dad added new telephones, but the old ones never moved. He added shelves, hung others on the walls, and stuffed the not-quite-ready-for-prime-time models into desk drawers. The 354, for one. Once in the telephony, a telephone stayed in the telephony.

Knowing the telephones couldn't be moved solved one mystery. Another unknown involved time. Could what was said in the telephony today change what had already happened seventeen years earlier? I should have paid better attention in my high school physics class. I remembered talk of bending light and time. One girl did a report on a rain-forest butterfly causing a cyclone in the Pacific.

"Tim, would you still want to see Amy if she has truly lived out your worst fears?"

He frowned at the question but answered resolutely. "Of course. My family will do anything to find Amy. We walked the back alleys of Seattle when we heard she might be there. We rummaged through dumpsters, looking for her, hunting for something to tell us she'd been nearby. We followed one kid's story to Boston and another's to Miami. If you want to know where to buy drugs in any major city, I can tell you."

I didn't want the telephony to be one more dead end for Tim and his family. "What you've said to Amy hasn't changed anything. What do you want for her?"

He looked over my head. "The places we looked. No one should have to live like that. If she had kept up her grades, if she hadn't gotten mixed up with the quarry crowd...They ruined her." He closed his eyes against whatever he saw.

I touched his arm, stepped closer. He met my gaze. "I agree. Amy would be a lot better off if she'd never started with drugs, but I don't know of anyone who has changed the past through the telephony. It's your choice. You can keep talking to Amy, a girl on the edge of destruction, or you can try to see the real Amy, the one who has lived to tell her story."

He clasped the back of his neck. "Amy knows where we are. My parents live in the same house she grew up in, and they've kept the same phone number. If she were alive and/or sober, wouldn't she contact them?"

"Maybe she thinks she can't come back because—"

"I'm too bossy."

"No, not that. But maybe the drugs, and the things she had to do to get the drugs, have changed her."

"You have a plan?"

Calling my hunch a plan seemed grandiose. "Come to the telephony tomorrow at your usual time. I'll close the bait shop before lunch. Let's try something different."

He lowered his voice. "I could come tonight. Anyone would buckle under Jerry's haranguing."

I wanted to say yes. "He won't call again tonight. Jerry's being cautious. He likes to catch me off guard. I have time. Let's get your sister home first. Besides, Connie is waiting for you."

"I should explain Connie."

"No need." I sat in the driver's seat and slammed the door closed. The driver's window had been stuck closed since I bought the Daewoo. Whatever Tim had to explain about Connie, he kept to himself.

IN MY DREAM, I packed a suitcase while trying to find my seat on a plane headed for Ireland, my dream destination, but I couldn't find my underwear or the socks Ginny had knitted. I couldn't find my purse either, which meant my ticket and passport were AWOL. An alarm went off. No doubt the TSA had discovered my 3.5 ounce container of shampoo.

I sat up in bed. The model 354 rang insistently. I threw back the covers and ran for the telephony. I held the receiver to my ear but didn't speak. I paced as far away from the base as the cord would allow.

"Hello? Jerry?" Think before you speak, Jenna.

"You got somebody tracing this call?"

"What? No! I wanted it to be you. And it was you. Hello."

"I ain't playing games here, girlie!" he bellowed.

My heart beat like a drum. How could I be so stupid? Be more careful. Jerry believed he was calling a week after Brian went missing. He expected to talk to a kid looking for his missing brother. Think!

"I wouldn't—I wouldn't play games, honest."

A couple sauntered by, laughing, stopping to kiss every few steps. Come on, Jerry, stick with me. Spill your guts.

"You sound winded," he said.

"I ran to the phone."

"You sound like an asthmatic. It's a sad state of affairs when a teenager can't run across a room without getting winded. You ain't even fat."

"Have we met, Jerry?" I said like a teenager trying to be polite to a smarmy uncle at the family Christmas party.

"Anyone who ain't young is invisible to you. Isn't that right?"

At thirty-four, high-school-aged clerks already looked through me. "I would have remembered you. You sound like a radio announcer."

"You're full of it."

"No, you do, honest. You could be a deejay." Oh brother. Ask him a question.

"I couldn't listen to that stuff you kids call music."

"Do you let your kids listen?" Tell me all about your children, Jerry.

"My daughter listens to nothing but crap."

I could add that Jerry had a daughter to the other things I'd learned about him, which amounted to very little. He didn't trust me. I needed to be more patient, let him slip up, tell me something I could actually use to find him in the present. He hadn't mentioned a wife. We all had our disappointments, including Jerry, I supposed. Most disturbing of all was that we'd met. Perhaps I needed to act like we knew each other.

"I like the old stuff," I said. "My dad plays Dan Fogelberg and VanHalen."

"That ain't old, girlie."

"I have a couple Patsy Cline…" I counted back through audio technologies. "…cassettes."

"Patsy was something. You like her, huh? Name one of her songs."

"'After Midnight?'"

"Good choice."

"I like 'Crazy' too. I wish I could sing like her."

"Won't happen. Not in this lifetime. Tell me about your parents."

"We've already talked about them."

"As long as I'm asking the questions, I get to choose the topic."

I shook off memories of the woman Mom had become and rewound to a time when Dad hadn't lived across town with another woman, back to the days after Brian disappeared, when we still pretended to be a normal family. "They're worried sick. Neither one of them sleeps or eats. Dad paces in front of the television. And he keeps the radio blaring. He's desperate for news, any news about Brian. He hasn't shaved in days. I've never seen him like this."

"Good."

Good? A dial tone sounded in my ear. "Hello? Jerry? Are you there? Hello?"

18

My dad showed up at the exact wrong moment.

I heard the bait shop's lock turn and the jangle of keys. "Jenna!" he called out, like he expected me to be on my way to Mexico since the bait shop door was locked. "What going on in here?"

I told Tim to wait by Snoopy. He'd been thoroughly briefed, but still I wanted to be there when Amy called, and I didn't want an audience, especially not my father. "Dad, you're early."

"Why's the shop closed? Have we made too much money this month?" He headed toward the cash register.

I stepped in front of him. "I'll reopen the shop in a half hour."

He narrowed his eyes, looked toward my bedroom. "You got a guy in here?"

I rested my hands on Dad's crossed arms and spoke softly. "I have one of our regulars in the telephony. He has an important call coming in. I don't want him disturbed."

"I'm opening up."

I rushed to stand between him and the door. Tim needed a time and place for his best effort with Amy. The invitation had to be extended today. "No, you're not. This is important. You can come back at the usual time."

"You're as crazy as your mother!" From his smugness, he expected the insult to sting. It did.

In the telephony, Tim greeted Amy. There was no time for hurt feelings. "Dad, you're probably right, but I'm not reopening the store. I'm asking you to leave. Now."

"If you don't want my help, say so."

"I don't want your help. Later would be good. Okay?" He considered my offer. "Dad?"

"You'll find out later, if and when I show up."

I locked the door behind him and hurried to the telephony. I'd borrowed a privacy screen from Larice, so Tim didn't have to sit in front of the window, and I'd turned off all the lights. I'd even taped a sign on the bait shop door that promised I would be back at one. We didn't need people pounding on the door.

Tim smiled gratefully when I stood next to where he sat. He looked like the boys from school I'd teased. Their faces turned red, but they never returned an insult. Those boys wore their hearts on their sleeves, and I'd punished them for their tenderness. I wanted to kiss Tim on the cheek and apologize for all of my sins against boys with good hearts.

"I have a fun idea for you, Amy," he said into Snoopy's handset, his voice bordering on exuberance. "Who knows what the future may bring."

Tim patted the seat of the chair next to his. When I sat down, he turned the receiver toward me and leaned closer. Warmth bled through his shirt to my shoulder. And amazingly enough, I could hear Amy talking.

He said, "I *am* getting sentimental on you."

"That's kind of creepy and a little scary." Amy sounded twelve, not sixteen. "What's happened to you?"

I mouthed to him to calm down, be natural.

Tim filled his lungs and let out a long breath. When he spoke again, he sounded more like himself. "You shouldn't be scared. Nothing's wrong, unless you call Philosophy 101 wrong. I hate that class." He mimicked a professor, "Just because you see a chair doesn't mean there is a chair."

"That's pretty stupid. I wouldn't tell Mom and Dad what they're teaching you. They complain about how much school is costing as it is."

"I've been thinking more about the future and how we can stay connected." Tim read from the script I'd scribbled, which made for an abrupt change in their conversation.

Her voice pitched upward. "Are you going somewhere?"

"I'm dying to hit the road. I've been in school forever." I wrote this bit, hoping she would believe Tim was the one slipping away, and she wouldn't blame herself for the years and distance that gathered between them. Believing he carried some of the responsibility might make her more likely to show up for a reunion.

"What's going on? You don't sound like yourself. You love school."

Tim looked at me, his face a portrait of panic.

I wrote on the script, "Experiences change us." He repeated the words to Amy, woodenly. I added, "Change doesn't stop love."

Tim dutifully read my words. They didn't sound like him, not at all. I put my hand over the mouthpiece. "Use your own words," I whispered.

"Are you kidding me?"

"You're the one she'll want to see."

Tim frowned, thought for a moment, and spoke to Amy. "Did you ever see the movie *An Affair to Remember*?"

What?

"Who sings the soundtrack?" Amy asked.

Tim pleaded with his eyes. I could only shake my head. I'd never seen the movie, except for the snippets in *Sleepless in Seattle*.

"It's an old film made long before soundtracks. Mom likes it. The two main characters plan to reunite after a long separation. They agree to meet on top of the Empire State Building in exactly one year."

I cringed. This was Tim's best effort at improvising?

"This is hard to explain," he said. He looked to me and I nodded, smiling my encouragement. I had nothing else to offer.

He said, "Suppose something happened and we had to be separated for a long time."

"Where are you going?" she said, her voice pitching ever higher.

"Forget about traveling. Let's say for unforeseen reasons that we don't see each other for a long, long time."

"Have you told Mom and Dad?"

"I will, if I go away for a long time, but that's not the point. Amy, listen, this is important. I don't want to lose you for any reason. You're the best sister—"

"Wait! Let me get a recorder."

"We don't have time."

"Timmy?"

"You're the best sister a guy could have. There's nothing in the world that could change that. There's nothing, *nothing*, you could do to stop me from wanting to be your big brother. In fact, losing you would kill me."

"Have you joined a cult?"

"Would you still want to be my sister, if I had three wives and twenty-seven children?"

"You're beyond weird, Timmy."

"Answer, *please*. Would you be my sister if I was that weird?"

"You're already that weird, and yes, I still want to be your sister. I love you, Timmy."

"Good. That's great. A good start."

"A start? What else is going on?"

"You must promise to do something that may seem a little strange."

I gave him a thumb's up.

"Stranger than three wives and twenty-seven children?" she asked.

"Much crazier but very serious."

"Go on."

"Someday, you're going to be forty years old."

"That's a long time to be gone."

"I know, it seems like forever, but the time will fly. I need you to write something down, okay?"

Paper rustled. She was crying. "Timmy, you can't go away for that long. Mom and Dad would die."

"Chances are we'll see each other this Christmas. Are you ready? Write exactly what I say: meet Tim at the end of the San Clemente Pier when I'm forty."

"On my birthday?"

We hadn't decided on a day. I pulled my cell out to search the calendar. "Tell her the Fourth of July. She'll remember a holiday."

Tim started to tell her, but I thought better of the date and waved my hands in front of his face. Tourists crowded the pier on the Fourth. And you couldn't walk all the way to the end. They staged the fireworks there. "Tell her the fifth of July."

Tim put his hand over the mouthpiece. "Are you sure? That's in five days."

I rolled my eyes. "She has twenty-four years to make reservations."

He spoke into the mouthpiece. "Just a minute, Amy. A guy needs notes from class today. Hang on." He held the receiver to his chest. "Isn't the fifth a little soon?"

"You've been coming here for two years, Tim. I thought you wanted to see her."

"I do. At least, I thought I was ready." He rubbed his forehead. "It's been so long."

I put my arm around his shoulders.

"We could do Thanksgiving," he said.

"And if the telephones should stop ringing again, and I don't stumble on why?" I shrugged. I couldn't give him the courage to try this experiment. I rose to lean against the wall to listen to his side of the conversation.

"I'm here," he said to Amy. "The guy across the hall missed Statistics. Did you get down what I said? San Clemente Pier. Fifth of July. The year you turn forty ... Yeah, this is cloak-and-dagger stuff, but I love you too much not to plan for the worst ... I am being paranoid. We'll be bugging each other at Mom's table every holiday until we're old and fat. You'll have bratty kids." He fingered his gray patch. "Forty isn't so bad ... Sure, but let me hear your promise one more time ... There's no possible reason you won't be there, right? I love you, Amy ... What time?"

He opened a palm, asking without words for the perfect time. Something must have occurred to him because his shoulders settled back into place. "When else? Five-thirty. You wouldn't want to be late for dinner. My treat ... Nah, we'll call the folks after dessert ... Good. Thanks. I'll see you soon."

Tim hung up and slid down in the chair and then back up again to pepper me with questions: "Was I convincing? Do you think she knows I want to see her, no matter what? Will she remember?"

Yes, yes, and I really hoped so. "We'll find out on Monday."

"Will you go with me?"

Interesting, I'd never thought I wouldn't. "Of course."

He looked at his watch again. "I've got to get back to work."

AFTER TIM LEFT, I reopened the shop. The regulars sat at their appointed telephones for their daily calls while I made a record number of iced mochas for parched beachgoers. Summer had finally arrived in San Clemente. We shielded our eyes from the glare on the water and children with pink noses and shoulders came to the bait shop for frozen treats. As the temperatures rose our sales improved—and not a moment too soon.

As I worked the espresso machine and sold tubes of zinc oxide, I replayed the telephone call with Amy. She'd sounded younger, sweeter than I had ever been. No wonder Tim worked so hard to save her from herself.

I worried, too, that by pushing Tim into asking for a reunion I'd upset the order of things to come. Maybe if Tim had tried one more day of talking to Amy his way, her future and Tim's history would change. But I knew better. The past had been written. My mother's conversations with Kevin proved that. She'd been talking to him for over thirty years— one way or another—and she still sat alone in the apartment day after day.

Dad did not return to the bait shop after I'd turned him away, and I handled everything just fine. I felt both pride and panic. Sure I could do the work, but did I want to be the sole dispenser of the things beachgoers craved? My future was a narrow tunnel with no friendly light to beckon me forward.

Something had to change.

During a lull, I rummaged through a cabinet below the cash register. The *Help Wanted* sign needed a good scrubbing, and I couldn't find the grease pencil to add the particulars. Never mind that I wasn't at all sure I could swing a part-time employee. In that moment, demolishing the house of cards we'd built as a family didn't seem all that dire.

While making Italian sodas and ringing up snacks for the folks rushing for the 5:02, Mom called to ask where I'd been. Her voice pinched around her words. When I told her I manned the bait shop alone, she asked, "Is this your father's doing?"

"Yes and no. I can't really explain now. I have a shop full of customers."

She hung up without saying goodbye.

Just as the girl who talked on the fiddleback slipped out and the 5:02 clanged, bellowed, and chugged over its departure, Tim called, a first. "I hate this mystical stuff. I've been trying all afternoon to wrap my head around what we did. Did we send a message back in time? If Amy misses the rendezvous, is it because we've broken a cosmic rule, or maybe all the counselors have been right about her all along, and we're wasting our time. How will we ever know?"

I leaned against the ice machine, feeling the full press of his doubts. "We won't."

"I should stay away from the telephony until the fifth. What I said today will be the last thing Amy heard from me. We're more likely to remember the last thing we've heard, right?"

I threw a wet rag into the sink. "I have to go, Tim. Restocking. Stuff like that."

I found a permanent marker in the back of the drawer and wrote on the *Help Wanted* sign: P-T, Flexible, Come in. And put the sign in the window.

I CLIMBED NOISELESSLY PAST mom's door up to Larice's apartment. Taylor sat at the bistro table, doing homework for a summer class at the junior college. The sun turned strands of her hair to white fire. Larice chopped and diced vegetables in the kitchen.

I stood inside the door to watch the mother and daughter tableau. Normal stuff like homework and dinner preparation happened in the same building that housed Mom and me. Amazing.

I leaned over Taylor to give her shoulders a squeeze and to see what she studied. Evidently, they'd invented a new language to teach math in the years since I'd graduated.

"Look familiar?" Taylor asked. Looking into her face, seeing the glow of possibilities there, I understood why Larice took mothering so seriously.

I closed the book to see the cover. Calculus. I'd barely

passed trig. "I better let you get back to your homework. Your mother hates when I distract you."

"Sit down," Taylor said. "You can distract me all you want. This stuff is easy."

"Taylor," Larice said with a warning in her voice.

"It's my fault." I kissed Taylor's forehead and entered the kitchen. "I can't get enough of higher math."

Larice didn't look up from the pepper she was chopping. She whispered, "I'm praying like mad she doesn't ask for help."

"She has the internet. Stop worrying."

Larice finally looked up. "I canceled cable. Something had to go. I can't keep taking money from my folks. They have their retirements to consider."

I sidled up to Larice and stole a piece of red pepper from her cutting board. She'd declared her fiscal independence from her parents before. She needed distracting more than her daughter. I explained the situation and my plans with Tim for the fifth of July. "You should pray for Amy."

"Who's Tim?" she asked with narrowed eyes. "You just joined the nunnery."

I reminded her that we'd talked about him when we were jogging. "He's one of my telephony regulars. He talks to his sister on the Snoopy phone. You'd like him. He's very nice. And he's old. Over forty. You know, the gray patch?"

Larice shushed me and looked toward Taylor. She whispered, "You say that like he has leprosy."

"Tim's like no one you've ever met. He's earnest, smart..."

"And very nice?" This from Taylor. "That's a definite disqualification."

Larice pointed her cleaver at Taylor. "Get back to work."

I turned my back on Taylor. "I was thinking of introducing the two of you. You'd be perfect for one another."

"No way, I'm going man-free until graduation, remember?" This she said loud enough for Taylor to hear.

I reconsidered my haste.

"He would wait," I said, doing jumping jacks with my eyebrows.

"If he's so nice, and you're so concerned about his feelings, maybe you should go into the prayer closet for him *and* his sister."

Larice did not always play nice. To be perfectly honest, I had no intentions of being a praying nun, in or out of the closet. "Mom's expecting me. In fact, I'm really late."

"For someone who doesn't wear a watch, you certainly have a keen sense of time." Larice followed me to the front door with the cleaver in hand. "Run with me tomorrow?"

"When?" I asked to be polite. No more running for me.

"I'm going early, around sunrise. I have to drive Taylor to Saddleback before work."

I put my lips to her ear. "I'm saying *adios* to Eric in the morning."

She backed away, her face blossomed with surprise. She pointed toward the prayer closet with her cleaver. "You don't want to face the him without fortification."

I hadn't read that much of the Bible, and what I had read scandalized me. God wasn't always nice, and he preferred the company of scoundrels. Prayer at knifepoint, however, seemed an unlikely strategy even of the God I'd encountered.

"Maybe when Taylor isn't studying."

19

Eric's hands ran up and down my back as he guided me closer to the bedroom. "I've missed you, babe."

I straight-armed him. "We have to talk first."

"I thought we settled all that." In one move he had my arms behind my back and we body smashed against the closed bedroom door.

Kissing Eric was like coming face to face with a running propeller—thrilling, terrifying, dangerous. One false move and there went my tonsils, and worse, my self-control.

Who was I kidding? I could not say no to the man.

ERIC PICKED HIS JEANS off the floor and something pinged on the linoleum and rolled across the room. I'd never seen him move so fast. He dropped to all fours to look under the dresser and the bed.

The gold band had rolled to the edge of a small shag rug by the bed and found shelter in the fibers. I reached from the bed to pick up the ring, holding it like the thing held dark magic. An inscription on the inside read, "Forever and always, Kate." Bile rose to burn the back of my throat.

I pulled the blanket up to my chin and leaned against the wall. Crossing over the line of infidelity broke something sacred, even for me. I'd avoided Eric's marital status to stave off loneliness, which put me in the shallow end of the nobility pool. And hating myself made me angry for being in such a stupid place to begin with.

"Why don't you have a tan line from your wedding band?" I asked.

Eric's head thumped against the box springs, and he let loose a string of expletives.

I closed my fingers around the ring. "Shh, my mother can hear us."

"You're telling me this now?" He stood and stepped into his jeans.

"Thin walls." While he was distracted by fly buttons, I twisted his shirt into a coil and tied it into a knot. "When were you going to tell me you're married?"

He caught sight of his shirt in my hands. His jaw twitched. "Look, I have to wear that today. Do you mind?" He spat the words. I welcomed his anger. Churning with disgust wasn't as much fun alone.

"A wrinkled shirt will be hard to explain to Kate, won't it?"

He sat on the bed to step into his boots. I put my feet to his back and shoved. He stumbled toward my dresser. Perfume bottles and picture frames tipped and clattered. When he turned back to me, Eric's veins bulged at his temples. What came next, I didn't know. We hadn't been in the same room long enough to find out. My heart thumped a warning, but he simply put his hand out. "The ring? My shirt?"

I threw the ring out the bedroom door and into the bait shop, hoping it would roll under one of the refrigerator cases. Doing so was childish, no doubt about that, but I felt awfully proud of myself. I'd taken a stand—a late, pitiful, and ineffectual stand—but a stand. Yay for me.

The feeling didn't last. First, I'd jumped at a sorry excuse of a relationship because he had incredible green eyes and pectorals rivaling those of gods. Second, he was m-a-r-r-i-e-d, married. Perhaps he was a father. I couldn't help but groan at the thought. And third, I was about to beg Eric's forgiveness—because I'm that weak—when the bell jingled over the bait shop door.

I hadn't intended for Eric to stay, so the door was open for the fishermen to enter. They could find what they needed and leave the money on the counter. I was in no mood to banter.

Tim called out, "Jenna, is everything all right?"

I handed the knotted shirt over to Eric. I pleaded with him in a forced whisper. "Please go. Please. Now. Go."

He looked toward the bait shop and back to me. A sardonic smile played at the corners of his mouth. "And the ring?"

"I'll bring it to the docks later. I promise."

"Jenna, I'm coming back there," Tim said.

"No!" I lunged for my clothes. Eric walked out, carrying his knotted shirt. The two men exchanged greetings.

The bell sounded over the door, and I prayed—with no sense of irony—they had gone together for coffee. They certainly had interesting stories to share of the two Jennas: the Good Jenna who championed lost causes, and Bad Jenna who could not keep her panties on. I shrugged into my hoodie and slipped into flip-flops.

Tim again, closer now. "Jenna, I'm sorry."

I froze, glanced toward the teeny tiny window above the bed. There was no retreat.

"The door wasn't locked."

Oh, God.

"Are you all right?" He was breathing hard. "You don't sound like yourself."

I leaned against the wall behind the opened door. "This isn't a good time." Please go away.

"I'll wait outside. I want to see that you're okay."

No, no, no. "You don't have to do that, Tim. I'm fine, really."

"Jenna, you don't sound fine."

I wasn't. I pressed a fist against my mouth. I must have stood there a long time because Tim said my name again. I managed to swallow hard enough to say, "I'm fine, Tim. I'm good. Have a nice day."

A dubious silence filled the space between us. "I'll see you Monday, like we planned?"

A briny hash percolated in my gut. "See you Monday."

When the bell above the door finally sounded again, I rushed out into the bait shop to watch Tim jog toward the walking path. He would eventually jog back this way and up the hill to his house. I stepped out into the swirling dampness, pulled up my hood, and locked the door. The fishermen were on their own for the day, at least until I knew Tim was safely in his tidy cubical at work. Until then, I hadn't noticed how irritating his kindness could be.

I ran hard for the pilings under the pier. I dodged surfers, dog walkers, and joggers. I could taste the salt pickling my mouth and feel the sand crack against my teeth before my feet hit the cooler sand under the pier, where I was krill in a whale's bony skeleton of pilings. A delicate spray wet my face as the waves echoed off the pier above to hush my senses.

I had just popped the third handful of sand into my mouth when Tim sat in the damp sand beside me, breathing heavily from his run. He handed over his water bottle. I should have waved him off and left. But he'd hunted me down. No one had ever done that, ever. Not even when I'd gotten lost at Disneyland. My family had picked me up at the visitor's station on their way out of the park.

Tim's presence comforted and scolded. I wanted him to leave and stay. I rinsed and spat twice before I handed the bottle back.

"Take a drink," he said, so I emptied his bottle.

He drew me in with his arm around my shoulders, as if he'd done so a hundred times before. I dropped my head to his shoulder and let the tears come. I do not cry pretty. My shoulders heaved. I gulped for air. Tim's shirt, already damp with sweat, now absorbed my tears.

He offered the hem of his T-shirt to blow my nose. That

would be a new low for me. I shook my head. His hand cupped the back of my head. He stretched his shirt to my face. "Blow."

I blew and blew again. Why not, I was being me—a blow-snot-on-your-shirt kind of girl. In one way, I was relieved he knew the real Jenna, but I didn't dare look at him. I didn't want to see what he was thinking.

He lifted my face with a hooked finger to my chin. Where I thought I would see disdain in his eyes, I saw something else, something unexpected and unknown. He brushed the sand from my mouth. Tears threatened again, so I stood up for a quick dash toward the shop, but Tim caught me by the wrist. Over the thunderous waves, he yelled, "You deserve better."

My tears dried up. My stomach hardened. My hands squeezed into fists. "How do you know that, Tim? Maybe this is who I am, the best I can do and exactly what I deserve. Maybe, just maybe, I prefer not getting sucked into relationships. That would make me a sociopath, right?"

"A sociopath wouldn't try to eat the beach."

"You know nothing about me." I shook my arm free and ran. The Metrolink warning bells sounded. The gates had lowered, but the engine was still a hundred yards off, more than enough time to squeeze through to safety.

Tim didn't know when to give up. And he was fast. This time he hooked me around the waist and pulled me to his chest. His embrace pinned my arms to my side. The train blared its warning. There was nowhere to go. I relaxed into his arms, breathed in the sour heat of his neck, felt the scratch of his morning beard against my cheek, and the pounding of his heart against my chest.

The train passed. A whoosh of air lifted my skirt. Tim did not loosen his hold. I'd never been more tired. If he hadn't held me, I would have sagged to the pavement. I closed my eyes and the world went silent.

I do not submit to peace all that willingly. Thoughts of the bait shop heckled me, along with the tax bill and my mother waiting for her first dose of Xanax. I stepped back and reached to touch the silvery patch of Tim's hair. I wasn't disappointed. The fine hairs slid through my fingers as soft as I'd dreamed.

"Sit with me on the beach for a while, get your bearings."

I needed to call the dairy vendor to order cream. "I want to. The shop. I should get going."

He looped a strand of hair behind my ear. "You'll be all right, promise?"

"Right as rain."

"Then I'll see you Monday?"

I should have explained Eric. But I couldn't help my cause, not really. "You're sure you want me there?"

He turned to look down the pier and then back to me. "I need you there, Jenna."

"Then I'll meet you right here."

Later, after Ginny had chatted excitedly to Frank and the world seemed to take a breath, I sat on an overturned bucket in the utility closet and allowed myself to consider what had happened that morning. Kicking Eric out of my life was meant to commit me to a state of being single, at least for the time being, maybe until Taylor's graduation. I'd come to terms with that. Instead, I'd been held by a man who let me blow my nose on his shirt. Although I tried to squelch the feeling, an effervescent sense of tomorrow bubbled in my gut, and I remembered, too, the optimism of Tomorrowland. All that sleek movement and new ways of talking. I felt just like that.

Only.

Only Tim had said nothing about Eric. How much had he heard? He'd seen plenty. Was the tenderness he'd offered out of pity or something else? Really, how had he found me under the pier? Had he watched me run from the bait shop? Talk about creepy. Or maybe he was different in a nice way. I decided to stick with a positive view of Tim until proven otherwise or Amy found her way home. Because thinking of the world without someone like Tim hurt too much.

THAT OPTIMISM LANDED ME in a strange space. I drank several shots of espresso with Larice—carried to her apartment in a Thermos—and a tall Americano when I arrived back at the bait shop. Caffeine is the drug of the perpetually buoyant. I would have to pace myself.

The fishermen would bang on the door early, but I remained bug-eyed at 2:17 a.m. Too much positive thinking and caffeine, I decided, plus a Patterson thriller. The main character was about to demonstrate outrageously bad judgment when the model 354 rang. I threw back the covers, and the book thunked against the closet door. I ran for the telephony.

"How's the vigil?" asked a cigarette-scraped voice.

"Jerry?"

"You don't know my voice?"

I knew his voice, all right. I despised his voice. He called to say absolutely nothing when he knew everything I needed to know about Brian. I almost shot off both barrels of rapid-fire sarcasm, but Jerry knew me as a young girl, a sweeter, less-tainted version of myself. I pulled on my Keds and jumped into eighteen-year-old Jenna.

"How have you been?" I asked.

"So we're friends?"

"You did call. I mean, you're the only one besides the reporters, and even they don't call as often."

"They've moved on to the next cat up a tree, have they?"

"If Brian were a cat, and he was up a tree, I would understand, but he's my brother, and we're all going nuts at my house. My mom's a wreck. I don't know how to help her anymore. She won't eat, and as far as I can tell, she doesn't sleep either. Dad's just gotten weirder."

Jerry coughed into the phone, a wet, rattling kind of cough.

"My company wants me to retire. They got younger guys willing to work for less pay. I'm getting too expensive for them."

Evidently, I'd dosed Jerry with too much reality. My mistake. I followed his lead. "You sound too young to retire."

"I don't feel too young, but I'm not happy about being ousted."

I wrote down that Jerry was shy of retirement age when Brian went missing. But I needed to know more. Maybe if I mined his far past. "Did you go to college, Jerry? Dad says an education is how to make money in this world."

"My son went to college to be an engineer of some kind. He graduated good, you know, high in his class. He'd been hired by some instrument factory in Texas. But he enlisted without telling me. He died of a busted appendix during basic. College didn't make him too smart or rich, just dead."

Reality had a way of biting back. "I'm sorry, Jerry."

"You ain't what I expected, girlie. Kids don't care anymore."

I'd found the chink in his armor. "Do you have other children?"

"I've got a good-for-nothing son. He never met a couch he didn't like."

"He has to find something he likes to do." I'd said the same thing to Dad about Brian.

"I don't think so. He'd have to get his fat butt off the couch. I'm not counting on that happening anytime soon."

"Maybe he would like what you do." Tell me about your work, Jerry.

"He would have to sweat. And Donny don't sweat."

I scribbled "Donny" on the notepad. "Would he need a lot of training to do your job?"

"What you getting at, girlie?"

Easy. "Nothing, just talking."

"My son is none of your business. Got that?"

"Sure, no problem. I didn't mean to upset you." He hadn't given me anything besides his son's name, and we'd already been on the phone longer than any other time. Keep him talking. "Jerry, what will you do after you retire?"

"I ain't staying home and watching soap operas."

"My dad would love to trade places with you. Before all this happened with Brian, he considered taking up golf or finding a hobby. Retirement's still a ways off for him, but he's already thinking about life after a commute. Do you have a hobby, Jerry, something I could suggest to Dad?"

A long pause. "No."

"You could travel. Lots of folks do."

"There ain't nothing I want to see outside of these United States of America." Jerry went quiet again, which made me nervous. Silence was his preamble to hanging up. "I won't be calling again."

"What? Why? I wish you would, Jerry. We haven't had a chance to talk about Brian. Is he okay? You can tell me that much, can't you?"

"I don't have to tell you nothing. I thought I would, but I changed my mind."

I repeatedly slammed the handset into the cradle. Thinking better of my behavior, I put the receiver to my ear. "Jerry, are you there?" I asked as sweet as pie.

Nothing.

I bludgeoned the desk with the receiver and put it back to my ear. Honestly, death made more noise.

I shouted into the mouthpiece. "Did you kill him, Jerry? Is that why you won't say anything? Or maybe your son did it. Is that why he slithered off to the military?" The words burned my throat. "Did. You. Kill. Brian?"

"Jenna? What's going on? Who are you yelling at?"

I held the handset against my beating heart to face Mom in

the telephony's doorway. She stood with her long toes curled over the metal strip holding the carpet in place. The light from the refrigerator case outlined her body under her flimsy nightgown. Once athletic, a serious golfer and tennis player, she now reminded me of the refugees I'd seen on TV.

"How long have you been getting telephone calls?"

I didn't know how much she'd heard, but I couldn't tell her about Jerry. She would never sleep again. I looked at the handset with as much incredulity as I could summon and placed the offensive thing back in its cradle.

"No one. I had a bad dream," I said. "A dream about Brian."

"And?" she said, her voice rising from a flat valley. I hadn't meant to raise her hopes.

"I got angry. A man in my dream knew exactly where Brian had gone and wouldn't tell me. It's silly, but I came out here, hoping a telephone would ring for me. I thought maybe the man from my dream would call."

She took tentative steps toward me. "His name was Jerry?"

I shrugged. "I don't know where that name came from. We haven't heard anything about Brian in so very long. I must be inventing names and people in my dreams. I'm glad you came down when you did. I might have thrown the telephone through the window."

Mom kneaded the back of her hand. "I thought maybe..." She looked up. "I'm beyond being much help to you. I see all that you do and how much falls on your shoulders. I'm deeply sorry. A mother should always be a mother. I can tell you this: don't ever wish for a call in this place. You will never be happy again."

I wrapped my arms around Mom. I feared if I squeezed her too tight, air would whoosh out and she'd collapse to the floor like a popped balloon. I rubbed her back, but my hand ran into her shoulder blades, so I kneaded her trapeziums, sadly atrophied. She settled her weight on me.

When my arms ached from supporting her, I said, "Let's go upstairs." We walked hip to hip up the stairs and through the apartment to her bedroom. The covers lay like the ocean on a windless day. I pulled back the comforter and fluffed her pillow.

She sat on the cool sheets and shivered.

"Will you sleep?" I said.

"I might."

"Do you want one of your pills?"

"They don't work anymore."

"Can I lay with you for a while? The dream upset me."

She scooted onto Dad's side, and I lay with my head on her pillow. She draped an arm over my shoulders. I watched the minutes and then an hour click past on her clock, and still her breathing remained shallow. She turned toward the far wall, releasing me from her care. Her breathing finally deepened.

I slipped from the bed and walked soundlessly out the door and down the stairs to my room, where I tugged a pair of sweat pants over my pajama bottoms and rummaged until I found Ginny's watermelon socks. With hoodie in place, I stepped into my running shoes and gathered up the model 354. Before opening the door, I reached up and yanked the clapper from the bell.

Some people are morning people. I'll never understand the allure. Others live for the plummet of the sun to the horizon when the day sighs into twilight. I choose the hours of impenetrable night just before gray tinges the east. Partiers have gone to bed. Babies sink into deep sleep. The streetlights hum. Old men shuffle to the bathroom glad for more hours of sleep ahead. This is alone time, fleeting though it be.

The fishermen would be hounding me for anchovies and squid before long, so I jogged across the street, over the railroad tracks, and between the restaurants at the beginning of the pier. I passed the lifeguard tower and the cantilevered restroom, and the shuttered curio shop. I met no one, which suited me fine. How would I explain jogging down the pier cradling a sorry example of a model 354 to my chest?

At the end of the pier, the darkness was a void with a beating heart and heaving breath. The edge of the world lay at my feet. I looked over my shoulder before I dropped the telephone into the black water. The splash came after I took my first step back toward the bait shop. I'd just broken about ten thousand state and federal laws regarding polluting the ocean, so I ran the near quarter mile length of the pier back to land.

I walked past my bed to the shower. Afterward, with my hair sticking to my bare back, I wrote out all I'd learned about Jerry. The list was disappointingly short.

What had I done?

By throwing the model 354 off the end of the pier, I'd sealed the fate of the telephony and me. I made a sign on a piece of cardboard from the dumpster that read, "Telephony Closed Indefinitely." I ripped a long strip of cloth from curtains I'd intended to make into a new cover-up and strung the fabric ribbon across the opening of the telephony like crime-scene tape.

If I could have lit a match to the place, I would have.

20

Saint or bug, my fate rested in the hands of Tim's sister.

Either I was about to become the most heroic figure since Joan of Arc or complete my transformation into Kafka's bug. If Amy waited for us at the end of the pier, I could polish my armor. If not, I'd better get used to scurrying under the fridge when the lights came on.

Tim looked down the pier, swiped the sweat from his upper lip. Tourists in broad-brimmed hats and sunglasses swarmed the pier.

"How fast can we walk to the end?" he said.

"With all these people? Five minutes, maybe eight to ten."

He looked at his watch. We weren't meeting Amy for another half hour. "We should probably get going. I would rather wait for her than have her think I'd forgotten."

"Tim?"

"Yes?" he snipped, but he repented immediately. "Oh, God, I'm sorry. I'm nervous, a little scared. If she's not there..." He looked down the pier. "She could already be there."

I wanted to tell him not to get his hopes up, but his hopes had already rocketed toward Pluto, the on-again, off-again planet. "She can't get away. If she's down there, there's only one way to leave the pier. She'll have to walk right past us. You'll see her."

"You're right. Of course you are." He gestured toward the throng. "Shall we?"

Lucky for Tim I'd had lots of practice being the levelheaded one. Never mind that my stomach roiled and sloshed with every step. To assure Tim and to steady myself, I slipped my hand into his and squeezed. "Whatever happens, we're in this together."

He smiled weakly. "Thanks."

We two-stepped around groups of people gawking at sea gulls and pelicans, surfers and paddle boarders, those who stopped to look into fishermen's buckets, and those who skirted away from fishermen's buckets. Inlanders were a tiresome lot, so easy to entertain and yet oblivious to those of us with a destination in mind.

A couple asked me to take their picture in front of Ol' Pete, who used the pretext of fishing as an excuse to sleep on the pier each day. Tim grimaced. I put up a finger. "Only a minute."

The couple tugged their T-shirts into place and smoothed wrinkled shorts. "Hold your stomach in, Gary," the wife said, backhanding his paunch. "And take off your sunglasses, for goodness' sake." She licked her finger and scrubbed at the corner of Gary's mouth. Fortunately, Gary complied and we continued down the pier within the promised minute.

This time, Tim took my hand. Our eyes met. "It helps," he said.

Our hands did fit together nicely, so I smiled and fixed my gaze forward. Besides, he was right. His touch did help, like being moored. I would not drift away that day.

"I don't know what will be harder," he said, "if she is here or if she isn't. My parents put their lives on hold for her. Why didn't she call?"

I stopped and he frowned, definitely annoyed by our sudden lack of progress. "You aren't thinking of asking her, are you?"

He studied my face but didn't answer.

"She's not a little girl."

"I may not recognize her."

"You probably won't."

"Then what do I say? I've lain awake for hours anticipating this moment and dreading what will fly from my mouth."

I placed my hand to his chest. His heart thumped under my fingers. "Say whatever your wildly beating heart tells you."

"Are you kidding? I spew stupidity when I'm unscripted."

Tim had nothing to worry about. I'd listened to his side of conversations with Amy for two years. "Tell her you love her. Simple. And hug her the whole time. Don't let go."

"I'll probably barf on her."

The late-day sun pressed us. Once we passed the curio shop, I reminded Tim to keep his eyes open, but I only wasted breath. He scanned the crowd like a beacon. "What color of hair does she have?" I asked.

"She was a brunette. We both were, but she could be like me. I started graying in my thirties." We walked to where I'd dropped the model 354 overboard and looked back along the length of the pier. "She could have forgotten," he said.

"We're early. Relax."

"Do you remember anything your brother said when you were sixteen?"

Brian had said lots of things I wished I could forget. He had an unparalleled way of getting under my skin. "He once told me a boy I liked had called, and I was to call him back. I should have known Brian would never be so helpful. So, you see, she could remember. Keep looking."

"Timmy? Is that you?"

Before us stood a woman I would put in her fifties with pale skin and shadows of scars over her hollow cheeks, but her eyes shone. Her hair was very brunette, newly dyed several shades too dark.

Tim studied her. "Amy?"

The woman covered her mouth, although clearly she smiled from the way her eyes crinkled in the corners. "I don't look the same."

"Amy!" Tim lifted her off the ground in a bear hug, which she returned, laughing and crying. "I've missed you."

"I'm sorry. I'm so sorry," she repeated.

Tim finally set her down, pushing hair back from her face. "Hush now. Nothing matters. You're here. Oh my God, it's really you. You remembered."

She dug into a pocket and pulled out a piece of yellowed paper. "I wrote the date down, just like you said. I've lost everything many times, but I kept this."

A crowd of people, mostly children, surrounded Tim and Amy. She introduced him to her husband—a slight man with a pictorial review of American history tattooed up both arms—and her stepchildren and foster children. I lost count at four, all dressed in crisp T-shirts and shorts. The boys and girls, varying widely in coloring and shape, greeted Tim with broad smiles and handshakes. He kissed the hands of the girls, adding a curteous bow.

Amy looked around. "Where's your girlfriend?"

Tim looked confused.

Her eyes narrowed, "The pretty girl you were standing with, Tim. You were holding hands, right?"

Tim blushed. "You mean Jenna," and he found me with his eyes, where I leaned against the rail. I stepped forward and introductions were repeated for my benefit.

Amy scanned the crowd and leaned toward Tim. "Are Mom and Dad around? I mean, are they...?"

He looked at his watch. "They should be at the house by now."

Panic widened her eyes. "Here? Now?"

"Just up the hill."

Amy blinked. "Do they know I'm here?"

"I'll text them. They'll be so happy to see you."

"You're sure?"

Tim gave her a brotherly punch to the arm. "Don't be

stupid."

Amy hooked his arm. "I thought you were a psycho, you know, back when we talked about meeting. I never dreamed we would need to plan years ahead to see each other."

Tim looked back at me, his face contorted by his trademark goofy grin, and winked. They took off toward the shore and their parents. I looked around. The husband, whose name I didn't remember—something ordinary and forgettable like John—carried a wiggling toddler on one hip and pried a boy's grip off his leg.

Two hands, sticky and small, grasped mine—one on the left and one on the right, Quinn and Clay—obviously brothers with their nearly black hair and eyes and lean bodies that trembled with excitement. I liked to think they recognized my heroic attributes and considered me trustworthy to escort them off the pier. When a fisherman landed a writhing leopard shark on the pier, they darted away. Glory was fleeting. So much for Jenna of Arc. But seeing Tim and Amy walking ahead, arm in arm, chatting and laughing, expanded me.

TIM'S MOM—smiling his smile—rushed out onto the lawn when the caravan of cars pulled up to the curb in front of his house. His father stepped carefully off the stoop and followed her. Happy, finally, to be together, the family huddled on the perfect lawn, peppering one another with questions and stepping into long embraces.

Seeing Amy reunited with her parents threatened to break my heart. I wanted to share their joy, but I could only think of Mom sitting at home, waiting for Brian. I thought of going home to be with her, but Quinn clung to me. The drama had set the boy to quivering again, and I admit to enjoying his confidence in me.

The two of us escaped the frenetic reunion by going inside to make hamburger patties. I nosed around Tim's kitchen for paper plates, napkins, and utensils, but once the ketchup landed on the counter, my culinary contributions came to an end. Tim came to the kitchen three times to thank me for getting his sister home. He studied me with approving eyes before kissing my cheek and returning to his family. Quinn and I had just settled in to watch SpongeBob SquarePants when Tim's tribe flooded in, all hungry.

After dinner, I played shadow tag with the kids under the streetlight. Clay darted out of my grasp more than once. I reminded the children—only moments before my heart burst from exertion—that Uncle Tim had bought ice cream. Once the bowls had been rinsed and counters wiped down, I whispered in Tim's ear that I needed to go home. Even more, I wanted to give his family privacy to remember good times and to skirt the bad.

He walked me to my car. "You're amazing."

"You're overstating my ice cream scooping skills. Perhaps you should turn your freezer down."

"You know what I mean."

"I had very little to do with your sister, if that's what you're talking about. You're the one who talked to her every day. You're the one she wanted to see. It's obvious she adores you."

"And you? Is there any chance—be it ever so slight—that I could evoke adoration from you?"

Speaking like someone from a Jane Austen novel did quicken my pulse. But if he meant did I trust him with my heart, then yes. I could probably do that, with minor reservation, of course. He had introduced me to poblano and spinach enchiladas, after all. That should count for something.

"You aren't saying anything," he said.

"I'm thinking."

"That's a start."

I was thinking that all this talk of adoration tiptoed into the area of the strange. Stranger than, say, arranging a rendezvous with a long-lost sister from the present to the past for the future? Probably not. Perhaps Tim did see me as a Joan-of-Arc type. I appreciated the promotion, however misguided the leap may be. He would figure that out soon enough. Plus the guy was ecstatic over reuniting with his sister. His endorphin-crazed brain must have been popping like firecrackers. He would wake up in the morning and ask himself, *what the—?*

"Yes," I said before I talked myself out of something really good.

"Yes? Good. A yes is very good." There was that goofy grin again. "Wait, is your yes a definite yes or a maybe sort of yes?"

I could easily have frightened him with the force of my yes, but standing that close, the scent of the sea in his hair, the memory of his exuberant love toward his sister, I knew I did not deserve the likes of Tim. Were we the same species? Full disclosure would remind him of our time under the pier.

"I'm a mess, Tim. In fact, I'm dangerous."

He silenced me with a finger to my lips and pulled me closer. "I'm going to kiss you. Do you have a problem with that?"

I didn't, not a bit.

What happened next almost stopped my heart. Something in me unwound. He pulled away much too quickly. I pressed in for more, but he put his hands to my shoulders.

"I wanted you to know I'm not Mr. Rogers. You've got some things to consider, Jenna, before we do that again. I'm older, so I come with my own messes and in some rather embarrassing ways I'm a fuddy-duddy.

"Keep in mind I'm not looking for a liaison. I'm not willing to share you. I'm looking for a friend, a companion, someone who can belong in my family." He looked toward the opened door as if to check the rationality of that final request. "I also want a lover, one who likes the idea of being a mother. I really want a family. To me, that all means marriage, eventually."

"Did we hit a worm hole here?"

"I've been considering this for a long time."

"Tim, you do remember the other morning? Me eating sand? Blowing snot on your shirt? And, oh yeah, a half-dressed man fleeing from my bedroom?"

"I remember."

I opened my mouth to remind him, yet again, that he didn't really know me. Before I could speak, he turned me by the shoulders toward my car and whispered in my ear. "My family will be here a week. I would love to have you here with us, but I need to trust your answer. Take all the time you need to think about what I've said. Okay?"

I turned back to him. The same Tim stood there. A totally different reaction ran through me. Think of electricity and a box of chocolates. We'd moved from talking on a Snoopy phone to talking total commitment in a blink. "A clarification, please."

"Sure."

The words were almost too preposterous to say. "Are you asking me to marry you?"

"I'm asking you to... Yes, I suppose I am."

"And you're sure?"

"Yes."

"That's not a maybe yes, is it?"

"A definite yes." No hesitation there.

"Holy cow."

"This must sound pretty crazy to you—out of the blue. A delirium. Perhaps desperation. I've been holding my breath forever. With Amy back I'm ready to jump in and live. And there's no one I would rather jump into life with than you.

"I wish the other morning hadn't happened. I can't lie about that. Maybe if I'd said something sooner...? I didn't and I'm sorry. Really sorry. Can we move on from here? Think about it."

THE SAN CLEMENTE BAIT SHOP AND TELEPHONY

I drove away, knowing I would be a fool to refuse an offer of marriage from someone like Tim. He'd been nothing but wonderful since the day I'd met him. But I was a fool, and that worried me.

LARICE EMPTIED THE WINE bottle into my glass. She settled back into the couch and savored a sip. "So what are you thinking? Are you going to accept his proposal?"

"When I left his house, I fought the urge to turn the car around to beg him to marry me."

"Don't do that. Desperation scares even the best guys." She cast an evaluating glance my way. "And now?"

"Larice, I've never seen a marriage up close and personal I wanted. My parents stayed married a long time, but I don't want what they had. I would rather die, actually."

"You are not your mother, and Tim is certainly not your dad."

What I believed about marriage and my ability to take part were the lesser questions, as always. The elephant lumbering through my strawberry patch was my mother. I couldn't imagine a future outside of the cloistered life of me and her. "I may not be Mom, but we're joined at the hip. I can't go off and plan a life without considering what's best for her."

"That's the great thing about having someone like Tim in your life. You won't be on your own anymore. He'll be there to help." Larice shifted to face me. "If only you could see yourself with Tim's eyes. You've welcomed him with no judgment. You've taken up the cause of his sister, thus lightening his load. Is any of this sounding familiar? When you aren't afraid of being hurt, you are kind, Jenna. And he wants to see your beautiful face first thing every morning."

I wasn't buying any of this.

She watched me over the rim of her glass. "You don't have to be perfect to have a good marriage."

"And you learned this where?"

Larice lowered her glass to her lap and stared into the glistening liquid. "I shouldn't answer you."

For not showing mercy to my best friend, I'd just failed my postulancy in the worst way. Forget the nunnery and the hope of being any kind of saint, including and especially Joan of Arc. I was Kafka's beetle, a bug—a big, legs flailing in the air, common to the point of annoyance, bug. With twitching antennae. And iridescent eyes with no pupils. "I'm so sorry. I should go." I rose to leave.

Larice grabbed my hand and coaxed me down to the couch. She said, "You don't have to be sorry. You're right. I've been a miserable failure, but I've been looking around, asking questions. I will get married again. The trick is to get there by a completely different route than I've tried before."

"Watching? We're not talking lab experiments, are we?"

She held out her hand. "Give me your glass. You're not so nice with more than one glass of wine in you."

I drew my glass closer. "And you're bossy on your third glass."

She set her glass down on the coffee table. "Point taken. Can we continue?"

"With what?"

"The couple I've been watching."

I put my glass down too. I was okay with being snarky, not so okay with forgetting what the conversation was about. "How do you know these people?"

"They've come to me since I started with dental hygiene— nearly thirteen years. Every six months, here they come, holding hands, talking like teenagers, always together. I clean her teeth first, because, according to her husband, ladies should always go first. When my fingers aren't in their mouths, all they do is talk about the other. And we're not talking Hollywood contenders here. They're average folks, who don't floss as often as they claim, but they prefer one another's company.

"That has never been my experience. The ceremony was like a starting gun for my husbands. From then on I had to compete for their attention. One sort of sport or another always won. Or the job. Don't forget their buddies at the golf course, or shooting range, or surfing. And the worst, the deal breaker, the one I never expected because I was too busy spending my husbands' money—the other women. Married men are magnets to single women. For all of my failures in love, I've never intentionally gotten involved with a married man. What is with these women? I'm done doing things the same old way."

She'd described me. I was the other woman, Larice's worst nightmare. But I hadn't wanted to be anyone's other woman. I needed—what?—I needed to feel something. Was that so bad? My God, I was horrible. Tears ran down my cheeks. "That's me. I'm the other woman. I'm so sorry."

Larice pulled two tissues from the box and scooted closer. She dried my tears and drew me into her arms. "Next time— and time is the key here—I am so getting to know a guy before I let go of my heart. I get stupid otherwise."

"Computer dating, then?"

She kissed my forehead. "I haven't ruled anything out. However love happens, I'm the one who has to be different— patient, for one thing, and not so concerned about presentation and more into substance. I can't be afraid to be alone. And I am. That's why I'm praying more and reading the Bible, which can be quite disturbing at times and utterly confounding at others. But more often, the very words I need to hear jump off the page." She slumped lower. "Oh man, I could sleep for a year."

"You don't hold your wine well."

"I should go to bed. Taylor will be home from the movies soon. I don't want her to see me like this."

"Go ahead. I'll stay until she gets home."

"Would you?"

"Only because I feel badly about the crack I made earlier."

Larice lifted her head with some effort. Her eyelids drooped. "Spend some time in the prayer closet. There's a verse written on an index card. Take it."

"Will this verse cure me of stupidity?"

"You might be shooting too high. Let's go for a good decision for yourself and Tim."

I pulled Larice off the couch and helped her into the bedroom she shared with Taylor. For a girl to put up with that kind of closeness to her mother, something good was happening here. Still, I had no intentions of stopping by the prayer closet. None.

Being a woman of conviction, I was surprised to find myself striking a match for the candle inside the prayer closet. Larice had taped about twenty index cards on the wall, and none of them had anything to do with testing a guy's long-term compatibility. I gave up reading and stared into the candle.

"I suppose I should start with I'm sorry. I remember some stuff from youth group, and I've pretty much blown everything." Sorrow wrung my heart and I started to cry again. But why? I ran my finger down an inventory list of heartaches. There was Brian, constantly and always. Mom often fought for first place on the list. Dad, which surprised me. He was an emotional putz, but he was my father, and he'd found happiness somewhere else. Also, I didn't feel worthy of Tim, God, or Larice. I'd been the other woman, for heaven's sake. I put my head to my knees and let the tears flow.

I must have fallen asleep, because the candle had gone out, and I had slumped to the wall. When I straightened myself, I swatted at my face, sure a spider poised himself to suck blood from my cheek. But one of Larice's cards had stuck to my face. The closet was too dark to return the card to its rightful place, so I folded it in two to slip into my pocket.

Before I left the closet, I said to the dark space where the candle had been lit, "Could you find it in your heart to help me find Jerry?" Once out of the closet, I slid the door closed and reopened it for one more request. "Please don't let him be dead. Amen."

Taylor snored quietly in her bed. I exhaled a long breath of relief. Tim wanted someone to mother his children? On so many levels I wasn't the woman he believed me to be, but more than I could have dreamed, I wanted to be that person. But first, I had some changes to make.

Back in my bedroom, I set my alarm for an hour early. Tomorrow, do or die.

21

I accomplished enough in the week after Tim's definite-yes proposal to fill a year.

For one, I hired a guy at the bus station to tear down the wall between my bedroom and the bait shop. We needed the income those extra square feet offered, and I didn't want to wait for a professional to be available. I paid the man minimum wage and all the snowballs he could eat. He must have felt guilty for eating a whole case of Snowballs, because he worked like a demon.

Adding the extra sales space galled me on one count: Dad would interpret the move as agreement. But I had my own reason. Eric—or some other muscled god—might wander into the bait shop. Not having a bedroom would make being a sexual pushover much less convenient. Sure, I should rely on my own sense of dignity, but that hadn't worked in the past. In this way, I hoped to show Tim I'd committed to being a better me, a me that might be worthy of him, someday. He seemed patient. He would have to be.

The help-wanted sign worked. I hired a high school girl to work part-time. I chose the smartest girl who filled out an application, definitely not the prettiest, which worked in my favor. I needed Ashley to focus on getting espresso orders correct and counting back change with accuracy, not writing her phone number on a guy's hand. I bought her help and twenty hours of freedom by reducing my draw. I would use that freedom to find Brian.

I ordered umbrellas, and surf riders, and bought myself a twin-sized blow-up bed. I inflated the mattress each night and stowed it in the closet every morning, which meant moving more stuff to my car. I also sat down to talk with all the regulars about closing the telephony, all except the girl who came in during the 5:02 rush. She'd stopped coming when the sign went up. I deeply regretted throwing the model 354 off the pier. Besides the possible wounding of a mackerel, Jerry could have changed his mind and called again. I would never know.

Ginny took the news the hardest.

"I know Frank and I didn't sound like we were having a loving conversation, but that was how we talked," she said, fingering the handle of her knitting bag

"Frank was your...?"

I'd listened to her conversations with Frank for years, but I'd never asked who she talked to, which was telephony etiquette 101. We didn't talk about what I heard, either. The silencing of the telephones changed the rules.

"My first husband. He died twenty years ago last month." Ginny barely moved her lips when she talked.

Suspicions confirmed: people did talk to dead people in the telephony. I said a silent prayer Jerry still lived and breathed. For all the changes I'd made in the last week, I hadn't come up with a way to find him.

"I'm sorry, Ginny. The connections have broken again." My reformation, evidently, hadn't completely taken hold. I wasn't past lying or omitting important details. I shrugged and opened my palms to the sky. "I've tried everything I know to get them working again, and nothing. I'll give the telephones a little more time. Maybe they'll come around like they did last time. The problem is I can't wait forever. I'll have to remove the telephones and do something else with the space soon."

"You can't!"

I heard the splash of the model 354 as I watched Ginny's eyes well with tears. I hadn't thought of anyone but myself when I tossed the telephone off the end of the pier.

"Would you like to take the 302 home? You've been so generous to me. This is the least I can do."

Ginny followed me into the telephony. I dusted off the 302 with a tissue and pulled the cord from the hole in the countertop.

Ginny gasped. "I always figured the thing connected to something." She felt for the chair behind her and sat.

"Can I get you a drink of water?"

Ginny stared at the frayed end of the cord. "How did the telephone work? How did I hear Frank's voice?"

This seemed like an odd question from a woman who spoke to a man who had been dead for twenty years. "I don't know."

"How could anyone?"

"I have a box. I'll pack the telephone with some bubble wrap, and I have a large bag with handles."

Ginny stood up quickly and started for the door. She spoke over her shoulder. "I can't take the telephone. I don't have room in my house." She stopped and turned back to me. "George would never understand. I couldn't very well try to explain. Thanks for everything. Bye." And she was gone.

I dusted the countertop and returned the 302 to its place. I'd already rearranged the desktop full of telephones, so Dad wouldn't notice one had gone missing. Such wasted effort on my part. Dad didn't step into the telephony when he did come. I suspected Sally kept his thoughts occupied. A bitter tang filled my mouth at that thought. Bottom line, anything that happened at the telephony or bait shop no longer interested him. This made the next step of my plan easier.

I would need lots and lots of boxes to pack away the telephony. The thrift store would be thrilled with the furniture, even send robust volunteers to cart all of it away. The space begged to be filled with something to generate income. That would silence the dead and the annoying completely. I wasn't sure how I felt about all that quiet.

TIM ARRIVED AS THE shop emptied of customers for the 5:02. My new girl had left early for a dentist appointment. Seeing Tim set my heart to pounding. He gave a little wave and leaned against the doorjamb between the bait shop and the telephony. I waited on the last of my customers.

His sudden appearance flustered me. We hadn't arranged a time or place, only a vague assignment of a week for thinking. I'd done plenty of thinking. I thought of Tim and what sort of life we could have together in the first moments of wakefulness and all through the day until I fell asleep. I'd even dreamed of him a couple times. I'd counted down the days and checked through the list of things he gave me to consider.

His age no longer bothered me. Tim was road-traveled but dependable. I liked that he fulfilled Larice's requirement for kindness. Also, his family enjoyed one another, even after years of pain and disappointment. Stepping into a family willing to forgive would be an advantage. More than any guy I'd ever been involved with, Tim wanted to be connected. He wasn't the hunkiest or the most exciting, but he'd awakened a part of me I liked. Sure, he claimed to have messes in his life. I didn't doubt him, but my life took the sweepstakes for the messiest, for which I was responsible. By comparison, Tim qualified only as an innocent bystander.

Tim waited while I washed my hands and toweled off the day's collection of espresso and pop splatters on my face. I locked the bait shop door and turned the closed sign over. I leaned against the closed door to catch my breath.

"Jenna?"

Tim's hair, which he always kept short and neatly combed, hung onto his forehead. He pushed the silver strands back into place. "It's been a week," he said and heaved a sigh, looking eager yet wary, as if I wielded a double-barreled shotgun.

He waited for my reply, looking vulnerable, which made him irresistible. My default setting for entertaining men in a locked bait shop had always been unleashed passion. But I'd heard Larice and thought often of her advice: proceed with caution; take your time. Sure, sure, sure—but in that moment I deeply regretted demolishing my bedroom.

"Can I show you something?" I said.

I ushered him to my remodeling project. Where my bedroom once stood, pegs filled a wall to hang surf riders. Those I would rent to beachgoers. The for-hire umbrellas would go in a large wooden box I was having made.

"Where do you sleep?" he asked. Oh my, was Tim thinking of full-press passion too? He was a man. Of course, he thought of sex constantly.

"My bathroom and closet are still here," I said. "But I added industrial strength locks. Lots of kids will come back here. I don't want them going through my stuff."

"And you sleep where?" he asked again.

This wasn't going to be easy. I unlocked the closet to show him my new twin-sized, self-inflating mattress. I wanted him to understand the changes meant no more sweaty rendezvous in the back of the bait shop with emotionally unavailable men. I was a new woman. At least, I was moving toward being a new woman. Anyway, I wanted to be new, the kind a nice man married. I kicked the mattress like you would kick tires on a used car. "The thing flattens in minutes to be stored in the closet, never to be seen by another soul."

"Jenna, you could always stay—"

"I know." My stomach warmed at the thought. But this kind of thinking headed in the wrong direction. If I engaged the old Jenna, the new thinking woman never stood a chance. "I knew you would offer, and I'm thankful. I'm fine here, really." He looked crestfallen, the exact way I felt on the inside.

All of my efforts seemed trite. Instead of giving Tim the

consideration he'd asked for, I'd rearranged walls and bought a toy bed. I said, "I would love some fresh scenery. Could you wait for me out front while I tell Mom I'll be gone for a while?"

"Take all the time you need."

Mom slept in front of the TV. I should have woken her. It wasn't like she slept to be refreshed or to heal. Instead, I wrote her a note and brushed my teeth and put on lip gloss. I really needed a shower, but I didn't have fresh clothes at Mom's. I spritzed some of her perfume.

Tim sat on the bench outside the bait shop, leaning forward, elbows to his knees, watching the dinnertime activity around the pier. Stragglers pulled tired children across the tracks and up the hill to their cars. New arrivers walked hand-in-hand toward the restaurant wearing beach chic, which included everything from swim trunks and tank tops to linen and silk.

He kissed me on the cheek, a very unfair use of touch at a time like this. "Should we get a drink? Are you hungry?" he said.

I couldn't eat. My throat squeezed around every word. "Could we walk along the beach? I've been inside all day."

We took off our shoes and walked toward the packed sand at the waterline. A wave covered our feet to our ankles with popping foam. The coolness shocked and delighted me, an invitation to run toward the breaking waves and dive headfirst through a glossy wall of water. Typical avoidance behavior on my part. I willed my head and heart back into the moment.

"How's Amy? Did you have a nice visit?"

"She's been through some horrific stuff, but she seems good. And she's been sober for five years this September. She works at a rehab center in Michigan, which worries me and fills me with pride. You were right about why she stayed away. She couldn't face our parents, even though she's come so far. Plus she was afraid of disappointing us again. I have nothing but admiration for her.

"Her kids are the greatest. Quinn, the one who helped you in the kitchen, he's got the knack with numbers. He can multiply triple-digit numbers in his head. The best part was watching Amy with the kids. She's a wonderful mother. My folks are downright giddy. I can't remember them laughing this much, ever. The husband is—how should I say this?—compliant."

That made me laugh.

"Thanks for laughing."

I must have screwed up my face.

"You've been so serious, like you were waiting for me to hit you." He stopped to face me. Another wave covered our feet and we sank into the saturated sand. "I haven't changed my mind," he said. "It's still a definite yes."

Another wave. Another inch deeper. "Tim..."

"I see."

"You don't see. You can't. This is a problem with me, not you."

Tim pulled his feet out of the sand and continued walking. When I tried to do the same, I fell onto my hands. A wave hit me in the fanny, soaking me from the neck down. Pulling myself from the sucking sand, I tugged my skirt into place and ran to catch up. When I did, he'd hung a closed sign on his face. I couldn't read him.

Anger?

Hurt?

Disappointment?

All of the above?

I stepped closer, took his hand. "Tim, my life is very unsettled. Mom is getting worse. If I could find my brother..."

"Let me help you. You don't have to do this alone." He took my other hand. We created our very own circle. "We can do the tough stuff together."

His words stopped me cold. Tim had ideas about love that, frankly, I could not reference. I nearly drowned in tough stuff every day. I wanted—*needed*—some parallel universe living, where my brother had gotten off the bus and walked home with me, and my mother traveled with Dad to paint the wonders of the world. And he'd never started collecting telephones or lashing out in anger. Slogging through more tough stuff with Tim or anyone held no appeal. Something had to be resolved. At least, partly. "I have to find my brother before I make any plans."

"With me?"

I should have said yes. I wanted to say yes, but he did deserve better. Instead, I stalled. "Could I have a little more time?"

He hung his head before he looked me in the eyes again. "We'll find your brother first."

"Thanks."

We didn't talk about promises anymore. We ate dinner on the pier. I heard more of Amy's story and about the trip the family had taken to Disneyland. We sat at the same table, but a new distance opened between us. I hadn't expected to feel lonely with him right there. He left me at the bait shop door.

As the blow-up bed grumbled toward firmness, I worried I was using Tim as I had used Eric, only in a much more pernicious (new word: having a harmful effect, especially in a subtle) manner. Would I have the courage to say definitely yes to Tim when the time came? And what if we didn't find Brian? How long would Tim put up with being my sidekick? To be fair we needed a deadline. I swiped through the calendar on my cell.

One month?

Two?

The air pump shifted to a higher pitch. I looked toward the sound of air rushing from the mattress. A seam had opened on the edge. I turned off the pump and opened the valve to release the remaining air. My new mattress, the very thing meant to save me from myself, lay flaccid on the floor.

And there was no plan B.

22

Dad inspected the new space I'd created for the rental items with his arms crossed over his chest. "You should've talked to me first."

Talking to Dad would have been difficult. He hadn't answered his cell or my texts in days, and I hadn't seen him in over a week. He'd blown in that afternoon, whistling his way into the bait shop, very surprised to see I'd hired help. Ashley introduced herself when he arrived, and he smiled his yellow-toothed smile at her. He probably saw his freedom in the stringy-haired girl with the thick glasses and the work ethic of a mule. Making Dad happy was easy. I needed to make him care.

"You're right," I said. "I'm sorry, Dad."

He looked at me out of the corner of his eye. "You'll get a drywall guy in here to finish this up nice, right?"

"When things slow down this fall."

He nodded his approval. "You're taking after your old man. You've got a business head on your shoulders."

Enough buddying up over business decisions. I didn't know how much longer I could behave myself for Dad's benefit. I was digging into my savings to pay his replacement, Ashley. "Mom's more nervous, agitated. I think she needs to see a doctor." Only the day before she'd stood at her easel without painting and slipped into bed before dinner.

Dad looked at his feet, clicked his heels together like Dorothy. There was no place like Sally's home.

"The doc won't refill her prescriptions without seeing her. Is she still on your insurance?"

"That was our agreement," he said, tight-lipped and

shooting furtive glances at the door.

"Could you talk to her?" I asked, making my eyes doe-like. "She's not eating much. I've bought all her favorites. Nothing seems to appeal."

"And you think she'll listen to me?"

"I'm running out of options. I could ask the plumber, the one she likes—Fred? Is that his name?—to stop by and offer her some mental health advice."

"Sarcasm isn't appreciated," he said, running his hand over one of the exposed studs. "This is rough. You better do some sanding until you get the wall repaired. The health inspector won't like this."

"I'm watching Mom dissolve into a heap of ash."

The visual proved too potent. Dad pivoted and all but dashed for the door. I didn't bother following him. Late-day travelers pushed past him to enter the bait shop for drinks and snacks. Watching him sidestep through customers spoke volumes: when matters of your mother come up, you're on your own, kiddo.

Fine.

I worked the espresso machine while Ashley took orders. The one man on San Clemente beach more miserable than I stepped up to the counter. He must have fallen asleep in the sun. The outline of his hand shone with neon brilliance against his blistering skin. He had worn his sunglasses. At least he would be able to open his eyes the next day.

"You got anything for sunburn?" he said.

I grabbed a travel-sized package of ibuprofen, two bottles of water, and my favorite aloe vera gel with benzocaine. "Ibuprofen for the pain, one bottle of water to drink and one to roll over your skin, and this gel will help you sleep tonight."

He winced reaching for his wallet. "How much do I owe you?"

"Nothing. Come back and rent one of my umbrellas next

time."

"If there is a next time," he said, walking gingerly toward the door.

Ashley and I dispatched the last of the day's customers, but one remained, leaning against the far wall, watching me and waiting—the 5:02 girl.

"I suppose you have questions," I said to her.

"Do you have time?"

I'd stowed Mom's dinner in the refrigerator, knowing she wouldn't eat, and I needed to shower before meeting Tim to strategize our search for Jerry. "I have a few minutes." Ashley, who knew how to read awkward situations—I hated to think how she'd gotten so adept—offered to come in early the next day to clean the espresso machine.

"I'll do it," I told her. "No problem. Be sure to lock the door." She looked at the girl, probably recognizing her from her regular visits, and raised her eyebrows. "Go on, really. See you tomorrow."

Ashley hung up her apron, gathered her purse from under the counter, and waved over her shoulder as she headed for the door. Her keys jangled in her hand.

I turned toward the young woman who stood with her body square to mine. I appreciated the chance to take a closer look at her. She'd always been a blur, rushing in and out of the telephony at our busiest time.

The shadows under her eyes increased her age from what I'd guessed, closer to thirty-plus, like me. She was angles and lines with blunt bangs and sleek hair that slid over her shoulders, a schoolgirl style that didn't work to soften her features. Her coloring brought dark chocolate to mind. Whatever she saw in me produced a bemused smile. Enigmatic described me perfectly.

We ducked under the barrier to the telephony and sat in opposing office chairs near the fiddleback. The young woman started to speak, and hesitated.

"I'm Jenna." I had no intention of becoming her best friend, but I wanted her to start talking. I'd thought all day about the prospect of finding Jerry, so I found this girl's timing more than inconvenient.

"Steph."

"Well, Steph, you had questions?" Come on, spit them out.

"It's been quiet."

I breathed deeply and let the air out slowly, a little trick I'd learned in yoga to calm myself. This visit would take a while. "The telephones have gone silent again. This time, I'm afraid, there will be no return to service." All thanks to my rash decision to send the model 354 swimming with the fishes.

"Do you know how the telephones work?"

"I haven't a clue. There's nothing we've done to make them ring. They just do, or they did." Steph smoothed her skirt. I prodded her with my own question, breaking telephony etiquette about minding your own business. "There seems to be a correlation between the caller and the telephone. A young girl from the early-eighties called on the Snoopy telephone. The fiddleback is over a hundred years old. Who called you?"

"You'll think I'm insane."

"This place has cured me of questioning anyone's sanity." If I didn't count Mom. "The regulars who came here loved the people they talked to."

"Well then," she said, as if admitting a state secret, "I talked with my great-grandmother. She thought I was her daughter. We must sound alike. I don't know. I never knew my grandmother. My mother refused to talk to her.

"Talking to Great-grandma Adele left us both confused. I figured out first who she believed me to be. It took longer to discover she was my great-grandmother. After that, I played the part of Grandma each time I came. I had to dig into family history with my aunt to be convincing. Mother has only spoken of her mother and grandmother with her teeth clenched.

"I invited my Aunt Rosie—are you keeping track of all the players?—to come with me, but she wouldn't. She was convinced the telephony was a bit too—and this is no reflection on you—but she believed the phenomena a source of evil." She dipped her chin to confide in me. "But Aunt Rosie demanded reports each time I talked to her grandmother, whom she also hated. She simply loved a good mystery more that maintaining her scruples. She gave me several notebooks of notes on family history. Otherwise, I never could have played the part."

Good or evil, I hadn't decided where the telephony fell either. Perhaps the telephony played with time to create opportunities. What we did with those opportunities, like Tim reuniting with Amy, is what assigned value to the place. Any thought given to the source of the telephony's power would have to wait, because I had another question, an important question, for Steph. "Is your great-grandmother—?"

"Alive? Heavens no, she died after my grandmother delivered her second child, Aunt Rosie, nearly seventy years ago."

This wasn't looking good for finding Jerry. Of the three callers I'd identified, 66.6% were dead.

"Do you have a caller?" Steph asked.

I startled and Steph opened her mouth to withdraw the question. I put my hand up and told her about Jerry. No one wants to believe they're the only one to skirt normalcy. "I'm hoping very much he's alive. He holds the key to finding my missing brother."

"I'll pray you find him."

I said nothing, smiled weakly.

She stood, looked toward the door. "I've kept you long enough." She rifled through her purse for a business card. "Please call if the telephones start to work again. I think I understand the craziness of my family a little better. I'll be marrying soon. I would like to avoid the mistakes my great-grandmother made." She put out her hand. "Thanks for this time."

I didn't want to see this girl again. "Would you like the fiddleback? I'll be closing down the telephony soon. Please consider the telephone a wedding gift."

She pulled out a credit card, but I told her the fiddleback held absolutely no value for me. "I'll send my fiancé for it." She chewed on her lip before continuing. "He knows nothing of what I've been doing here. I would appreciate—"

I drew a finger across my lips. "Mum's the word."

"And if the telephone should ring?"

It wouldn't, but tripping her plans for a happy marriage seemed cruel. "You'll have to decide to answer or not."

She ducked back under the barrier and I followed. "Have you seen families helped through the telephony?" she said, waiting for me to unlock the door.

I thought of Tim spinning his sister in his arms. A definite yes to that.

I PESTERED, BEGGED, AND wheedled Mom to eat. She'd not eaten the lunch I put beside her chair at noon. Now, bits of chicken, pepper, and pineapple congealed in the sweet and sour sauce of her dinner. I offered to reheat the food. She flipped a dismissive hand. I kissed her cheek, asked one more time if anything sounded good to her. "Don't be so pushy," she said. "I'll eat when I'm good and ready."

I left the apartment more angry than worried, not a great start to the evening, so I walked slowly down the stairs, reminding myself that finding Jerry was the first step toward better days for Mom and me.

I carried a new legal pad, complete with a list of everything I'd learned about Jerry. And I wore an outfit I'd bought in one of the Del Mar boutiques in about five minutes. Staring into my closet for an hour had left me desperate from eliminating T-shirt and jean combinations for being too low, too high, and too me. I meant to wear makeup, but the mascara came out of the tube as a solid clump. And the eye shadow had pulverized. I threw the mess in the trash.

Tim's first words to me were: "You look different."

Preparing for our time together, I'd miscalculated a simple choice like what to wear. "Should I change?"

"You already have." He said this with his eyebrows pressed into a question.

I looked down at myself and saw my mother in one of her QVC finds. I felt like a stranger to myself. "You don't like it?"

"A wise and beautiful young woman once unbuttoned the top button of my shirt and said, 'You should be comfortable.'"

If comfortable meant not being choked by your own clothes, I was plenty comfortable. But if comfortable meant not feeling conspicuous, I felt like a pimple on prom night.

"I can wait," he said.

I should have been upset. He pretty much said my attempts at fashion had flashed and fizzled. And what message had my new outfit sent him? Trying to impress him seemed cruel. I'd put him off indefinitely when he had said yes so definitely. To be a grownup, emotionally secure woman, I needed to move past playing such games. On the other hand, the outfit had invited Tim to affirm a change in me, and he'd ushered me back to myself. I really appreciated his generosity.

I held his hand as we walked to his car, a Ford Fusion. It smelled new. A compass, a stack of maps, and several pens in the console were the only evidence the car had left the showroom floor. By contrast, my Daewoo smelled lived in, probably because I used the car as a storage shed. I rotated boxes of clothes from the car as the seasons changed, mostly from lighter to heavier hoodies.

Tim pushed a button to start the car. A chime sounded and the dashboard lit up. I prepared for him to be upset, because no vibration or engine noise followed. We pulled away from the curb. Ah, hybrid. Sensible. Very Tim.

WE SAT AT TIM'S dining table, a piece of furniture I likened to an indoor picnic table made of exotic wood—long with benches down both sides and upholstered chairs on the ends.

I'd been in plenty of bachelor places. If they owned a table for eating which was rare, it was something they'd picked up off the curb. None of those guys had used coasters under their beer cans. Tim offered one for my iced tea. Yet more evidence that we traveled in nonsynchronous orbits.

There I went again. I'd promised myself not to think about us as *we*. *We* didn't exist, except in a narrow sliver of shared experiences—lunches on opposite sides of the bait shop, a drink on the pier with a bonus dinner attached, and an odd incident—the oddity being me—under the pier. Add helping him to connect with Amy, and the subsequent kiss and the out-of-the-blue proposal. I doubted all that equaled *we*.

Also, I wasn't to think about the kiss anymore. Thinking about the kiss made me stupid.

"Jenna?"

I looked up to Tim's questioning gaze. "Yes?"

"What do you know about Jerry?" Something in his voice hinted he'd already asked this question.

I pulled the legal pad from my bag and turned the list toward him.

1. His name is Jerry.
2. He knows where Brian is, was, or wasn't.
3. He's a suspicious, old-sounding man.
4. He has a wet, rattling cough.
5. He has a daughter.
6. He has a son named Donny, who loves couches.

7. Another son is dead
8. He got hot where he worked.
9. He's keeping a promise to someone. Who?
10. He did not go to college.
11. I met Jerry, at least once, when I carried a book bag.
12. His company forced him to retire.
13. His grammar sucks.
14. He's very, very, very secretive about Brian.

Tim tapped his pen against the paper, frowning at the list. "There isn't much here, but you've been very thorough."

"That cough," I said. "He's probably dead."

"Not necessarily. He could have had a chest cold. Nonfatal. Usually."

"Is there anything helpful?"

"Some. We know his first name. Did you get the sense he owned his house?"

"I never thought to ask."

He stood. "We should go for a drive."

IN THE CAR, TIM asked, "Where did the school bus drop you off?"

"What are you thinking?"

Tim explained that Jerry must have seen Brian and me walking home from school because he mentioned the book bag I'd been carrying.

"That's brilliant." The bus stop had changed at the beginning of the year Brian disappeared, so he and I had a longer walk home, which gave us plenty to grouse about the moment we walked into the apartment door.

"The bus dropped us off at the corner of Monterey and Ola Vista. If we had money, we stopped at the convenience store for something to snack on, which we never told Dad about. He expected us to starve until we got home to buy snacks in the bait shop."

"He made you buy snacks?"

"You're beginning to see my life more clearly. Scary, huh?"

Tim came to a complete stop, waited for an elderly man to step onto the opposite curb before he drove through the intersection. My pulse pounded. A churlish dread settled on me at the thought of coming face to face with Jerry. I thought to ask Tim to stop the search before it began.

Instead, he stepped on the gas to zoom past parked cars. "Did you walk home the same way every day?"

Shouldn't he slow down? "Brian and I studied a street map and picked the shortest route possible. So, yes, we walked home the same way."

"Perfect. You've narrowed down our search area. We'll go to the county courthouse and look for Jerrys who owned property along this route the year Brian went missing, but maybe driving the route will help you remember something too."

Tim turned onto Monterey and slowed. We landed smack dab in the middle of beach town architecture—pseudo Spanish-tiled apartment buildings mixed with beach cottages, which for this part of town meant they were small, not quaint. Most had flat roofs, and if they had squeezed their house onto the lot just right, a one-car garage. Because of the uptick in property values, most were well maintained.

I asked Tim to stop in front of a turquoise house with a picket fence and an overgrown lawn. A golf cart with a flat tire sat parked in the driveway. And while sidewalks had been installed in front of all other houses, only a worn path connected the sidewalks on either side of this house. I wrote the address on the legal pad.

"Are you remembering something?"

I remembered nothing, but the house looked like a cranky old man with a rattling voice might live inside. "Just a hunch."

We kept driving through the winding streets, slipping into driveways of strangers to let an impatient driver pass on the narrow street. Occasionally, we stopped to note an address, mostly because I wanted something to show for our effort. Everything looked familiar but nothing triggered a memory of Brian and me talking to an old man. Tim finally turned onto Avenida Victoria and parked in front of the bait shop.

"Disappointed?" he said.

Yes. "Not yet. I'll go to the courthouse."

"I'll go with you."

His eagerness set off an alarm. I wrapped my fingers around the handle. "You have work. Ashley can cover for me."

"Before you go, I should clarify. You look beautiful in everything you wear. How about we go out to dinner, give you a chance to show off? Do you have time?"

Dammit! Who talks like that? I pulled up hard on the handle and pushed the door open. I stepped from the car and closed the door before I talked to him through the opened window. "Thanks for today, but I've got this."

He leaned over the console, frowning. "Jenna? What? Did I say something? We should talk."

"No. No, we shouldn't."

"No?"

"I'll find Jerry and retrieve my brother from God knows where."

"Jenna—?"

"You're confusing me. I need my head on straight. This is the most important thing I'll ever do. You've been great, but…"

"Definitely, no thanks?"

His words bit. I'd hurt him. The kindest thing to do was cut his losses. "Definitely, no thanks." I turned toward the bait shop. I did not want Tim to see me crying.

LARICE STARED AT ME agape. "Let me get this straight. A nice guy with no criminal record or a wife has asked you to marry him. You told him you needed time to consider. I track with you up to that point. In fact, I'm proud of you. You're learning. But now you've told him to take a hike? Jenna, that's just—"

"Stupid?" I'd been sabotaging relationships with guys since high school. I was very good at it.

Larice took me by the shoulders and turned me toward the prayer closet.

"A closet won't help what's wrong with me."

"You don't know that."

I dug in my heels.

Larice hugged me from behind and whispered in my ear. "Tell him what you need."

"God? All I do is cry in there."

"Which happens to be a language he understands well."

I settled onto the cushion and Larice lit the candle. "This is dumb," I said, like walking away from Tim qualified me for a Nobel Prize.

"Not as dumb as some stuff we've done."

"Close the door." I managed to stifle my sobs until Larice whispered through the door she was leaving to pick up Taylor. Once the apartment door clicked shut, I let the tears and the snot run wild.

I yelled at the candle with its perky flame. "Fix me!" In a great demonstration of faith I blew out the candle, left the closet, and poured myself a tall glass of wine.

God, definitely yes, knew that.

23

The ladies of the clerk and recorder's office of Orange County loved a mystery. Before I got my legal pad out, I possessed all I needed to find Jerry—thanks to Juli and Holly. One step completed toward bringing Brian home.

Someone with the first name of Jerry—or something like it—owned three homes on Avenida Monterey and Avenida Victoria. Jerry Dryden had bought his house the previous year, which was too recent, so I ruled that Jerry out. A couple, Gerry Ashcroft and Bruce Larson—also bought their house too recently. And Gerry, in this case a derivative of Geraldine, was the wrong sex. The third home, located within a hundred yards of our bus stop, had been bought by a Jerzy Budney in 1972.

Okay, so I stretched to make Jerzy into Jerry, but the year worked out about right. I did some math on an In-N-Out bag. If Jerry retired close to Brian's disappearance, he would have bought the house around his fortieth birthday, which fit well. Maybe he'd bought in San Clemente for his eventual retirement. He'd wanted to live in a smaller town, and his wife loved the beach, I reasoned. I couldn't imagine Jerry loving anything but perhaps his wife nagged him into submission, although no wife was named on the deed.

Jerry would now be in his early eighties. People lived into their eighties, no problem. And chances were I could outrun a man in his eighties, if he turned out to be as objectionable in person as he had on the telephone. I liked that mobility worked in my favor. I drove straight from the county courthouse in Santa Ana to the address I'd written down.

The house turned out to be worse than I'd expected. I

hadn't bothered writing down the address while driving with Tim earlier—thinking of Tim wrung my heart—because the place looked like a meth house, and nothing inside a meth house would make me ring the doorbell. What had once been someone's seaside cottage had decayed from lack of care. Draperies hung rotted and torn. Nicotine tinted the windows. The mailbox swung with the breeze.

No one could live in such a house. The lawn hadn't been watered in years. A broken palm tree with a pouf of crispy fronds bent toward the ground like a supplicant. I didn't need my dad's girlfriend, Sally, to know the wreck was worth close to a million dollars, even in its withered state. If Jerry's children didn't like how he'd handled his will, the property could have been frozen in probate for years. That might explain its sad condition.

On closer inspection, much to my surprise, a purple bucket of Gerbera daisies squatted by the front door. The exclamation of color sparked hope in me. Someone actually lived in the house, someone who liked daisies but didn't mind dead trees. That sounded like someone who had been influenced by Jerry and survived.

So this had to be *the* Jerry I was looking for. I didn't have the luxury of considering he wasn't.

I knocked on the door.

Lumbering steps challenged the floorboards on the other side of the door. A chain slid and two locks clicked open. A woman with innumerable chins and skin like an orange looked back at me. My luck, a troll guarded the way to Jerry.

"What do you want?" She sounded exactly like Jerry.

"I'm looking for Jerry Budney."

She closed the door until only one eye, her nose, and mouth showed. "Who are you?"

I hadn't expected suspicion. I deserved a medal for courage and perseverance. From the sneer on the troll's face, she didn't appreciate my efforts as much as I did. I imitated a sweet schoolgirl. "Jerry used to talk to me and my brother all the time. Does he still live here?"

I didn't remember talking to an old man on the way home from school, ever. But I might have, especially if Dad had promised a long list of chores when we got home. "We got off the bus right there," I said, pointing toward the corner. "Could I see him?"

Her eyes narrowed to slits. "Why are you really here?"

"It's hard to explain."

"Did my brother send you?"

A question I could answer with complete honesty. "I don't know your brother."

"You can tell that low-life that Dad is not dead yet. If he wants money, he should get a job."

The door caught on a rug, which the woman, evidently Jerry's daughter, pulled away with a grunt, and the door slammed closed. Our first encounter didn't go well, but Jerry was still alive. Or he wasn't dead yet, as the troll had said. His condition sounded tenuous. I knocked again.

Jerry's daughter turned the volume of the television to high and yelled, "I don't have time for you!" I recognized the theme music of *The Dr. Phil Show*. My mother watched the show daily. Mom and Jerry's daughter had something in common. How weird was that?

I could hear Dr. Phil getting down and dirty with a deadbeat dad through a window left open by the front door. I put my face to the screen. "I won't take any of your time. I would love to see Jerry," I said, switching to my Girl-Scout voice.

"He's sleeping!"

I doubted anyone could sleep with the noise in the house. "It's important!"

The sound of the television muted. "Are you from the

power company?"

"No, I'm a friend!" I said. "I'll come back when you're not busy!" I waited for a response. "Okay?"

"Don't bother. Dad doesn't have friends."

I stood within fifteen feet of the one and only person who knew my brother's whereabouts. Retreat was unthinkable, but I had nothing to offer the daughter to gain entrance into Jerry's house. I couldn't exactly tell her I'd talked to a much younger version of Jerry just days earlier, and that I needed to interrogate him about my brother's fate. She would nominate me as a guest on *The Dr. Phil Show*—Grieving Sister Reduced to Delusional State. Stay tuned!

The only person who could help me find Brian lay near death in a house reeking of cigarette smoke and guarded by a contrary—and fearful—daughter, a troll.

BY THE TIME I closed the bait shop and made my way upstairs to Mom's apartment, I was scheming ways to find Eric. Doing so numbered among my worst ideas ever, but if the new Jenna was a bust—as my poor treatment of Tim had proved—I didn't see the need to settle for cold sheets.

Besides abandoning my conscience, a rendezvous with Eric would mean getting creative. I slept on a duct-taped, blow-up bed that lost enough air to land me on the floor most mornings. I'd already dismissed the idea of rebuilding my bedroom walls. The surf riders and umbrellas brought in good money. Being practical, or at least being someone with a strong survival instinct, proved especially inconvenient at times.

I knew exactly where to find Tim, but I refused to drag the poor man back into my life. As I'd said so many times before, he deserved better.

Mom slept in her chair with the television cranked up for maximum hearing damage. I added getting her hearing checked on my list of impossible goals. I slumped into Dad's chair and drew up my knees to watch her sleep.

Her eyes rolled wildly under her lids. Who or what did Mom dream about? My stomach reminded me I hadn't eaten since breakfast. Otherwise, I might have fallen under the spell of Mom's rhythmic breathing and tumbled off into dreamland myself, which would have been easier than wrestling with my conscience—to hunt the elusive Eric or not?—that was the question.

The pungency of linseed oil and turpentine caught my attention. A cigar box sat on Mom's easel with the lid propped open. I rose to see what kind of light she'd captured, and, more truthfully, to see evidence of life coursing through her veins.

The scene before me weakened my knees. She'd painted the morning Tim had walked into the bait shop to find me with Eric and then eating sand under the pier. There we were, center stage, embracing by the tracks.

In the painting, my skirt lifted from the turbulence of the train's passing, and the train receded from the scene toward the north. She'd caught everything. I touched my check, feeling afresh the roughness of Tim's morning beard on my cheek and smelled his exertion and the barely-there soap.

I closed the painted box.

"That man would never make you eat sand," Mom said through the fog of sleep, her eyes only half opened.

No, Tim certainly would not.

Mom's eyes closed again, so I carried the cigar box to the bait shop, where I took another look at the scene. All eyes had been on us that morning. Some smiled. A teenager rolled his eyes. A woman held her hand to her mouth. Perhaps she alone recognized the anguish powering the embrace, or she remembered a scene from her own life, one she wished had gone much differently.

I cleared the spot on the closet floor for the cigar box painting to dry, which meant carrying several pairs of flip-flops and boxes of feminine products out to the car for storage. I propped the box open, so the edges would dry without sticking closed.

Leaning against a surf rider to study the scene, I knew I wouldn't look for Eric. I would go upstairs to fix dinner for Mom, sit in Dad's chair to watch TV, and figure out a way to get inside Jerry's house.

I also stifled an urge to run back to Tim. In a few days, maybe a month or two, the punishing claw in my chest would cease its ripping. The wound—self-inflicted—would scab, itch for a time, and scar over.

24

I knew two things about the troll: she liked Gerbera daisies and Dr. Phil. The acerbic doctor couldn't help me, but maybe the daisies could. After I knocked five times, the door opened.

"Like I said, Jerry does not want to see you."

I played dumb. "I'm so sorry. I didn't hear you say that. I thought you said he was sleeping." I held out a pot of flowers to the troll. "I saw that you like Gerberas. They're one of my favorites too. It's got to be tough taking care of a sick parent. These guys are so cheerful. I hope they help."

She settled her marble-like eyes on me, not even glancing at the daisies. "Let me see if he's awake." She slammed the door closed.

I stared at the sun-bleached door, wondering if God would mind hearing a request to get me inside. I didn't have a chance to ask. The door opened and the troll crossed her doughy arms. "He wants to see you. I don't know who you really are, but if you have any plans on sweet-talking your way into his checkbook, you should know there's a gun in the house."

She opened the door and a tsunami of scents washed over me—cigarettes, urine, mildew, and rotting food. The toxic slurry only intensified in the closed confines of the room, where a gun lay nearby, somewhere out of sight. The temptation to run for higher ground tugged at me. When and if I found my brother, he would hear about this and pay dearly.

I stood by the door like a mannequin.

"Do you want to see him or not?" the troll asked.

I could not continue this sweetness-and-light routine without knowing the troll's real name. I introduced myself. She did not offer her name in return. Fine, her name was Troll. "Thank you. I really appreciate the opportunity to see Jerry."

I followed her shuffling steps through the living room, past the bathroom—worse than can be described—to a room with a grinding and hissing oxygen machine. When Troll stepped aside, I saw the real Jerry for the first time, so very small in the hospital bed. The Jerry of my imaginings had been impossibly tall and muscled, his face contorted by a menacing grin. The corners of this Jerry's lips sagged nearly to his chin. Gray skin draped his withered arms and shoulders.

Troll squeezed her bulk between the far wall and the bed. "The CNA came this morning. He's had a bath. Otherwise, you can barely breathe in here."

My mind was too busy reconciling the two Jerrys to say a word. Where I'd imagined dark slicked hair, his white hair formed an enviable pouf far back from his forehead. His eyebrows hooded his eyes. Only his black pupils shifting between me and Troll convinced me he could see. The man had no lips. His face hung like a tarp over a spear of a nose, and a dimpled chin jutted out to dare me to misspeak. But this Jerry could not hang up on me.

He spoke in sentences punctuated by gasping breaths. "I know...who...you are."

To Jerry, years had passed since we talked on the telephone. For me, only days. Troll stood on the other side of the bed, watching and frowning.

"Good." I looked for the outline of a handgun under the sheets. The sheets lay smooth.

"How do you know each other?" Troll said.

Jerry said to her, "Make yourself...useful. Put up...those postcards...like I asked."

Troll left the room. Jerry hefted himself against his pillows. "You want...to know...about your brother...before I die."

I had no reason to pretend otherwise, not with Jerry. "Yes."

Troll returned with a stack of postcards and a plastic box of pushpins. "I don't like putting holes in the walls."

"Don't matter. They'll tear…the place…down."

"You're crazy. Why would anyone tear the house down?" she said and glanced at me.

He sucked in a breath. "Stinks."

Troll set the postcards on the far nightstand and turned toward the wall. "Look who's high and mighty after his bath."

"Put…the damn…postcards…on the wall." Jerry broke into a coughing fit, which his daughter ignored. I looked around for a glass of water and found none.

"I don't see why this has to happen now," she said, taking another postcard off the pile and impaling it with a pushpin. I wanted to look at the cards, look at anything but Jerry's face gasping for air, but I couldn't take my eyes off of him.

"Do you need a drink?" I said.

He shook his head.

The coughing fit gradually ceased, but Jerry labored for every breath. He sunk into his pillows and slipped down the mattress. He did not look comfortable. His eyes shifted to his daughter and back to me. "She's…a vulture."

"Jerry, please…" pleaded Troll.

His cough boomed. Troll pinned postcards of Cozumel and Sapporo to the wall. Ketchikan. Nassau. Singapore. Dakar. Hobart. Istanbul. Whoever sent the postcards really got around. Perhaps Jerry had a pen pal, or he'd discovered the joys of travel, after all.

I remembered why I'd come. "Do you need anything, Jerry?"

"Tired."

I leaned over him, my nose practically touching his. "Is Brian alive?"

Troll spun around. "What the hell are you asking him?"

I ignored her. I didn't want another coughing fit to

interrupt my time with Jerry. "Nod or shake your head."

"Get out!" Troll had shuffled around the bed to pull on my arm. "Get out of here before I call the police."

I kept my eyes on Jerry as long as I could, looking for a nod or a shake of his head. He closed his eyes and his chin sank to his chest.

TROLL COULD NOT BE anywhere near Jerry the next time I visited. Surely she went to the grocery store regularly. I asked Ashley to work early mornings until two. Dad agreed to work one afternoon. That gave me plenty of time for surveillance and another visit.

"You're the one who insisted on hiring help. I don't see why you need me at all," Dad said when I'd asked him this small favor.

I dipped my head to tell him I needed time for my yearly gynecological exam. No more complaining from him.

My plan was simple: arrive at Jerry's house before dawn, park across the street, and wait for Troll to leave the house. The second she was out of sight, I would go inside to have Jerry all to myself.

But to get a parking space along any street in San Clemente meant parking the day before, no later than four, when people started leaving the beach and before residents came home for the evening. Then I would walk back to the bait shop to return to the car the next day to watch and wait.

Time and opportunity. Simple.

AN INSISTENT KNOCK ON the bait shop door woke me after midnight, this according to Brian's alarm clock, the one I plucked from the closet each night as my bed blew itself into a tantalizing if eventually disappointing firmness.

My thoughts flew to Mom. Something had happened, but who would be knocking? Dad slept soundly with Sally, and besides, he carried a key. As I threw back the covers and reached for a hoodie, I stopped.

Maybe it was Tim. I combed unruly curls with my fingers. The knocks came again. Wanting Tim to show up in the middle of the night proved how confused I'd become. He hadn't called or dropped by since I sent him away. I did not appreciate his unwavering respect for my wishes.

Larice stood at the door, her hands forming binoculars to look inside. I waved. She started crying. Once inside, she paced the narrow path between the refrigerated cases and the wall of snacks. She'd dressed for a night out—a snug halter top over tight black capris and strappy stilettos.

"I went out with a guy," she said. "I thought he'd be safe. I met him at church. Jayne introduced us. I've put him off for a long time, told him all about my pledge to remain celibate until Taylor graduated and I could focus on finding a good guy. I thought—and don't you dare make fun of me—that maybe God had sent someone early.

"Zack said he was cool with celibacy, said I sounded smart. He quoted Bible verses at me. Can you believe that?"

"What happened?" I asked, but I already knew.

"I liked him a lot, right away. I believed we were on the same page. Oh my God, it was heavenly to let my guard down. The next thing I knew, we were making out on the couch."

"In your apartment?"

"Is what I'm trying to do even possible? And what's the big deal? This isn't Victorian England. Who really cares? It's not like what I'm doing is wrong, right?"

"I don't think so."

"I'm tired of being lonely. I deserve to be loved, don't I?"

"Sure. Of course."

"I'm beating myself up for nothing. No one should feel bad about wanting to be loved. It's human, right?"

"You loved this guy?"

Larice froze. "No. I liked how he looked at me. I liked...I liked feeling special and wanted." Her bottom lip trembled. "God, I sound like a middle-schooler. Why is this—you know, guys, me, life, everything—why is it all so hard? Why do I even try?"

"Is it possible that it isn't that hard? You may not have had the start you dreamed of, but maybe Zack is the one."

"How can he be? He knew what I was trying to do, and when I sabotaged my own success, he took advantage of my weakness. How could I ever trust him again?"

I had absolutely nothing to offer my friend. I felt disappointed, though, which was weird but understandable. How was I supposed to expect a genuine, long-term, mature relationship, if Larice, the mother superior of our ragtag nunnery, settled for much less? So I rubbed her back and let her tears soak the shoulder of my hoodie, as she had done for me through plenty of heartaches.

"God must be sick of me. I can't get anything right."

Her words reminded me of the verse that had stuck to my face when I fell asleep in the prayer closet. I released her and wiped her eyes and nose with the cuff of my hoodie. "I have something to give back to you."

I worked the tape loose from the index card inside my closet door. Larice's teeny tiny printing crowded the card. I kissed her forehead. "I took this from the prayer closet." I held the card out to her.

Larice waved me away. "Not now, Jenna."

The words were meant to help. If not now, when? "Do you remember the 'miserable person' verse?"

"Jenna," she pleaded.

"This is really good. You'll like it."

"I know the verse." She buried her face in her arms.

"Whoever wrote this struggled and failed to do what he wanted to do all the time, just like us."

"So now there is no condemnation for those who belong to Christ Jesus," she recited with oozing sarcasm.

"Exactly," I countered with Tigger-like enthusiasm. Seeing Larice dismiss the life preserver she'd offered me started my heart racing.

"So maybe I don't belong to Christ Jesus, whatever that means."

"We prayed together at camp."

"That was a long time ago."

"But you've been trying, really trying, just like this guy." I waved the card at her, probably not a kind thing to do. "Maybe belonging is more important than trying."

"I'm such a fraud."

Larice reeked genuineness, but now I was angry and desperate. "You blew it. I'll give you that. Maybe you would feel better if you talked to that lady you work with about this."

"I couldn't!"

"Then ask her what this guy means," I said, pressing the card into her hand. "Maybe you'll be given chances, just as he was."

She crumpled the card in her fist. "I could do that."

Larice washed her face in my bathroom and came out ready to face the executioner, who happened to be her daughter.

"Do you want me to come with you?"

"This is not the lesson I wanted to teach my daughter."

"Listen, I haven't been as supportive as I could be. Let's do the celibacy thing together, for real. No half measures. It can't be worse than what we've tried before."

Larice looked away, blinked away tears. "This probably isn't a good time for me to commit to anything."

"It's less than a year."

"Jenna..."

"Hey, we can do anything together. Don't forget Chemistry."

"We cheated."

"Then we'll do a lot of running. Movie nights. Road trips. High adventure."

"And your mom?"

"I'm getting real close to finding Brian. That changes everything."

Larice pulled me into an embrace. She whispered in my ear. "I can't do this alone."

"Me neither."

ACCORDING TO THE CLOCK, I had three more hours of sleep before I walked up the hill to where I'd left my car parked on Monterey, only a few doors down from Jerry's house. I refilled the mattress, feeling reasonably certain I would remain suspended over the concrete floor until the alarm went off. I stared at the ceiling. Without a door to close, the refrigerated cases filled the area with blue light.

I stalled all efforts at sleep to replay my conversation with Larice. In the realm of improbable likelihoods, I was the last person to be handing out Bible verses. Did church people know an ancient guy with a habitual sin problem wrote part of the Bible? They couldn't, could they?

Before I gave sleep one more try, I studied Mom's painting of me and Tim. The fluorescent lights of the refrigerator cases distorted the colors. Still, there we were clinging to one another as if expecting a giant squid attack. In the painting, I would never push away and run back to the bait shop. I wished life had imitated art. I closed the cigar-box painting and stowed it under the scrapbook in my closet.

I prayed: "Lord, I can't handle this pain one more minute. Please take all of it away."

Nothing happened. The glass that shredded my heart continued to slice away. The sinner in the Bible sounded like me, but he must have had God's home number.

25

By sunup I deeply regretted drinking an extra-large latte.

To pee meant leaving the car and my vantage point for watching Troll's movements. Also, I'd worked like a maniac to orchestrate this opportunity. Was emptying my bladder worth squandering a chance to see Jerry?

The decision—to pee or not to pee—became moot when a sneeze threatened.

I power walked up to the corner convenience store, the one where Brian and I had bought our afterschool snacks. I snaked my way back to the bathroom. The clerk, probably Indian—the kind from India, not the Great Plains—watched me from the moment I walked through the entrance until I closed the bathroom door, just as Dad had trained me to do with our customers. With the door locked, the paper cover in place, and relief realized, the thought of watching for shoplifters for the rest of my life brought tears to my eyes.

I gave myself a speech in the mirror over the sink: "You will talk to Jerry. You will find Brian. You will have a life. Tears don't help." I blew my nose before I left the bathroom to buy water and a newspaper.

The clerk tried to make small talk in English that rose and fell in all the wrong places. I caught every third word—drink, sometime, my place.

I walked from the store empty-handed.

By ten, my butt ached. I'd missed Troll, no doubt about it. Maybe a friend had picked her up to go wherever Troll and her friends had fun. I restructured my mission to wait for her return. This would accomplish absolutely nothing, which played into my average nicely.

The morning haze dissolved enough to allow the sun to drill through the windshield. I now regretted leaving the newspaper on the convenience store counter. And my throat ached for water. I chose the largest library book from the backseat stack and opened the pages against the glare. I had to peek around California wildflowers—a book Mom had requested—to watch Jerry's front door. While gaping over a two-page spread of lupines, the door opened.

Troll waddled toward a sun-faded sedan of indiscernible make and model and squeezed behind the wheel. The engine resisted starting. I stifled a whoop when it finally roared and coughed exhaust. She backed out, almost hitting a Lexus parked across the street, and rumbled her way down Monterey toward the shopping district. My guess, she was headed for Ralph's. I didn't have much time.

I knocked on the door a few times, calling through the screened window beside the door. "Jerry, it's Jenna! Can I come in?"

No answer, so I tried the front door. Locked. I walked along the garage toward the back of the house, winding around trashcans. As finicky as the city was about codes for this, that, and the other thing, they had dropped the ball on Troll's hazardous waste. Why hadn't the neighbors complained?

Maybe they knew about the gun.

My heart thundered as I checked the windows around the house and a door into the garage. Anyone else would have taken the fortress-like house as a sign to go home, but I returned to the window beside the front door—the only window left open.

I looked up and down the street for curious eyes. Only bees hummed and birds sang. Possible outcomes of crawling through the window ranged from being shot dead to cracking San Clemente's biggest unsolved mystery to being arrested for breaking and entering.

And so, I removed the screen.

The window tilted in its track, wedged solidly in place. I pounded at the aluminum frame with the palm of my hand. That smarted, but the window didn't move. I took another look up and down the street. Breaking the window would be noisy and tough to explain. I loved my brother dearly, but I sure hated the idea of being dead or serving time. The prospect of looking for shoplifters for the rest of my life, however, redoubled my efforts to open the window.

I wrapped my hand in the hem of my cover-up and walloped the frame of the window. The frame straightened ever so slightly. I hit it again and again, each time the window moved closer to square. I also had to pee again, as if I needed another reason to hurry.

I took one last swing and the window slid open. Unfortunately, all the odors of the stagnant space wanted out as badly as I want in. I braced myself against a swoon.

After one more look over my shoulder, I held my breath and climbed through the window. Once inside, I talked constantly, like a hiker in bear country. "Jerry, it's Jenna. I'm here to talk with you. Remember? I'm Brian's sister. We talked on the telephone a long time ago. Jerry? Are you awake?"

At Jerry's door, I stopped to watch him sleep and looked around the room for any evidence of a gun. Jerry was nothing but a gray cave of flesh and bone. Troll had been busy. She'd covered the wall opposite Jerry with postcards from every port of call, some I recognized, most I didn't, all I wouldn't have minded visiting.

I stood before the wall as if visiting a gallery. Someone Jerry cared about must have done the traveling. His wife, whom he never talked about? His son who lay on the couch most of the day? Someone else? A lover?

Eew.

Some of the postcards had served as coasters, not exactly treasured but in some way important to Jerry. Not all of the postcards rated the wall. A stack of postcards stood on Jerry's nightstand, where Troll had left them.

Jerry's fascination with the postcards made him a perplexing riddle. They didn't fit the Jerry I'd constructed through our telephone calls. People who traveled consumed life and its treasures, the wonders of the newly discovered. I doubted Jerry approved of a change in toilet paper, let alone a change in latitude or longitude. Jerry seemed to be a man stuck.

I knew the feeling well.

This was no time to satisfy curiosity about Jerry's state of mind about traveling or anything else. His breathing came in gooey gasps. I wouldn't touch him, so I shouted into his face. "Jerry! It's Jenna!"

His eyes popped open. "What—?"

"Hey, Jerry. It's Jenna, Brian's sister." I handed over his smudged glasses from the nightstand. "We don't have much time. I need to know about Brian."

"Fat...cow...here?"

Such a tenderhearted father. "She's gone. I don't know how long."

"Time?" he asked, his eyes wide opened now.

I looked around the room for a clock. Pill bottles stood like silent soldiers on his nightstand, along with a package of Depends, and a ceramic cat with one eye missing. No clock ticked away the minutes. "Before eleven, I'm pretty sure."

"Watches...*The View*."

Mom also religiously watched *The View*, at eleven.

With every shallow exhale, Jerry whispered. "Tomorrow...doctor...two. Come back."

"Is your daughter going to the doctor tomorrow?"

He nodded.

"Jerry, do you have a gun?"

He shook his head.

Good. Fabulous. "Will you tell me about Brian tomorrow?"

He closed his eyes and nodded again.

I considered asking him not to die before the next day. Instead, I said, "I like your postcards."

Before I left, I unlocked the garage's side door, which took climbing over piles of boxes and squeezing between more trashcans. I doubted Troll would go through the trouble to lock the door again.

At the front of the house, I waved at a couple of kids who rode by on their bikes, trying my hardest to look like I belonged. Finally, I re-jammed the window, replaced the screen, and walked down the street toward my car, all the while looking over my shoulder for Troll to return.

Back at the bait shop, I held my hand up to Dad. There would be no exchange of pleasantries or requests for help with the packed store until I showered off what clung to me from Jerry's house. Once I shampooed and let the hot water rinse the stink down the drain, I leaned my head against the tile and weighed the risk I'd taken against the possible benefit. If Jerry lived through the night, I would know what happened to Brian.

But could I live with what I discovered?

DAD MUST HAVE TOLD Mom I'd taken the whole day off. She peppered me with questions about who I'd been with and what we did. Over the years I'd developed skill at lying on the spot, so I made up a day I wished had really happened.

I told her Tim had taken me on a long drive along the coast to a botanical garden in L.A. County.

"A botanical garden? You know nothing of flowers."

I knew more than she realized. I'd once dated a guy who worked at a garden center. The more she interrupted my story with questions, the more creative my lying became. "Tim surprised me too. I didn't know he had an interest in gardens. I wasn't even sure how he knew about the place. The grounds lay at the end of an unmarked road. Not another soul walked the garden paths."

"Did he hold your hand?"

"He took my hand by a display of succulents." I squeezed my eyes to remember the plant names from the California wildflower book I'd hidden behind earlier that day at Jerry's. "There were miniature hollyhocks with wide-eyed magenta blooms, and a ceonothus called California lilac covered with blue spires—the color was amazing—and fried egg flowers. They looked exactly like sunny-side-up eggs, only they were daisies. We stopped at every numbered sign and read about the plants. That's why I was gone so long."

"Imagine flowers that look like fried eggs!" Mom purchased my lie with her whole heart. "Did you see poppies? Poppies are my favorite."

"You can't very well go to a California native garden without them. An entire hill glowed orange."

She lowered her voice, her eyes brightened to welcome me into a confidence. "So you like this man?"

I caught a whiff of Mom. She smelled of soured sweat with a hint of urine. "You need a shower before dinner."

"Tell me more."

I then committed my most flagrant transgression of the day, a laudable accomplishment on a day when I'd broken into a house and lied to my mother. "I could take you to the garden. We could find it. You have to take your paints." I said this, knowing she would never agree to such an excursion, but I wanted to get her off the subject of Tim. What I'd considered harmless redirection, she'd recklessly misinterpreted.

"You've forgotten about Brian!" Her face flushed with anger. "One man walking through poppies has made you abandon ship. Fried-egg flowers, indeed!" Her rant of accusations went on and on. I was an unfit sister, a gold digger, an ungrateful daughter, and disloyal to the family.

Given how I'd spent my day, I came close to slapping her. I needed out. "Mom, I'm going to check on Larice and Taylor."

She rose from the recliner and shuffled toward the bedroom. "Sure, take your sorry self up to your slut of a friend."

"Mom!"

She turned back to me, chin lifted. "You might remind her how thin the walls are in this place."

"I will not. But I will only return when I hear the shower running."

She wagged a finger at me. "This Tim has made you into a disrespectful child. I doubt you went to a garden. You holed up in some motel all day. You're no better than your friend."

Her irrational ranting was new, but I didn't have the energy or the patience to tell Mom the truth. I didn't want to raise her hopes to a height I couldn't support, either. I doubted she would listen anyway. Instead, I told her through clenched teeth, "I'm very sorry you believe that about me."

I PASSED TAYLOR COMING down the stairs. "Your mom is upset," she said.

The walls were definitely thin. "She's getting worse, crazier."

Taylor stopped and turned back. "That's harsh."

I almost suggested Taylor walk a mile in my shoes, but I wouldn't wish that on anyone. Besides, I'm the cool friend. I continued up the stairs.

I found Larice on her balcony with her ankles crossed on the top rail, looking more like the Larice I knew and loved. Her eyes reflected the metallic blue of the sea. Most of the redness and swelling around her eyes had vanished. As much as I came to check on her, I needed her to be herself, which wasn't fair. But the day had been very long and very weird.

The 5:02 had come and gone, so the street scene had quieted to dinner-goers and a few kids who clung to the summer light like a lifeline. Larice told me to pour myself a glass of wine and join her. The bottle was empty, so I poured a glass of water.

I listened for the shower downstairs. Instead of showering, Mom probably smoldered her indignation toward me and felt sorry for herself. The storm of her rage would pass with time. It always had.

I sat beside Larice and put my feet up. I couldn't talk about my day, except that I'd seen Jerry. Sadly, there wasn't much to tell. I figured Larice had plenty to talk about, and I was right.

She looked at me and back to the expansive view before us. She spoke in a slur as flat as the sea. "Taylor's been seeing a guy. When she told me she was going to Jessica's, she was meeting him. I don't even know the guy or where she met him. She won't tell me. After the other night—she heard everything, by the way—she feels justified in doing whatever she feels like doing. God, I've been so stupid."

If children needed a role model, I was underqualified. No kids for me. But deciding that didn't absolve me of my responsibility for Taylor. I'd held her when she was still slick with blood and goo after her birth, and I wiped her face before handing her to Larice. When I looked at her, my heart swelled for the future. She was fresh, smart, a daughter any mother would be proud to claim.

"Is she going to meet him now?" I asked.

Larice shrugged. "I don't know. I don't know where my very sweet, very naïve, very intelligent, very hardheaded, self-righteous brat is going. I would give anything for a night of walking the floor with a colicky baby just now."

I didn't know about the colicky baby part. But I knew a girl could be surly, sleep around, and fail home economics. I had. I drove my parents mad with anxiety, all while they grieved the disappearance of their son. Larice did not need to hear about that kind of truth at the moment.

"Anyway," she continued, "I don't know where she's going. I used to *think* I knew where she was going." She flailed her arms. "Taylor could be heading for heaven knows what, and I'm completely clueless."

Clueless didn't describe Larice. Together, we knew all the best places to park. Sure, the town had grown, but that only meant kids had to drive farther. When I explained this to Larice, she said, "They could be at a friend's."

"Let's drive around. At least we'd be doing something."

Larice slipped deeper into her chair. "I've failed my daughter. This is what comes of collapsing under pressure. Your kid jumps under the train right after you."

We could find Taylor. Most likely, she'd headed for the hills, literally. If nothing else, Larice needed to move. Despair rooted itself in inaction.

"Let's go," I said, pulling on her arm.

No amount of finagling would pry Larice out of the chair. I suspected she had already finished more than one bottle of wine. There was nothing quite as inviting as oblivion when disappointment hit. After she promised not to jump off the balcony, I left her where she sat and headed downstairs to make Mom dinner and to dose her with Xanax.

She surprised me by being in the shower. I dug through the freezer to find one of her favorite frozen entrees. I set up a TV tray in front of her chair and left a note saying I would be back soon. I didn't expect her to be happy when I returned. Her approval mattered less than finding Taylor.

I DON'T DO WELL more than three miles from the coast.

The farther I drove inland, the more I sweated. I turned on the headlights as I drove past the high school and shopping centers. My Daewoo struggled up the hill past housing developments to the drought-scarred hills, where the parking spaces I remembered lay in niches of brush.

Without knowing the make or model of the car Taylor rode in, I doubted I would find her and the scumbag. But the word impossible didn't mean the same thing to me anymore. My car was a closet on wheels. That worked, right? So I asked God to help me find her.

God had good reasons to help, which I dutifully listed for him: "First, Taylor—I'm pretty sure—is a virgin. You like virgins. Think of Mary and Mother Theresa. Second, finding Taylor will prove to anyone interested I'm a changed woman, if you don't count the break-in, which is a new thing and shouldn't count against me. And third, leading me to Taylor is the merciful thing to do. And isn't mercy your middle name? Neither one of us wants Taylor ending up like me, spitting out regret like broken teeth. Amen."

I turned onto a dirt road off Christianitos Road, a track leading to a scrawny chaparral growth of sage and manzanita. I pulled up behind an SUV of some kind to fill the interior with light. I beeped the horn. Two heads popped up in the backseat. My headlights glinted off Taylor's coppery hair before she slumped into the corner of the seat.

Now what?

I honked again. "Taylor!"

The boy turned to squint into my headlights. I laid on the horn. He jumped and hit his head on the roof of the car. This was getting fun.

"Taylor! Let's go home!"

The back door opened on the boy's side. He looked more manlike than I remembered high-school boys being, especially in the confidence department. He fastened his belt as he sauntered toward me. I hadn't counted on such cockiness. I got out, so he could see I wasn't some crazed middle-aged mother. I was young and hip. We could talk this out.

"Taylor needs to go home with me."

"You aren't her mother." Boy, he was a mouthy hotshot. Didn't she know better?

"No, but I care about her future, her dreams."

Taylor yelled out the window. "Those are my mother's dreams, not mine."

These kids had been watching television long enough to believe adults were stupid, and that was exactly how the boy looked at me, but the longer I looked back at him, the less boy-like he seemed. His jawline was too defined for a high-school kid.

"How old are you?"

He hesitated. "Eighteen. What's that to you?"

"Eighteen? You look older. I placed you at twenty, which would make you almost four years older than Taylor."

He lowered his voice, gestured toward the car. "How old is she?"

"She'll be seventeen in December. She's young for her class. She skipped a grade."

"Shit." He hurried back to his car, where he opened Taylor's door. She stumbled out. "You gotta get outta here." He opened his palms to me. "She said she went to UCI."

Taylor walked toward the Daewoo like she'd been sentenced to the electric chair, but I refused to lecture her. I wanted her to think about how close she'd come to starting a journey she would surely regret. As we drove down from the hills, the temperature slid back to the bearable range.

When I slowed for a light at El Camino Real, she said, "Drop me off here. I'm going to a friend's."

"Your mom is waiting for you."

"She's a hypocrite! She says one thing and does another."

"You're right. She is a hypocrite, but she loves you, and she's learned a lot from her past. She made a huge mistake, and no one knows that better than her." And then I thought that maybe I hadn't saved the day, that I'd arrived after the fact. "Uh, Taylor, did you use protection?"

"I'm not discussing this with you."

"There are, like, a million diseases out there."

"I do not have a disease, okay? You didn't give me a chance."

"Taylor, you've made me very happy." The car died but revved to life on the first try.

"That's rich coming from you."

"You can't tell me anything about myself I don't already know. I'm stuck in the vortex of doom, and I'm not looking for company." I parked a block away from the apartment. Taylor pulled up on the handle, but I put my hand on her arm. "Stay for a minute."

Taylor crossed her arms and stared out the windshield. People lugging beach bags, towels, and chairs slogged by. "When you get inside, your mother is going to be angry, and she'll say some angry woman stuff. Keep in mind she's mostly angry with herself. She'll get past this."

"So why didn't she ride with the posse?"

I'd never ratted out Larice before, but this situation required honesty and humility. I'm not sure how I knew that. "She's been too busy being a hypocrite."

Taylor turned toward me. "She's drinking, isn't she?"

I was out of my depth. Taylor needed someone she respected to explain that we all experience the chipping and splintering of our parents' veneer. They're not super-human, and we have to love or hate them as flawed people. Maybe if I texted her later.

"Are you going to tell her where you found me?" she said.

This question assured me Taylor the Wonderful still resided in her skin. As for telling Larice about Mr. Older-than-dirt, I always told Larice everything. In fact, I would tell her every stunning detail of Taylor's near miss. "I think you should. I'll ask her what you said tomorrow. I'll give you that chance."

"Can I go now?"

"I'm not sorry for what I did, Taylor."

She slammed the car door and walked ten paces ahead of me back to the apartment, up the stairs, and through the front door. I wished someone had delivered me to hyperventilating parents long ago. Maybe things would have turned out much differently.

I opened the apartment door to talk my own flawed parent into eating a bowl of ice cream with me.

26

Life in the bait shop droned.

The usual fishermen came for coffee and bait, but besides the arrival of Ashley at ten, the melody of my day had lost its underlying rhythm without the regulars coming in and going out of the telephony.

My heart chimed noon as regularly as Big Ben. Although I fought the impulse, my eyes rose to where Tim had sat, talking to his sister on the Snoopy telephone. Snoopy's grin became more of a smirk with each passing day. If he weren't careful, he would find himself at the bottom of the ocean with the model 354.

And yet, the meeting with Jerry loomed. I set Brian's alarm clock to alert me to prepare for our meeting, which meant washing my hands and putting on a clean hoodie. I left the bait shop under Ashley's watchful eye and drove to Jerry's place. I found a parking space within sight of his house—a minor miracle—with little time to spare.

I watched Troll drive her car down the street before I entered Jerry's house through the garage door I'd left unlocked. I chattered away, as I'd done the day before. I wasn't convinced there wasn't a gun in the house. Troll had been so adamant.

Jerry sat propped up by pillows. When he saw me, he sucked in a breath and exhaled, "Not sure…" another breath, "you'd come."

"You're surprised to see me? Jerry, of all people you know how desperate I am to learn anything about Brian."

"Hold…horses."

"I've been holding my horses for seventeen years. I came

for answers. You owe me answers."

"Could...leave."

A heart of stone beat underneath his fading form. "You know I won't," I said, moving toward the window. The afternoon sun baked the room to ripen the stew of odors trapped inside. I tugged hard to move the window along a track full of dust and dead flies. The room sighed with the rush of fresh air.

When I looked back to Jerry, his eyes were closed. "Jerry!"

He sucked in a breath. Waited. Sucked in another. "Need...trade."

"From me? For news about Brian? You better be kidding."

"Go...La Jolla."

"Why La Jolla? We have a perfectly good beach down the hill. I'll take you there," I said with no idea how transporting Jerry even that short distance could happen.

"No...deal."

I stepped closer. Jerry wasn't the same man I'd seen the day before. His hair flipped and spiked. The sheet had slipped down to reveal his shirtless chest. His supraclavicular fossa and the jugular notch sank into cavernous hollows. And his diaper needed changing. "Traveling doesn't seem like a good idea, Jerry."

"Not...far."

He'd made me wait all these years, and now the man wanted a joy ride. What a ridiculous and maddening demand. And yet, what could I do? From the outline he made under the sheet, I was pretty sure I could carry him, but the oxygen machine was as big as a filing cabinet. I scanned the room for a portable oxygen tank, something small enough to fit in the Daewoo. "Do you have a smaller tank?"

"Con...denser...yes."

"And your daughter? She hates me. There's no way she'll let me take you anywhere."

"My...problem."

The enormity of what he asked pressed me into a corner I didn't appreciate. "I'll try. But after La Jolla, no more tricks and trades. No more delays. You will talk. Are we clear about that?"

His gaze moved to the wall plastered with postcards and back to me. "Promise."

Even if I emptied the Daewoo down to the floor mats, Jerry with his condenser and wheelchair would be an impossible fit. Plus, I needed someone to help transfer him from the car to the wheelchair and keep track of the condenser. I refused to think about diapers.

"I'll need to take someone with us," I said, hoping to discourage him. "I can't maneuver you around by myself."

"Big...boyfriend?"

No such luck. Eric would have been perfect, if muscle alone qualified a man to care. Dad was out. I didn't want to raise his expectations, and Mom, well, how many ways can you spell impossible? And Larice weighed less than me. Now I was depressed. My life had gotten too small to know helpful people, and wasn't life one odd assignment after another?

"I have someone in mind," I said, "but we'll have to wait until the weekend. He works weekdays." Not to mention I would have to convince Tim to go somewhere with me and a smelly old man, not an easy task after I'd been so unabashedly me. But I had no other choice. At this point, I would sign over the deed to the bait shop to find out something, *anything*, about Brian.

Jerry's irises were dark shadows under his papery eyelids. What could possibly be calling him to La Jolla? Wading in the surf was out. Could he stay awake long enough to see the beach? What if he died on the way?

Perhaps the postcard wall held a clue. Palm trees aplenty filled the scenes, bending over every shade of tropical sand and every hue of aquamarine lagoon, nothing looking like La Jolla's rocky shores and sheltered coves.

I nudged his shoulder until his eyes opened. "I'll figure out a way for us to get to La Jolla. We'll go on Saturday. You make sure your daughter will open the door for me, and if there's a gun in this house, I want it gone. I'm not walking into an ambush."

"No…gun."

"You're sure? Because your daughter—"

"Sure."

His eyes slid closed.

Jerry could have overpowered my brother seventeen years ago. Brian hadn't a muscle to his name at fifteen. But brawn wouldn't have been necessary to draw him into Jerry's house. Promises of beer and cigarettes would've done the trick. Brian loved his beer. And then what? A Mickey in Brian's drink? Did Jerry have his way with Brian and Brian struggled? Did Jerry put his hands to Brian's throat to quiet him, but his strength and fear pressed the life from him? How ironic that Jerry now fought for every breath and how easy it would be to exact revenge.

"Jerry!"

His eyes popped open.

"I'm losing my patience for games. I consider your request especially cruel. I'm only doing this for information. You must give me your promise I won't be disappointed."

He nodded and I left his house through the front door, leaving it slightly ajar. I wanted Troll to feel as vulnerable as I did.

The moment the engine of the Daewoo rattled to life, I regretted agreeing to Jerry's conditions. His jaunt meant I would have to talk to Tim to ask a huge favor—all varieties of awkward in one encounter. And my parents couldn't know. That meant careful timing. It took about an hour to drive down the coast to La Jolla, two hours with the return trip, plus loading Jerry and his gear in and out of the car, twice. Add however long Jerry needed to be in La Jolla. I could leave the bait shop when Ashley arrived and be back by three when Dad might drop by. Such a schedule cut things close.

What to do about Mom?

I would have to trust her to dose herself. Anything else? There was the librarian to sweet talk into a double stack of DVDs for Mom to watch in my absence. I didn't want her speculating on my whereabouts. Six seasons of *Heartland* would stupefy her as well as any sedative.

If everything fell into place—and we're talking momentously miraculous here—I would know everything Jerry knew about Brian in just a few short days.

God, please, let that be enough to find him.

27

The receptionist wore a sleek black dress with white trim, which accentuated her impossibly tiny waist. She looked more New York than beach town. I stood before her in my latest experiment, a gored skirt of vintage fabrics with a tulle flounce. By comparison, I looked like the tooth fairy. If only I could sprinkle myself with fairy dust to disappear.

"Do you have an appointment?" The receptionist sounded dubious.

I didn't have an appointment, but I'd cleaned out the bait freezer in anticipation of the next day's delivery and told Ashley I would be back in an hour. Despite scrubbing my arms up to my elbows, I smelled of mackerel. I stepped back from her desk. She took my name and suggested I make myself comfortable.

Tim made me wait a long time in the reception area of Mellecker Industries, the medical supply company where he worked. From the magazines on the glass table, the medical community couldn't get enough of prodding and poking the vascular system of perfectly healthy-looking people.

I leaned back in the leather chair, and my skirt popped up. I tucked its excesses under my thighs and looked around the room, which oozed cliché office swank in leather and chrome and glass. I pretended to read a professional journal article, "Greater Endothelial Apoptosis and Oxidative Stress in Patients with Peripheral Artery Disease." Time slowed. The air thickened. I fought the urge to flee behind a group of well-dressed employees leaving for a late lunch.

With a buzz, the door opened and Tim finally emerged

from the bowels of the building. He wore an orange Dreamsicle shirt. He looked positively delicious. But he wasn't smiling, so I stood, trying to be as businesslike as any professional tooth fairy would.

"We should go outside," he said, leading the way out the tinted doors and toward a lawn area surrounded by a low privet hedge. The sun pressed through my hoodie and sweat collected at my hairline.

He pivoted in the middle of the grass. "I'm surprised to see you."

I wiped at my lip. "Tim..."

He looked at his watch. "I have another meeting in five minutes. It's audit time. Everyone's a little uptight."

"Oh. Well then. I should get to the point."

Tim looked up, shielding his eyes from the sun. "Let's get to some shade. I haven't been outside since yesterday. It's hot."

We walked toward the east side of the building. I apologized to his back for interrupting his day. He leaned against the brick and crossed his arms. "Well?"

He wasn't even trying to make this easy. Good. I didn't deserve his kindness. "I shouldn't have come."

Out of habit or—and this thought nearly broke my heart—because he was genuinely good, he asked about my mother. "Is she all right?"

Why not be honest? I had nothing to lose. "No, she's getting worse, I think. She hasn't painted in weeks and she's stopped getting dressed, and she rarely eats. I don't know what else to do."

"How can I help?"

We weren't friends anymore. I hadn't seen him in ages. What I'd said to him haunted me in every quiet moment and squeezed my heart. The bottom line: Tim and I weren't anything definable. I'd put an end to all possibilities. I'd been the jerk and he, as always, was the noble one, even when he clearly didn't want to be, which, for some reason, made me angry. "Don't be nice to me, Tim."

He looked at his shoes, rounded up an errant pebble and toed it back into the shrub bed. "What do you want?"

"I've seen Jerry."

He looked up, surprised. "So you know something about your brother. That's great."

I told him Jerry's life hung by a very thin thread and about his troll of a daughter. And then I told him about Jerry's demand to go to La Jolla.

"He's extorting you."

"I can't manage Jerry on my own."

"You're going to take him?"

"What choice do I have? He's old, an obstinate old fart, but he's my only hope of finding my brother."

Tim stuffed his hands into his pockets. "I'm feeling used."

A decent person would have thanked Tim for his time and walked away. "I'll be out of your life after this, I promise."

"I'm not sure I want that. I'm confused."

"Oh, Tim..."

"When do you want to go?"

"Really?"

"I would still be talking to my sister on a Snoopy telephone if not for you."

"You don't owe—"

"When?"

If Jerry didn't die between now and then—hang on, Jerry!—and Troll cooperated, I would be one step closer to finding Brian. I couldn't speculate whether the idea of finding Brian or spending several hours with Tim made me happier. Before I had a chance to suggest we take Tim's car, he offered to pick me up.

"There will be a wheelchair."

"The back seats fold down."

A ping sounded from Tim's pocket. He pulled out a smart phone and turned the screen toward me: "Meeting with Kent Frieling."

I pushed back the cuff of my hoodie to read the watch I never wore. "I have a meeting too," I said. "See you Saturday. Thanks."

The heat from the parking lot bled through my flip-flops. My hands shook as I unlocked my car. I wanted to lay my head on the steering wheel for a good cry, but I wanted to get some air moving through the car even more. That meant driving.

A vast emotional chasm separated me from Tim. It was a physical thing, an ocean more expansive than the Pacific. I would drown in those waters, if I dared to jump in.

I pulled the Daewoo over three times on the way back to the bait shop to pound the steering wheel and scream obscenities at myself for showing my worst, most unforgiveable side to Tim one time too many.

I PUSHED PAST LARICE when she opened her apartment door.

"What's up?" she said. Her words slurred.

I looked over my shoulder at her from the prayer closet. She held a near-empty glass of wine. Her hair hung limp and stringy. She still wore her scrubs. "Tough day?" I asked, but to be truthful, I wasn't interested in her answer.

If Larice had had a tough day, mine had been hideous. Seeing Tim, feeling his indifference and his compassion simultaneously left me a knotted mess. I'd waited until the last customer had collected his snack for the train trip home. The peace of the prayer closet beckoned me.

I slid back the door. Plastic tubs filled with shoes, sweaters, and Christmas wrap covered the floor. The cushion no longer sat on the floor. The Bible verses had been removed.

"I needed the space," Larice said, walking past me to the bistro table. She filled her wine glass and held it up to me. "Can

I pour a glass for you? You look awful."

She looked beyond awful. Mascara had collected in the folds around her eyes. Something green lodged in her tooth. "What's happened?"

She took a long draw of the wine and shrugged. "The usual."

I looked around for evidence of Taylor. "Where's Taylor?"

Larice shrugged again.

I closed the gap between us in three steps, took her glass, and threw the wine in her face. "Wake up! You are the mother. Act like one."

She blinked and looked down at her white scrubs, now stained a bland rose. Her face puckered. "I'm a horrible mother."

I took her by the shoulders. "One day does not a horrible mother make. Try again. Do not give up. Never, ever give up." Now I was crying. I pointed at my chest. "This is what you get when a mother gives up, Larice." I turned for the door. "I'll call the carpet cleaner in the morning."

I leaned against her door until her sobs and my tears abated. As much as I wanted to go back inside to her and remind her that we were in this together, I couldn't gather the strength to do so.

I FOUND MOM, YET again, asleep in her chair with the TV blaring promises of not one but two revolutionary mops to the first five hundred callers. I opened the sliding glass door to let in the breeze. With the ocean only a hundred yards away, she didn't need to live in stagnant air.

I stood over her, studying her breathing, looking for a sign she had drifted closer to shore. The breeze played with her hair and lifted her robe to reveal the swell of her knees and the sharpness of her shin under nearly transparent skin. My mother was fading before my eyes. I had no time to coax her to eat.

Ashley would want to go home soon, and I had one more thing to do.

I opened Mom's closet. The scent of Estée Lauder hung softly on her clothes. It took effort to push between the animal print blouses and the pastel golf shirts. At the back of the closet, I rested my head against the wall.

"I've got to talk to you, whether you're here or not, whether this is a prayer closet or not. First, don't let Jerry die before Saturday. Second, let Brian be okay. Third, if Tim could stop hating me, that would be great. Thanks, I guess, for listening. Oh, and help Mom. She needs to come home too. And Larice. Help her too." I stepped from the closet, straightened Mom's clothes, and ran my fingers across my forehead. The wall had embossed its texture into my forehead, which somehow reminded me to add an amen to my prayer.

I was such a poser.

28

Tim folded the seats down to fit Jerry's wheelchair into his car.

That left the driver's seat for Tim, the passenger seat for Jerry, and the cargo area for the wheelchair and me. I lay behind Tim's seat with an arm rest pressed into my back and the handle of Jerry's wheelchair threatening my left eye.

This was not the picture I'd carried in my mind since Tim had agreed to drive Jerry and me to La Jolla. Scrambled expectations should have been routine to me by now. Had I become optimistic? Cozied up to a wheelchair, while speeding toward La Jolla on the 5, didn't leave much room for positive thinking. We'd been en route for less than ten minutes and my left gluteus maximus cramped angrily.

Getting Jerry into the car had been tricky. He was a marionette with severed strings, awkward and ungainly. Beyond Tim's grunting of instructions for transferring him safely, we hadn't really talked.

Grunting would have been a huge improvement over the rumble of the freeway and the frequent *ka-thump* of the Botts' dots whenever Tim changed lanes. Could someone turn on the radio? Tim seemed in a hurry to fulfill his commitment. So I didn't ask for any more favors.

"Jenna?" Tim said, a pound of panic in his voice.

I rose to my elbow. "Is there a problem?"

"Jerry is slumped forward. I can't tell if he's breathing."

I pushed up to my knees and hit my head on the dome light. Poking my head between the seats, I inched as close to Jerry as the wheelchair would allow. He looked dead. And if he was? The temptation to kill him a little more would be tough to resist. He'd dragged out his big revelation about Brian's whereabouts far too long. "What do you want me to do?"

"Check his pulse."

Perfect. That meant touching Jerry. I'd done plenty of touching already that morning in the struggle to get him out of the bed, into the wheelchair, and inside the car—all without the help of Troll. His skin had been cool to the touch and downright slippery over his bones. I felt for his carotid. His pulse raced under my fingers.

"His heart rate is high."

"Can you sit him up?"

I'd read all about emphysema on the internet. Jerry was a classic soon-to-be expired case. "His heart is working harder to keep his blood oxygenated."

"Still, if he were sitting up..." Tim and I exchanged glances in the mirror. His eyes pleaded with me.

We sped south along the part of the 5 that drew a line between Camp Pendleton and the ocean. The Marine Corps did not appreciate cars stopping on the freeway for any reason, not even to open an old man's airway, so I traded places with the wheelchair, a bit of gymnastics only the car behind us could appreciate, given I flashed my heiny in their direction. I worked my arm under Jerry's and across his chest. I pressed him into the seat. His head dangled over my arms.

"Can you get his head back?"

That did it. I was driving the return leg of this circus. Jerry's head could bobble all it wanted with me at the wheel. I spoke through my teeth. "Sure, if I had one more arm."

Tim reached over and pushed Jerry's head into the headrest.

My shoulders burned from the effort of holding Jerry in place. "I can't stay this way much longer." Beyond duct taping Jerry's head to the head rest, I didn't see a solution. "We have to let him go."

"Slowly."

"You go first."

Tim lowered Jerry's head back to his chest, and I pulled my hands away.

Jerry fell forward and popped back up. "What!"

Tim explained to Jerry our heroic measures to open his airway.

"How...I sit...none of...your...business." And Jerry commenced to cough violently. We waited him out, me praying he would catch his breath soon.

With the handicapped parking placard we'd snitched from Troll's car, we found a parking space close to La Jolla Cove, the beach Jerry had insisted on visiting.

I pressed for a plan before we opened the passenger door to get Jerry out. No more grunts or nods of the head by Tim for me to interpret. Words, gentlemen, we needed to use our words. And so we did. And Jerry landed in his wheelchair like a bird lighting on a branch. I upped his oxygen and tied him upright with a piece of cloth I ripped from the hem of my skirt.

I looked for a ramp but only found thousands of stairs—give or take a hundred—going down to the beach. "So, Jerry, we can't get you down to the beach."

He raised a hand. I think he said okay.

"Is this a good spot?"

Jerry sucked in a breath. "Over there."

I followed his gaze. "On the point?"

He nodded and Tim pushed him on the arc of sidewalk that outlined the cove to the point, the best possible view of the beach and rocks and people. Behind us, Scripps Park spread out like green icing ringed by a crown of palm trees—some with Lorax-ish tops that swayed atop pencil-thin trunks. In front of us, sandstone formed a cove around a diminutive sandy beach. The water's color intensified from well-worn jeans to gray-blue to dark indigo as the water deepened.

With no waves to speak of, divers walked in and out of the water weighted down by their tanks, and swimmers floated like planks over languid swells. The water beckoned me into its coolness.

Perhaps another time.

Probably never.

Once we had Jerry parked to take in the view, the three of us watched the mini dramas unfolding below us. No one said a word, although I saw plenty warranting comment. Lifeguards flirted with one another while their young charges swam farther out than they should. A man left an empty chip bag in the sand when he folded up his towel and left. A fair-skinned girl, who had lived in a cave all of her life, had moved long past pink to fire. Day two of her vacation would be spent in a motel bathtub of cool water.

I waited for Jerry to say he wanted to move or needed a postcard. Tim stood with his arms crossed over his chest. Did he worry about the sunburned girl? Was it the chip bag cartwheeling along the sand? Were his eyes seeing? Did his thoughts tumble and churn? Was he speculating on the cost of getting involved with me in the first place? Who could blame him for taking a self-protective stance? He deserved a medal for being there at all.

It killed me to be that close to the water and not jump in. This was a rare treat for me. There were no espressos to brew, no sunscreen to recommend, and no telephones to dust. Only me—forever and always in my bathing suit—and the sparkling sea to beckon me. Even the screech of gulls sounded musical in this place. The scent of sunscreen mixed with salt and sun. I was almost home but far enough away that a dip in the calm waters would be an adventure. I looked to Jerry to see if he might tolerate my absence for a few minutes, maybe fifteen.

I wasn't prepared for what I saw. Jerry's shoulders heaved

and streams of tears flowed through the deep canyons on his face. I dropped to my knees beside him. "Jerry, are you in pain?" Troll had sent along a dose of morphine, just in case.

He shook his head and shooed me away. I stood, looked to Tim for direction.

"Maybe we should let him be."

People slowed to watch us, and I feared Jerry would start coughing again. I followed his gaze, this time to the beach below us. What on earth could have happened here to reduce an obstinate, foul-mouthed, and insalubrious (new word: unclean and unhealthy) man to sobbing goo? Had he lost his wedding ring here? Perhaps a friend had betrayed him. Had he met a mermaid face to face and forgotten to get her phone number? None of those things had happened to Jerry. I knew the cadence of his cry, like a mother will know a hunger cry from an I-need-my-diapers-changed cry. He'd hugely disappointed himself.

Just to be sure, I bent to speak in his ear. "Does this have anything to do with Brian?"

He shook his head sharply and continued crying.

I squatted next to him. "Then you won't cry alone." It didn't take long to compile a list of my own bad choices and the disappointments that followed. Soon I joined Jerry. I put my forehead on his bony shoulder and wept.

Tim lowered himself close behind me, his chest to my back, like two bowls in the drainer. He combed my hair from my face with his fingers. And then his arm held my waist and our heads touched, which only made me cry harder.

Jerry fell asleep before he stopped crying. I leaned back into Tim to whisper we could go. He brushed my cheek with his lips and stood, extending a hand to help me up.

The day did not go according to any of my modest imaginings. For once, my expectations had fallen far short of reality. An old man went to the sea for reasons he could not, or would not, share. But something—a memory, a sight, a sense of something bigger, which the ocean certainly is—pried open his heart and a dam crumbled before our eyes.

As for me, I'd gone to the tiny cove thinking Jerry would tell me something about Brian's whereabouts. More distantly, barely a hope, I'd seen the trip as a chance to melt the freeze between Tim and me. That happened, I think. A little. I don't know how.

Something else happened inside me that had nothing to do with Tim. Something loosed, more like Jerry's dam than I would like to admit. I think I felt relief, because it felt like last-year's jeans snapping easily after a summer of ice cream.

I still knew nothing of Brian. And wouldn't that day. Jerry slept the whole way back to San Clemente, and Troll dosed him with morphine the moment we tucked him into bed. I wouldn't leave without a promise from Troll that I could see him the next day.

Tomorrow.

Tomorrow I would know about Brian.

29

Larice sat across the table at Fisherman's Restaurant. She flicked pieces of napkin at me she'd torn, crushed into tiny balls, and soaked with cola.

"So, you're still angry?" I said, making shields of my hands.

"You threw wine in my face."

"Are you going to forgive me?"

"I'm thinking about it." She launched another ball, which I batted away.

"Have the lobster, on me." Lobster was her favorite. I offered it wanting to remind her that she truly loved irascible ol' me.

This could not be a day for animosity. The sky yawned magnificently blue. The haze had lifted so completely we could see Catalina sharply outlined against the sky. Not one gull had strutted by to eye our chips. Magic laced the air, Larice. Come on.

"You're paying, right?"

She'd had lots of experience forgiving me. I made out with her boyfriend at a football game and arrived at one of her weddings late, hung over, and in the wrong ugly bridesmaid dress. I also missed Taylor's birthday party right after one of her divorces became final. I'd had a good excuse—Mom had gotten a telephone call from someone pretending to be Brian and nearly popped her cork.

We didn't talk for months, not until she needed a place to live and came looking for a roommate. So warmed had I been by her need for me that I kicked a gaggle of surfers out of the third-story apartment and let Larice and Taylor move in. I couldn't bear to lose her to some bland inland locale, where I might never see her again.

"How's Taylor?" This question would surely open Larice's heart to me.

"I know what you're trying to do. Not yet. We're not ready for pleasant conversation." She flipped her perfect blonde hair over her shoulder and took a long, slow pull on the straw of her cola. She sat back in her chair, pushed her sunglasses onto her head, and levelled her gaze at me. "You must suffer until we reach the bottom of the chips."

Larice dumped the chips onto the table and held up the empty basket. "There are 65,000 people in this town, Jenna, and only one person cared enough to confront my drinking and sucky parenting." She leaned across the table to grab my hand. "I forgive you, Jenna. In fact, I invite you to throw wine in my face any time you see me sliding toward the abyss."

Behind my sunglasses, tears pooled. I let go of her hand to pile the chips back into the basket. "If you won't talk about Taylor, how are you?"

"I feel stupid. Ungrateful. Childish. Have I learned anything at all?" She cocked her head. "Did I mention stupid? You can see why I need you."

Being needed was better than being forgiven. "I won't disappoint you."

I signed the charge receipt minutes before eleven. Larice had already left to pick up Taylor for church. I had an hour to check on Mom and Ashley, brush my teeth, and start the climb up the hill. I planned on getting to Jerry's early.

Today was the day, finally. Brian. News. Truth. Exultation or crushing disappointment. I left the waitress a larger than usual tip. I needed all the karma I could get.

MOM SAT ON THE top step of the stairs, just outside her apartment. She wore a seersucker capris outfit with embroidered butterflies flitting about the lapels. She carried a paper umbrella, the kind from Japan we used to sell in the bait shop.

"Did I forget a doctor's appointment?" I didn't have time for such a protracted event.

"It's Sunday," she said sharply. She picked at the frayed carpet on the stair where she perched like a swimmer waiting for the starting gun. "I was thinking, maybe, seeing as it's been awhile, that we could go out, during the day, for a walk. You know," and she pointed toward the street, "there."

"Out?" Mom needed a week to gather courage to visit the doctor, her one and only somewhat voluntary outing—besides her tryst of sorts with Kevin in the telephony, which didn't seem to count.

"It's a lovely day." She meant to sound chirpy, but her voice was stretched to the breaking point.

"It is." I told her about Catalina.

"That sweet girl in the bait shop said she was covering for you until one-thirty or two. That should give us plenty of time, don't you think?"

"You talked to Ashley?" This was huge—and untimely.

"You don't have to sound so surprised."

No, perhaps not, but I was extremely disappointed Mom had chosen this very day to muster her courage. "Mom, I have an appointment at noon. It's important." Please gather yourself up and march yourself back into the apartment.

She rose. "Then we better get going."

This wouldn't last long. I could still get up the hill to Jerry's on time, no problem. I put my hand out to her.

"I'm not that old." She took the first three steps like the mother I remembered from nearly two decades earlier. And then she stopped. "Is it windy? Perhaps I should take the other umbrella?"

"No wind. Well, there's a little breeze. The usual." We

didn't have many days without a breeze. The curtains twisted and writhed constantly. My stomach twisted too. Had she forgotten the breeze? What else?

She took another step. "Do I need a hat? They say such horrible things about skin cancer on the news."

"The umbrella is better. You'll be fine." We would step over the line of no return faster if I played along. "I could go get your hat, if you like."

She studied the umbrella in her hands. "This will work." She reached for the next step with her foot but quickly withdrew. "I've been watching from the balcony. There's a group of young people milling about the pedestrian underpass. They should move on, don't you think?"

"I didn't see them on my way home."

"Would you mind?" Which meant, would you look to see if the young people still stood where they had every right to be?

"I'll take a picture with my phone."

"What a great idea. Thank you, honey."

Four steps down, ten to go. At this rate, I would arrive at Jerry's in time for a midnight snack with Troll. The prospect soured my stomach, but I hopped down the stairs and took a video of the sidewalk from the Beachcomber Inn to the parking lot. If anyone or anything objectionable moved out there, we could cut this expedition short. But the crowd of young people had moved on. Drat.

I replayed the movie to Mom, shielding my cell from the sun's glare. "How do we know someone hasn't come since you climbed back up the stairs?"

"If you're not ready…"

She drew herself up and squeezed my arm.

"Okay then, let's take another step or two."

We continued on, working down the stairs one by one, anticipating and strategizing for all contingencies until we stood on the last step before the sidewalk.

As inconvenient as her burst of courage had proven, I couldn't help but marvel at seeing Mom outside the apartment—without having been coerced, cajoled, or coaxed. "Wow, Mom, you're superwoman today."

Our gazes met. She bit her bottom lip.

"Only one more step, Mom. Where do you want to go?"

"I don't know."

She'd showered, chosen a fresh outfit, and hunted down the umbrella. A destination was a small item on such a colossal list of accomplishments.

"We could walk down the pier," I said.

"No."

"Part way?"

She heaved an exasperated sigh. "Brian could come."

"How about the bench across the street? You can see Catalina, and Brian can't miss us. He'll come right over and join us."

"I never liked Catalina much."

"Really?"

She stretched her neck to look up and down the street. "Your father. It's a long story."

There were many long stories about my mom and dad I would never hear. At any rate, safe options were scarce, and by safe I meant places she knew or where she wasn't likely to come in contact with too many people, especially friendly people striking up a conversation.

Suggesting a walk down the pier had been like offering Mom a chance to stroll through a mine field. My mistake. What were our options? The grass, which Mom would say was unsanitary, thanks to dogs. Every picnic bench had been claimed, and sun-wearied beach-goers occupied the low walls of the pier entrance.

Hardly anyone visited the Marine Corps memorial on the hill, but doing so meant crossing the street and walking past a picnic area. Probably not a good choice. Not for today. On our side of the street, only Canaletto's or a splintery bench in front of the bait shop remained.

When I suggested the bench, Mom stepped off the stair and practically dove for it. She sat, all right angles, looking as though someone held a knife to her chest. I sat next to her and she scooted close, weaving her arm through mine. She released her breaths in rapid puffs.

When your son has been gone for seventeen years, not knowing if he is alive or dead, not even the faithful heartbeat of the ocean, the squeals of children running from the surf, or the once-in-a-season appearance of Catalina offered comfort.

"Why don't you close your eyes?" I said.

Her eyes flitted up and down the street. "Is that wise?"

"Yes, of course. I'm here, and I'm not going anywhere. Think of someplace calm." My knee bounced. I was certain I'd missed my appointment with Jerry.

"This is supposed to be a calm place, but it's not. Not at all." A car with a throaty engine inched by. Mom stiffened.

"Are you ready to go back upstairs?"

"No."

"You've accomplished something amazing, Mom. You shouldn't feel like you've disappointed me. I'm very proud of you. This is nice. I enjoy sitting here with you, but we should probably start moving toward the apartment."

Mom gripped the edge of the bench, whitening her knuckles. "I can't breathe."

I stood up and pulled her along. "Then it's definitely time to go."

She crumbled into a tight ball before I could get my arms around her. I sat on the sidewalk to rub her back. "You'll be okay. We'll get you back to the apartment in a minute. For now, breathe into your tummy and hold that breath as long as you can. Soon your tummy will be soft and breathing will be easier."

A woman ran across the street toward us. "I'm an EMT. How can I help?"

I shook my head. "Panic attack. We'll go back upstairs when she's ready."

The woman gave me a knowing look, but she could not have known how Mom's panic attacks, even the threat of her attacks, felt like a vise. "Have a nice day." Several more people offered help, not knowing their kindness rekindled Mom's panic and prolonged our return to the apartment.

I searched Mom's pockets, hoping to find Xanax or one of its cousins. I found a wadded tissue. People sidestepped us, gaping but trying not to be noticed. As much as I found their stares intrusive, I would have done the same thing.

By the time Larice and Taylor returned home, Mom had fallen asleep with her head in my lap. The three of us led her upstairs and put her in bed. I slipped a couple Xanax under her tongue, a trick I'd learned from my dentist.

"Didn't you have an appointment at noon?" Larice said.

"Could you stay until the pills dissolve and she falls back to sleep?"

Since I was over an hour late for my appointment with Jerry, I gave Ashley a lunch break and asked her for another hour. She agreed quickly. She was saving for something geek girls couldn't live without. I hadn't a clue what she was talking about.

SPOTS FLICKERED IN MY vision as I tromped up the steep hill to Jerry's house. I should have stopped and taken the breathing advice I'd given Mom. But this was the day. No stopping for me.

Red and blue lights bounced off the surrounding houses as I rounded the corner to Jerry's. I arrived in time to see a uniformed man slam the back door of an ambulance and walk slowly, head down, to the passenger side of the vehicle.

I ran the rest of the way and pounded on the door. Troll's car was parked in the driveway. Perhaps she sat in the back of the ambulance with Jerry.

"Don't die!" I yelled as the ambulance rolled away in no particular hurry. "Hey! Wait! Where are you taking him?" Of course, Saddleback Memorial, the closest hospital. I needed a car.

Jerry's door opened behind me. "You killed him!" screamed Troll.

I turned toward my crimson-faced accuser. Her veins throbbed purple at her temples. I couldn't muster an ounce of trepidation. I'd frittered my only chance to find Brian. The grass crunched when I slumped to the lawn. "Jerry's dead?"

"You took a sick old man on a joy ride. What did you expect? How could you have been so stupid?"

Had I been stupid? Had I killed the only person with the answers I craved? "He needed to go. He said so."

"And now he's dead, all thanks to you."

He'd sat in a nice car for two hours and rode in a wheelchair at one of the most scenic spots on the California coast. Some would call that therapeutic. Still, he had cried pretty hard.

I pulled at the dead grass. "And now he's dead." The full force of that irreversible truth socked me in the gut. I covered my face with my hands. "You're right, how could I have been so stupid?" Jerry was dead and I knew nothing about Brian.

Troll, fists to hips, dipped at her middle over me. I met her red-rimmed eyes. "Pretty freakin' stupid, I guess, because Jerry would still be alive if you and the munchkin hadn't driven off with him."

Did she not know her father at all? "Wait a minute. Jerry wasn't the most lovable guy on the planet, but he deserved to see the ocean one last time." And Tim was no munchkin.

Arguing over Tim's height missed the point. My only lead to finding Brian had taken vital information to his grave. I'd been too soft. I should have insisted on Jerry telling me everything he knew. He'd bullied me, probably lied about knowing anything. I could be such a sap.

"I don't know what you're talking about." Troll's voice softened. "Dad hated the ocean. It was Mom who wanted to live here. She would have loved a trip like that. But Dad?"

Troll's face had returned to its usual mottled hues. If I wasn't going to discover anything about Brian, I decided to satisfy my curiosity about Jerry. There would be plenty of time for self-pity after the bait shop closed for the day, and I could sneak off to sit under the pier with a soup spoon to eat as much sand as I wanted.

"What happened in La Jolla? Why did Jerry want to go there so bad?" I asked Troll.

"You mean the cove?"

"Exactly."

Troll searched the sky for answers. "Mom grew up near there. That was her swimming hole. Jerry couldn't afford La Jolla, even back in the seventies, so they ended up here—as close as possible but too far, evidently, to actually take his wife there. And then she died. Dad hated me and Steve for still living. There was no making that man happy."

"I'm sorry," I said and meant it. "How did she die?"

"Twenty years ago. Ovarian cancer. I feel like I have a monkey on my back. I have the gene."

"And you're alone?"

"My brother lives in Culver City. He'll be down here like a bullet once he learns Jerry's dead. Everything goes to me. There's really only the house. Not much else is left. Steve scares me to death. He had a meth problem. Maybe he still does. He's changed."

I couldn't very well continue to call her Troll. She still

mourned her mother, felt hated by her father, feared her brother, and lived with mortality hanging overhead. "What's your name?"

"Me? Heather."

She looked more like an Agnes or a Fergus. "Pretty name."

Heather, whether her name suited her or not, was my last link to Brian. "Heather, did your dad ever say anything about a boy named Brian?"

Her brows lowered. "Why?"

"He's my brother. Jerry said he knew him, said he'd seen him on Brian's last day in San Clemente. We walked to and from the bus right by your house. Jerry was going to tell me—"

Heather stepped back into the house and moved to shut the door. I jumped up to shoulder the door open.

"Go away!" She pushed back hard against the door.

"I'm not accusing Jerry of anything. I want to find my brother. Please." My feet slid out of my flip-flops from the force of her pushing.

"Go away and don't come back!" She gave ground but came back with all her weight to slam the door shut.

I pounded on the door and yelled. "I'm sorry! I should have waited. I'll be patient, give you all the time you need. Heather?"

She spoke through the screen of the jammed window. "I'm dialing 9-1-1."

Touché, Heather the Troll! You've held the line on your family's secrets today, but you'll consume your supply of Cheetos and Coke soon enough, and I'll be waiting. You've underestimated me. I will find something about Brian in your house, if it's the last thing I do, girlie.

30

My favorite book from age five through middle school was *Alexander and the Terrible, Horrible, No Good, Very Bad Day*.

I begged and begged for my own copy. The library only allowed two renewals, so I felt cheated of Alexander's consolation for most of my life. Mom considered the book too negative for young minds. Children, she'd believed, should savor their days of innocence like chocolates parked in their cheeks.

I didn't remember my childhood like Mom recalled my childhood.

I wrote to the fictional Alexander and had the good sense not to give the letter to Mom to mail. Instead, I gave the letter to Mrs. Newton, my beautiful, always smiling, wished-she-would-take-me-home fourth-grade teacher. I'd snitched a stamp from Mom's address book. All that was required of Mrs. Newton was to drop the letter in a mailbox. She promised me she would.

I believed her.

Understandably, I never heard back from Alexander. I'd thought my most terrible, most horrible, most no-good, very bad day had happened the day Brian disappeared. The day Jerry died was worse. I lay on my air mattress without a dash, not a pinch, not a grain of hope of finding Brian and regaining my life.

And the cherry on the sundae? Tim hadn't called as he'd promised. I watched Brian's clock change to 11:48.

My cell rested on my chest, the vibrator and ring tone set to high. The piped music of Canatello's seemed especially melancholy, a selection of suitable tunes for people who had eaten bad meatballs.

I threw back the covers and slid my legs over the edge of the mattress. Enough air had seeped out for the sides to rise and encase me. For the third time that night, I turned the air pump to *fill*. I would be sleeping on concrete by morning, if I slept at all.

A glass of wine would help me fall asleep, but I'd finished off a bottle the night before. Clawing up to Mom's apartment to tap her box of wine felt too much like standing at the base of Mount Kilimanjaro with only a peanut-butter-and-jelly sandwich for an eight-day ascent.

I lay back down. I would wait until midnight, the last possible moment for Tim to fulfill his promise. He said he would call and he would. He always came through. There would be time to ascend to Mom's frig afterward. For now, I lay surrounded by a forest of beach umbrellas. My life was all kinds of strange.

The red numbers of Brian's clock read 11:51. Three whole minutes had passed. I rubbed my eyes hard with the heels of my hands. I would go to the library and look for *Alexander and the Terrible, Horrible, No Good, Very Bad Day* the next day. Perhaps I could still find comfort in other people's misery. Perhaps I should ask the librarian for a good Greek tragedy too.

I startled at the sound of my cell humming and playing the Peanuts theme, my ringtone for Tim. "Hello?" I said, with Nancy Drew enthusiasm.

A garbled and slurred voice spoke back. I looked at the screen again: Tim. "Hello?" There were female voices in the background, and then one of them said into my ear, "He's been driving us bonkers about calling you the minute he arrived in his room."

"Who is this?"

"This is his nurse. Mr. Rainford just got out of surgery. We're going to keep him overnight. That's all I can tell you. I've already said too much. HIPAA, you know."

HIPAA *schmipaa*. I knew everything about HIPAA. I'd been to every one of Mom's doctor's appointments for years. "Hasn't he given you verbal consent?"

"He's still a bit loopy to give consent."

"Put him back on the phone," I demanded. And then thought to say, "Thank you." But what was I thanking her for? Before Tim's call, I'd been in despair. Now I was frightened. I should have asked her which hospital, if his prognosis was good, if he would live to see tomorrow.

"—ro?" he said.

"Tim, do you know where you are?"

A long pause. "Bed?"

"Is the nurse still there?"

A longer pause. "Nope."

"Which hospital, Tim?"

"Home –morrow."

"Do you need a ride?"

More nurses talking on Tim's end. They sounded far away. "Tim?"

One of the nurses said, "He didn't hang up." And the line went dead.

NOTHING KILLS A GOOD night's sleep quite like an ambiguous call from the hospital. And unreturned voicemails and texts.

Noises I'd never noticed in the bait shop now whirred, clanked, and pounded. The bait shop had never been a quiet place for a bedroom, not with piped music only feet away. But the place didn't need to rival Times Square for brightness as well. I unplugged the two glass refrigerator cases. The only perishable items—frozen burritos—needed culling anyway.

I firmed up the air mattress and lay back down. The bait

shop was eerily quiet without the buzz of the refrigerators. Larice had shared a meditation technique from her birth classes, so I closed my eyes and imagined large statues of white numbers, one through ten. I painted them with a large paintbrush saturated with red paint. The paint slid off the numbers into the blackness.

My eyes popped open.

Add failure at meditation to my list of disappointments.

There are nearly forty hospitals in Orange County. I called all but the children's hospitals in hopes of finding Tim. Some refused information; others announced rather perfunctorily that he was not a patient. That left waiting as my only option, not my best trait. Only sleep, if attainable, would make the hours pass quickly. This called for the big-gun of relaxation— Savasana. My happy place. Giant sequoias and ferns. Spears of light through the canopy. Spongy earth under my feet.

My breaths deepened.

Keys worked the door lock, and the bell jingled softly. I opened one eye to make sure it was Mom. How she could move with ease in the middle of the night and yet be paralyzed in the brightness of day, I never understood. And probably could never forgive.

I considered intercepting her, reminding her that the telephony had entered a hiatus once more. I hadn't told her about throwing the 354 over the rail. Doing so then meant I would be up the rest of the night adjusting the balance of her world. I'd designated my wakefulness for self-pity and fear, and I wasn't about to surrender my precious time. That left me with one option: wait her out. Mom would tire of the silence and return to the apartment. I feigned sleep with deep, slow breaths.

Mom shuffled through the bait shop and into the telephony, back into the shadows, where she sat to talk to Kevin.

"Hello, darling," she said, although I hadn't heard a telephone ring. I wouldn't. "No, I haven't a thing to do but wait for your call."

I sat bolt straight. Either I'd misinterpreted telephony protocol, or more disturbing, Mom had become delusional enough to believe she was talking to Kevin without the aid of telephony magic.

She lowered her voice. "I have some good news for you." To hear better, I skated toward the telephony in my watermelon socks.

"You have to guess ... Ron *is* a drudge ... Oh my, I could never call him that." She laughed. "Kevin, you're being absolutely wicked ... All right, I'll give you a hint. By July, someone will call you by a new name ... Another? You can't guess? Let me think. Okay, here, but this will give the surprise away: a very tiny someone will arrive in July who looks just like you."

Brian's birthday was in July.

"I don't know what you mean ... You said you wanted a child. I thought you'd be happy ... Legal or not, this is my child, your child. I would never!"

Mom's voice tightened to a shrill. I held my breath, waited. Privacy, of a sort, was all I could give her.

When she spoke again, this time matter-of-factly, in charge, collected. "That's fine, Kevin. I don't see any reason to continue this charade." She pronounced charade like the French. "Of course, I mean every word I say. You've asked me to make a choice and I've made it. I will love this child. Goodbye, Kevin."

Mom's chair scraped against the floor. I ran back to the mattress and pulled up the covers. I watched Mom through one squinty eye as she walked calmly out the bait shop door. I followed and climbed the stairs silently. I pressed my ear to the closed door. If she'd been crying with any intensity, I would have heard her.

I leaned my back against the door and counted to a hundred. By then I figured she would fade back into sleep. She had a gift that way.

Counting gave me time to wonder how many times Mom had had that particular conversation with Kevin. Had she always been calm and resolute when giving Kevin his marching orders? Or had she begged him to stay with her, saying she would do anything to keep their relationship together? Had the telephony changed her, given her a chance to rehearse her life until she got things right?

And then I marveled at the idea of Brian being my half-brother. This explained how Dad's hostility toward Brian grew as Brian grew more and more into someone else's son. Brian didn't look anything like Dad. Brian was slight, a reed. Dad was a sequoia, stubbornly strong and perpetually angry. Brian bent with the wind, saw the best in people, until he couldn't anymore, about the time he got hormones.

This clarified a lot. Holding baby Brian must have been like holding a piece of Kevin for Mom, which went a long way toward resolving her unreasonable devotion to him, not that babies didn't deserve an absurd preoccupation. But perhaps Brian's parentage explained why Dad could not partner in Mom's loss and why she blamed him for driving Brian away.

I stood over Mom, watching her sleep, her mouth slack, a diamond of drool caught on her lip. Dad and I hadn't been enough for Mom. And Mom and I weren't enough for Dad. The common not-enough in those equations was me. I was not enough to keep my parents faithful or to hold their marriage together. But I was plenty enough to clean up the mess they'd made.

Yep, I was angry.

But still inextricably tied to Mom. Maddeningly so.

I couldn't leave her to face the darkness alone, but I

wouldn't—more truthfully, I couldn't—give up on my own future of love, maybe a family. Education. A job that didn't make me smell like eau de squid. I longed for a bigger world, maybe even a few traffic jams or deserts with wide-open vistas. Many fewer pharmacies. Air that didn't smell like mildewed towels. I wanted a life too unwieldy to tame, to be busy with something else besides the bait shop and telephony.

The starting place for all change was Brian, which made me even angrier. I would have to reconcile his persistent role in my life even with him gone. And the role my parents played as two people with ruinous foibles who had given me their DNA and part of a brother. While I wanted to shake my family off like a dog shimmying after a swim, they populated every atom of my being.

I would give Heather a few days to gather herself and to bury her father. Whether she liked me or not, if Brian was the starting place, she was the map. I needed her to welcome me when I showed up on her doorstep. If not, I had some money left in my school fund. I could hire a cheap private investigator to discover the one place I hadn't thought to look. Spending the money on an investigator meant an early end to Ashley's employment, and I truly hated losing her.

Once I had settled on a plan, I allowed myself to consider a life with Tim. What I imagined wasn't exactly unwieldy but it wasn't a chokehold either.

31

Tim had fallen off the planet.

He hadn't called again, so I used every spare minute to expand my search. Not one hospital could confirm he was a patient. I kept my cell tucked in my bikini top in case he called. The cell finally rang as I pushed through the library door with a stack of books and DVDs. I dropped everything on the lawn and sat on the grass to talk to him.

"I've slept the day through," Tim said. He sounded more alert than the night before, but his words were still pillowy.

"Tim, are you okay? What's going on?"

"You knew I'd hurt myself?"

"You called last night," I reminded him. The nurse certainly hadn't underestimated his state of mind.

"I did?"

"The nurse called you loopy."

"I was probably calling to apologize for not calling. Did I say anything stupid?"

"Tim, should I be worried?"

Tim told me the story. He'd taken a misstep at an orienteering event, which sent him rolling down a hillside. He spoke of cracking sounds and searing pain in his ankle, of dislocation and pins and narcotics managing the pain but keeping him loose, of staying with his parents in Newport Beach until he could control the pain with Tylenol.

"Can you come and see me?" he said.

"Jerry died."

The phone went silent.

"Tim?"

"I'm so sorry. I should be there."

No, he should not have been there. If he'd been sitting with me on the lawn, caught in the embracing warmth of the afternoon, I would dump my whole day in his lap—everything about the erratic behavior of Mom, her conversation with Kevin and the great revelation of Brian's parentage, how I felt the jaws of Mom's illness clamping down on my neck. That seemed like an awful lot to unload on someone. Instead, I said, "There's still Jerry's daughter. I'm going to see her tomorrow. I'm sure she'll let me look around. I'll find something."

His words slurred. "I haven't been much help."

Hadn't he? Tim and Amy's story had fortified me with an unexpected prospect that, on second thought, would probably never be realized. Perhaps he was more right than wrong. He really hadn't been much help. He'd found his sister. I was left to scour the library for the perfect cookie recipe to bribe Heather into helping me find Brian.

Still, Tim had given up a whole day to drive Jerry to La Jolla to help me gain vital information about Brian. "We may not have gotten the lead I was looking for, but whatever Jerry had to accomplish before he left this world, you helped him do that. You should feel good about that."

"So, can you come?"

Tim demonstrated remarkable persistence for a drugged man. I imagined driving the Daewoo full throttle along the coast to Newport Beach. Before I answered, though, I made myself think about what to do next. This was a new skill for me. My brain hurt from the effort.

Talking to Tim was too much like swimming in the surf. The water heaved and lifted, tugged and pushed. All in all, a very pleasant experience until a wave caught me off guard and slammed me to the sandy bottom. I didn't know which way was up. And I needed to know which way was up for Mom's sake and Brian's. Maybe Dad's. Definitely mine.

"You sound tired," I said.

"I am."

"Let's talk tomorrow. Maybe I'll have something to report, and you'll be more comfortable." If I couldn't do the right thing and define the relationship, I could put the whole mess and heartache off for another few hours.

"Sounds like a..."

"Tim?"

He snorted. "Yeah?"

"Go to sleep."

I slipped the cell into my bag and lay back in the grass. The colorless sky reflected far less than an ounce of good will, but I decided there and then to love Tim forever, even if I couldn't in good conscience allow him to love me back. Until I found the courage to release his heart again, in a kinder way than before, I would be the best me possible, just for him.

It seemed like a good plan at the time.

I TOSSED THE INGREDIENTS for Toll House cookies into the grocery basket. If I was baking to bribe Heather for information, it only seemed fair to cook something for Mom too. With a cookbook opened to a sweet-and-sour chicken recipe, I hunted for canned pineapple.

At home, I diced and chopped. Grease splattered the stovetop. Pots and pans collected in the sink. When Mom and I sat down to what I considered gourmet fare, she pushed the vegetables and chicken around her plate.

I spoke to the top of her head as she inspected chunks of carrots and peppers. "So, Mom, I got to thinking about why Brian looks so different from the rest of us. I mean, his body type is nothing like yours or Dad's. Even the color of his eyes, which may or not influence the way he sees the world, are so dark. His sense of humor. His total lack of athleticism. His school troubles. Was he washed onto the beach after a storm and you and Dad took pity on him?" To torment me?

Her eyes came up from her plate, her lips tight, her eyes wary. "He's a carbon copy of his father."

"He looks nothing like Dad," I said, holding to the pretense I knew nothing about Brian's parentage.

Mom slapped the table. "I don't know what game you're playing, but you're a smart girl. You've known for a long time your father could not have had anything to do with Brian."

"You've overestimated me," I said, fighting to cork a hot retort. The constant measuring of words and motives wore me out. "I heard everything when you talked to Kevin. As you've told me before, the walls are thin around here."

"I don't know what made me go to the telephony last night. I'd sat there enough nights to know whatever worked down there had vaporized." She wagged a piece of impaled chicken at me, imploring with her eyes. "Does knowing Brian has another father change anything? He's still your brother, isn't he?"

After listening to Mom's side of the conversation with Kevin, I'd thought of little else. Brian and I shared fewer genes but other things, more important things, bound us together. I'd fallen asleep to his snores. We cooked hot dogs over the gas burners when Mom went out. I was the one who reassured him about his first wet dream, and set down rules for the care and handling of his new trick. We collected cigarette butts to smoke under the pier. He convinced surfers to buy us beer. And on the day he disappeared, I'd planned on telling him I'd won the race to lose my virginity. If shared genetics proved scanty between me and Brian, we were confederated by our secrets.

Brian was my brother.

"Knowing about Kevin changes nothing," I told her.

She sighed and a moan came from a deep place. "I've given up on finding him."

"Kevin?"

She frowned, looked confused. "Brian, of course. The

police are idiots. They've long forgotten my boy. Kevin is…"
She twirled her fork like a lasso, as if she might snag
something—Brian, Kevin, an idea—by the horns. She leaned
toward me. "You're looking, aren't you? You never could leave
a puzzle unfinished. What have you found?"

I set my fork down and pushed the plate away. I struggled
over what to tell her. I feared bolstering her with false
expectations. "I tried. A little. I have one more idea. Nothing
that will amount to much."

Knowing I hadn't given up seemed enough for Mom. She
stroked my hand. "I'm going to bed. I'm so very tired. You
don't mind, do you? The stroganoff was nice."

Stroganoff? I'd put enough red food coloring in the sweet-
and-sour chicken to give me a headache. "Mom?"

She came around the table, swept my wild hair away from
my forehead and pressed her lips to my skin. Before she
reached the bedroom door, my mouth opened and out popped,
"I could find Kevin. Do you know his last name, when he was
born, where he lives?"

Had she heard a word I said? Had she floated away? Where
was she going? Tonight? Tomorrow? The day after? This had
been the strangest conversation I'd ever had with her.

Mom turned and stepped back into a square of light from
the bathroom. "Honey, Kevin is dead. He died only months
before Brian disappeared. Besides, I wouldn't want to talk to
him." She closed her eyes and lifted her face to the ceiling.
"I've given this a lot of thought, and it's pretty clear God is
punishing me for my unfaithfulness to your father. Kevin died
and then your brother disappeared. And then there's divorcing
your father. Asking him to leave may have been the last drop
from my portion of mercy."

My breath came shallow and rapid. I stood up fast enough
to overturn my chair. "*You* divorced Dad? You told him to
leave?" Mom slipped back into the shadows. She would not

find a hiding place, not tonight, not with my life in a vise. "Had you given any thought to what divorcing Dad would mean for me?"

"I waited through all your father's dalliances, waited for you to grow up into an independent woman."

"Making runs to the library and the grocery store doesn't make me independent."

"You went to the botanical garden with a man. And there's the bait shop."

As quickly as my anger had erupted it receded into a swallowing despair. I sank to the floor and my chin hit my chest. Mom would never understand why I lied about visiting a botanical garden with Tim, or how a timer always ticked in my head when I needed to leave her. I lived under a constant deadline. She needed her Xanax at 6:00, 2:00, and 10:00. She didn't eat unless I prepared her meals and not always then. I deliberated every word to avoid a meltdown and failed too many times. Dad's absence granted me all the responsibility of parenting a young child but none of the sticky kisses or refrigerator art.

I felt robbed.

And she felt punished.

I could clear that up. "I don't think God works that way. The whole friend of sinners thing, you know?"

She looked at me as if I'd sprouted a second head.

"It's a long story. Larice had all these index cards in her closet."

Her eyes narrowed.

"There's this guy who can't stop sinning."

She cocked her head.

"He asked Jesus to rescue him. And you're not near as bad as him."

By the way she chewed her lip, she kept silent with some difficulty. Finally, she headed for her bedroom again, which, truthfully, was a relief. I had nothing more to say, and I couldn't answer any of her questions.

I leaned over the sink, poised as if I might lose my dinner but not feeling sick as much as startled by my own words. Did I believe them? Did God forgive? I had decided that if there was a God, ignoring him probably wasn't a good idea, but I didn't exactly want him telling me what to do. Still, I worried I would be the one outlier to God's ability to forgive.

God: too important to ignore, too big to understand. Highly inconvenient. Kind of irresistible.

I DOSED MOM WITH Xanax at ten and preheated the oven to bake Heather's cookies. With all that butter and chocolate, she might find the cookies magically transformative. She might even forget she hated me and threatened to call the police. She could turn into a princess. This kind of thinking came from eating too much cookie dough.

I left a plate of cookies on the counter for Mom and headed for my sleeping space in the back of the bait shop. Inflating my air mattress at midnight raised the probability I would still be suspended above the concrete floor when I awoke for the fishermen.

Sleep proved impossible. I blamed the caffeine in chocolate chips until I owned up to how disturbing my dinner with Mom had been. The plan had been to weasel information from Mom, not to watch her swing from indifference to seething anger to helpless child. Doing so cracked something inside me, and I felt the light spilling out.

To distract myself, I tried to picture Brian. He must look like Kevin. That would explain Mom's unparalleled devotion to him. Conjuring Brian didn't work. He would not materialize. I clicked on the flashlight and reached for the scrapbook.

And there he was, just as I remembered. A deep apostrophe between his eyebrows was the only bit of my mother he possessed. Everything else—his questioning eyes, the fortress of a chin, the god-like straightness of his nose— these things had to have come from Kevin, not Ron Archer.

I held a picture of Brian beside my face in front of the bathroom mirror. My face was round, and my cheeks turned into dinner rolls when I smiled. My eyes, also round and too small, were a half-hearted blue. Brian's were as brown as Junior Mints. His face was an enviable oval.

At fifteen, dark stubble shadowed his lip and dotted his chin. I'm pleased to say a razor has never touched my face. His hair is straight, thick, and tamable. Mine came from a recessive gene contributed by a hermit who never combed his hair. Wild does not begin to describe my locks—not exactly curly but not straight either. Wavy would have been nice. The color is tolerable, a salted caramel.

I clicked off the light, satisfied Brian and I were still as different as I remembered, but he was my brother, my only brother. I doubted finding him would cure Mom, but now I wanted to find him for me. I missed him. I needed to share the memories of our fractious family with someone. Isn't that the connectedness of families?

My determination set my resolve.

Heather didn't stand a chance.

When I picked the scrapbook off the floor to return to the closet, a stack of loose papers splayed across the floor—a few pictures, a program from Brian's eighth-grade graduation, and several postcards.

The postcards made me smile. Brian sent one whenever he got to go somewhere I did not, like Big Bear with his Boy Scout Troop, the Huntington Library with an art heritage class, and one from San Juan Capistrano, not ten miles from our front door but far enough away for Brian to write "Sucker!" on the back and spring for a postage stamp. He'd sat across from me while watching television that night, smiling like he'd swallowed a canary...or a swallow. When the postcard arrived the next—

Brian sent postcards.

Jerry prized stacks and stacks of postcards. Heather had pinned them to the wall while I stood waiting for Jerry to spill his guts. Had Brian bought Jerry's silence with a promise of a postcard from wherever he traveled? Was that Jerry's promise?

Sleep proved erratic. I finally gave up about three to clean the cabinets under the espresso machine and the cash register. Their refreshed orderliness soothed me in a most therapeutic way. By the time Tony—new guy, bald and pudgy, grizzled, definitely not a temptation—delivered the fresh bait and the fishermen begged for burned coffee, I'd made up my mind.

Those postcards would soon be mine.

32

Rolls of carpet, pad, and lengths of splintered baseboard spilled from a dumpster parked in front of Jerry's house. Hip-hop music blared from the painter's truck. A gaping hole yawned where the front door used to be.

I stepped over the threshold onto paint-splattered concrete. Not a lick of furniture remained. I stood in the middle of the room, watching the painters put the finishing touches on the new molding around the front door. The wall between the kitchen and the living room was gone. Boxes of wood flooring waited to be laid.

A painter nodded at the plate of cookies in my hands. "Them for us?"

I considered the cookies stacked on Mom's one and only china plate. "Is the owner here?"

"The gal from the real estate office left about an hour ago," he said, looking with longing at the cookies.

"No, I mean the owner." How to describe Heather?

"The one that's in a snit all the time?"

I could not have described her better.

"We haven't seen hide nor hair of her since day one."

I should have defended Heather. She'd just lost her father. But where was she? Jerry had been dead for three days, and her attention had turned immediately to cashing in his one and only asset, and to do so before her brother took notice. Could something have been left to help me find Brian? As unlikely as that was, I had to try. I held out the plate of cookies to the painter. "Eat your hearts out. Mind if I look around?"

"Heck no. Knock yourself out. Take all the time you need."

I ran my hand over the wall where Heather had pinned postcards onto Jerry's bedroom wall. Someone had filled in every hole and painted the room a shade too light to be beige but too warm to be white. They'd also removed Jerry's hospital bed along with the nightstand and stool. No oxygen machine heaved and sighed and clicked.

And no postcards. Not one.

Nothing remained of Jerry. His existence had been carried off and painted over, which meant I was back to knowing nothing about Brian, but harboring a sense of violation. What had been taken from me? Simply a tidbit of information to unlock my future, more than enough to siphon the lifeblood right out of me.

The painter stuck his head in the room. "You lookin' to buy this place? I'm supposed to give you this here flyer." He held out a glossy paper with pie charts of population demographics and average incomes.

I took the flyer. My eyes focused on the price printed across the top in red numbers. "You're kidding about this price, right?"

"There's a peek-a-boo view of the ocean from the back stoop." He pointed at the flyer. "Says so right here."

That was when I noticed the Realtor: Sally McCallister, Dad's girlfriend. Maybe she would know where to find Heather. "Can I keep this?"

"You can have every last one. We'll be done tonight, moving on to the next flip. Sally keeps us busy."

"Well, you've done your job. You've transformed the place." The painter didn't seem too eager to hurry back to his work. My deflated heart longed to hear how horribly Heather had left the place. "So, she left the place trashed. Were you part of the cleanup?"

He threw up his arms. "You've been here? This place smelled like an outhouse. The first thing we done after all the junk got thrown in the dumpster was strip out the drywall, then we sprayed a special coating on the studs to seal in the stink. This here's a brand new house." He crossed his arms over his chest. If his work hadn't meant the postcards were gone, I would have patted him on the back.

Out the front window, now much bigger with a transom for ventilation, the dumpster bulged with debris. Was it possible the postcards still waited for me among the bags of trash and discarded drywall? I'd been strangled by lesser hopes. Why not go all in? "Jerry's postcard collection meant a great deal to me. Do you remember seeing anything like that?"

"They was stuck all over the wall in the back bedroom. I hauled them out with the drywall."

"Could that drywall still be in the dumpster?"

"The waste folks can't get here too soon, if you ask me. I just now gave 'em a holler. They shoulda been here by now."

My heart thumped against my ribs. "You're sure Heather didn't take them?"

"Ol' cranky pants? Couldn't tell ya, but if she didn't, they're out in that there dumpster. You're welcome to take a look. I'd get out there right quick. Those trash guys are fast as sharks when they expect payment."

I stood on an upturned bucket to look into the dumpster. Mostly construction debris, and a few trash bags of who-knew-what, filled the thing. And didn't Jerry wear diapers? I would have to move whatever got thrown on top of the drywall scraps. Where were rubber gloves when you needed them? I climbed onto the edge of the dumpster. The acrid odor of decay nearly knocked me over.

Behind me, the painter said, "You're lucky. The drywall's only 'bout halfway down."

I didn't feel lucky. I flung my leg over the side and lowered myself into the shifting crud. As the painter had promised, the waste guy showed up before I reached the drywall. I paid the driver fifty dollars (part of the deposit I hadn't taken to the bank yet) to buy ten more minutes of hefting aside stained carpet.

I came across the pieces of drywall with the postcards right where the painter had promised. When I whooped for joy, he jumped into the dumpster to help me haul the drywall onto the brittle lawn. I breathed in deeply of the fresh air before I plucked a postcard off the drywall to read the back.

The only message written there was, "Sucker!"

I held the postcard to my chest and wept. Completely mystified by my show of emotion, the painter backed into the house. When my tears slowed to a trickle, I harvested the remaining postcards and stashed them in my purse. Many more of Brian's postcards would head for the landfill, but I felt triumphant with the stack of forty-seven postcards I'd managed to salvage.

I was a mess. Drywall dust powdered my arms and clothes, and I smelled like an abandoned fishing boat. I thanked the painter and retrieved Mom's plate. I needed to get back to the bait shop. Ashley would be waiting for me to return. School started right after Labor Day, and she would be gone. What would I do without her? I slumped to the curb in front of Jerry's house.

His mailbox lay on the ground beside me. The waste guy should have taken it with his load. No more junk mail for Jerry, but maybe—could it be? I bent down, tugged open the door, looked up and down the street for snooping eyes, and pulled out a stack of glossy advertisements.

And ran the whole way to the bait shop.

Ashley stepped back from the counter to hold her nose. "Ew 'mell terwabull." Customers parted as I walked toward the back of the shop and the shower. As long as I showered before or after hours, privacy hadn't been an issue. Now, with a half-dozen people watching, I pushed an umbrella display to the side to unlock my closet, where I collected clothes and a pair of flip-flops, pushed the umbrella display back in front of my locked closet, and unlocked the bathroom door. I felt curious eyes burning into my back. I promised myself to never gape at an aquarium again.

I turned on the light and the fan, which rivaled a jet engine. The roar of the fan rather than the door provided the sense of privacy I needed to strip down to my bikini. I sat on the toilet to flip through Jerry's mail. I dealt a thick sheath of coupons— for everything from lube jobs to a baker's dozen of muffins— into the trashcan.

Near the bottom of the stack, I found a glossy postcard. I held my breath. What were the chances? Besides, the postcard didn't look anything like what I'd fished from the dumpster or seen on Jerry's walls. No palm trees or outlines of ancient buildings, only a row of impossibly red, yellow, and white clapboard buildings stood shoulder to shoulder along a cobbled road. One bland brown building leaned forward as if to align itself with the others. "Bergen, Norway" was written across an impossibly blue sky, the kind you see on postcards from Ireland to Yosemite.

I turned the card over slowly to find one word: "Sucker!"

Oh my gosh, he was alive, truly alive.

I wanted to kill him.

While he'd traveled to places with tidy rows of buildings, I'd tried to maintain a sense of normalcy in an ever-shrinking, ever-crazier world. I admitted—since I was alone in the bathroom—that our family had been odd and insular long before he'd left, but not this fractured or detached. His disappearance had lifted us to a new level of familial decay, increasing our dysfunction exponentially by the day.

And he had been so close. At least his postcards had been close. Would sending a postcard to his mother have compromised his sense of rebellion? Or to me, his only ally in this chamber of horrors? He seemed okay sending the wretched postcards to the most contrary man on the planet. Jerry was a beast.

This kind of thinking got me nowhere.

I traced Brian's scrawled letters and read the description of the place in the picture. "Known as the city of the Seven Mountains, Bergen is the second most populated city in Norway and the busiest port in the country. Founded before 1070 AD."

The postmark was only ten days old. Brian had plucked a postcard from a rack just over a week ago, signed and addressed it to Jerry, and found a post office somewhere in Bergen to lick a Norwegian stamp into place. He'd completed this ritual—by my best guesstimation—hundreds of times.

Hundreds of times he'd bypassed his family for a man connected to him only by a childhood promise. What would have made him do such a thing?

I didn't have a clue.

I added the Bergen postcard to the stack in my purse and turned on the shower. I washed my hair three times to remove the smell of cat urine. Scrubbed pink I stepped from the shower with a hot anger brewing. When I pictured myself seeing Brian for the first time after all these years, I now saw myself kneeing him in the groin. Take that for leaving me alone with a mother immobilized by her grief and a father who stuffed his complicity with old telephones and Danish oil.

Brian would pay for his selfishness.

I CHANTED AS I waited for Tim to hobble to the door. "I am a nun for a year. I am a—"

A young girl, maybe twenty, opened the door. She wore scrubs emblazoned with characters from *Frozen*. Her blonde hair was pulled back into a severe ponytail.

"Can I help you," she said with genuine glee.

"I'm here to see Tim." I assumed this ponytailed darling to be Chrissy, the CNA hired to help Tim through his recuperation. "You're Chrissy?"

"I fix his meals, help him with meds, and anything else he might need. I just gave him a bath."

"Oh. Well. Can I see him?"

"Of course. He's doing great." She opened the door wider and gestured toward the back of the house. "The bedroom is on the left. I have some paper work to do. Don't feel like you have to hurry."

I felt compelled to set the record straight for the girl. "We're good friends. We've been working on a project. I think I may have made a breakthrough." I wanted to continue, tell her I'd made a vow to myself and God to love Tim from afar, the only chance he had at a happy life. But the girl was already busy shuffling through papers on the counter.

I took a deep breath and walked toward Tim's bedroom.

"Jenna! It's so good to see you." He patted the mattress beside him. "Have a seat. You look wonderful, really fabulous."

He looked good too. His hair, still damp from his bath, had been parted too far to the left, but his eyes shone and focused right on me. And he hadn't slurred one word. He took my hand when I sat down. I already felt an overwhelming desire to negate my vow. I was so easy.

With his free hand Tim pointed the controller at the TV to silence *Sports Center*. He sat propped up against a padded headboard with his foot elevated on about a dozen pillows. One of those moon boot sort of casts encased his foot and shin. He wore shorts that revealed defined quads. I hadn't expected that. Oh my, better get the pleasantries over and move on to the real reason for my visit.

"Are you comfortable?" I asked.

He squeezed my hand. "Very. Thanks for coming. I'm more than a little antsy. It's just me and the TV."

"There's Chrissy."

He leaned forward, lowered his voice. "She does her job quite efficiently, but only so she has time to text."

A pair of crutches leaned on the wall. "How's getting around?"

"They're bringing me a scooter later today." He waggled his eyebrows that were carefully trimmed and quite feminine in the symmetry of their arc. "I paid extra for a basket." He held up his phone. "And speaking of texts, Amy doesn't keep one thought to herself. We've slipped back into our roles of big brother and little sister quite nicely. I suppose some things aren't meant to change."

Enough chat. More than anything, I longed to reach out and finger his silvery spot of hair. That would be a mistake, like the Paul guy from the Bible verse who kept doing what he didn't want to do. "Tim," I said in my most businesslike voice, "Brian is alive. At least he was ten days ago."

Tim's face brightened. "What did you find? How do you know? Or did he call?"

If only learning about Brian had been so easy. I told Tim everything. He'd forgotten about Jerry's death. The drugs must have erased that bit of news. How nice for him. He'd probably forgotten he'd asked me to visit him at his parents, which was just as well.

"I wish I could have helped you, especially with the dumpster. You wore gloves, right?"

"You can help me now, if you feel well enough."

Tim asked for his laptop. "Let me see the postcards." I apologized for how they smelled, and he brushed my concern away. "These are all ports of call. Either he's a mariner of some sort or works on cruise ships."

"The locales make me think he's working on cruises," I said. "A life of endless parties would suit Brian, at least the Brian I knew. I see him as a bartender or a dealer in a casino, nothing too domestic."

Tim scooted over and shifted pillows, so I could sit next to him to see the computer screen. He smelled of soap with a hint of lavender, probably something Chrissy carried in her supply kit. Tim typed in a search for cruise ships that docked in Bergen. "There can't be too many," he said. "Bergen's a bit off the beaten track."

He clicked and read and clicked some more. I used his preoccupation with finding Brian's ship to take in his room. It was painted a silvery blue with espresso-colored furniture and a watercolor of what looked like Cotton's Point. Normally, I would want to jump into the scene, listen to the growl and fizz of the surf, and dive into the turbulence of a wave.

But leaning into Tim contented me, so I enjoyed the crisp whiteness of the trim work and studied the pictures of his family on his dresser, including Amy and her brood. They all looked so happy, together, joined. This sentimentality took me off guard. I would have to think about that, do some observations, ask Larice.

The room was tranquil. There were no humming refrigerator units filled with sodas, vitamin-packed drinks and water, no neon OPEN signs, and no threat of a ringing telephone from the past. I closed my eyes. I fell asleep breathing deeply of Tim's scent.

"JENNA, DO YOU HAVE a passport?" Tim sat up and I fell into the warm place on his pillow.

The light in the room had changed. Shadows of palm trees fell across the bed. I sat up. "What time is it?"

"Nearly eight. Is there a problem?"

I bounded from the bed and stepped into my flip-flops. "I'm late. Really late. Mom should take her meds at six." I stopped to make eye contact with him. I owed him an explanation, and I needed to remember why leaving was better than staying. "She gets a little crazy." And coaxing her into being less crazy was getting impossible.

Tim's face was a map of concern. "Call me later when things settle down. Don't worry about waking me up."

I remembered his internet searches. "You found something?"

"I'll know more when you call. Go on. Take care of your mom. I'll be here."

No one, not Mom or Dad, not any boyfriend I'd ever had, and certainly not my brother, maybe Larice—yes, Larice—had given so much to me without asking for the impossible in return. He'd brought me lunch every day for two years. He'd wiped sand off my face as I wallowed in regret under the pier. And now he'd found my brother while I sat on his bed. That was a first, a first that scared me to death.

I took a step back.

Tim set his laptop aside. "Should I come with you?"

"No!" I said too loudly.

"You're crying. Have I...?" Tim reached for his crutches.

I put up my hands and backed toward the door. "Don't get up. I have to go. I'll be fine. Right as rain. Lovable and capable."

"Will you...?"

"I'll call you in a few hours, maybe tomorrow." I turned to scurry like a mouse caught when the light clicked on.

I revved the engine of the Daewoo, meaning to cover the pounding of my heart. No such luck. Couldn't Tim see how very different I was from the people he treasured in the photographs? He occupied a space with them far higher on the continuum of human nobility from me.

I was nothing but trouble. If Tim wanted to step into my arena of craziness, he would have to convince me I was worthy of the trouble. And, oh yeah, wait twelve months.

God, I prayed he could do that.

IT TOOK A SECOND Xanax to calm Mom into sleep. I was spent and more than a little resentful of her theatrics. She'd tried my patience, and I'd failed miserably.

I hadn't changed at all. I could sit in a closet and talk to God for a hundred years and still remain the same old Jenna, the Jenna who let her good-for-nothing brother slip away for the sake of her own pleasure and misguided sense of competition. Mom took the brunt of my disappointment. Add that to my list of shame.

To regain a sense of purpose, I restocked the refrigerator cases. Tim called just before midnight.

"Do you have a passport?"

"How long are they good for?"

"Ten years."

Larice and I had taken a weekend trip to Mexico one winter. The trip had been a twenty-fifth birthday celebration. The passport was good for one more year, if I could find it.

"You've found Brian, then?"

"I called a ship that docks in Bergen and left a message for him with the operator. She promised to give the message to him personally. That makes me reasonably sure he's working on the ship. But when I pressed her, she wouldn't say more. If he's not on this ship, we'll hunt until we find him on another."

For a second, I allowed myself to believe the journey to find Brian was about to end. But what was I thinking? I couldn't go anywhere. Who would care for Mom? I explained my dilemma to Tim.

"There has to be a way. Your brother will dock in Bergen on the thirty-first, the last day of the cruise season in Norway. There's no way to know where he'll go next. I'm sorry I can't give you more time to think about this. You'll have to leave tomorrow night to get to Bergen in time."

"And you're sure he's on the ship?"

"I'm not a gambler, Jenna. I'm a CPA. I find blessed

symmetry in balanced books. So no, I can't be one-hundred percent sure Brian is on that ship. I'm about eighty-seven percent sure. Under the circumstances, that's a reasonable risk." When I didn't respond, he added, "I bought you a plane ticket and booked a hotel."

"Tim..."

"Your dad has to help you."

"Tim..."

"The fastest way to the harbor from the Bergen airport is a taxi. I've printed out everything you'll need. They have a terminal where all the passengers will disembark from the ship. There'll be lots of people, probably a place to buy snacks and coffee. People have posted pictures. It looks nice. You should be comfortable."

I couldn't reconcile Tim's generosity. Besides, I'd fanned a pretty good resentment toward Brian. "Tim..."

"Tell me you wouldn't do the same for me."

My heart would not spark. Every ember of hope that had resided there was ash. "It's a longshot."

"He'll be off to the equator and then the southern hemisphere, if the pattern of his postcards continues. Your brother is a vagabond, a man of endless summers. If we don't find him in Bergen, I don't know where else we'll look. Jerry won't be receiving anymore mail."

"Can you get your money back?"

"Nonrefundable tickets, I'm afraid."

I was going to Norway on a fool's errand. How suitable. "I'll pay you back." That would take about a hundred years.

"We'll talk about details when you get back, when you can tell your mom Brian is alive and well."

I worried about convincing Dad to step into my shoes for a few days. Tim was waiting for me to thank him. Again, I'd misjudged him. "Jenna, this has nothing to do with squaring a debt. You know that, don't you?"

He still believed I was his definite yes. "Are you nuts? I have a mentally ill mother who keeps me shackled to a very small life. And I do things I hate and eat sand for penance. And have I told you I've been sitting in closets to talk to God? *God*, for heaven's sake. If you think this is the kind of life you want to step into, you'll have to convince me with something more than plane tickets, although plane tickets, in this case, are exactly what I need. I'm grateful."

"How can I convince you?" he said. "I'll do anything." He sounded like I'd doused him with a bucket of heartache.

I had no idea what to tell him. My gaze fell on a magazine in a rack by the counter. Article teasers encircled a photograph of Jennifer Garner on the cover of *Elle*. One promised ten proofs of a guy's love. Tim's love wasn't in question here, but my lovability was.

"You need ten rock-solid reasons why I'm worthy of your love."

"Only ten?"

"Ten indisputable, testable, provable reasons. No fluff. Nothing that can't be referenced."

"Do you need those annotated?"

He seemed awfully cocky for someone with an impossible task before him. Did he know something about me I didn't? Once again, Tim's assurance bewildered me. "I need to talk to Dad. I'll come by in the morning for the ticket." I sucked in a breath to staunch tears. "Thank you."

And I pressed the end call button.

DAD SAT ACROSS FROM me. His long hairy legs sprawled out from under his robe as he slouched in the chair. What little hair he had on his head stood at odd angles. He listened with detachment to my sudden plans for international travel.

"And you want to leave tomorrow. Is that right?"

"My plane leaves after one. I'll need to be there by eleven."

"Jenna, I have plans. I'm going with Sally to a development for retirees in Mexico. We're seriously considering a home there."

This news disturbed in two ways. First, there was no one else to care for Mom. Second, if Dad moved to Mexico, there would never be anyone to spell me. I swallowed down a sob. "I know this is a huge favor to ask. And sudden. But could you reschedule? I will never ask you to do so again."

"Our calendar for the next few months is full. We'll be in and out of town, visiting Sally's family, attending conventions, and doing some personal travel. You couldn't have picked a worse time. Maybe you should have talked to me before buying the ticket." He said the last part with a hint of parental condescension. The temptation to stomp out like a child pulled at me.

Out of desperation, I told him almost everything, certainly not the part about Jerry or the postcards, only about the very slim window of time I had to find Brian.

"How sure are you it's him?" he asked, now leaning forward.

"About eighty-seven percent."

"Does this have anything to do with the telephony?"

"I talked to a man who saw Brian on the day he disappeared. Through some simple investigating, I discovered the man was still alive and receiving correspondence from Brian. That's how I found out where Brian might be."

"The telephony?" He sounded dubious.

"I agree with you the trip will probably prove disappointing, but this is the best and only chance we have left of finding Brian." Please, Dad, play along just this once.

Dad rubbed his face and his beard scritched against his hands. "It's time to find him. Do what you have to."

Had I not been sitting, I would have fallen down. I stood and turned for the door. "I won't ask again."

He followed me. "Your mother will hate having me around."

I'd forgotten the most important instruction, and Dad didn't take instruction well. "We can't tell her where I've gone. If she knows I'm off to find Brian, and I don't succeed, she may never resurface."

"What should I tell her? You know she'll ask."

"I'll take the heat. Tell her I left nothing but a note saying I would be back soon. Good news about Brian will soften my return."

"How long will you be gone?"

"I travel on the day before he docks. I'll hang out in the terminal until I see him on the thirty-first. My plan is to have the rest of the day with him. Maybe we can arrange a visit home."

"Do you think he would?"

I hadn't had a chance to consider what Brian might think of all this. I only remembered Tim and Amy's reunion on the pier, how they had walked off arm in arm. Such expectations would probably prove unrealistic, but that's exactly what my heart demanded.

"I don't see why not." Except he'd had plenty of chances to do so already. Brian probably worked cruises to Catalina, for all I knew. He could have driven to see us from Long Beach in less than an hour.

Dad planted his hands on my shoulders. "Okay, but this is it. If Brian is a no-show, he's dead to me. I can't keep on like this."

I rose to my tippy toes to kiss Dad's rough cheek. I felt the weariness of a million miles I hadn't known I'd traveled, while a million more lay ahead. "You're the best. Thanks."

I stood outside the courtyard and listened to the drum roll of the waves. I pictured myself perched high above a blood-thirsty crowd on the Tower of Doom. A margarine-sized tub of water awaited my dive. Sure, I would hit the tub, but a belly-flop was probable.

Finding Brian could be the greatest disappointment of all.

33

I used to think of international travel as passengers in form-fitting suits of shimmering fabric who carried Italian-leather briefcases. Jet-setters. The rich. Those who crossed the globe like I crossed the street, only more frequently.

It's nothing like that.

People plod along like cattle in their pajamas. I fit right in, although with Tim's coaching I switched out shorts for yoga pants and kicked off my flip-flops for tennies, so I wouldn't do a face plant on a walking sidewalk. I could have joined any number of elder tours and no one would have been the wiser.

I stood in front of the customs agent mimicking a wide-eyed cow, hyper-vigilant about answering their rapid-fire questions. I'd heard stories of well-meaning tourists getting gabby and ending up in a windowless room, backpedaling through their mundane lives just to get on with their vacations. My vacuous gaze worked because I slid right through security without any embarrassing pat-downs or interrogations.

Tim texted every step of the way.

Where RU now?

10 feet farther

RU past security?

Getting dressed

Ha!

Miss flip-flops

Call from gate.

My mother hadn't been this attentive when I left for my first day of kindergarten. "Are your underwear clean?" she'd asked, and off I'd plodded up the hill to the bus.

The plane I flew from LAX to Heathrow seemed like a shoe two sizes too small. Passengers squeezed by along narrow aisles, forced bulging bags into overhead compartments, and wedged themselves into ridiculously cramped seats. The passengers released a collective sigh when the cabin door slammed shut and latched, for everyone had settled into their diminutive piece of real estate for the flight.

After a late dinner, the lights dimmed for sleepers. Most watched movies on seat-back screens or plugged themselves into their personal devices. The plane went deathly—a poor choice of words, I know—quiet for the rest of the night, leaving me to rehearse everything I wanted to say to Brian. I ran every possible scenario of what seeing him might be like, including not seeing him, which in my sleep-deprived brain had proved to be a huge relief.

Not finding Brian meant ignorant bliss for me. Why he hadn't contacted us in all those years could remain his secret. How he'd survived during his late teens, when he was too young to work on the cruise ships, would also remain veiled and unknowable. Not finding Brian meant no begging him to visit Mom either. He would have done so by now, if he'd given a hoot. Tim or Dad or Larice had not dared to mention the deliberateness of Brian's distance. I'd thought of little else.

Because it would be me who told Mom.

What would I say? "Hey, Mom, I found Brian! He's great, really healthy. But he's too busy—or too angry or too selfish or too much of a putz—to come home. I wouldn't expect him until there's an estate to settle. Or never."

All of my motivations for finding Brian suddenly seemed cruel and self-punishing. I could not imagine a happy ending to our story. Maybe clarifying sleep might help. I actually considered nudging a snoring woman and asking for a dose of whatever I'd seen her pop. Instead, I told my occipitofrontalis muscle to give up the ghost and both temporalis muscles to turn to butter and the masseters to go slack.

They did not.

TIM HAD SCHEDULED A full day of Bergen before Brian's ship arrived to rest. He said sleeping on the plane would be nearly impossible, and I told him I could sleep anywhere, which until I'd boarded a transatlantic flight seemed to be true. I slept in a bait shop, after all.

I arrived at the hotel on the Bergen harbor at Norway's seven-thirty p.m., my ten-thirty a.m. I think the date was August 30th, somewhere. Anyway, I'd planned on arriving on the thirtieth. I was all kinds of screwed up and no closer to sleep. I ordered two cognacs through room service. If two stout drinks didn't put me down for the night, I would re-up my zombie membership.

I WOKE UP FOURTEEN hours later, only one hour before Brian's ship docked. I'd missed my chance to stroll through the city to gain equilibrium. Instead, I showered and dressed quickly. I slid open the security lock on the door. My knees turned weak. I'd longed for this day for most of my life. Now that it was here, I knew I wasn't strong enough to face Brian. I bolted the door again.

I stepped into the hotel room's closet to stand with a wooden hanger bumping the back of my head and the ironing board as a resting place for my forehead. I squeaked out a plea for help. I felt wonderfully certain I was heard. In Norway. How about that? I left the room still wobbly in the knees but not as alone as I had once felt.

In the lobby I asked for directions from a blond-haired god at the concierge desk. He spoke unaccented English, which, truthfully, disappointed me. Since I'd endured a long flight, I felt entitled to experience the exotic. My disappointment didn't last long. The concierge had me believing I was the queen of

Norway with his blue-eyed attention. He'd probably learned how to coronate women in concierge school.

"Don't panic," he said. "If your brother is on the crew, he'll have lots to do before he disembarks. You probably won't see him until later tonight. Is there anything I could do for you to make your wait more pleasant?"

I spoke as if I'd swallowed my tongue. "Could you point me toward the terminal?"

"Have you had breakfast?"

"I haven't seen my brother in seventeen years." I had no idea why I thought this beautiful specimen of Scandinavian manhood needed to know anything about my brother's absence.

He picked up the telephone. "Bring a take-away breakfast, ASAP." He put his hand over the receiver. "Do you drink coffee?"

At the mention of coffee, weariness sat on my shoulders like a gorilla. "Yes. Black. Huge."

Once the concierge hung up the phone, he opened a map, drew an X where the hotel stood, and highlighted the route to the terminal. "I could call you a taxi, but the walk is lovely. The fresh air and sunshine will help you adapt to the time change. You should arrive at the terminal in about ten minutes."

I instinctively looked at the watch I never wore.

"You have plenty of time," he said through a reassuring smile. A man dressed all in white delivered a bag with the hotel's embossed gold insignia. "Ah, and here's your breakfast. Good luck to you."

With his cheerful dismissal, I was off to find the terminal. I had slept fourteen hours, but I looked at the world with rheumy eyes that longed to close for a few more minutes. In spite of the view of Bergen I'd stored away from Brian's postcard, the cacophony of color insulted my tired eyes. The houses and shops stood boldly like the tips of brand new crayons. The sky spread every bit as blue as the postcard's sky, and the lawns sparkled a deep emerald. I pulled my hoodie up against the onshore breeze. I longed for Ginny's watermelon socks. I walked faster.

The scent of the sea struck me as very friendly and familiar—salt, fresh and musty, old and new, home. If I closed my eyes, I could have been standing at the end of the pier. The gulls squawked. A shorebird whistled sharply. The smells and the sounds offered enough confidence for me to put one foot in front of the other.

I walked on a broad sidewalk of cobbles past quaint stores and small parks blooming with vivid pinks and yellows and purples. Beyond the park a stone wall rose, very worn yet sturdy. I wanted to lean against the stones to absorb its warmth like a lizard.

No time for slacking. Brian was coming. Maybe. I walked on.

Huge ships awaiting their cargo parked along the quay. I snapped pictures on Tim's cell phone—he declared mine unfit for international travel—every few steps. Maybe I should have asked him for five reasons he found me lovable. I worried he couldn't think of ten.

I didn't have time to ponder my misjudgment. I arrived at the terminal in much less than ten minutes, so I asked a uniformed man eating a pastry if I was in the right place. He brushed crumbs from his mustache before answering. "Every cruise ship disembarks right through those doors. You're definitely in the right place, young lady."

I settled in a terminal chair. I winced at the blinking sea outside the floor-to-ceiling windows. Arthritic fingers of land rose in the distance, sheltering the harbor from the North Sea. I admit to reading about the harbor on Wikipedia while Ashley had stocked the freezer case, which now seemed like another lifetime ago. I opened the coffee, hoping its magic would prepare me for what lay ahead.

I woke up to the sound of suitcases rolling across the tiled lobby, exuberant goodbyes, and promises to stay in touch. I sat up and swiped drool off my cheek. The clock on the wall confirmed the hulking ship filling the windows with sparkling white was Brian's.

In a panic I realized I didn't know what Brian looked like as a man. He'd been shy of his sixteenth birthday when he took off. I remembered a boy with hands and feet like a clown. He could walk right past me, and I would never know.

I fished a pen from the bottom of my purse and rummaged through a nearby trashcan for cardboard. I wrote: "Brian Archer, San Clemente, CA" in anemic blue ink. I scribbled each letter darker, while scanning the rush of people coming through the doors.

Brian? Hello? Is that you? Have you grown nose hair? Do your eyebrows connect in the middle?

The tension of not knowing where Brian had been and why he hadn't bothered to contact us had ripened like an angry pimple that needed to be popped. Only hearing the story from him would bring relief.

I lifted the sign over my head and stood directly in front of the double doors, where cruise ship passengers entered the terminal from the ship. Some smiled. Others grumbled as they parted to walk around me. I envied all of them their loose gaits and relaxed shoulders.

The rush turned sporadic. The lessening crowd made seeing each face much easier, but Brian hadn't walked by. At least, I didn't think he had. Not many of the passengers were in their early thirties. Most wore sensible shoes and Garanimals for adults. Not one person in a crew uniform had walked past. I expected the likes of *The Love Boat* crew, my only experience with anything related to cruise ships.

When twilight waned into dusk, I stepped outside the doors

of the terminal, where signs forbade anyone but passengers and crew. I breathed deeply of the sea air, hoping the positive ions would refresh me for a night of examining faces and doubting my ability to recognize my own brother.

As the sky inked itself toward blackness, the planets illuminated odd points of the sky, and then the first far-northern stars spilled like salt across the celestial sphere. I recognized a few constellations, but they leaned at uncommon angles. I'd never given the stars much thought. Now that they side-stepped their positions, they accused me of trespassing.

I didn't belong in Norway.

What an idiot I'd been to think I could find Brian.

He did not want to be found.

Well, too bad for him.

A new wave of people pushed through the terminal doors, and I stood taller to study their faces and to hold the sign. This group laughed heartily and called to one another. They hefted stuffed duffels, lit cigarettes, and made plans to join up later. Not one of them used a walker. This had to be crew. I stepped in front of the herd to flash the sign. They laughed and shook their heads.

"Come get a drink with us, pretty lady," said one dark-skinned boy with a mysterious accent.

"Do you know a Brian on this ship?"

He stopped, put a finger to his chin. "I could. Or not. There are so many."

I shooed the man away and turned my sign back to the doors. And waited. From hunger and weariness I sagged to the floor. I fell asleep sitting with my head propped on my hand and awoke with a start at the shouts of more crew members disembarking. This group looked foreign. Slender faced. Shadowed eyes. European—Northern? Southern? Eastern? Maybe North African. What did I know? All looked as though they had been scrubbed for Sunday school.

None of them were Brian.

I couldn't sit there forever. I would wait until midnight, a half hour, and call a taxi—Tim would insist—to take me back to the hotel.

I woke to someone nudging my toe. "What are you doing here?" The voice sounded perturbed. He sounded like Brian.

I stood up as straight as a fence post to look at the man with the voice of my brother. But he didn't look like Brian, except for the eyes. If this were my brother, his cheeks had rounded out, softening the edge of his jaw and chin. His hair had darkened. He wore it shorter. His hairline, unlike Dad's, stood its ground. Muscles plumped his arms and broadened his shoulders. A tuft of chest hair peeked from his collar.

"Brian?"

He shrugged. "Who else?"

He had my muddled thinking—lack of sleep and all those faces—to thank. Otherwise my knee to his groin would have been a quick answer to his condescension. The stronger impulse was to throw my arms around him. Let's blame that on jet lag. I stuffed my hands into my pockets.

He shook his head. "I should have transferred sooner."

"You've been gone a long time," I said, fighting to keep an accusatory edge from my voice. My original goals were moot. This I saw in the tension around Brian's eyes, the way his shoulders reached for his ears.

"I'm not going back."

Not ever? "Would you consider a short visit?"

"I don't have time." He turned and strode toward the exit.

I ran after him. Boundaries voiced or implied did not apply after seventeen years and one transatlantic flight. And waiting for him to jump into the game didn't appeal either. I tugged at his arm and pleaded for a chance to talk.

He shook my hand free, stopped to look down on me. When had he gotten so tall? "Jenna, I'm happy. Home made me miserable. I won't go there. Nothing you could say will change my mind. Besides, I was the problem, wasn't I? I drove Dad to the brink. Mom, she did her best to shelter me. The job proved too much for her. I could see that. You know things are better without me."

The apartment definitely got quieter without Brian. From the outside we looked like a united family, clinging to one another in our time of grief. Underneath, the buzz of tension had only intensified. Although no one said the words, each of us blamed the other for Brian's disappearance and swallowed our own pills of regret.

And he'd never been happy? That stung. Hadn't he and I schemed together? Hadn't we shared secrets and dreams? Hadn't we laughed ourselves stupid with the help of one joint? That was what brothers and sisters did. Wasn't that fun? I watched as he pushed through the doors and faded into the night.

The heat rose from my gut, through my chest, and broke a sweat on my brow. The turd was walking away from me. Guilt over leaving him alone on the bus had cemented me in place for nearly two decades. He could simply turn and walk away from me.

I dropped everything and ran with arms pumping toward the doors. I hit with enough force to bounce the door back at me. I jumped aside to run harder. Ahead, on the very same sidewalk I'd taken along the quay, Brian walked jauntily.

I didn't slow down as I drew nearer. I jumped onto his back and wrapped my arms around his neck and my legs around his thighs. A long list of deficiencies followed my name, but I was strong. He would talk to me, and he would hear what I had to say.

"Jenna! Get off!" He clawed at my arms and spun around. I closed my eyes against dizziness.

I yelled into his ear. "Mom is crazy with grief over you.

And I mean completely unhinged."

"Jenna. Off."

"She hasn't left the apartment in years—not willingly, not comfortably. She's afraid she'll miss you."

"I. Can't. Breathe."

Now he knew how I'd felt for seventeen years. I squeezed harder and his knees buckled. "You left us to decay, Brian. Nothing is better without you, not one solitary thing."

He fell to his face, with me in tow, in a great expulsion of air. "My God, you're crazy. Get off of me!" He tried to roll me off, but my legs still clamped his legs like a vice. My knees throbbed from our fall to the cobbles.

"You owe me one conversation, Brian. One stinkin' conversation." Then I did the last thing I wanted: I cried like a baby. "Please, Brian. Please. Talk to me. I've missed you."

His body relaxed. "Get off and we'll talk." He executed some impressive moves to undo our tangled limbs. He rose to his feet first and offered a hand. When we finally stood face to face, Brian was laughing. "You haven't changed at all. You're still scrappier than any guy I've ever known. Do men fear you?"

"Not a topic for discussion," I said, breathing hard.

Backlit from a streetlight, I could not read his expression. He could have been sneering or queasy. "You've seen me. I'm alive, gainfully employed—Dad will like that—and living life on my own terms. Mom can go back to her double life. You can do whatever you do. That should make everyone happy."

"I have questions, Brian." When I found out all I wanted to know, he would—what?—follow me back to San Clemente? Never. Perhaps transferring the agony of guilt I carried onto his shoulders would be enough. But I doubted that would happen either.

He stepped back. "I won't be interrogated."

"Of course not." Oh, yes, you will!

"I know a bar," he said and started walking.

"My hotel is that way, The Haven-something or other."

"The Clarion. Don't worry, I'll get you there."

I felt too light and unencumbered. I'd dropped everything to chase after him. "We have to go back to the terminal. I left my purse."

To my surprise, he stopped, turned around, and walked beside me. "You're limping."

My right knee pressed against the seams of my pants. "I fell pretty hard."

He put his arm out to stop me. "Wait here. I'll get your stuff and be right back." I must have looked doubtful because he dropped his duffel at my feet as collateral. "I'll be right back."

I watched him trot across the street and disappear into the terminal. I nudged his duffel. His whole life was in there. Surely, he would come back. Surely. The lights inside the terminal went dark.

A taxi crawled by, looking for a fare.

The streetlight hummed. Dimmed.

My knee throbbed.

I stood there until the terminal's crew came out with arms weighted by lunch boxes and newspapers. The tallest uniformed man locked the door. His team walked away from me toward the town's center.

Brian wasn't coming back.

I hefted his duffel and limped back to the hotel. The blonde god had been replaced by an officious woman with draped eyes and hair like steel wool. She called a bell hop to carry the duffel. Inside my room, I sat on the bed and stared at the bag until my vision blurred.

How did I ever think I could convince Brian to reconnect with us? In hindsight, the task seemed gargantuan. Impossible. Futile. If he'd wanted to be part of the family, he knew the way home, didn't he? He did. He definitely knew the way home.

The weight of thousands of past days and all the days to come settled on my shoulders. I shaped a bag of ice around my knee, sunk into the pillows, and nestled under the comforter. Almost instantly, the nonsensical half dreams of twilight sleep beckoned me deeper. I saw no reason not to follow.

THE CONTENTS OF BRIAN'S duffel covered the second bed in the hotel room. He sure liked his fancy underwear. I didn't want to think why. I unzipped his shaving kit. He used a straight razor, which seemed awfully risky for smooth cheeks, especially a smooth neck. He'd also developed a taste for Nike sportswear and Hawaiian shirts, where he preferred his dancing girls in coconuts. And there was a pirate costume, complete with a stuffed parrot. No pictures or books. No camera with tale-tell pictures. Not even a to-do list. Three pairs of athletic shoes. About four dozen pairs of socks. A Walkman with a Bee Gees CD. I didn't find one clue to reveal who my brother had become. There was absolutely and positively nothing to tell Mom about her son.

I could always lie.

"Mom," I would say, "Brian is a fun guy, incredibly well-liked by everyone on the ship. He feels terrible—he cried, actually—about skipping out on us and all the heartache he's caused. He would come home, but he can't bear to see the disappointment on your face. I tried to tell him differently. He just couldn't believe you've forgiven him.

"His psychiatrist is part of the problem, Mom. He insists Brian commit himself to a facility for six years of therapy and rehabilitation. He sees no other way for Brian to become any kind of man at all. He's a jerk of the most colossal proportions. That's the official diagnosis, by the way. And six years may not be enough. More like a century and there are no guarantees."

I couldn't even lie nicely about Brian.

I stuffed his belongings back into the duffel and wrote him

a note on hotel stationary to tuck in one of his shoes. I apologized for the tackle and promised to leave him alone. Actually, the thought of his face soured my stomach.

The bell hop came within a minute of my call. I toed the duffel. "My brother will probably be by looking for this. Is there somewhere you can store it?" As if a duffel bag the size of a small car was typical fare, the bell hop hoisted it onto the cart and left for the elevators. Too late I remembered to tip the guy.

My plane was to leave the next morning. When Tim had run me through the itinerary, he suggested Brian and I could find a park and catch up. I'd let myself picture Brian and me reminiscing over the bookmarks of our lives, sitting under a shade tree. Memories, time, and anything resembling a schedule now unwound before me into a shapeless tangle.

Could I get an early flight home?

What was the rush?

The bed was soft. Brian had cleared my schedule of familial obligations. This was my vacation, pitiful though it was. I closed my eyes.

I woke to a soft knock on the door.

"Jenna?"

I opened the door to find Brian holding my purse at arm's length. I did not reach for it. "Jenna, you shouldn't carry your passport with you unless you wear it around your neck. It's not safe. Purses get nipped all the time."

"Thanks."

"You don't want to mess with the embassies."

"I'll remember that."

"Have the concierge print your boarding pass. You'll be glad you did."

"Brian, what are you doing here?"

He dropped his arm to his side. "How about lunch?"

"I haven't had breakfast."

"It's nearly two. A beer?"

I snatched my purse from his hands, dug for my passport, and slid it into my bra. "Coffee."

As we walked along narrow streets, more like alleys, I watched Brian for any signs of bolting. There are just so many times a person can be left in the dust. I'd reached my limit.

He walked slightly ahead of me, turning back every few feet to see if I was still there. I did not reassure him with a smile. Brian looked as if he wanted to say something. I was determined not to make that easy. I'd been dreaming of this moment for seventeen years, and, so far, nothing had happened as I'd played out, and I could be as pessimistic as anyone.

He stopped in front of a heavy wooden door. "How's your knee?"

"Bruised. The swelling's down, though."

"Good." He pushed open the door.

The bartender raised a hand to him. "Bro." Such a sparse greeting was reserved for friends who didn't need to say much or talk about the weather.

"Are you sure you don't want a beer?" Brian asked me.

My skin vibrated with fatigue, not from loss of sleep but from an emotional marathon that had left me empty. "Coffee." The moment called for alertness, not sedation. "Make it a tall one, please," I said to the bartender.

We sat at a table near the back, where the only light came from beer signs. "By the time I get off the ship, I'm ready for a little quiet. You can answer just so many questions about the fjords and the oil platforms. This is my home away from home in the North Atlantic."

The bartender brought our beverages. Brian took a long pull on his beer and stared at its froth. "I started a million letters," he said. "I even dialed our number. My reasons for leaving were good ones. I don't have to explain myself. You were there, right? My reasons for staying away are much more complicated."

I thought of Amy and the shame that kept her from coming home to Tim and his parents. "You're much more welcome than you can imagine."

He looked at me. "Mom would suffocate me. Dad...I would rather not find out."

"You could set boundaries, tell them what's okay to talk about and what's not."

"And this is something that's worked for you?"

My heart sagged. "You know it hasn't."

"I can't do it, Jen. I wish I could. I wish I could show up and change everything, give you the freedom you want. Things would only be worse when I left again."

"Do you have to leave? I mean, there's no law saying you can't find a job in Orange County and come home for Sunday dinners."

Brian blinked a few times. "This is my life. I'm good at what I do. The passengers like me. I get along with my shipmates. I've been able to save up a good chunk of change. No one expects very much from me, just that I do my job well. If I get a better offer from another line, no one gets their feelings hurt. I leave on good terms with an invitation to return. You can't ask for much more than that."

Were slick exits and re-entries enough? To show him the other side of that question, I told him about Mom's vigil, how she had pulled ever tighter on the belt that held up her life. And mine. Dad's story was much easier to tell. He'd gone crazy for telephones and other women. Also that he'd mellowed and seemed to be happy with Sally.

"Telephones?"

"Enough for a museum."

"That's weird."

"You don't know the half of it."

"And you? How are you?"

"I'm…" I longed to torture Brian with the stunning details of how living life on his terms had robbed me of a future, but I wasn't sure Brian would care. I couldn't blame him for my unhappiness. I'd managed my misery fine without him. I needed him to give us enough of himself to open the door to a new kind of happiness, especially for Mom and me. I took Tim's cell from my purse.

"I'm most interested in helping Mom. In truth, doing so will get me back into life. You could help."

He pushed his chair back from the table. "I'm not like that, Jenna."

"I agree," I said, laying my fingers lightly on his hand. "I'm not like that either, not really. And I'm right there."

He rubbed his face. "Then why did you come?"

My reasons for finding Brian had changed since I'd boarded the plane in Los Angeles. Even earlier, really. I knew when Brian had trusted his fate to the likes of Jerry that he wouldn't come home. Brian could not change the trajectory of my life or yank Mom back from the brink or give our Tin Woodsman of a father a heart. So why had I traveled across the world to see him?

"I came because only you can speak with authority about your happiness and health. Hearing from you might be enough to start Mom toward a better place."

"Which would help you?" he asked with a sardonic smile. I wanted to smack him.

"Maybe. I have other options." One thing I'd learned about guys who lived life on their own terms—as this seemed to be the kind of guy I'd repeatedly fallen for—was they liked to be noticed to the point of worship. I leaned toward Brian, lowered my voice. I picked through the truths about the last seventeen years and fought against the emotion those truths flamed. "Brian, it is good to see you. You've become a man outside the family's scrutiny or help. Doing so couldn't have been easy.

You look wonderful. And you're happy. That pretty much makes you the winner. I'm glad for you. I've also missed you."

He finished off his beer in a swig and backhanded his mouth. He smiled like a demigod. "You're buttering me up."

"We're older. We don't have to posture for one another. I'm only saying what I've wanted to say for a long time."

Brian studied my face. Was he seeing my gray hair? Counting my freckles? Looking for the unabridged truth?

"I thought you'd be fat with lots of kids by now," he said.

"I'm glad you've been thinking of me."

"What do you want? What's with the phone? I'm not calling the folks."

With all of the mental rehearsing I'd done of this moment, nothing had prepared me for Brian's dismissiveness. We'd been confidants, coconspirators, sworn enemies of our parents. We'd been as much like friends as a brother and sister could be. Could he still see the world through a fifteen-year-old's eyes? Who could look good through that sort of angst?

I tapped a few icons and arrows to get to the recorder function on Tim's phone. "Let me interview you."

"What kinds of questions?"

"There are things I really don't care to know about you, Brian, especially if we part ways after today. I don't need extra stuff rattling around in my head. I have plenty of my own junk. But if we could talk about some of the things you've seen on your travels, if you would be willing to show even the smallest sliver of your life, I think that might be enough."

"And I should be willing to do this because...?"

"Because I'm not asking much, not really. Just a few minutes of your time, nothing personal. Your secrets are yours to keep."

Brian looked over his shoulder to the bar and raised a finger. The barkeep filled a glass and brought the beer to the table. The two fist bumped. Blessedly, the barkeep also brought the coffee pot. He poured the black brew to the top of my cup and winked. Oh brother.

"Well?" I prompted when the bartender had stepped behind the counter.

"Sure. Why not?"

I tapped on the record button. "Brian," I said in my chirpiest top-of-the-morning voice, "what is the most amazing thing you've seen in your travels around the world?"

Brian sat straighter and looked around to see who might be listening in. Only a half-dozen people scattered about the bar, none of them taking notice of us. He reflected back my cheerfulness. "First, Jenna, it's good to see you. I can trust you'll say hello to the folks for me?"

"Of course." Gag.

"Your question isn't as easy as you might think. I've seen a lot since I left home, and I've made some great friends all over the world."

"Let me make this easier on you. Is there any one place you've visited you could recommend for a vacation?"

Brian played the travel agent from then on. He convinced me to visit at least five destinations on each continent, excluding Antarctica. He sounded genuinely enthusiastic and excited about his life. I prayed this proved to be the healing balm Mom and Dad needed. It would have to do.

I noticed a low-battery warning on the phone. "I see you're looking at your watch. We're both heading out later. Thank you so much for answering my questions. Is there anything I missed?"

Brian's head popped up. I turned the recorder off. "I'm sorry, Brian. Do you want to end the recording there?"

"No, I should answer your question. I froze for a minute. Any ideas?"

You could tell Mom you love her, which could be a lie or simply a benevolent misdirection. From the way his eyes flitted to every corner of the bar, Brian was a caged animal in that moment. I put the key in the lock. "This is all about you, Brian."

He splayed his hands before him and took a deep breath. "Okay, I think I'm ready."

I tapped the record button.

"I should tell Mom about a lady on the island of Moorea. She had a figure like a barn, but she painted beach scenes inside the lids of cigar boxes just like Mom, only Mom's are much better." He looked up at me, biting his lower lip. "That's all."

Brian walked me to the hotel. The air had cooled and thickened into a moist soup. "So, come on, tell me what you're really up to?" he said.

"Me?" I refused to give Brian the satisfaction of my lost life. He didn't want to know, not really. Besides, I wasn't feeling quite so miserable after seeing him, the real him, again. He'd composed his exit from our lives just fine. "I'm in transition."

Before we said goodbye, we posed for a selfie, all smiles and wasn't this great.

I wanted the recording to flip a switch in Mom. I dared not consider which one.

34

A jet plane is not a transporter beam. There is no swirling of glitter and—*poof!*—you've arrived. No, I landed at home in the same mess I'd left.

I stood across Avenida Victoria, studying the front of the bait shop, the telephony, and the stacked apartments with eyes that had, for a short time, broken the bounds of my culture and country. Evidently, flying 5,000 miles—not even halfway around the world—had reminded me why I'd done such a crazy thing. The bait shop and telephony were no place to call home.

Paying Ashley and chasing after my brother, however, had emptied my savings account. That left exactly nothing to make a move. Thinking about the months and years it would take to rebuild my stash brought tears to my eyes. I swiped at them, angry at my weakness.

I would begin again. I would hoard pennies and continue to tempt Mom back into the world. At the intersection of Mom-can-stand-on-her-own and first-and-last-month's rent, there would be a place for me. There *had* to be a place for me.

First things first. With no small sense of doom, I climbed the steps and let myself into the apartment to tell Mom about my visit with Brian. Inside, the air of the apartment squeezed me. I opened the glass door to welcome a cleansing rush of sea air.

"Mom?"

Half-eaten frozen food trays filled the table beside Mom's recliner, along with cups, glasses, and bottles of water, all untouched. A paused movie—Meryl Streep looking into the camera—filled the TV screen. From the count of food trays, Dad had given up on Mom about midway through my absence. Not much had begun and nothing was finished.

My life and homecoming had swung far afield of anything Rockwell ever created, but I could not stop myself. I turned the bedroom doorknob slowly. The optimist in me believed Mom simply slept a dreamer's sort of sleep. Behind the closed door, however, Mom lay under the window in a tight knot.

Oh God.

I checked her pulse. Her heart beat a steady rhythm. I expelled a trapped breath.

Getting her into bed required serious wangling. Once safely deposited between the sheets, I wiped Mom's face and hands with a cool cloth, pushed damp bangs off her forehead, and counted the Xanax remaining in the bottle, which set off an alarm.

I called Dad.

He was driving toward John Wayne Airport to join Sally in Puerta Vallarta. He spoke vaguely of his time with Mom—she wouldn't cooperate; nothing seemed to calm her; she was ungrateful.

"When did you last see her?"

"You're breaking up."

Cells made the untethered life so convenient. "When. Did. You. Last. See. Her?"

"It's been…awhile."

"She only has twelve Xanax left. Does that seem right?"

"She takes that stuff like candy."

"Dad. Please. Does twelve seem right to you?"

I heard him muttering, probably counting off the days, doing the math, estimating. "She may have taken an extra dose, maybe two, nothing to worry about."

"Thanks, Dad, have a fabulous time." I hung up before he

had a chance to opine on Mom's behavior. Funny he hadn't asked about Brian, not funny in a ha-ha way but in a heart-crunching way. Nothing new or terribly surprising there.

I didn't want to stray too far from Mom, so I did a quick check with Ashley to see how things had gone in my absence. "Your dad's bossy," she said as she handed an iced mocha to a customer. She leaned against the counter and looked at her shoes. "My parents want this to be my last day."

"I'm sorry I put you in a tough situation."

She looked up. "Did you find your brother?"

And so, Ashley heard the story first.

"Have you told your mom?"

I ran upstairs to find Mom was still breathing. I washed the dishes, took out the trash, and ran the vacuum cleaner. Before heading up to Larice's, I felt Mom's pulse again. I deliberated about calling the EMTs, but if she took extra Xanax to calm herself, a trip to the hospital would only land her in the psych ward. And I wasn't sure our Band-Aid station of a hospital even had a psych ward. However she'd dosed herself, her carelessness with meds felt like my punishment for daring to have a life. I should have spent my free hours more extravagantly.

I SHOWED LARICE THE picture of me and Brian.

"He's gotten good looking."

"You won't think so after you hear him talk."

Larice turned off the recording after a few questions. "Did he ask about his family? Does he ever mention coming home?"

"He's not that kind of person," I said, and the truth of my words sapped the last bit of energy I owned.

Larice pushed the cell toward me. "How did you keep from ripping his eyeballs from his skull?"

The thought had crossed my mind. "He gave me all he could. Drinking beer and talking about his travels was a heroic effort for Brian. He does say he likes Mom's paintings better than some lady's in Moorea. She might find that warming."

"Well then, we should thank him for saving us a trip to Tahiti, the toad."

Larice's apartment, with its calming colors and purging light, beckoned me to curl up on her couch and sleep for a day or two. "I have to get back to Mom. If she doesn't wake up soon, I'll take her to the ER."

Larice laid her warm hand on my arm. "I met Tim."

Heat rose to my shoulders, neck, and face. "How did that happen?"

"Relax. You didn't tell me where you were going. Your father looked like he'd swallowed a bug every time I asked about you, and your mom wouldn't answer the door. I got worried. Taylor and I did a little cyber investigating and found Tim within minutes. He knew everything. I, your best friend in the world, knew nothing. I'm carefully considering forgiving you, yet again." Larice leveled her gaze on me. "Have you seen him yet?"

"I'm not quite sure what to do about Tim."

"Well, he certainly likes you. And he's so cute. What's there to be sure about? Is he a mass murderer? A scam artist? Does he kick dogs? No, he's a very nice man with a steady job who thinks you're the sun, the moon, and the stars. What are you waiting for?" She squeezed my arm. "Love him back, Jenna. He's fabulous."

"It hasn't been a year."

"Are you kidding me? Love him back. Now."

MOM WAS SITTING IN her recliner when I returned to the apartment. She held a full glass of water and stared out the window. Her hair didn't move in the breeze. That meant more wheedling on my part to get her into the shower.

"Did you find him?"

Dad had never been able to keep a secret. How could I expect him to stay mum about the great Brian hunt? "Yes, I saw him in Norway."

"Norway," she expelled with a breath and turned her eyes on me. The full cost of loving a displaced child contorted her face. "Is he all right?"

I'd determined on the long flight home to keep my answers about Brian nonjudgmental and brief but true. "He seems happy."

"And healthy?"

I sat on the arm of the recliner and pulled Tim's phone from my pocket. "I have a picture."

Mom gasped when she saw Brian. "He looks exactly like..."

Like Kevin. "He's definitely a man. Gone are his scrawny arms and outsized hands and feet."

"Did he explain...?"

I couldn't tell her how Brian held both her and Dad in utter contempt or the pathetic sense of self-sacrifice he'd voiced. "I recorded an interview. He's been everywhere. He loves to talk about the things he's seen." I reached for Tim's phone in her hands. "I could play it for you."

She held the phone to her heart. "Jenna, I don't like the way this is sounding. Is he coming back, or did you scare him away forever?"

"Mom—"

"You told him I was crazy, didn't you?"

"I told him you missed him." Did I?

"You're lying! You warned him off, told him I'd lost my marbles, become a pathetic scab of a person. You are the last person I would have sent to find him."

I lowered my voice to a rehearsed place of calm. "You can hear everything in the recording." She loosened her grip on the phone. I tapped an icon and then the recording's title. I was about to tap the blue arrow when Mom grabbed the phone from my hands and threw it out the door to the balcony, where the cell skidded to the edge and disappeared.

I arrived to the railing in time to see a square-built teen with a pimply back stoop to pick up the cell. I called down to him, "That's mine."

He looked up, showed me the cracked screen. "Bummer."

Inside, Mom sat with wide, saturated eyes, her hands to her mouth. "I'm so sorry, Jenna."

I pulled Mom to my chest. "Don't worry, Mom. Those phones are cheaper by the dozen. Are you okay?" I didn't offer her more Xanax. She seemed calm, now that she knew a measure of truth about her caitiff (new word: a base, despicable person) son.

"I don't know what happened."

"Mom, listen, everything's okay. But I have to go get the cell and help Ashley with the rush."

"Who?"

"The girl who works in the bait shop. Today's her last day." From the closed-door look in her eyes, Mom had receded to a safe place. "I'll be gone about an hour. Do you have what you need?" I didn't expect an answer. I inventoried the essentials on the end table—remote, water, catalogs, a bowl of roasted almonds.

"I could use a blanket," she said.

I tucked Mom in and collected the cell from the teen. "I powered it up, ma'am," he said. "My brother used plastic wrap to hold his screen together, but his didn't look so bad as this. I sure hope you got insurance."

I carried the phone into the bait shop as if carrying a fragile heirloom on a teeny tiny tray. Ashley groaned when I laid the phone on the counter. "You have insurance, right?"

"It's not mine."

"That's gotta suck."

More than she knew. I wanted to see Tim, but not to tell him I'd killed his cell. My time with my brother had come dangerously close to what he'd expected from Amy— knowledge but not connectedness, heartbreak for him and his parents. Tim and Amy, however, had accomplished their happy ending.

Tim wouldn't harangue me about a shattered cell, not because he was reckless about his belongings. Tim wasn't reckless about anything, except his heart. I should have stopped by his house on my way home from the airport. He'd asked me to do just that through texts, and the many voicemails he'd left on the cell.

The problem was me. I wanted Tim to see me as responsible and capable, an equal partner, not a project. Seeing Mom folded into a heap had undone the sense of accomplishment I'd felt finding Brian. Tim would have to settle for a phone call after I closed the bait shop for the night. I couldn't leave Mom, not yet. She'd taken a hard blow.

"HOW'S YOUR MOM TAKING the news about Brian?"

I was learning a lot about people by what questions they asked. Tim valued family and understood the tremendous burden Mom's mental state had become.

"She threw your cell out the door. I'm so sorry."

"Do you want me to come over?"

"Mom's on the edge. And I'm exhausted. Can you give me a few days? There's so much to tell you." And I needed time to process how I felt about all of it.

His voice stepped away from me. "Sure."

"I need time, that's all—for Mom, to gather my wits, to get the bait shop back in order. I'm really sorry about the cell."

"Take all the time you need. And don't even think about the cell. I have insurance."

Of course he had insurance.

35

With Ashley back in school and Dad off to points unknown, I soldiered on with the bait shop, but I used every spare moment to dismantle the telephony. There would be no more voices to tether people to the past.

I dusted and bubble-wrapped each telephone before taping the box lids closed. I even labeled the boxes with everything Dad would need to list the telephones on eBay. The finality of all those sealed boxes proved intoxicating. I pictured a French bakery in the space with a glass case filled with fruit tarts and buttery cookies. A boutique or a surfboard shop would work too, anything other than the telephony.

A rap on the window made me jump. There was Tim, leaning on his crutches, looking real good but not particularly happy. Maybe I'd finally stepped past the line with Tim. The thought of his disapproval deflated me.

"Hey," I said, wiping grime onto my sweatpants. I realized with a start that Tim needed a place to sit. I ushered him into what remained of the telephony, where I pushed aside several boxes to release the desk chair. I wheeled the lumpy-seated thing to him, making sure he faced the impressive fortress of boxed telephones I'd built. "Can I get you something to drink? A burrito? Lip balm? You look really good."

"You've been back a week. I thought I'd see you before now." He said this as if commenting on a rise in gas prices, painful but not unexpected.

I filled him in on how Mom had come unhinged listening to Brian talk blithely about his world travels without one mention of ever coming home.

"Your brother is an ass."

To my utter surprise, I came to Brian's defense. "The recording was my idea. I asked him to tell the folks about his world travels. I should have asked him to talk to Mom."

"He's not a puppet, Jenna. He's a grown man. He could have said anything he wanted. He made the recording about himself, and I'm not saying what he did was a bad thing.

"Your mom learned from her son's lips how self-absorbed he's become. I can't imagine anything more painful. But at least she knows the truth. Dreams can be prisons."

True enough. I'd been hammering away at a rock pile most of my life, but I didn't want anyone rescuing me either. But why in the world not? I wished I knew the answer.

"I won't help unless you want me to."

Tim knew me far too well. "You wouldn't see me as a damsel in distress, if you knew my part in Brian's disappearance."

"Whatever role you played—at age seventeen—doesn't exempt you from being loved or supported, neither of which have anything to do with being rescued. I'm no Prince Charming, but I can offer you a safe place to land at the end of the day. Can you see yourself in a place like that, Jenna?"

To make sure Tim knew exactly who he offered to catch, I told him all about seducing Ryan in the hills to win a bet with Larice. "If I had been on the bus with Brian, we would have walked right past Jerry's house and on to the apartment. No police. No reporters. No scooping Mom up to face each day."

Tim didn't blink. "Brian would have left anyway, some other day. Most likely, he'd been thinking about leaving for a long time. You said your dad held him to an unreasonable standard, that your mom practically smothered him. Brian's smart. He made his exit look like his family had let him down. That way he wouldn't have to blame himself or feel obligated to keep in touch."

Brian had talked about running away lots of times. I'd never taken him seriously. He was too young to get a job, and he looked even younger. The minute his stomach grumbled, he would have run home, or so I thought.

"You have nothing to prove to me." He pulled a tightly folded paper from his pocket. "You asked me for ten reasons why loving you is a good idea. It's enough for me that you're you, that your heart's beating, your lungs are pumping, that you're beautiful and far too vulnerable." He smoothed the folds of the paper against his thigh. "I came up with many more than ten, but knew you wouldn't stand still for such excess, so I highlighted my favorites. Are you ready?"

There was no less romantic place in the world than the telephony. And I was a mess. Dust stuck to my skin, and I could smell myself. On the other hand, I'd made an important step by boxing up the telephones. I'd begun to breathe easier. There would be no more telephone calls to remind me how careless I'd been.

And Tim. He denied being a Prince Charming, but he'd already saved me. Out of curiosity more than believing he could pull off those ten rock-solid reasons, I pulled a box from under the front window and sat in front of him. "I'm ready."

"Good. Number one: Jenna is unflinching in her kindness toward people caught in highly improbable situations."

"You mean the telephony?" How could anyone not be kind to the regulars? They'd been gobsmacked by their pasts. Smothering them with kindness was my only option.

He continued, "The regulars came in here completely vulnerable. You made us welcome, acted as if nothing out of the ordinary happened here. Doing so required tons of empathy and compassion. I'm not the only person who noticed."

And now the telephony was gone, the room completely emptied of the meddling telephones. On to the ordinary for me, like falling in love with a man who made lists about my disparate set of qualifications. I deserved that kind of goodness, didn't I? But then, there was Mom. "I can't consider the future with Mom in such a bad place."

Tim nodded and smiled knowingly. "You're thinking of taking care of her alone." His smile faded. "You don't have to be alone anymore."

I rose to pace in front of Tim. "We're quite the package, Mom and me. Am I worth the hassle? I want you to really think about this." I stopped, opened my hands to him, prayed he would think I was.

"I'm more calculating than you give me credit for. Can I continue?"

I sat down, resigned to hear what Tim had written. He ran a finger down the list, but I still caressed the idea that I wouldn't be alone. From the outside, I hadn't been alone, not ever. There had been Mom and Dad, the fishermen, the regulars, the inland shoppers. But their preoccupations had left me terribly alone.

I didn't need to hear anything else, but Tim had worked hard on his list. I owed him a good listen. "Please continue."

"Number two." He stopped, looked up. "I'm sorry I have to read these. I don't want to mess up. Number two: Jenna revealed my true shallowness without crushing me."

"When did I do that?"

"I couldn't think of Amy as a drug addict and love her."

"Tim, you wanted to save her heartache and pain."

"If I'm completely honest, I have to admit I was more interested in saving myself from regret. I brushed Amy off when we were younger. I was the older brother too busy for his sister. You convinced me we're our best selves because of the mistakes we make. That includes Amy, but it also includes me."

I did that? Maybe I did, but I needed to learn that lesson more than Tim did. All through the time of packing the boxes,

I'd written imaginary postcards to Brian. I pressed hard on a pen to write every expletive known to man as I put Brian in his place, and then I remembered the look on his face as he tried to break free from me. As far as Brian was concerned, he'd done us all a favor by slipping away. He'd made a huge sacrifice for the yelling to stop.

I squirmed under Tim's gaze. This conversation needed to be directed back into familiar territory. "I thought you'd say I have a nice butt."

He shuffled through his papers and pointed to a line of his precise printing. "Number thirty-seven."

"My butt only rates a thirty-seven?"

"I cannot tell a lie. As butts go, yours is right up there with the best. I'm aiming for the high ground here. I figured lots of guys have admired your backside. There's so much more to you. On the other hand, if you want to be loved for your butt..." He grabbed for his crutches.

I put a hand on his knee. "Your list isn't at all what I expected. Maybe one more and we could take a break?"

Tim smiled like he'd called my bluff. I'd admired similar looks of victory on many a man's face, which usually led to a frenzied and quick-to-fizzle relationship. What was I to do with a man who loved me at least thirty-seven different ways and actually wanted to marry me?

The old Jenna would have found someone with lower expectations, had some fun, and moved on to the next loser guy, eating plenty of sand along the way. The Jenna that Tim loved sat poised between running, her usual, and squirming through the list. Tim had changed the rules, upset the usual game plan. He controlled the ball.

He held up three fingers. "At this rate, we'll be at this all night. Should I continue?"

"Yes. One more, please."

"Jenna is willing to risk everything for those she loves."

"That's not exactly true. I hoped finding Brian would mean freedom for me."

"So you didn't risk arrest to find your brother? You haven't bent and twisted your life to be available to your mom? You never gave a thought to her peace of mind as you ran all over Orange County looking for the right hair dye?"

"I told you all that in confidence."

"Traveling to Norway proved costly for you in other ways, didn't it?"

Tim had watched too many courtroom dramas. "Are you a lawyer or an accountant?" A long-winded, lawyerly answer would provide time to consider his questions.

He winced. At first, I thought the reference to lawyers had offended him, but he reached for his broken ankle and his face twisted in agony. "Jenna, could I get some ice?"

I knelt beside him. "You're way past ice. Why didn't you say something?"

"I wanted to get through the list," he said through clenched teeth.

I kissed the warm place behind his ear. "I've heard enough."

He looked up. His face drained of color. I knew exactly what to ask. The nurses in post-op asked me the same question every five minutes after my rotator surgery. "The pain? On a scale from one to—?"

"Nine."

I'd been to nine on the pain scale. And then I passed out. I got Tim home and medicated. While slipping into oblivion, he asked with garbled words if he'd convinced me I was lovable.

I stayed by his bed until the time came to dose Mom. Chrissy the CNA had been replaced by Broomhilda, so I felt as good as I could leaving Tim in her very large, cell-free hands. I wanted to stay, to be there when he needed another pill and bring him scrambled eggs and toast in the morning.

Back in the bait shop, I lay in the blue light of the refrigerator cases. My air mattress already showed signs of letting me down. I didn't care. I shuffled to rearrange the way I thought about myself, trying to get Tim's picture and my picture to line up. I did not know the woman he loved, but I wanted, more than anything, to become her.

36

There are places we are not meant to visit, like viper pits and the bedroom your dad shares with his girlfriend. Against my better judgment, I followed Sally to their bedroom after she greeted me at the door.

She hefted a leopard-print suitcase onto the bed that rose high above the floor. The bedspread draped across the carpet like a bride's train, which screamed of drama. My face got hot.

The contents of Sally's suitcase heaved upward. "I hate this part. Some people loathe the preparation for a trip, getting all their traveling ducks in a row. Ducks don't scare me. It's finding a place for all the stuff I bought—and don't need and can't imagine why I ever thought I would—when I get back home."

When I'd traveled to Norway, I'd counted the days I would be gone and packed that many T-shirts and underwear. I wore the same yoga pants all five days. Everything I bought I ate. Like Sally, I wasn't afraid of ducks, but a needling dread settled over me about Dad's reaction to the U-Haul truck I'd just parked in the driveway.

Sally sorted the contents of her suitcase into three piles. She looked up. I felt like a tourist who had found her way into the White House bathroom. "You look, I don't know, worried? Afraid?"

"I made some changes while you and Dad were gone."

She gave a little hop to sit on the bed and patted the spot beside her. As unappealing as touching their bed was, I needed an ally. Sally certainly kept a smile on Dad's face. What could I lose?

I joined her, and I told her all about emptying the
telephony and filling the U-Haul—with the help of two surfers
in dire need of a year's worth of board wax—to dump in her
driveway. "I thought you'd still be in Mexico."

"You're a smart cookie. It's a sin that storefront is
collecting dust. You're sitting on a gold mine with that
location."

I expected Sally to understand my motivation. What I
hadn't expected was such enthusiastic support. I blabbered on,
"I have a new tenant, a crêperie. They're anxious to get into the
space. They've already hired a contractor. I had no choice. I
had to get the telephones out."

I actually had plenty of choice about what to do or not do
with the space, but the crêperie people came along as I was
vacuuming up the debris of years. They were nice. They had
money. It all seemed so meant-to-be.

"Of course," she said, sliding off the bed. "Do you want
me to look at the contract?"

I felt guilty about my original plan to park the truck and
run. "Maybe I should move the truck before Dad gets back."

"Don't you dare. I've parked a few trucks to get men
moving. It's a time-honored modus. You've done what you've
had to do, I believe."

"Dad won't be happy."

"No, he probably won't." She took my hand. I resisted the
urge to pull back. "Your father isn't perfect. I knew this long
before we got close. But I'm not perfect either." She waved a
hand over her suitcase. "This isn't the only baggage I carry
around."

Sally plucked a dress from her suitcase. Her admission
made her seem vulnerable to Dad. I didn't want her hurt
because of my actions. "I'm willing to stay here until Dad gets
back. I never intended for you to absorb his anger."

Sally dismissed my offer with a shake of her head. "Your

father has a temper on him. He's tried to fling it around here. I suppose he's made a habit of using his voice and his stature, since that's what worked for him. Do you understand what I'm telling you?"

She noticed the dress in her hands and stepped before the mirror to hold it up to her neck. "What was I thinking?" She tossed the dress into a wastebasket by the dresser. "It's embarrassing. My usual purchasing savvy turns to mush when faced with a bargain in a distant land. Please don't tell anyone, will you?"

I assured her I wouldn't, and she picked up the conversation seamlessly. "We treat people in whatever manner works to get the things we want and need. Such manipulations are okay if love and kindness is what works for us."

I sucked in my lips so my mouth wouldn't gape open. How would things have been different if Mom and Sally had been friends years ago? Dad's rage could have been channeled into something entirely different. Brian would have found home a safe place. Mom might have been content to stay in Dad's arms. And an amazing man like Tim would not be compelled to construct lists.

Sally hadn't been there for Mom, but, perhaps, and this line of thinking astonished me, she was here for us now. Dad's girlfriend could teach us some things, especially about Dad.

I slid off the bed. "I have to go."

"Do you need a ride?"

"Your garage is totally blocked. Besides, I'm looking forward to the walk home."

"He'll come to see you. When he does, let him know what works for you." She let me out the sliding glass door on the beach side of the house. I hurried across the tracks and climbed down the boulders to the water's edge. The sun glinted off a wave's curl.

I kicked off my flip-flops and ran full tilt into the hiss of the foam and on to where the water pressed against my thighs. A wave rose above me and pulled against the back of my legs until I nearly buckled. I dove into the glistening green curtain. The breaking wave thrummed against my body and glugged and churned. I pulled and kicked myself deeper into the water past the breakers. When my lungs could not resist taking a breath, I turned toward the surface and kicked.

I swam hard for Seal Rocks with no intention of ever reaching the barnacle-crusted outcrops. I'd already done so on a dare in high school, probably from Larice, and cut myself badly trying to climb from the water to rest. I was older now, more than capable of swimming the distance, but I didn't have anything to prove. The near presence of the rocks was enough. Knowing that something enduring lay within my reach soothed me. The rocks achieved their purpose by simply being there.

The swim cleansed me of Murphy's soap and the grime I'd accumulated by packing up the telephony. And I felt lighter. Perhaps because I swam for no better reason than the water had beckoned me.

I stopped clawing at the water to tread and catch my breath. I turned onto my back. Each roll of a wave lifted and then sighed me into the next trough. I breathed with the ocean's pulse. A strand of seaweed wrapped my ankle, and the insides of my eyes flamed red from the sun. I tasted the salt on my lips, soaked in the sun's warmth on my face, and felt the tug of the deepening water on my legs.

I returned to treading, but I hadn't been pulled by the current as I'd thought. I bobbed in front of Sally's house, right where I'd begun, feeling cleaner, ready for what may come, braver. That seemed a big enough accomplishment for one day. I swam for shore and walked along the water's edge to the pier and the bait shop.

ERIC SPOKE MORE WORDS in ten minutes than in the whole

time I'd known him. He stretched out every detail of his wife packing up all they owned, how only stains on the carpet and a bag of trash remained as evidence that anyone had lived in their apartment. She even took his clothes. That was just mean. All that remained of substance was a note.

I'd agreed to have a drink with Eric for three stupid reasons: 1) He didn't smell of fish. 2) He looked amazing. 3) He was a known commodity. The man had low expectations I was more than qualified to meet. He was here today, gone tomorrow, and he went well with a chaser of sand.

So much for being brave. Or noble.

This was all justification on my part. The past enticed me, which in a blood-sucking way made sense. What we know, no matter how self-destructive, comes with an old-shoe comfort that teases us into believing we belong in the familiar.

Still, I wasn't the woman who threw his wedding ring under the refrigerated case weeks earlier. "What did the note say?"

"'Feed the dog.' But she took the bowl and the food, and I can't find Growler anywhere. What kind of woman leaves the side gate open?"

An angry one. "So she found out about us?"

Eric grimaced.

"Someone else?"

"Probably."

"Oh."

"You look beautiful."

I hadn't combed my hair or changed my clothes since diving into the ocean. My skin felt sticky from evaporated sweat and seawater. "Do you have kids, Eric?"

"What's that got to do with anything?"

"You've lost a lot."

He squeezed his eyes shut. "A boy and a girl."

"Tell me about your little girl. How old is she? What's she like?"

"Abbie? She's seven. She looks like her mother, only she's sweet and not fat. She never gets tired of combing my hair, or stroking my cheeks, or, for that matter, sitting so close I can hardly breathe. She won't go to sleep unless I read to her."

I climbed down from the barstool and pulled a soggy ten out of my pocket to slap onto the bar.

"Hey, wait, you don't have to go. We've got the whole night ahead of us."

"I would have given anything to hear my dad read to me." I hefted my purse to my shoulder.

Eric lassoed me closer with an arm around my waist. Pressed against him, I struggled to remember where I was headed or why I was leaving. His hands moved up and down my back and lower. "Let's find someplace."

I felt myself shift into autopilot. And I did not want to fly on the wire. Too dangerous. I put my hands to his chest and pushed out of his embrace.

"What's up?" he said. "Come on, don't leave me hanging here."

If I tried to explain why I was leaving, he could have argued me back into his arms in a flash. I was that weak and that scared. I walked out with Eric's pleas following me through the bar and out to the pier. He called out, "You bitch!" as I walked over the railroad tracks toward the bait shop.

I needed a closet.

Mom slept in her room and the entry closet bulged with the detritus of our lives. Larice wasn't home. I had a key, but it seemed wrong to use a master key to talk to God. It would have taken an hour to empty my closet and three times that long to put everything back. I headed back to the beach.

The crowds migrated toward their cars. Parents overloaded with beach gear herded toddlers. Fishermen hefted their catches, tangling every few steps in their tackle. I walked against all of them toward T Street, to the stretch of beach in between there and the pier. I sat down in what passed for isolation on a California beach.

I squeezed my eyes shut to conjure the embracing walls of a closet.

Nothing.

"Okay," I said and looked around for eavesdroppers. Only a couple, him in a hipster hat and plaid trunks and her in a tiny bikini, lay facing one another—talking, laughing, locked in an impenetrable cocoon of togetherness. They wouldn't hear a word I said. I continued, "This is your big chance to whip me into shape. I'm tired of being the worst version of me. I'm up. I'm down. I'm stupid." Only the relentless pounding of the surf responded. "Hello?"

The ocean—had it always been this big?—sprawled like a winking blanket of light. If I could grab its edge and pull the swirling stew of life over me, not to hide but to be in and under its presence, something might rub off on me...or eat me. I fell back in the sand.

"This isn't working."

An image came to me unbidden. I saw Eric sitting on a sofa. Blue light from the television held his attention. The vision wouldn't go away no matter how hard I swatted at it. Not even when I pictured Tim on his sofa, waiting for me, which he was, probably.

In my imaginings, I walked toward Eric. A plush carpet cushioned my toes. The sight of him, sitting there and waiting, drew me ever closer. I closed the distance without a self-conscious bone in my body. The sofa was huge. I hefted a knee onto the edge. Eric noticed me, looked down, smiled. He lifted me to his side, where I fit under his arm perfectly. I pressed into his warmth. He covered me with a knit blanket and tucked it under my chin. He rubbed my back but not like before. No urgency hurried his touch. I'd never felt safer. A pressing fatigue pulled me deeper into the comfort of his presence.

When I surrender to the peace, I realized I'd gotten it all wrong. Eric had nothing to do with the vision. Nothing at all.

I left the beach reluctantly, afraid I would lose whatever peace had been granted me.

37

Tim wouldn't sit down. He paced—*thud-thunk, thud-thunk*—in front of me as I sat on his sofa. "I never should have made the list," he said.

"I like the list."

He stopped, planted his crutches. "I've totally screwed up, Jenna. I've freaked you out. I'm incredibly clumsy. Can we start over?"

And I'd freaked him out, asking to wait on a wedding date until Mom shifted closer to herself. Not a year. "Absolutely not. I'm not going back. We can start right here, thank you very much."

"I totally jumped the gun. Is there any way—"

"If we—you and me—are going to work, we can't be backing up all the time. And since I'm the queen of screw-ups, you'll have to trust me on that one. This is going to be messy. I'm much more concerned with you getting tired of me."

"How could I? You're the bright spot of my life."

"*Ack*, Tim, you sound like a Barry Manilow song."

"You have your messy and I have mine."

"No 'Mandy,' okay? I'm good with everything but 'Mandy.'"

"And I won't get tired of you."

"You might. And I would understand. Others have."

He took that revelation into consideration. "It's not like I haven't worried."

"Seriously?"

"Only for a minute. Once we learn to trust one another—"

"You don't trust me?"

"You don't trust me."

I drew a breath to argue with him, but he was right. I didn't trust him. I didn't trust anyone. "I want to."

"You will."

No one's mental health can be counted out on a calendar. How long could I expect Tim to wait for me?

Perhaps when Mom started living in the twenty-first century, that would be the sign Tim and I were looking for. But that was too vague of a marker. Going to coffee with friends, that would be a colossal leap forward, but how was she supposed to make those friends without leaving the apartment? Any goal had to be realistic. Redecorating the apartment out of the distant nineties would unequivocally prove her forward progress, but Mom still curled up in her mauve recliner each night to watch *Full House*.

I hadn't a clue how to know when Mom crossed the line from caged-by-fear to reasonably-concerned-yet-functional.

I did know that I wouldn't choose between Mom and Tim, so I stepped into a closet at every opportunity to pray for Mom. Her unnamed prison imposed no sentence and, more worrisome, provided no keys to release her. So that's what I prayed for, a key.

WAITING FOR DAD TO storm into the bait shop after I'd left over two hundred telephones in his driveway was like waiting for my own death.

The bait shop counted out its rhythm each day. The fishermen came. The beachgoers hurried in and out. The espresso machine hissed, gurgled, clacked, and hummed. The end-of the-day rush came and left behind a cavernous silence. Nothing had changed and everything had changed.

I wished Dad would march through the door to spew his insults, all red-faced and indignant. The sooner the better. Nothing was more familiar. Instead, the waiting stretched my stomach over a hollowed log. Yes, I could have gone to him, but I would have lost home-court advantage. To follow Sally's advice I needed that strength. I should have known that practicing arguments didn't work. That didn't stop me from doing just that—over and over and over. Part of me believed Dad's no-show act was part of my punishment for dismantling the telephony. Changing his standard operating procedure at this stage of our relationship seemed terribly unfair.

But so typical of Dad.

I woke to find him sitting on the one remaining office chair in the telephony. The contractor would be there at eight to start the process of transforming the telephony into a crêperie. He looked up at me, his face drawn, his eyes gauzy. "I thought I was doing something good here."

I leaned against the partition between the bait shop and the bare room. "We can't afford to do that kind of good anymore, Dad. It's time to take care of our family, don't you think? The income will secure a place for Mom, and, maybe, get her the help she needs."

He shook his head. "Telephones. A man dreams of many things when he's building his life. I'd never given telephones a second thought. Who would? You dialed from one place to another, got your business done, and hung up. End of story.

"Brian hadn't been gone a month. I went to the flea market to lose myself in the hubbub of the place. I loved the kettle corn. There was a booth nearby with a huge, wooden box—maybe six feet by six feet—full of antique telephones. The vendor rubbed oil into the wood of an early coffin telephone when he noticed I'd stopped to look. The wood took on a luster, the grain deepened. I fell in love with a stupid telephone. It didn't even work, but I bought the whole box. I won't tell you how much I paid.

"The telephones felt wonderful in my hands. They responded to the care I gave them." He brushed his hands together and stood. "I'll sell what you delivered, and then, I don't know. It might be time to move on. I'll help Sally flip houses or something." He turned in the middle of the room. "A crêperie, huh? Sally thinks you're a genius."

After Dad left, I busied myself with restocking while the fishermen filled their thermoses and left too much cash on the counter. The storm I'd expected from Dad was a drizzle at best, not the usual tempest, which proved pleasantly unsettling.

The contractor, a scraggily old surfer with the work ethic of Henry Ford, arrived right on time. He shoveled the last of the drywall dust into a wheelbarrow by the time I offered him three burritos and a smoothie for lunch. Not one speck of telephony remained.

I stood in the middle of the empty room. I'd never been more tired in my life.

38

I woke to the *swish, swish, swish* of a whisk against a copper bowl.

The walls between the crêperie and the bait shop were still thin, but the sounds coming through the walls were happy and productive. This was so much better than the silent stare of the telephones. The crêperie's success had landed us in a better place financially. Swish away, oh beaters of eggs and flour and butter!

The influx of cash allowed me to hire two CNAs, Kim and Karla, to keep Mom company, dose her as needed, and to cook her meals. She only grunted at me for three weeks. She claimed she hated me, accused me of abandoning her. But I could see that the CNAs had managed to reach Mom in a way I never could. Daughters are horribly limited by shared genetics and a history of disappointments.

Within days of hiring the two Ks, Mom laughed out loud with Kim over coffee and gossiped with Karla about people I didn't know. I heard every word from Mom's balcony above the bait shop. By the middle of the third week, Mom started painting again and taking her pills on her own, without complaint.

To be perfectly honest, I sometimes hated Kim and Karla for doing what I'd tried and failed to do for Mom over the years. I was the drudge. They were the party girls. And then Kim enticed Mom into the kitchen to bake a mandarin orange cake. It's hard to be resentful of anyone who creates a dessert that evokes ecstasy.

One day, as I decorated the bait shop's window with

cobwebs and spiders for Halloween, I looked up to find Mom sitting across the street. She sat on the very edge of the bench, her gaze fixed on the curtain of fog that veiled the pier.

I trotted across the street. "Mom, hey, how did you get here?"

She looked incredulous. "I walked."

"It's just…" There was no sense explaining her limitations, not to her. This wasn't high school. No hall pass needed. I sat down, scooted close against the dampness of the morning.

Below us, a bulldozer pushed sand from the low tide line up to the walking path, storing sand out of reach from winter storms. A trash truck beeped its retreat from the lifeguard station. Walkers pumped their arms. Runners wove between city workers blowing sand off the pavement. Near the railroad crossing, a man conducted an invisible orchestra while his dog slept at his feet. Just the usual.

"Fall is my favorite season," I said.

"Karla told me about another patient of hers. The woman hides in her house all day. I almost told her the patient was a nut case." Mom looked at me, a wry smile on her lips. "That's the pot calling the kettle black, isn't it?"

I did not want to answer her question. Fortunately, I didn't have to. Mom kept talking.

"The woman's daughter told her teacher that her mother had died. How else could the girl explain her filthy clothes and grumbling stomach? In the girl's mind, I suppose, only a dead mother would send her to school that way." Mom searched my face.

I picked up her hand and kissed it. "I'm not mortified over my childhood, if that's what you're thinking."

"I'm thinking about a lot of things."

"You're my mom. I love you. I want you to be happy."

"Happiness is fleeting, Jenna. You should know that."

Happiness was as ephemeral as a sunset—an explosion of

radiant color to soften the coming darkness. Not bad if you're okay with evanescent (new word: vanishing) outcomes. "Okay, let's hope for something more durable, like contentment."

"Contentment," she said, chewing on a cuticle. "I hardly remember...maybe when I was a very young girl. In my swing. Not at the beach but under an oak tree. I wasn't a high flyer. I preferred twisting with my head back."

That Mom could reach back to touch contentment in her memories was a very good sign, not *the* sign, but a good place to start.

Mom pulled a glossy postcard from her pocket and handed it over. Pictured on the side meant to evoke envy was a clam-shaped bay with white sand lips. I fingered the line where the water shifted from emerald to sapphire.

"Go ahead, Jenna, you can read it."

I turned the card over.

Dear Mom,

Life is good in Tasmania. You should come here sometime. Take Jenna to a shrink.

Love,

Brian

"He doesn't say much, does he?" she said.

I put my hand to my chest, where my heart beat wildly. "But he sent it."

"He did that."

I inventoried the changes in Mom over the last month or so—laughing, gossiping, baking, a walk across the street. Had one postcard from Brian held that much magic? "How long have you had this?"

"It came yesterday."

I returned the postcard to Mom and edged closer. She clasped my hand. "It's a start, the postcard," I said.

"Yes, a start."

39

Tim found me staring into the closet of our guest bedroom. He stepped behind me and wrapped his arms around my waist. I leaned back into him, enjoying his warmth and the smoothness of his freshly-shaved cheek against mine.

"I'm glad you're enjoying the view."

"You have a superior closet, that's for sure."

"It's your closet too."

Tim stored about twenty suits in the closet, mostly shades of gray, plus one questionable green, a couple of blues, and one black. They hung in eerie uniformity. "Do you wear these?"

"Only if someone dies. I've been told by reliable sources that they're grossly out of date. If you need the room…"

"Someone could die."

"I'll buy a new one."

I thought I knew everything there was to know about men until I married one, and now I'm sure I know nothing. Tim has surprised me daily. For one, he offered the use of his toothbrush on our honeymoon. I didn't see that coming. If I'd needed a confirming sign that Tim was the one—I didn't—the use of his toothbrush would have worked.

Another thing, he's always glad to see me, even if I step out of the room to go to the bathroom. I return to his full attention and that goofy grin. I could eat him when he does that. And he doesn't keep track of who does what. There are no ledgers in his head that attest to my indebtedness. In fact, he insists that he's the constant debtor. I'm not buying that.

Tim is my sweet, boy-faced warrior. He's stepped between me and Dad, me and the unsuspecting bureaucrat at the DMV, and me and the produce guy, who couldn't be bothered to retrieve a fresher rendition of lettuce from his storeroom. Last semester, I negotiated a truce between Tim and my English professor over a B-. Tim doesn't always differentiate between the times I do need a knight in shining armor and when a listening ear will suffice. This will take more practice.

Very surprising to me was to discover that men are tons more vulnerable than I could ever have imagined. More than anything—maybe more than sex, but he would never admit so—Tim needs me to respect him for being capable of superhuman abilities when he is really a child longing to please. This makes things incredibly complicated and confusing. I've spent many hours reassuring him that he is more than enough for me. I will do this until the day I die, and I won't grow weary.

He warned me about being a fuddy-duddy. I should have asked for specifics. At first, I saw his preoccupation with bread crumbs in the cutlery drawer as entertaining. I'd never vacuumed out a drawer in my life. Tim did so weekly. He also bought a hamper for my dirty clothes, where he deposits what I've left on the floor, dropping the lid like a guillotine. He's quite particular about his car too—such a waste of good storage space. On the good side of fuddy-duddiness? I never have to worry about falling in the toilet.

The aftermath of arguments is the hardest. A great emotional rift opens between us. We are polite, but we don't say more than we have to. We are opposing magnets. I'm lonelier than I've ever been in my life, more desperate than when Brian was missing. This is the hurting side of love. Walking past the slashing burn of words to reconnect is a vote for our marriage. It's usually me who takes the first step, not that Tim doesn't want to. I don't think he feels the rift as acutely as I do. I don't mind. I would do much worse to ford the chasm.

Marriage is hard work. Yes it is.

"I'll take the suits to Goodwill," he said. "I can't be the only 42 short with poor fashion sense in Orange County." He kissed me again, which put my whole day in serious danger of being sidetracked. My smart watch chimed an alarm. The train to Santa Ana left in half an hour.

I hefted my book bag and grabbed the lunch Tim had packed for me. We stood nose to nose at the door. "I need a place to pray."

He blinked.

"The closet. Is that too weird?"

"Most women want shoe storage."

"Mine are in front of the TV."

"So they are."

"I should have told you about the praying."

"I hear you. At night."

"Sorry."

"No, don't worry. It's good. You know you can pray anywhere, right?"

"I sort of like the closet."

"Then, goodbye suits."

"Goodbye suits."

I KEEP THE LIST Tim made about all the reasons he loves me in my nightstand drawer. If I can linger in bed after he goes to work, I read the list like holy script. I'm beginning to see the woman he wrote about in me.

I'm still not sure how that happened.

ABOUT THE AUTHOR

Patti Hill lived in San Clemente during her high school years. While she has left the beach, the beach has never left her. She's the author of *Like a Watered Garden, Always Green, In Every Flower, The Queen of Sleepy Eye, Seeing Things,* and *Goodness and Mercy.*

Made in the USA
Charleston, SC
25 May 2016